Advance Praise for *Ballad of the Gangster's Daughter*

"*Ballad of the Gangster's Daughter* is a sweeping, cinematic tragedy. Slingsby writes with meticulous humanity; from fire-hydrant Bronx to fluorescent Florida. Serena Magic is a protagonist of depth and resilience, and her journey is rendered with polished, astute prose. A haunting, compelling read."

—John Reed, author of *A Still Small Voice*

"Slingsby boasts a keen eye for social observation across classes, age groups, and professions, and plots that engage the reader with the many elements of power. He has a natural flare for language that manages simultaneously to propel his narrative, provide insight into his characters' minds, and advance his thematic agenda."

—Dale Peck, *New York Times* bestselling author of *Now It's Time to Say Goodbye*

"Zachary Slingsby is a gifted storyteller who has created an irresistible narrative peopled with characters who live on the page."

—Patrick McGrath, award-winning author of *Asylum*

BALLAD OF THE GANGSTER'S DAUGHTER

ZACHARY SLINGSBY

A POST HILL PRESS BOOK
ISBN: 979-8-89565-685-3
ISBN (eBook): 979-8-89565-686-0

Cover design by Conroy Accord

This book is a work of fiction. People, places, events, and situations are the product of the author's imagination. Any resemblance to actual persons, living or dead, or historical events, is purely coincidental.

Post Hill Press
New York • Nashville
posthillpress.com

Published in the United States of America
1 2 3 4 5 6 7 8 9 10

For Julia: my angel

TABLE OF CONTENTS

TABLE OF CONTENTS

PART ONE

Connecticut Girls Don't Say "Daddy"

At a young age Serena was taught that some men do business at night.

She and her sisters would be sent to bed in that great Connecticut house just as her father's guests were arriving. Ricochets of laughter and business would rattle their bedroom floor. Serena learned to fall asleep to them. Like most kids, she could not remember her dreams. But when she could, and when they were nightmares, she would wonder, much later, if they were dreams or memories.

The people who came over brought gifts: wine or delicacies from the old neighborhood, cigar boxes, earrings for their mother, baguettes, rugelach, amaretti, eight-tracks. Though Serena watched these visitors carefully, she could never find any category to hold them all. They were from different places, drove different quality cars, were all different ages and backgrounds, and spoke with different cadences and varying manners. Some came back often, and some once and never again.

The pattern of the visit was rigidly the same: The Magic family finished their dinner around 7:30. Uncle Jimmy, her father's brother, who lived ten minutes away in a bachelor's townhouse, would show up by 8:30, play with the girls before bedtime, then take out a long yellow legal pad defaced with scribbles to show their father a few minutes before the night's meeting.

At nine sharp the doorbell would ring. Their visitor, invariably male, would say something pleasant about the home and present his gift. As Catherine thanked him, Uncle Jimmy would rush their small talk and usher the guest into the dining room where Gerard was waiting, seal the sliding doors behind them, and a conversation anywhere between twenty minutes and three hours would ensue.

Sometimes they would have port and cigars. Sometimes Horace Eaton, another of her father's associates, would join, and sometimes other men.

It made a kind of sense that the different industries her father was immersed in might attract different characters, though none of his endeavors was terribly colorful: He was involved in real estate; a commercial lighting business; and oversaw, under contract agreement with the municipality, a depot along a few miles of the Connecticut pier. She couldn't imagine that other families, whose fathers worked on several things at once to provide, were hosting this company of wanderers so many nights a week.

When Serena asked him about it, Gerard said, "People are busy during the day. So they like to do business at night."

Doing business at night became an explanation that ossified in the family culture. Her other sisters didn't pay it a thought. But Serena watched these men when they arrived. She saw their evening smiles and the swell Hollywood way they held their hats and stomped their feet on the runner. Everybody is uncomfortable the first seconds in someone else's home, but these men lingered in it. As Jimmy ushered them into the dining room and their eyes would flit to their host, already seated, Serena could see the guest suck in a short breath, awaiting the *tick* of the sliding door lock.

One afternoon cleared everything up.

Her mother took twelve-year-old Serena into the attic to sort New Year's decorations. Serena poked at a brown panel in the floor, looser than the rest, with a sense she might find something under it. Catherine said to leave it be. Serena asked, as though it were a related subject, "Mom, do you ever feel afraid living here?"

Catherine Magic said, "Of course not." Serena could feel the weight of her pause, as though coming to terms with how much older her daughter was now than she'd ever been before. "The country is a stranger place than the city. We're still getting used to it." She had said this many times. Then, "I am not afraid of anything anymore because your father has proved to me you can get anywhere in life by being strong."

There was only one explanation that would satisfy the many moving parts of her parents' life—her father's visitors, her uncle's cars, their recent exodus from the Bronx to Southport, Connecticut, this thrilling house, her mother's loyalty and faith—and it crystallized itself to Serena that afternoon in the attic, hearing the pride and comfort in her mother's voice. The lighting company and the docks' business, these were a ruse.

You see, Serena's father worked for Richard Helms.

Serena had read a magazine piece about Helms that went on forever and made many allusions she couldn't comprehend, but the upshot was that the man was an information glutton. Whereas previous directors of the Central Intelligence Agency were enthralled with covert missions of the 1960s, empire-toppling assassinations, and poison-squirting pens, DCI Helms's reign was characterized by a lust for knowledge as its own end. The CIA's charter anchored its activity abroad, but plenty of American enterprisers had been enlisted to report intelligence here at home—from antiwar groups, investors, and salespeople spending time in Eastern Europe to exporters, importers, wholesalers, and capitalists rubbing shoulders with cretins who had no use for patriotism.

It was Helms's job—and the CIA's mandate—to gather *official secrets*, and Serena knew he was partnering with private citizens around the country to tap into their reservoirs of hearsay. After she read this article, it very suddenly made perfect sense why her father took pains to associate with so many kinds of people, some of them strange, even chilling.

It made sense that the docks' business would afford him access to international chatter. Of course Helms would kill for Gerard's connections to importers arriving from possibly hostile territories with stories to share. It made sense, her mother's cool admiration, mixed with apprehension about how far her husband may have to stick his neck out for his nation. It made sense of Uncle Jimmy's fidgety focus, as though much more were at stake than a simple business deal. And it made perfect sense of that list Serena and Madeline had found in Gerard's briefcase two Christmases ago, which they made out to be the names and ranks of cops in Fairfield, Greenwich, and Westchester—officer, sergeant, lieutenant, chief—with dollar amounts beside each entry. Surely they were tracking which cops were paid off by foreign influences.

Men of secrets ran America. Not Serena's America, which consisted of school, the town, her bike, her frog Puttsy, her music, recent memories of the bakeries and sidewalks of the Bronx…but the America on TV and in glossy print, the banks and law firms, academies, Goldman Sachs, PBS, *The New York Times,* and the CIA. Every week men came and told her father secrets. And he told his government. He was an American leader.

After that day in the attic, when it hit her all at once, she stopped wondering about the evening visitors and their gifts and her father's overnight trips to New York or Jersey or other parts of the country. She was relieved when once he went to Canada. *International work.* The profile piece on Helms tied the disparate observations of her childhood into a neat domestic bow and avowed what she long knew in the crypt of her youth: Her father loved people and tried every day to help them.

* * *

In April 1970, just a few months after Serena's heartening revelation, another sister died.

Catherine had taken Jane, closest in age to Serena, to South America for help treating an autoimmune disease of which American experts claimed no understanding. Gerard had strongly encouraged the trip, believing that all things could be cured, while Catherine was suspicious of foreign interventions of any kind, medical especially.

Catherine and Jane had been in Paraguay three days. Catherine wrote a letter of glowing progress on the second. And on the fourth, their commuter bus tipped over on the way to the clinic. It rolled down a hill, and the splash of fuel and steel ignited the engine.

Jane died first, they said. Serena did not know how they could tell for sure. In the case of a bus fire, the sequence of casualties seemed untellable. She supposed they'd both survived long enough to meet the medics, then succumbed one at a time; Jane first. That would explain it. At least, she thought, Jane would never actually know life without a mother, not for one gory minute.

A few hours before they got the news, here in charming Connecticut, Serena was making the case to her father that her younger sister, Madeline, was evil.

"Daddy, she told me she was going to kidnap Puttsy and kill him—in those exact words."

"I did say that," said Madeline, "but I didn't do it. I'm not even saying I wouldn't have done it. I just happen not to have."

Gerard was reading the paper. "I believe her, Serena. The frog is probably in your room. Go take another look."

Emily Magic, Serena's oldest sister, chose this moment to return home through the back door, towing her groveling boyfriend, John McClusky, behind her. John was wearing a uniform of some kind and tried to stiffen his posture as he entered their kitchen, even though no amount of self-seriousness could make him any taller than five-six. Serena had not heard Emily leave and now wondered where they had been.

"Daddy, I looked everywhere. Madeline *tortured and buried him*."

Gerard stated calmly, "I know Madeline's voice when she lies. Check. Your. Room."

On her way out, Serena heard Emily say, "Madeline, can you go, too, please? John and I need to talk to Daddy." Emily added, "Serena, I know you're still standing in the hall—please beat it."

Serena tiptoed off as not to suffer the indignity of predictability.

Within minutes all the other sisters became aware of a showdown in the kitchen and floated in and out of neighboring rooms.

Their house was yellow, three stories, down the end of an alpine road and long driveway at the western edge of Southport, Connecticut.

Southport was a coastal New England town rich in driftwood cafes, marina captains, cardiologists, Cape Cod houses, and onions. They had moved here four years ago. The peeled linoleum table, at which Gerard now sat with Emily and her slouchy suitor, was the only piece conveyed from their four-room apartment on the Grand Concourse. It was a wincing reminder of the old standard of décor, of the tiny hexagon tiles lining every vestibule along the Concourse and the sooty smell of those Bronx hallways, whatever it was that caused it, mold or filth or the entwining sensorial histories of many nations and many nations' ghosts.

Serena came back to the hall outside the kitchen, stopping a foot from the creaky panel.

"I don't want to go without your blessing," Emily went on. "But it is not a dangerous place, Daddy. Most of Ireland is still peaceful, and the parts that aren't, the parts seeing riots and terror, they need help. The man I love, the man I want to marry, has enlisted in a war to help his countrymen."

"Emily, he grew up in Pelham."

"Don't talk about him like he's not standing here."

"John," Serena's father said, "I'd like to ask you, as a man," speaking to him as a boy, "to wait outside."

Serena hadn't seen boys or men defy her father in his own kitchen and waited to see if John would have the temerity to make history.

"The conversation will be at least partially about me," John said, "so I'd like to be here for that part."

"We'll come in and get you," said Gerard, "if we make it to that."

Serena heard the boy trudge across the room, followed by the sigh of the swinging parlor door.

Gerard said, "You aren't moving to Ireland, Emily. And you won't be marrying that young man."

Serena waited for the sob. It came.

She could picture Emily through the wall, her bright blonde hair tied back, her tears flowing freely. She was skinny by right, her chin a delicate point, wide blue actress eyes with thin lashes. She wore simple house dresses if she had nowhere to go and sometimes if she did. She'd turn twenty in a few weeks and seemed to have decided that Ireland held her hope of a life of duty and pride.

Young John McClusky was a dues-paying member of the Northern Ireland Civil Rights Association and had gone overseas three times to plot his entry into their conflict. He had ideas and wanted Emily to marry him and share them. The Troubles, so called, had claimed a few thousand lives so far, and while believers branded it a faith-persecution episode, much of the world thought it had more to do with land than God. Nationalism complicated everything, and Belfast riots roused the batons, which roused more rioters, and an ancient feedback loop ensued, spitting up angsty headlines about "peace walls" and prejudices. Bloody Sunday was still two years away, and many Americans were confused about the IRA's manifesto and didn't like happy hour poisoned by talk of this quirky war.

"He is a *Catholic* man," Emily shouted. "A man who believes in something. He is trained to fight—and is going to fight for the people being discriminated against because of their faith."

"Where do you think our name comes from?"

"You've never been to England, you hate culture, and you don't eat fish." She was louder now, and Serena felt embarrassed for her. "Everyone we grew up with was Catholic. Mommy took us to church. I want to go and help them organize, tend the wounded, *fight* if they'll let me."

"No one who knows anything about The Troubles thinks it is as simple as you're saying," said Gerard, back in his even pitch, the unshakeable tenor of people with big oak desks and mysterious medals glassed-in behind them. "John has no business in an Irish war. He can pray for his people at St. Anthony's. You have two or three paths open to your life and have my blessing for each of them. Protestants and Catholics can slaughter each other without the help of any of my seven daughters. Bring the kid back in or tell him yourself."

Emily Magic had, over the last few seasons, gone from known quantity to reticent mystery.

She once prized her family over every invasion of reality. But in the salt-sea air of their new life, all that had changed. There were no more card games, no more checkers, no more making up stories together about alien galaxies. The changes in Emily were not original. They were changes only people who knew the loveliest version of a girl could feel shocked by. Emily had been Serena's best friend. Now she was some gaunt thing, obsessed with a stubby toy soldier, who couldn't care a cent about gin rummy, the old neighborhood, her sisters' opinions, or Puttsy's fate.

Emily was kind in 1964 and mean by '68. She liked boys in '62, kissed them in Van Cortlandt Park, hated them by '65, *understood* them in '66, and narrowed them to one by December '69. One can uncover the lies of life easier in the Bronx than in most other places on earth. And Emily dug them up.

Serena watched all this, that fondling of crude lies, and knew she'd lost her sister in the process.

"What's going on?" whispered Madeline, creeping behind her.

"Emily's moving to Ireland, and you killed Puttsy," answered Serena. "Admit it now, and the revenge will be less."

Maddy smiled, and her eyes twinkled. "I didn't, but if you find him, and he's still alive, I will kill him tomorrow."

Serena shoved her, and Maddy stuck her arms out backwards, palms flat to catch the floor. The thud was minor compared to John McClusky's bursting back into the kitchen.

Before Maddy could get to her feet, Serena betrayed her hiding place, swinging in to see John a foot from her father's face, screeching with a brogue that was something of an anomaly for a bricklayer's son from the boroughs. Words like *republic* and *loyalist* slid out of John's mouth with the soapy mettle of the cadet whose favorite soldiers were from movies and not history books.

"The poet Juvenal said it best, Gerard." The brogue came in burlier, "'Count it the greatest sin to prefer life to honor, and for the sake of living to lose what makes life worth having.'"

Gerard paused to be sure John had finished, then whipped his palm across the boy's face, so the carpal bones connected first. John tipped backwards and clutched at the pain, making sounds that were more or less squeals. The brogue was gone.

"What soldiers do, John? They don't scream," Gerard said. "They don't holler speeches. Soldiers watch. And act. That's all. Watch and act." He looked at Emily and aimed a thumb at her boy. "He's going to save Ireland?"

Serena caught a glimpse, smaller than a toothpick, of a lime-green hind leg twitching in the triangle shadow of the spice cupboard. "Puttsy!" she cried. She ran to scoop him up.

"You made a false accusation, Serena," Maddy said, stepping into view. "Dad, tell her how bad that is."

"Both of you get outside," he snapped.

Emily came around the table, took John's hand in hers, and looked at her father. "I already have a passport. I'll come back in a week to explain it to Mommy. She'll see things."

Holding Puttsy to her heart, Serena shouted, "Just let her go, Daddy. She's too busy dreaming of becoming a war wife to care about this family. Let her go and see what it's like. We don't need her."

Gerard studied the young love in his kitchen. An idea blossomed behind his eyes, and his face took the same form as when you'd permitted his king to double-jump your checkers and hadn't yet noticed. He crossed the room and snatched Emily's wrist. "Where is it?"

Emily said, "What?" John finally was quiet. Serena waited to understand.

Gerard screamed, "Where!"

Serena tightened her hold on poor, terrified Puttsy. Emily's free hand dipped inside her loose wool pocket, and she held it up. Serena heard Madeline gasp. She moved left until Gerard's shoulder no longer obscured it: a tiny golden ring.

"Yesterday?" whispered Gerard.

"This morning," said Emily.

Gerard released her wrist. He looked at John like there were a million things he was thinking of doing to him. Instead of doing any of them, he left. Serena left through the other door, bumping Madeline out of the way with her bony shoulder. Emily called after them all, but no one came back.

News of the deaths from abroad came within the hour.

***

Now it happened that the day Emily gained a husband was the same she became motherless. They would be inextricable after that, marriage and death, and perhaps they already were.

When Gerard came out of his study with the news, there appeared no relationship between age and composure. Some of the youngest girls cried least; the oldest longest. Emily had been crying all day, so it wasn't much to keep going.

She sat with John at the far end of the patio. He rubbed her ringed hand. "I know it changes things."

"It does?" she asked. Every few minutes a new surf of torment rolled through her abdomen. She stared past him at a few of the youngest girls, sitting out in the middle of the lawn, their bodies joined in knots of incompetent consolation. Madeline was eleven, Daphne eight, little Beth only five. Beth had lived five years in a full family. Maybe she'd remember one of them. "I guess it does."

"Doesn't it?" he said.

"I want to be strong for them," Emily told her new husband, "but the only thing I've been happy about is going with you and joining this cause. If that idea also dies today, it may be more death than I can survive." Another wave taunted her muscles. "Don't you still want it, John? Tell me you didn't lose your nerve."

"I want it, Em. I want it all, and I'm ready. Let them doubt us." He held her.

John knew that Emily knew what she meant to him. His shortness and his stutter did him no favors in the stolid mayhem of a Bronx childhood, a warzone even in its splendor, that place where peers used your insecurities against you not because you deserved it or even because they wanted to but because the cost of not doing so was too high: If you weren't strong and cruel, you were vulnerable and weak. The boys threw John McClusky around those streets like a Spaldeen, bouncing him until his skin grew pinker than its rubber flesh. It was years until he could look a neighborhood girl in the eye, knowing as he did what she would've seen, the exhibitions of shame that engulfed him on Fordham Road, on the handball courts, in the alleys behind the Ascot Theatre. He didn't think he could be known, by a woman, as a man.

On the abraded marble steps of Our Lady of Mount Carmel Church, he would sit and watch sharp Italian men go into one grocer, buy a bouquet for their dates, go into the next and buy a cannoli, and they'd smile at people on the street—milkmen or mothers with strollers—and grimace at anyone who resembled themselves. John studied real gangsters on Arthur Avenue and Hoffman and Crotona, unable to imagine how they walked around unafraid of each other—more than unafraid, eager for a chance to become a maniac. They were unkillable.

When John was seventeen, his father moved them to rural Connecticut on a pension earned by fulfilling Robert Moses contracts in Staten Island and New Haven. John was a junior when Emily was a senior. She could've been with a lot of guys. Guys her age or older. She could've been by herself and would've been fine with that too. She gave him a chance to show who he'd become since the Concourse. He invented who he wanted to be and sold it to her, and every day since had tried to become it for real, a boy in the lilac dusk of boyhood, that finale when dreams and nostalgia and vocation meld and, like the Apollo, erupt into dangerous glory.

The problem with John was that he had seen *Casablanca*.

Emily poured herself an iced tea from the pitcher Mrs. Wolinsky had set out. "I was worried about everything this morning," she said. "I was scared to marry you, scared of what Daddy would say about Ireland, what my sisters would say. Now I'm not afraid. It just feels like some door closed, and I couldn't get through it in time."

She got up, walked to the patio's edge and leaned against a white wooden beam. John stared from his seat. He stared at his wife.

He'd wanted to be that boy on the verge of eruption. But when he looked at himself, he saw no traces of the bouquet-wielding gangsters or Rick Blaine or Gerard and Jimmy Magic. He saw a short boy with thin wrists and undisguisable shame. What was worse, his father who had grown up poor, knowing only poverty, had, in John's teen years, graduated to middle class. True, this had brought them to Connecticut, which brought John back to Emily. Simultaneously, however, it had robbed him of his only hard-knock claim: that he came from nothing. How he wished, sitting up at night, thinking of ways to keep Emily, that his stupid father had waited only a few more years to blunder into basic financial stability.

Despite it all, Emily gave him his great chance. She was happy when he arrived in Connecticut two years after her own family. She'd remembered him. They began spending all their time together. She didn't treat him as worthless. He could tell she liked that they shared an extradition story, a common set of references and that inherited pigheaded pride their other classmates would not relate to. She waited, sweetly, for him to become who he said he was about to be. In the long interim, stunningly, she claimed to love him.

One day John's father spoke of The Troubles. That was all it took—one mention of one article dissecting the quality of mercy in Belfast—to spark the chain of logic that enjoined him to a new fate. His people were Catholic. There was a war—well, a kind of war—being fought in the same territories that nested the origins of his family. If he went over there, despite his own neutered government's policy, despite rationality itself, people who knew him all his life would call him a countryman. Others would say soldier. Emily would see that all her hopes for him, all that sat dormant in his marrow, could finally be galvanized by a blood cause. The other things he had done to try to evoke this impression—joining a classmate on some petty theft runs on department store stockrooms—had only resulted in an arrest and an adjournment of court dismissal, meaning if he got in trouble again, the court would make the trouble stick.

His draft lottery number had been favorable. His grades were good. He was unlikely to be called to Vietnam, and if he was, he would probably receive a deferment. If that happened, and he didn't go to Ireland, he would simply be a boy who couldn't fight, who would never disprove or rewrite his origin story. One set of Troubles solved all of his.

"Emily," he said, "let's get in the car now. Get your bag; let's go to my house and get mine. We'll catch whatever flight we can to anywhere in Europe. It doesn't matter where; we'll get to Ireland by the end of the week. They'll reimburse us travel costs, and we'll get salaried." He went over to her and put his arms around her waist, trying to render imperceptible the two inches he had to lift his chin to gaze into her eyes. "It's the worst tragedy I ever heard, what happened to your poor mother, to sweet little Jane. But there's nothing for us here—and God is in Ireland tonight. Let me take care of you now."

She kissed him. "I don't know. OK. Tomorrow, we'll go. I have to hold my sisters tonight, just tonight."

"Emily, so much can happen in one night."

"So much has already happened," she said. "I owe them a night. I owe it to Daddy too." She ran her hand through his hair. "Tomorrow morning, everything will be new again. We'll go see God."

***

Serena went into the attic. She pushed around some boxes, found that panel and pried it up. For a placid minute she stared, then replaced it, went downstairs past the pantry closet and heard her father in the dining room with his company men.

She went into Hannah's bedroom. "Daddy's laughing in the dining room."

Hannah, the oldest sister behind Emily, closed the door. "You're too young to understand how he deals with things. Or what he deals with." She lifted a purple bottle of fragrance and sprayed her opposite wrist. She sniffed the vein. "Besides, he's all we have now."

When she had woken up that morning, Serena was the fourth oldest daughter in the family—by evening the third. It would not be the last time death promoted her.

"He isn't all. We have Jimmy and Mrs. Wolinsky and the Tully uncles and each other. *He's* going to focus on work, so I think we should count him last. And Emily, she won't go to Ireland anymore. She can't."

Hannah sat with Serena on the bed. "Whether Emily really goes or not, she's already gone. She's part of the world now." She kissed Serena's forehead. "You and I can do it, Serena. We'll hold everyone together. We'll need to love Daddy, not turn on him. If we can go on that way, maybe we can all be all right." She wasn't looking her in the face anymore. "There's a chance."

Emily, Hannah, Jane, and Serena came of age in the Bronx and called Gerard *Daddy*. Madeline, Daphne, and Beth grew conscious in Connecticut and said *Dad*. Connecticut girls were too self-serious to carry on the diction of toddlerhood. But in the Bronx, it wasn't sentimental to say *Mommy* and *Daddy*; it was just calling them proper names. While Emily made no effort to recondition herself, Hannah had been trying to speak like a New England woman now. She'd inherited their mother's nasally pronunciations with short *Rs* and coarse *yeah*s but tried to refine each tic into a transatlantic elegance—like the radio stars from her parents' youth—that might land her a country club husband sometime before forty.

Jane sounded like the Bronx, but she was dead. The younger girls, Maddy, Daphne, and Beth, had the inflections of suburban teacher's pets and would grow up with no geographical clues in their speech. Serena was not so young when they moved that she'd ever take on some fancy boathouse elocution, and now, her mother gone, she longed to imitate her in everything. The way she said *honey*, *radiator*, *cigarette* was a fine start.

"I miss Mommy so much I want to be dead. If Emily leaves...this morning I didn't care at all. Now...I think I have a plan."

Hannah took both her hands. "Look at me, Serena. Forget it. Forget Mommy, forget Jane, forget Emily. It's up to us to be happy."

"This is how we can be happy," she said. "Stick together."

Hannah, in her new voice, said softly, "That's not what life is."

Emily came in and sat on the floor. She asked if they might listen to some records together.

They went to the den, and Emily put on some of their mother's favorites. Emily held Serena on the Lucky-scented chaise. Hannah sat at their feet. During one spectacular refrain of a Peggy Lee track, Serena said, "I can't believe how pretty this is." She asked her big sisters, "How does she think of this?"

"Most singers don't write their own songs," said Hannah.

Serena lifted her chin. "Who writes them?"

"Well," said Emily, her cheek resting on Serena's hair, "other people."

Serena felt a tug inside her chest. She slipped out of Emily's grip and stood up. "Really?"

"It's still beautiful," said Emily. "Come back to me."

Serena couldn't sit down again. She began trying to explain what she felt but struggled and grew quiet.

She only knew that all these people on the records that she'd spent all that time with—who sang to her through the chemistry of needle and vinyl—were fundamentally liars. A song, she thought, was a way to express a feeling unconveyable with words alone. It now turned out that this was in no way the purpose of a song.

How could everyone not be furious over it?

"Serena," Emily called, "come back."

She went through the dining room where men in dark suits were still talking, talking, always talking. Down the hall she saw the screen door and the dimming green world beyond it. She turned into the parlor made sloppy by the light spring coats of all their guests, splayed over armchairs.

How many days and nights this room was full of the suit coats, shawls, and scarves of her father's guests.... Serena imitated her mother's voice and named each coat aloud by its owner. One name stopped her.

If lyrics and melodies were a deceit, what other perfect things were sham? She had thought the men and women on the covers of those tender records were poets. But they were syrupy impostors, slick and raspy, drunk people who liked pretty words but had no regard for the roots of truth from which they grew.

She made another visit to the attic and then, without being seen, left their estate through the backyard. On the street, she took Puttsy out of her dress pocket, kissed his gray-green nose, and dropped him in a sewer.

***

Many came to the house to say what a horror. By dusk the guests had pared down to Gerard's inner circle. He sat at the head of his dining table.

There were six other men around him, all in suits. They leaned on doorframes or stood with their hands pocketed. An open bottle of Redbreast sat on a silver serving tray with glasses dealt around it, none filled.

"Let's discuss what this means for the rest of the year," Gerard said.

"Why don't we talk about the arrangements first, Gerard?" his brother said. "Business can wait."

"I'd like to settle business, Jimmy, so I can focus on arrangements. But thank you for helping sort my thoughts."

Jimmy sighed. He was older, skinnier, and funnier than his brother. But it was precisely the instinct to discuss sentiment before business that made him second in command, lieutenant, operator instead of architect. Gerard's nature was business. Jimmy's was relations. They were good at different things—and together, at many—and neither coveted the other's possessions or position. This was perhaps Gerard's only perfectly self-sustaining relationship. For Jimmy, it was the closest thing he had to a wife and the closest he was interested in getting.

"Catherine ran the estate, and she ran the books with Horace," said Jimmy. "She was as good at both of those things as anyone. We'll need somebody we can trust to step in. Personally, I like the idea of it being another woman; I think that had a gentle way about it, made a lot of things neat that could've been sloppy, and never seemed to draw questions. But like I said, I think that's talk for another day.

"Then there's the house and the girls," he went on. "The way we have things now, you're traveling a quarter of the year coming. I don't see how we can keep to that, even if you lean on Mrs. Wolinsky. Besides, the girls are going to take their time coming to deal with this. Losing a mother at the age most of them are, it's a little like being separated from your head. At least I'd figure. Then you throw poor Janey in. A mother and sister the same cursed day. I think we need to keep you off the road long as we can, keep you close. Lean on the two oldest, Emily and Hannah, to help the others through it."

Gerard had been tapping two fingers on the ashen tablecloth as his brother spoke. He said, "Emily's leaving. Going to Ireland. She got married this morning."

"John McClusky?" said Jimmy. "Emily married John McClusky? Today?"

"Go on in and look at her ring." Now he got up, got the bottle, and filled the glasses for the rest of the men, his own last. After his first sip he told them, "We can't nix the road. I need to go to those places and sign them to our pier. If I don't, we're set back. We'll start to lose…" he looked up, "things we've built."

They stood around, sipping the Redbreast, and the mortuary drinkers' tradition took hold. The sweet bite in the esophagus after it rolled over the palette reminded them there was no occasion more naturally fraternal than facing death together. This sentiment entrapped them all save the widower himself.

Whatever Gerard felt, he felt it alone. He was no more publicly emotional now than in any other meeting he was eager to end. His richer thoughts, his business insights, they came to him in the solitude of his study. His celebrations were tempered and brief. His torments he worked out at night, standing alone on the small flagstone balcony overlooking his yard. Even in those moments, breathing loud as a beast, he did not permit himself to name the causes of his unrest. He treated any twinge of inner pain the same as he did a migraine, a condition both physiological and temporary, a thing to be outwaited. He distracted himself by dreaming bigger. If his girls couldn't sleep, if they were worried, lonely, scared of monsters, he told them to do the same: Dream away your demons. Then get strong enough to realize the dreams.

"Can I raise a glass, Ger?" asked Jimmy.

The others looked at the widower. Gerard nodded.

Jimmy said, "To my sweet little niece, Jane. She loved this house; she loved her father. She was a good kid through and through." He held up his drink. "To my sister-in-law Catherine Magic, born Catherine Tully, that funny little woman from the Bronx. She gave it to all of us if she saw it needed giving. She wasn't afraid of any man." He seemed to think of what to say next. "Stood up to her own family when she saw they had the wrong ideas about our life." He nodded at his own words. Some of the others nodded with him. Gerard waited for it to be over. "She married my brother. And in twenty-three years and eight tries, they couldn't squeeze out a single boy." The men erupted in laughter. "She had a head for numbers, boy. She played the piano like some Broadway hustler. Nobody taught her nothing about it either; she just sat there and danced with it and filled the room up until everybody got punchy… She sang to her kids. She never laughed at anyone in a jam. She was my brother's girl. I'm sorry, Gerry."

Jimmy drank. So did the rest.

Around a minute later, Gerard said, "I'll need two eulogies. Maybe one of you can start on that."

Jimmy said, "Sure. You want one of us to stay tonight? Another pair of hands in case anything needs doing."

The youngest in the ranks, a dock manager named Brighton, said, "What for? He's got John McClusky."

Gerard's eyes darted up. There were a few seconds when it could've gone either way, then the widower's lips fell apart, and a peal of laughter spilled. The others joined one by one, their shoulders dancing.

***

The newlyweds were back on the patio when night fell. One or two at a time, the sisters had come to talk to Emily. She hugged and kissed them and answered questions about heaven. After a while, she found herself describing a familiar place—a wide and boundless thoroughfare with heavy lights and songs and the young faces people owned in the prime of their lives. It was full of all humanity yet uncrowded. She described games, candy, and strangers who became like brothers and sisters. She said once a night a big ice cream truck plows through and blares lullaby music as it feeds the masses. She said everything smells like bakeries, tobacco, and the sun, and everyone's parents sit on happy perches a few stories up, waving and cheering.

Heaven, Emily realized, sounded much like 178th Street in June.

One of her father's company men, Brighton Salk, stood at the edge of the garden, puffing a Marlboro. Madeline began needling John McClusky about all their grand plans. Emily stared into the yard as night settled on it. The birches were distinct in the fading yellow spell, and she wondered if Ireland's greens were quite this stubborn in the prologue to dusk. She went on wondering as Maddy got meaner to her new husband.

Uncle Jimmy swung open the deck door. "Your father wants to talk with you, Emily."

"I don't know if I'm ready, Jimmy."

"Well, we'll find out. Let's go." He gestured at the house.

John piped up, restless under the mass of hours between them and daylight. "She'll be in when she's ready, Jimmy. Tell Gerard I'll come in and talk with him if he likes. I'm ready to offer my condolences."

Jimmy and Brighton traded looks, and Jimmy said, "Maddy, honey, take Johnny down to the fishpond, show him how you catch the tadpoles."

John McClusky shot out of his chair and started for Jimmy when Brighton stepped casually in his path. Neither of them moved a hand above the waist, but their noses were closer than lovers'.

Brighton nodded. "Going somewhere, Johnny boy?"

"Just the hell out of this sorry country."

"Mhm. Don't let love stop you."

Madeline watched with great restlessness, rooting no doubt for a fast fight that would take them all out of the moment into a new one.

Emily tried not to take it personally, this easy disdain her siblings seemed to feel for the man she'd married. She knew they were only mad at her for being willing to leave. But she was also aware that her sisters didn't require the stimulant of tragedy to bare their teeth.

From Gerard they'd inherited candor and from Catherine morbidity, and the two instincts had welded in every one of them. The result was that if they stumbled upon a reason to feel resentful or, worse yet, some clear articulation of how you were deluding yourself, there'd be no delaying them telling you. And the release you'd see in their faces shouldn't be mistaken for glee in giving offense; it was simply the joy of getting that toxic discovery out of their minds, letting it soar into the world where it could make better sense of reality.

Not one of the Magic girls was harmless.

Neither Brighton nor John had flinched when the door opened again, and Gerard Magic appeared. "Emily, get inside," he said.

Emily stood up, and as she did, Hannah, behind her father, asked, "Serena's not out with you?"

Maddy looked around. "Not unless she's hiding like a creep."

Hannah turned and called her name inside, the shout echoing up through the floors hiding the youngest siblings.

"Does no one know," Gerard said, "where Serena is?"

Just then Mrs. Wolinsky called from the foyer. She said they'd all better come in.

***

The high ceiling in the foyer made everyone's voice important.

Serena stood just inside the house. The front door was still open. Immediately to her right, hovering two feet taller, dressed to his rank, was Sgt. Kenny Prince of the Southport precinct. He looked at the patriarch of the five-thousand-square-foot home. "Hiya, Gerard."

Gerard didn't say anything, so Jimmy Magic said, "Sergeant."

"My condolences, Gerard."

"What do you want, Sarge?" Jimmy continued.

The family was bursting through the parlor doorframe behind them, no one all the way through except Emily, her fiery little husband, and the young, tough Brighton Salk, still rank with smoke and firefly dust.

Sergeant Prince said, "I have to do my job still, boys, and this girl brings me here, tells me the kid, McClusky, is wearing contraband. Only she doesn't call it contraband—she says something else, I don't know, but she knows it's no good, a little package in his coat." He nodded at the Irish lad. "How about it, kid? You bring something in this house you shouldn't have?"

Gerard and Jimmy, then the others, looked at John McClusky.

"She's lying!" screamed Emily, pointing a long vile finger at her sister who was hunched without any expression beside the lawman.

Walking back from the precinct in Sergeant Prince's portly shadow, Serena had prepared herself for Emily's wrath; even so, she found it improbable that her once-best friend could choose this man over her, someone so disgusting and pathetic, someone who'd grown up without a single friend. He'd yet to shed one tear over their mother.

"Look," said Jimmy, "you know you got no cause coming into a private house and harassing the kid. Whatever he has or doesn't have, you got no call, Sarge."

"Fair enough," the sergeant said, "but she practically drags me here, says she's afraid he's bringing danger on you. Gerard, I don't want trouble for you today. If you want me gone, I'll go. If you want me to frisk the kid, I have reason. But it's your house."

Gerard was staring at his new son-in-law while Emily harangued him for taking so long to answer. "Send him away, Daddy! These are lies. Serena, you are a liar. And today. Today, Serena?"

Gerard watched John throughout her tirade, saw him keep a soldier's composure. It seemed the boy had decided he had too much honor to refute the charge. He would trust the truth to vindicate him. Gerard said, "Mrs. Wolinsky, go to the den, get John's overcoat and bring it to the sergeant."

Emily found her lungs again and protested louder than any Belfast militants.

The housekeeper was back in a minute and handed over the tweed coat. Sergeant Prince found it in the inside breast pocket, a handkerchief-wrapped pistol, silver, white-gripped, smaller than Puttsy, looking like something you'd see hidden in a muffler shop in some grainy movie.

"No serial number. You keeping a permit for this, McClusky?" Sergeant Prince asked. John held to his silence even as the facts eviscerated its effect. Jimmy Magic looked at the marble foyer floor like a winner who wanted to win a different way. "All right, then," said Sergeant Prince, "against the wall."

Emily rushed the cop, but Jimmy and Brighton collected her limbs one by one and managed her off into the sitting room. The boy was cuffed and marched out the front door.

It took several minutes for Emily to settle enough that Jimmy agreed to call in Serena. All the sisters watched from behind the bars along the stairs. Serena started with an apology. She was sorry not for the action but the manner in which it was taken, although, thinking out loud, she couldn't see another way.

Emily kept asking *why.* By the time Serena got it out, it was guessable. "He's been in trouble before. So…a second time and…well, he can't leave the country. That means you're not going anywhere."

The confession set off another demon in Emily's nervous system, and everyone had to replay their parts in containing it. They pinned her, whispered, and stroked her hair. If she'd gotten hold of Serena.

Gentlemen in Little Italy drove old blue Camaros. In Southport the cardiologists had nice cars but didn't handle the wheel with any style. They didn't trade in charm; they weren't suave or dangerous; they wanted to be seen and envied but not respected by reputation. That may have been an important difference between the old neighborhood and the new one: The Bronx was about who you were; Southport was about what you had.

The Magic girls never got the chance to be very happy in Connecticut. When there was no tragedy, and if good fortune came, it came with fireworks and glitz, entourages and clatter. But excitement did not resemble happiness any more than silence promised peace. And Emily and Hannah and Serena, they would think fondly of that tiny life from whence they came, misremembering the past as only the best-willed people can do. They would ache for the cascading simplicities of eight hundred square feet when morality asked nothing of their minds, when they had no choices to make, only chores and heroes.

At the end, when Serena was the only one left, she would sometimes think of this April afternoon and the two hours they'd had in the backyard before their father came out from his office, bearing news of the endings that began everything. She would think of the games they'd invented on that sprawling six-acre lawn, weaving through the yellow-pink eulogies of winter.

That night was the start of an absurd family pattern—Serena's sisters' premature and inconsiderate deaths—which would go on to become the delight of fiction writers, a beguiling interest of half a dozen talk show hosts, the curiosity of ancestry journalists, a footnote in the speeches of two governors, and the shadowing curse of coming generations who'd done nothing to anyone.

They would all die. For different reasons and in different ways. And with no more glory than history will grant you or me or the few we truly love.

Leaving Emily screaming like a bird at dawn, Serena carved a route back through the kitchen where the day had begun with a lost frog and an itchy ring finger, through the sitting room where her mother had spent many sunrises feeling grateful for her husband's strength, and out onto the patio where fireflies lied that it was a simple good night, and thirsty mosquitoes told the truth.

Serena aimed her chin up at the stars. She heard someone join and knew who. She heard his heavy soles on the panels. His voice was not hoarse or tired. "You got that gun from the attic?" She didn't answer. "How'd you know it was there?"

"Mommy showed me once. She didn't mean to, but we were up there, and she was staring at a little piece of the floor. She looked scared. She said to forget it. I didn't tell anyone. But I didn't forget."

The crickets sang the long song of suburban nights. Amid one of their choruses, Gerard said, "Turn around."

She turned. He clapped her across the face. Her shriek was calm. She held the sting with one hand, catching her breath. This one, she knew, would bruise. Her mother wouldn't be here to see it.

"Don't ever bring a cop into my house again." Then he said, in his way, "Say, 'Yes, Daddy.'"

Little Serena Magic whispered, "Yes, Daddy."

PART TWO
Blood Before Magic

Emily Magic's relationship with lying matured.

In her twenties she had a respect for the truth that caused her great suffering. Now she thought it was only people who understood no more than half of life who'd use a word like *lying*. Emily was getting to know all of life. Lying was another color in its tapestry.

That morning in the kitchen in 1970 was her first lie—she got married without telling anyone—and really that was more of an omission. But within a few years lies became a casual power that defied the weight of accountability. She realized many walls of the world were made penetrable by massaging reality.

Today Uncle Jimmy waited outside her house, only twenty minutes from her father's estate. It was near 10:00 a.m. when she pulled up in her Chevrolet wearing square pilot sunglasses and a backless satin jumpsuit. She climbed up the hood of his Jaguar.

Jimmy yelled, "Em, your heels are on the paint; that ain't funny."

"You're due for another car anyhow. All the widows of Danbury have already ridden in this one."

The Jaguar was black, a V-12, and Uncle Jimmy kept the top down even now in true October. Cars and leather shoes were his biggest expense outside of gambling losses and loans to losers in whom he found something lovable.

He said, "Your father wants you to come home. Go on in and pack a bag for a few nights. Bring the boy—Beth can watch him. Leave McClusky for now; he can join tomorrow night."

Emily said, "Can you pretend at a bit more respect for my husband than that?"

Jimmy looked at his niece's clothes, left over from the night before. "You first."

"I'll come to the house, but I won't be there until late tonight," she announced. "And I'll be bringing Serena."

Jimmy perked up. "You spoke to her?"

"Not exactly. I'm going to drive up to New Hampshire and tell her she has to come home. That her family needs her." She could read the skepticism in his face. "Our sweet sister Daphne is in the hospital. However Serena feels about you or me or Daddy, she loves Daphne. And she should be by her side. Now. When every minute counts."

"Daphne is doing better," said Jimmy. "The docs say she might be released next week—maybe this one."

"Serena will have time to forgive me for not mentioning that—when she's home. *Home*, Jimmy, is a powerful source of forgiveness."

Following the day of her marriage, Emily tried to abandon her family. They never made it to Ireland, but she clung tight to John McClusky and kept distant from the other Magics for around a year.

Many small things happened after that which made daily life difficult—hardly unbearable, but difficult and quiet and unexpectedly stale. Gerard wrote to Emily with an offer to help them put a down payment on a house close to home. They met with a realtor as an exercise, an information-gathering experiment, and within a month decided to settle in a township a few miles west of Southport. Now, in 1979, both she and John worked for her father.

In her bedroom, Emily packed a bag as John held their two-year-old son.

In answer to his many questions, she offered the following synopsis: Daddy and Uncle Jimmy needed Serena's help. The family was in a spot of trouble, and they, Emily and John, along with it. They needed Serena home immediately. John could help by minding their son, taking the messages of anyone who called, keeping her appointments with the dock supervisors tomorrow, and meeting her tomorrow night at the family estate. God willing, she'd be there with her baby sister, solving all their problems.

At the end of this monologue her bag was packed, her car keys rattling eagerly in her palm. John McClusky had been sitting on the edge of their marriage bed, their napping child contoured to his frame.

"Emily, I haven't seen you in two days. I don't know where you've been. You make a fool of me out there, then you come home, tell me some vague business about your sister, and make a fool of me in here."

"I answered every one of your questions like I always do. All you do is ask questions, John, and I answer with the patience of a saint. You know where I've been: I've been working. I'm sorry you can't fathom what's going on with this family, and I am sorry my father doesn't trust you enough to bring you into it. But I won't be made to feel a horrible woman before I have to drive four hours to put out a fire that could burn down everything we're working for."

The silence of the morning in any house, punctuated by nature's warbles and trills, a bird, a breeze, a rustle, was enough to drive all a man's demons into the dry light. Nobody but a psychopath could stand up to that volume of peace.

John, a man who once lived by the beat of Irish fight songs, stood up to the quiet morning, shouldered the weight of his boy and crossed the room to his wife. He kissed her cheek. "I am devoted to you, Emily. I love you." He stroked her hair as he'd done in the first year of their marriage, when the world was against them, and they cared nothing for its affection. "But you're leaving the best parts of yourself in the past. For no good reason. For the love of people who have the worst ideas on how to live."

"You mean the people who pay you? Who took you in? Them?" Her voice was colder when it questioned you than when it stormed answers.

"The reason you don't understand me is that you are a warm man without courage."

She left the bedroom without kissing either boy goodbye.

In the car she went over her plan, the way she would talk to Serena, the harsh and earnest appeal she would make.

There was nothing to be gained, she thought, through timidity, through bargains, through weakness of any kind. John, were this his charge, would show up on Serena's doorstep with soft eyes begging consideration. That was not the Magic way. That was not who Emily was anymore. That was the way of people who believe, in their bellies, that they have no say whatsoever over the outcomes of life. Emily would never be confused for one of those people again. She would not cry over an Irish war, mourn victims who'd chosen not to fight, or give a dollar to a downtrodden man capable of a day's labor.

Emily believed that Serena owed her a debt from those early years when Emily was her hero and their house was a wonderful place. She was driving to New Hampshire, she said out loud, to collect this debt. She stepped on it.

* * *

Serena had graduated Dartmouth that May of 1979. She was twenty-two and living in her first home outside the dormitory. Her sister, Hannah, twenty-six, a young lawyer in Boston, had just spent the weekend. She was packing to leave when the phone rang.

Serena was in the shower, so Hannah answered it and spoke with Beth, the baby of the family. When Serena came out of the bedroom, she was dressed in Sunday clothes, a soft white sweater and jogger's pants. Her long black hair was still soaked.

"I am not going to be leaving yet," said Hannah. "That was Beth. Emily is driving here. Right now. I think I'll hear what she has to say."

Serena went on drying her hair with a bath towel and looked through the curtains down at the street. She draped the towel over a kitchen stool. "What did Beth say?"

"She said she wasn't supposed to warn you, but overheard Jimmy tell Daddy. Emily left this morning, so she can't be far. Beth thinks she's coming to try to get you home. Beth hopes you will come home but doesn't know what Emily's motive is. She also said Daddy and Jimmy were talking seriously, not lightly. That they wanted you home too."

"Fourteen-year-old Beth talks a lot like a twenty-six-year-old lawyer."

"I'm reiterating in summary form."

Serena's lease on this third-story walk-up in the Northern Quarter, which she shared with a roommate, would end this month.

After graduating as salutatorian from Dartmouth, she became the recipient of an unlikely fellowship in Washington, DC. By dint of a long letter she'd written to her congressman regarding the efficacy of term limits, her information had been passed to the fellowship director at the US Capitol. Serena received a call at her off-campus apartment asking her to participate in the inaugural class of congressional fellows. The program would run two years and consist of six four-month placements on various committees, from steering to transportation to defense. Serena had never been to Washington. The prospect of her first visit being as an official of the Capitol building was not one she was prepared to pass up for all the vermilion foliage of Manchester.

Hannah was visiting to help her box up and say goodbye. They both felt they had taken enough advantage these last four years of living just an hour from each other, between picking halfway points to visit museums and spending weekends like this, dining, watching foreign films neither of them loved, and sleeping in the same bed again, where nothing could get them.

Serena was never prepared for Hannah to leave. And she was never prepared for Emily to arrive.

"If Daddy wants to talk to me, why not call?" Serena said.

"Does that sound like Daddy?" Hannah asked. "Call you and ask for what he actually wants?"

"He congratulated me on Washington."

Hannah took off her jacket and set her keys on the counter.

"You don't have to stay for this, Hannah," said Serena. "I know you have a big day tomorrow."

Hannah shrugged. "I haven't seen Emily in a while. I'll stay."

Serena knew her true motives were unlikely in the way of reunion. Hannah, the second oldest, was the only one to have left home before Serena. She felt, Serena thought, a constant responsibility to see her younger sister uphold this decision to live a life separate from their old one. She enjoyed helping Serena assert her independence as though by fortifying Serena's autonomy, she could further demonstrate how successful her own had been.

No one was prouder of Serena's date with DC than Hannah. It was through Hannah's persistent counsel, absent her hourly retainer, that Serena worked up the resolve to end her relationship with Max, her college boyfriend, before she left. To their consensus thinking, Max, for all his strengths, wasn't likely to end up in Washington, and though perhaps Serena wasn't either, she was sure to meet many men who might; this was a season of *mights*, and Max was a *maybe*, never a might.

The buzzer rang. Emily's voice shouted, "Surprise!" Serena buzzed her up.

They heard her trudge on the weak wooden steps. She appeared in the doorway with her sunglasses pushed up into her hair and a heavy leather purse slung over her arm.

Emily looked first at the room bathed in the daylight of the large Victorian windows. She dropped her bag with a thud and scooped Serena up in her arms, lifting her clear off the ground, Serena objecting through real laughter. Emily let her down and peeked at Hannah. "You aren't going to let me do that to you, are you?"

Hannah said, "Not likely."

Emily nodded fiercely. "Counselor." She saluted. "Counselor, thank you for seeing me, your honor, counselor, sir-ma'am, may it please the court, serious lawyer, big shot."

Serena laughed again to intercept Hannah's silence.

"Emily," said Hannah, "what are you doing here?"

Emily tried to drain her voice of all its unrelenting humor. "Daphne is dying."

***

After he left his niece's house that morning, Jimmy Magic visited his brother and explained Emily's plan to get Serena home as best he could follow it. Then he drove down to the docks.

He spent a little of every day at the docks, even the days he had to drive to Westchester or the city or Jersey for some bit of business. He spoke to his foreman, reviewed the cargo statements, then went up to the seaside bistro, Henrietta's, overlooking the bridge, for a glass of something and a tuna melt or some crab soup.

Today he skipped the foreman's office and went directly to Henrietta's. Brighton Salk waited in a booth. He saw Jimmy come in and checked his watch.

Despite spending most days of the week together, Jimmy and Brighton didn't speak much. They knew each other as well as any fifty-seven-year-old man can know a man in his late twenties, a boy. Though Brighton didn't speak like a boy, that's what he was to Jimmy. His unspoiled face didn't match the width of his shoulders or the callouses on his hands. His voice was plain, and he never used many words on any subject. He woke up at 5:00 a.m. every day and hadn't missed a call time in thirteen years working for the Magics. Jimmy missed meetings as often as he made them. He felt that was his prerogative at this stage of his life and was not likely to suffer Brighton's judgments of his punctuality or any other vices however subtle Brighton thought his judgments were.

People who see each other every day need to develop an understanding that can carry them further than loyalty or fondness. To truly coexist, to thrive, they needed to comprehend the core differences of their natures and relinquish all judgments of the same. The biggest reason Jimmy thought Brighton was still a boy was that he did not understand this necessity. Brighton still believed there was one right way to live. This was, thought Jimmy, the defining quality of children.

Together they went through the kitchen and down a short hall toward an airy, unfinished back portico that looked out onto a row of dumpsters and a stretch of unused pier.

Sitting at a bare wooden table waiting for them was a man about Jimmy's age, heavy in the gut and neck, wearing a gray suit. His name was Angelos Lykaios, known in Southport as the Greek Banker. He represented the portfolios of many clients in New York City and had come to the ports, the acknowledged terrain of the Magics, to discuss one client in particular whose interests had intersected violently with Gerard's.

Jimmy and Brighton sat across from him.

"I thought I was to meet your numbers man." The Greek dialect had diminished over his years in Connecticut, in the States. What remained was a broken-up vernacular with a lot of character in the verbs.

"Horace couldn't make it," said Jimmy, "he's with the big man all day, all week in fact, trying to work his way out of the pickle jar you put us in, Angelos."

Angelos pointed to himself. "I am not the power man, Jimmy. You know this. I am a man who gets his bread, his wine, enjoys his family. You have seen my office. My client tells me to give your brother a letter. I say, yes, I know Gerard and his family. I can give him this letter. Do I know what is in the letter? Do I know what is in store for your family? I know nothing. Not until this boy, Brighton, comes to my house and tells me to visit with you here, today. Then I find out. He tells me, and I call my client and find out the rest. But I am not hiding, Jimmy. I am here to talk with you about what can be done. A man in my line comes between two angry parties every day. I have learned to respect people who find themselves put in a corner, as I respect you today. For if you do not respect those people, the hopeless kind, you may find how dangerous hopelessness can make them."

Jimmy peeked over at his colleague. "I guess he just threatened himself on our behalf. Guess we can go home."

"Guess so," said Brighton, parting with words like each one cost a million bucks.

"I would not know how to manage a threat. What I propose is to cast the situation you face in a new light. I will do that now: My client believes he has been wronged. You know this—yes. He believes he has a claim against your brother for a great sum of money, likely more money than Gerard has to his name, or at least as much. He intends to bring this claim, which he has good reasons to believe will be vindicated, unless your brother consents to selling a fragment of his corporation to my client at two times its current market value. The choices are: On one hand," he lifted one hand, "your family stands to lose a lot of money. On the other," he lifted the other, "they stand to be paid handsomely, more than fairly, for a fragment of one business."

"You keep saying 'fragment,' Angelos," said Jimmy. "What you mean by fragment is fifty-one percent."

"That is the figure stated in the letter, I am told." His already-pink face blushed behind his mustache.

"Fifty-one percent is what our numbers man Horace Eaton, if he could've been here, would call a 'controlling interest.' And this *one business* is Gerard's stake in the Jersey City boulevard development, a land deal that'll quadruple over three years. Your client wants to pay a million tomorrow for what'll be worth four or five by 1982. That's greed. Sneaky greed. He knew my brother would never go for it, so he went out and found a patsy to sue us as a strong-arm to take a bad deal. And you're here to tell us we'd better take it."

The Southport air was salt-tinged and crisp. Everything was mesmerizing in October in New England, but the chill from the water wind seeped into your lungs and prepared your guts for winter. People were surrounded by beauty yet in constant mind of its annihilation.

The financial adviser type, or whatever type Angelos Lykaios really was, was always prepared to explain someone's circumstances in as many turns of phrase as it took. He leaned his arms on the ratty wood. "The Magic family has a clever name. That has worked in your favor since you came to Connecticut. Me, I am a small man. But I know big men in that big city, and I work for many of them. Some know you, some do not. You charm those that have heard of you. With your cigarettes, your drink, your happy way of friend-making. You do your business harmlessly." Now he smiled. He spoke slowly, like a storyteller. "But do not pretend to me or to each other that you do not know you are all tap-dancing on a cliff. Any day anybody in that city decides you are becoming a bother, they will blow one gust of wind and *poof:* You all tip over…crash into the sea."

Jimmy hadn't reacted to any of the Greek Banker's flourishes. Brighton said, "We happen to be from that city. Just about all of us. Borough called the Bronx. A place you might not understand."

"The Bronx has a reputation," said Angelos, "but so does my client. And many people come from the Bronx who are sad, dirty, or silly. And my client is none of these things. Talk to your brother, Jimmy. Fifty-one percent will be a great loss for your family. But you will survive it. If you choose this other path," he shrugged his dumpy suited shoulders, "who can say how long you dance for."

"You should see me dance," said Jimmy, and he got up and Brighton followed.

They took Brighton's car to their next meeting, across town, out here in peaceful Connecticut.

At a long red light, Brighton said, "Why don't we go visit this guy right now?"

"What's that gonna get us?"

"We'll show him how we deal with things. He finds some skell to sue us, we go to right to his lobby." Jimmy didn't answer. "Say the word, I point this car south."

"Rispoli's cousin is mobbed up."

"What's that matter? Rispoli's not; he's a shmuck."

Jimmy laughed. "How long since you been back to New York? Who someone's cousin is always counts. I'm in no mood for Manhattan today." Jimmy shook his head. "And we don't have a plan."

"Does Gerard have a plan?"

"Half a one," said Jimmy. "It's sittin' somewhere in New Hampshire."

***

At an oyster bar a few blocks from her apartment, Serena sat with Emily and Hannah.

"So why did Daddy bring this doctor back in," Hannah said, spooning some vegetable soup she found sour, "if he misdiagnosed Daphne's symptoms to begin with?"

"Daddy likes him; he thinks he just got confused by all the notes in her file. It's a long file now."

"Sounds like a quack."

Emily told them the rest of the facts the way their uncle Jimmy would've, crisp, to the point, with spurts of analysis mixed into data. It reminded Serena how much time Emily must be spending at his side.

"You know, you don't seem too upset, Hannah," Emily said, "considering the news I've brought."

"How I deal with things," said Hannah, "is to understand them and understand how to improve them. You don't know what's in my heart."

"That's a cheap thing to say, Emily," said Serena.

"Don't get mad at me for guessing the truth. Sad times call for it. And college is the last place you'll hear it, so soak it in, child."

"How would you know?" said Hannah. "You didn't finish college."

At twenty-nine, Emily differed from Hannah in as many ways as there were colors in New Hampshire's tree line. Hannah believed in experts; Emily believed in the testimony of her eyes. Hannah believed in new friends and the utility of acquaintances; Emily believed in few friends and extending to those the benefits of family. Hannah was serious and worried about self-delusion; Emily was joyful and worried only about their father's problems and how to make them disappear.

"See," said Emily, "you expect me to hear the truth as an insult. Nope. It's just the truth." She drank her wine and licked her lip of an errant drop. "Didn't finish college. Didn't care to. Don't care now that someone reminds me I didn't care then."

Emily accepted the waiter's offer of another glass of chardonnay, then said, "I have a suggestion. I think we should all go home and keep Daddy company for a few days. Until we hear more news."

Hannah said, "Well, I just can't do that, Emily. I'd like to, but I have cases, and I'm—I won't be able to."

"OK. I expected that or something like it." She looked at Serena. "How about you, Mr. Smith?"

"I leave for Washington in five days. I don't see how.... What I'll do is I'll call Daphne. Tomorrow I'll try to get through, and if things look worse..."

"All right, I only thought I'd ask," said Emily, "what with our widowed father facing the loss of yet another daughter—but there I go again with my non-college-educated notions of right and wrong. Is it sophomore or junior year when they teach you that sympathy is an invention of the bourgeois?"

"You asked, you got your answer," Hannah snapped. "Leave it there."

Serena said, "I can respond myself, Hannah." She cleared her throat. "Emily, can I ask you a question? I really have missed you, but I need to ask you something."

Emily stiffened her back. "Go ahead."

"Are you committing crimes for Dad and Jimmy?"

Emily snorted and followed it with a gravelly laugh. "That's balls, Serena. Don't come home if you don't want, but don't accuse me, you screwy brat. Who paid for Dartmouth, I'm curious? Do you remember?"

"She got a scholarship," said Hannah, calmly, knowing Emily had genuinely forgotten.

Emily looked at her food.

"I am not accusing you," Serena went on. "I am asking because I am worried for you if you are. I don't know what's going on with the family, neither does Hannah. I don't know if they are clear of all that horrible business or if...I don't know what any of you are doing."

"I run the real estate portfolio. I work with Jimmy, sometimes Horace. If people don't pay us what they owe, I develop collateral arrangements. There's nothing illegal about it. Ask your lawyer."

"I am not attacking you. I love you."

"But what?"

Serena hesitated. "I know you're cheating on John. I know about the incident in New Haven. And I know you go to the city every weekend now." She looked across the table with the most obvious pain in her face. "You're a mother of a little boy, Emily."

"And you're a robot," she replied instantly. "You're both robots." Back at Serena: "Big job in Washington? Put on a badge, tour the Capitol? You know what I remember you as, sister? On those lazy home days? You were a songwriter.

"Both of you think you're important and respectable. All you are is lost. My days are messy, but I know who I am. I look at you, I see women without the first clue. You traded identities for résumés." She really smiled. "You're guessing and acting—calling it a life."

Serena left the table, then the restaurant.

The waiter handed Hannah the bill; Emily snatched it and handed it back with a lump of cash.

Hannah said, "You know, I find it odd, Em, that you didn't answer most of my questions about Daphne. It has me wondering how near to death she really is. And how near to desperate you, Daddy, and Jimmy are to get Serena home that you'd gin up a story about our sister's respiratory condition."

"That's awfully sick, Hannah," Emily said.

"Right." Hannah's napkin slid off her lap onto the floor as she rose. "I'm sick, Emily, so is Serena; the two sick ones in the family who had to move to different states so none of you would catch what we have."

Emily stayed behind to finish the oysters and chardonnay.

Hannah found Serena a block from her apartment. It had begun to drizzle. She said she doubted very much that Daphne was at death's door. Serena said she didn't think so either but was troubled by what other problem could make Emily desperate enough to tell that lie.

They sat together on her front stoop—what their family would call a stoop—and Hannah tore open a new pack of Rothmans and dealt one to Serena. They smoked in the weak rainfall.

At Dartmouth Serena's friends would sit on manicured lawns surrounded by ancient buildings and ask questions there were no sure answers to—about the afterlife, the origins of love, the impulse of genocide, whether ghosts could touch us. Everyone Serena had known before she turned eighteen asked questions with definite, knowable answers: How do we turn five thousand dollars into fifty? How are the eggplant heroes at the new deli on Burbank? What's behind the attitude of that neighbor with the pink Cadillac? What's the spread on the Cowboys?

Her mind was now a fine mix of both lines of inquiry, the fuzzy, indefinite, eternal kind and those pragmatic, streetwise interrogations. She was a dreamer who had seen what action *is*.

Emily sauntered down the sidewalk and stood before them, tipsy and smirking, as the drizzle let up. She held out her hand, and Hannah gave her a cigarette.

They smoked together in street silence for a while, three girls who grew up around so much smoke they could barely smell it anymore.

"I know neither of you is buying what I'm selling on Daphne," said Emily. "So she may not die. Probably won't. Hannah, you belong in Boston. We both know that. But, Serena, your family needs you. I am going to get the car and pull up across the street." She stood up and dusted off her skirt. "I know you'll come. The world may be your oyster. DC, then Neptune. Go ahead. It won't be surprising. You may really be capable of magical things. But blood comes before magic. And today you're coming home."

She went for the car.

Hannah started to say something, but Serena held up her hand. She went inside.

She left a note for her roommate. She phoned her contact in Washington and gave the phone number of the Connecticut house should they need to reach her. She wrote another note to Max, who would just now be enduring the worst of their breakup. It read:

> *Max,*
>
> *I hope you are OK. I will truly miss you when I am in Washington and am sure I will live to regret losing you.*

I know you'll be very happy soon. You have a cheerful heart. Don't let someone like me take that from you.

I will remember being yours,
Serena

When she returned to the street, Hannah was in the back seat of Emily's Chevy. Serena threw her bag in the trunk and climbed in beside Emily. "Shouldn't I drive? You had twice as much to drink."

"Close the door," said Emily. She ate a breath mint.

"What time will we get there?" said Serena.

Emily put on her sunglasses even though the sun had long set. She sped off the curb. "Before midnight."

***

Two strange things seemed to be unrelated.

First, Brighton's hand was bandaged. This was strange because it was usually not.

Second, there was a pool service truck in the Magics' driveway. This was strange because the Magics' house didn't have a pool.

Gerard was the one who would at last connect these two pieces of strangeness. But he would be a few minutes too late.

It was 10:00 p.m., still an hour when the house was expected to be busy.

Beth, Madeline, and Daphne still lived there. Friends and friends of friends came often, and business was regularly conducted in the dining room or on the patio, and the cook, maid, and two full-time chaperones milled about the kitchen and played rummy on the portico. Jimmy regularly hosted whiskey carnivals for their extended family and merry network of acolytes, bar bums, and the portly impresarios of New Haven and other harbor towns.

The estate was a festive place seen from a bend in the road on a moonful night when ritzy visitors in cashmere or velour tripped on the lawn lights, spilling champagne on the magnolias, and those bar bums laughed from their driveway dice game. Like in the great capital cities of the world, the Magics' home was always a place where both extremes of the caste system rubbed elbows, where the sherry-sipping dealmakers nodded nervously at streetwise louts wielding rusty flasks, each more afraid of the other than they would admit, and three-piece-suits and alligator attaché cases were as common as greasy jeans, slang, Bushmills headaches, and switchblades tucked into ankle belts.

Gerard himself didn't enjoy parties. He didn't have his brother's gift of affection for groups of people eager to hear and tell stories. Yet privately he enjoyed that a bustling atmosphere still reigned in his home. He knew it wouldn't always be so. He slept well, alone in his bed, with the property alive outside his master window.

After nine years widowhood wasn't foreign to him. It was a condition with which he had learned to coexist, like astigmatism or a limp. He'd never remarried or thought to.

Tonight, as his three oldest daughters, unbeknownst to him, drove south toward home, Gerard, behind his cherrywood desk, told Horace Eaton to get some sleep in the guest room. They had been turning over their dilemma for two days, and he said they'd face it better in the morning.

As Horace rose, the double doors of the study slid apart, and Jimmy and Brighton came in.

The housekeeper, Sonia Maude, poked her head in after them and said, "There was a pool truck in the driveway; they've finally left. The delivery man insisted this was his service address. Show me, I said. Show me where we have a pool."

Horace Eaton laughed.

Gerard said, "The McCanns have a pool."

"I told them that, and he kept showing me a form with our address. I took him to the yard and said, 'Here, show me, where is our pool?' His truck was louder than… Anyhow, did you order a pool and not tell me?"

"I didn't," said Gerard.

Jimmy and Brighton sat down. Sonia Maude said she'd give them some privacy and there was some finger sandwiches in the kitchen, and really, what kind of failing company is doing pool service on an October night?

Horace stuck around as Jimmy gave a report on the day, including their meeting with Angelos Lykaios. Gerard noticed Brighton's hand wrapped in green gauze and tape. "What's that from?"

Before Brighton could answer, Jimmy said, "We visited that property on Brunswick. Kid had to reach through a broken window to pop the door. Well, it's not worth a real look from us, too gutted." Jimmy put his feet up on the red leather ottoman across from his brother's desk. "That new Pope is in Boston. Then he's on to New York. Think we can get him to stop in for some vodka? Catherine would've loved that, huh, Ger?"

Gerard still had his eyes on Brighton's hand. The reference to his dead Catholic wife tweaked his attention. "Communists don't let themselves get smashed," he said. "They don't trust what they'd say." He checked the time on the wall. "I haven't eaten dinner."

"Neither have we," said Jimmy.

"They'll fix you something out there; I need to eat alone. Ask them to send in anything, and some iced tea."

They left him alone.

That Greek Banker Lykaios held no power to help them. Gerard knew their meeting would be wasted time.

When they first got leaned on by the Greek's clients, two men you would never figure for partners, none of the Magics was too concerned.

They had been leaned on by heavier weights than Ronnie Rispoli and his bedridden ex-monk partner, Simon. Though these men had prime Manhattan addresses and ran bookmaking operations around the boroughs, and glad-handed true dangerous men at nightclubs, they were not themselves connected to any outfits. They were independents.

Simon was a cloistered monk for eleven years before he left the brotherhood and took up with his childhood chum Rispoli, finding in himself a zest for crime deeper than his Zen. They built themselves something modest and sturdy with gambling and probably drugs, and now they were edging into land development and sought to cut in line.

A few months earlier they asked for a meeting with Gerard. Gerard asked Jimmy and Emily to check them out. Satisfied it was possible they had something interesting to say, he invited them to lunch in the backroom of Henrietta's over the docks.

Simon kept to himself, incapable, it seemed, of aggression; Ronnie Rispoli showed all his cards at once, incapable of subtlety.

They wanted majority partnership in the Magic's Jersey land deal and were willing to make one offer and only one offer, and far from a fair one. Rispoli, in true five-borough-businessman fashion, convinced himself that the deal was fair and then spoke from a place of conviction that the Magics were missing out on the chance of a lifetime. Simon sat silent, his stoic smirk a tell that he respected Gerard enough not to pretend this was anything other than a shakedown.

This was before Simon's sciatica confined him to his penthouse. Months passed and Gerard forgot all about them, dismissed them as fumbling sewer rats, men without real strategy or strength. Then the Greek messenger dropped a letter in Gerard's lap.

Rispoli was suing them—by proxy. At first glance, this too seemed like a wild haymaker. But the more Horace dug into it, the smarter the move began to seem.

Simon and Rispoli had gotten hold of a man who'd worked briefly as a longshoreman for the Magics on the Southport docks. Their letter contained a copy of this man's sworn statement detailing unfair treatment and menacing work conditions. Most to the point, he alleged that the men on that dock crew were expected to be violent with the Magics' enemies. He wrote that all the rumors were true: that most of the dockworkers were also thugs and that Gerard and Jimmy were not businessmen, but criminals.

So Rispoli's note to Gerard said that this man, this disaffected dockworker, had come to him seeking counsel on how to proceed. What was Rispoli to tell him? Should he tell him that a lawsuit is the only way forward and that he himself would help fund it? Or was that really, terribly unnecessary?

"He is a good young man who saw things, and did things, he wishes he didn't."

The dockworker's statement was an affidavit. Its filing would possibly initiate criminal proceedings, but the lawyers doubted those would get far.

All he had were reckless claims of nighttime shenanigans, and the other longshoremen would contradict them a dozen times.

The most concerning leverage they felt the worker had—and by extension Rispoli and the ex-monk—was in the claim of damages for how and why he was fired. He had gotten injured on an after-hours task Emily sent him out on, perhaps too soon for how well she'd gotten to know him, which it turned out wasn't well at all. The worker's leg was broken by a worthy opponent. Two of his teeth were knocked out. His eye socket suffered damage, and he couldn't see clearly, according to his fancy medical note. Gerard believed about half of it. The core problem, however, was that their foreman, with Emily's blessing, then fired the guy for being useless on the job and "more useless in a brawl."

In a civil case, Horace said, Gerard would lose, and he may lose splendidly. Threatening the worker seemed off-limits, considering Rispoli's backing. In a usual year, Gerard wouldn't mind losing a lawsuit. He kept very little money in his own name for exactly this reason. But this time was different. After six years with the bulk of the family fortune nested under a trust controlled by Emily, Gerard had asked Horace to put their assets back under his own control only three months earlier. He spoke to no one about the rationale for his decision, including Emily, but she was made aware of it when Horace asked her to sign some papers one evening at home. She signed quietly and didn't bring it up again.

And the final problem was this: While they weren't afraid of Richie Rispoli or his lame, smart partner, they couldn't go out and hurt them either. See, there was a bit of hereditary context missing from Emily's initial investigation of Rispoli that shed more light on his confidence.

He had hardly earned the loyalty of the Italian crime bosses in New York. They had probably never heard of him. But he was indeed the chirping cousin of a prominent Mafia figure, Vincent Tagletti, who, while never one to intervene favorably in Rispoli's business, would not be able to ignore an act of violence against his own blood. It would be a matter of honor, not affection. Nobody could *like* Richie Rispoli, not even his own family. But this tied Gerard's hands. Being stronger than your opponent is not a relevant measure if strength is not demonstrable.

So he couldn't fight them. He couldn't win in court. And he wouldn't surrender a controlling interest in his most profitable venture in thirty years. What all that added up to was eating alone in his office at 10:00 p.m., wondering where Emily was and thinking about the towel on Brighton's left fist.

Madeline came in, a bit out of breath, "Is Beth in here with you?"

His mouth was full of a sandwich. "No."

She closed the door, and he heard her talking to the cook and some others in the hall. A few minutes later he heard many sets of footsteps on the stairs that ran over his study.

He went out and saw Jimmy by the window. "What gives?"

Jimmy waved at the wall. "Beth must've gone down to the neighbors and not told nobody. Madeline went out to check."

At fourteen, Beth, Gerard's youngest, walked where she pleased and rarely told anyone. Gerard took a glass from the cupboard and filled it with water. After five minutes, he said to the housekeeper, Sonia Maude, "Beth told me she was going to do her algebra. She said it around eight when Horace was still in there with me."

"She isn't in her room."

"Is the bed made up?" he asked.

"I didn't notice."

Gerard, feeling silly all over, took the steps two at a time and looked in on Beth's room. The covers were neat and untouched. He went back to the kitchen as Brighton came in from the patio, huffing, Madeline behind him.

"She's not at any of the neighbors, Dad," said Madeline, "and she goes to sleep by now or watches TV. When's the last time you saw her? I hope she didn't, I don't know, fall down somewhere."

"That girl makes her calls late at night; I bet you anything it's a boy," said Sonia Maude.

"She doesn't have a boyfriend," said Madeline. "She calls Serena and Hannah. She calls them all the time. Daddy, this doesn't seem right."

Jimmy was drumming his fingers on the faucet. He inhaled, clicked his tongue, stared at Sonia. "What were you saying about a pool man when we came in?"

Sonia reiterated the story about the man, his big chlorine-stinking truck, its deafening engine, and Jimmy cut her off with questions she couldn't understand. She racked her memory, trying to describe the man, his uniform, where the truck had parked.

Gerard's heart beat in rhythm to Jimmy's questioning, thumping until it hurt his breastplate. He saw Brighton's pale face.

At that moment, the front door made its loud noises followed by heavy footsteps. They all let out a breath, Jimmy loudest, expecting to see Beth turning the corner holding an ice cream cone. But the face that rounded was Serena's. Emily and Hannah came behind her.

"Hi, Daddy," said Serena. "I came home."

Gerard turned around, tossed a chair out of his way and gripped Brighton's blazer. "Who did you fight today? Don't think of anything—get it out."

Brighton looked at Jimmy, then his boss. He said naturally, "I banged up Rispoli. Didn't plan to, but we went down there, and he got the jump on Jimmy, so I braced him."

"How bad?" Jimmy said something, and Gerard screamed over it, "How bad!"

Brighton's face sank. "I broke his jaw."

Gerard took up a fruit bowl and pitched it into the dish cabinets, smashing the wooden frame and glass to the tune of Sonia's screams. The three oldest in the doorway didn't scream.

Anyone else in the house rushed in. Gerard wet a hand towel and ran it down his face. He sank into a chair.

Serena went to her father and tilted his chin up. "What happened?"

"They took Beth."

"Who?"

"Got her from her own house," said Gerard.

Serena looked around the room. "Sonia and Madeline, go outside." They left trembling. Serena said, "Jimmy, who took our sister? Say it or I walk out of here!"

"In all likelihood: the Italian Mafia. But possibly just two crazy men from New York." He walked over to Serena and touched her arm. Then he leaned over Gerard and gave him a light smack on the face. "They just got her, OK? We got a shot. Let's go into the dining room. It's time to work now."

***

In about a month, Ted Kennedy would declare a challenge to Jimmy Carter for the Democratic nomination. All Kennedys were popular with the Magics, with most of the English of their time, and with every Irish American who lived on or near the Grand Concourse in the Bronx between 1955 and 1970. Gerard would not forget his wife's brothers' four-day bender through the saloons on Gun Hill Road following JFK's assassination, or the way they called him Jack, a buddy, a guy they might've served with in the Pacific. Catherine's brothers were street cops—one had made sergeant. Gerard liked them all right; they loved Jimmy.

Gerard shared the Irish view of politics to a point, the neighborhood view, but he understood the academics' view of wars, the hearts of college-aged children that broke for collateral deaths, babies without limbs in luckless Asian cities. Carter was all speeches. And the family's money was worth less under his reign. But something in Gerard, as in Serena, ran fond of the president's ramblings on the sweetness of peace.

Some of his daughters would cast a vote in the primary. All of them—the five still alive—would vote in the general the following year, one for Reagan, the others not. Gerard despised election years for the focus they stole from business and the otherwise placid joy of Connecticut life. This election year would be particularly harrowing. Nobody in his family would agree about anything. And everyone he'd ever met would send him flowers.

"The Italians have codes about things like this," said Jimmy.

Serena, Emily, Horace Eaton, and Jimmy sat around the long dining table with Gerard at the head. Hannah stood by the door. Brighton and three other young dock guys waited in the hall. Two others sat in a Cadillac at the top of the driveway. It was 1:00 a.m.

Jimmy explained the course of events that had led them to Manhattan that afternoon and got them tangled up with Rispoli's footman at his office. They hadn't planned on Rispoli himself being there—they'd gotten a tip from a west side contact that one of Rispoli's men was dissatisfied, in debt, liable to disloyalty. They thought they would mine him for anything they could use as a countermeasure. Rispoli and his crew, Jimmy said, came down the elevator and "it went to fists and alarms," and Brighton, who was incapable of throwing a punch any weaker than as hard as he could, laid Richie out on the vestibule tile. Then he crouched for a follow-up before Jimmy could stop him.

Hannah had changed in the bathroom into more serious clothes. Still refusing to sit, she said, "Nobody has explained to me why the police have not been called. And if I don't hear an explanation that satisfies me, and I mean now, I'll call them myself."

At the far head of the table Emily said to Jimmy, "Imagine four hours of her in the car."

"Beth," said Hannah, pointing at them all, "has never done one wrong thing on this earth. And now she's in a closet somewhere, or worse, because of the games you play. What do you think, Daddy?" She walked toward him. "You think she's crying? I bet she fought back, because she's tough, because you raised us tough. I bet she fought them, and they smacked her. What would a man like you do to a girl who hit you? Would you hit her back?"

"You're a manic woman," Emily shouted. "Go back to Boston. We'll call you when we solve the problem."

Hannah reached for her worst words yet, but Serena said, "We cannot call the police. They won't get her back. Cops will fish around for her, and that will drive whoever has her further underground. They took her because they want something. Dad, what do they want?"

Gerard didn't answer. Serena asked Emily.

Emily looked at her father, then said, "There are two men in New York who are trying to cheat Daddy out of a deal. They've been picking at us, coming around, taunting. A few days ago, they got a guy who used to work our docks to sue us. Horace and the lawyers think they might win, and it might cost a lot. A lot as in…I don't know, millions, I think."

"Millions," repeated Hannah, "a deal. Beth is gone, so we can protect a deal."

Emily ignored her, addressing Serena. "We didn't do anything to provoke these people. They targeted us and are trying to steal a fortune either outright through muscling us or indirectly through a court system that hates us for our success."

Horace Eaton picked up the thread of the story. "Serena, the reason Emily brought you home is that our plan was to create a family-owned trust and make you the executor. If we put these assets in your name, your father could stand up to a lawsuit, lose, and not have to forfeit the family's wealth."

Hannah started laughing. "That's too perfect. Put a ton of money and properties, obtained illegally, under Serena's name to protect you from an employee you screwed ten times over."

"Why couldn't they go in Emily's name or Uncle Jimmy's?" said Serena.

"Emily and Jimmy are as likely to be named in the suit as Gerard," said Horace, answering with most of the truth.

"All of this was from before," said Gerard, "before they took her."

He was wearing suspenders over his crisp white shirt. His cufflinks were black, his eyes blue.

Jewish men with whom Gerard owned part of a bowling alley typically joked about the guilt that was their birthright. Gerard had never waded into guilt for anything he had to do. He saw his actions as the logical steps for any father set on getting his children from the neighborhood he was from to the one he lived in now—things any modern American man, sufficiently capable, would do to defend against creatures who would love to see you broke, servile, desperate, and dead. He was not a guilty man. But shame carried a different sensation than guilt. Shame was the cornerstone of his widowhood. He was disgraced, for nine years and five months, that he could allow his wife to die. And now he was shamed by a stolen daughter. By the men who took her. By the faces around him who now knew he could let it happen.

Horace looked at his boss of eighteen years. "Gerard, we drew up the papers. Regardless of how the next few days play out, if Serena is willing, I'd like her to sign them. This is a protection we ought to put in place for a hundred reasons. Serena," he said, looking at the girl he'd seen grown up, "do you need to think about this?"

Hannah said she didn't need to think about it, that it'd be ruinous to her career, and she wouldn't do it. Emily threatened to have Hannah removed from the room. Hannah shouted back and—the phone rang.

Horace got up and lifted the receiver onto the hutch. After about a minute he hung up.

"Well?" said Jimmy.

"The mob didn't do it," he sat down and aimed everything at Gerard. "Our guy in Midtown spoke through a liaison. The Bonanno family knows nothing about it. Rispoli and the monk are acting alone."

"That crazy son of a bitch," said Emily.

"It's good, right?" Serena asked. "That it isn't the Mafia?"

Horace was silent. Jimmy squinted his eyes and said, "In a way, yes, but in a way, you can count on the mob to be reasonable. This Simon character, he's twisted. We braced his partner, and his first play was to snatch a kid. What else did your man say, Horace?"

"They use a Hell's Kitchen crew for their jobs. Smart to think they used them for this. We know where their social club is, but they're not going to bring a fourteen-year-old girl in there. We have a few of their names, but…we don't have much."

"All right," said Jimmy. "So the step is to make contact with Simon. We propose reparations for Rispoli's jaw, we offer something on the land deal—doesn't matter what it is, we just need to get Beth home."

Gerard was not listening anymore. He asked Hannah to open the door and call in Brighton and the other men. When they were all before the table, Gerard said, "Get another car full of guys and drive into the city. Pull off somewhere in Hell's Kitchen and call the house from a payphone in two hours. We'll tell you what's next."

Brighton led the men to the driveway without a word. In half a minute engines rumbled.

"Ger," said Jimmy, "if we kick down doors without knowing what's behind 'em, we risk getting the Bonannos involved. Or worse, we risk this psychotic monk bastard starting to hurt her."

"I want you to find another car," said Gerard, "and send it to Simon's home and another one outside the hospital they dropped Rispoli."

"Sending twenty-five-year-old dockworkers up against killers is how we'll end up in jail or on the news," said Horace. "We can get the girl back, but Jimmy has the way. Let's find a price we can live with, or at least agree to for the moment. That will make it unfeasible for them to hurt the girl."

Serena said, "Please stop calling her *the girl.*"

Gerard said, "Jimmy, pick up the phone and get more men to New York." He stood up. "Serena, go into the den and think about the papers we want you to sign. I don't know what I'm going to do tonight, but my name may not be worth much when it's done. And whatever you think about me or the way you were raised, the rest of your family doesn't deserve to lose the life I've tried to give them."

***

Serena was alone.

She thought about the music she'd heard in this room, the family den. Her mother instructed her on the piano from the age of four. Catherine Tully-Magic wasn't a virtuoso, and she wasn't a snob, but her own mother had taught her piano on a beaten-down Janssen spinet, and she taught her girls, the ones she'd had time to teach, what keys made which sounds and how to sew some songs out of them.

Jane was a wonderful player. Hannah had become talented, but her skill was a dry one: the most proficient and least memorable. Emily had forgotten most of what she learned. None of them had taken the time to teach Beth. The Magics' musical talent, it seemed, more or less, died in that bus fire.

In many families, Serena thought, the youngest child arrived into a vivid world, a family formed by repetitions of love. In their house, the youngest girls had gotten short shrift. They were born into stability but grew up in the wreckage of tragedy. They had never known the Bronx, like Emily, Hannah, Jane, and Serena. The upper-class life they found was friendly and seamless yet lonely in a way they wouldn't likely admit. Or perhaps they didn't know how lonely they were, Beth, Daphne and Madeline, the princesses of Southport.

A knock at the door startled Serena. Horace Eaton came in and sat across from her.

"Where is my father?"

"He is getting ready to go out. Brighton hasn't called, but Jimmy's expecting the address of a mechanic's shop the Hell's Kitchen crew runs in Manhasset. There's a good hope it may be where they're holding Beth."

"Does anyone think it's wise for my dad himself to go there?"

"I've known him a long time, Serena. His youngest daughter is missing. What's wise will matter as much as all the other things richer, more powerful people have told him never to do."

Horace's wooden leg was visible where his pants cuff folded up at the ankle. He had been the numbers man for her father for as long as Serena was alive. Like most of their inner circle, Horace was a Bronx guy who had moved to Connecticut to follow Gerard and Jimmy. There must have been fifty people who left their old neighborhood to move to Connecticut the same year the Magic family moved. Horace was operating a dry cleaner when Gerard met him. They would talk for hours about the way small businesses were misrun. They knew they could do better. They did.

Horace was skinny in the shoulders, somewhat hunched, and his belly had grown in New England, relaxed as he had become with their rising fortunes and grimeless houses. But when crises visited the family, as one had tonight, Horace was as sharp and agile as he would've been the day he sold the dry cleaner and shook Gerard's hand on the corner of 183rd and Hoffman. Many famous leaders would've failed spectacularly if not for a man like Horace Eaton, watching out for sharks, filing timecards, understanding the ingenuity of the IRS and outsmarting them in their own tradecraft. The only problem with operators like Horace was guaranteeing loyalty, and the absence of bitterness, relegated as he was to counselor.

But Serena doubted if Horace had been bitter a day in his life. He was a man who thanked the sky for its blueness. He loved Gerard and his many daughters with a ferocity that made it untenable to think poorly of him—even if you could be sure, as Serena was, that he'd done rotten scum things to good people for the sake of money.

"Why do you love Dad so much, Horace?" said Serena.

"I know him. How many people can you really say that about? Even people you say you love. I know your father. He knows me. That's about as beautiful a thing as has ever happened to either of us."

He stretched his real leg. He laid the folder he'd brought in on the plaid cushion.

"Serena, the day of disillusionment comes for all the kids. My boy had his, and it was a sad one. But he got through it, and we love each other. I suspect your disillusionment has been a slow process. One day you saw something, and you wondered about it. Maybe you had a nightmare. Gerard would be the first to say he ought to have done a lot different. But whatever you think you know about him, your uncle, me, the docks... there is something I need to impress on you.

"To you kids, we own the world. But we are not scary, powerful people. We have done a great job with what we had. We were Bronx kids. We never had a start. We came up buying dry cleaners, gas stations, and eventually pool joints. We still make a good chunk from bowling alleys and car washes. We were merchants. We learned to get violent because that was the way."

He slid to the edge of the couch and steepled his fingers. "We survive by carving out the little bits of action that the real big guys, the real scary guys, haven't noticed. If the Italians or the Russians in Brooklyn or the Irish in Woodlawn, or any of a dozen crews in White Plains, decide we get too big for our britches...they'll knock us over like a sandcastle. And they'll be no one to complain to.

"Your father's genius has been knowing when to stand up and when to sit down. Only right now, he's not listening to his genius. He's going to stand up to anyone who gets in the way of getting your sister back." He opened the folder to reveal the forms establishing a new trust. "Whatever

Hannah is telling you, I know she means well. But this does not make you liable for any crimes. It makes you a steward of legal assets. It protects this family. And when Beth comes home, and she will come home, it will protect her too.

"Now, what would you like to do, Serena? We won't force your hand. But we need an answer now."

She looked at the pages. She reviewed the columns of assets, liabilities, and the total sum of money that would legally become hers. She said, "I have questions about the businesses. About the kinds of crimes you, my father, Jimmy, and Emily commit. If you answer them all to my satisfaction, I'll sign the papers tonight."

Horace smiled and eased himself back on the couch. "Have at me."

They spoke alone until 2:30 a.m. They were interrupted only once by Jimmy, who was agitated Brighton still had not called. When they were done talking, Serena took out the first page of the trust agreement. Her pen hovered. She had one more question.

"Has my father ever killed anyone?"

A certain relief came over Horace's face. All the dignity in the world went into his answer. "Never."

She signed the first page. She initialed the second and had more to go when they heard shouts in the foyer.

Emily and Jimmy stood in the doorway blocking two uniform policemen from entering. Gerard was in the center hall. The harsh beams of cruiser headlights framed his chest.

Three uniforms pushed through the door, and a couple detectives came in behind them. The taller one showed his badge. They came from Portchester and had been escorted by these local patrolmen. A tip hit their squad that Gerard and Jimmy were taking an action against a crime syndicate in New York; to hear the tall one tell it, he was here for Gerard's own good.

"You don't understand," Emily shouted—and Serena flashed to the last time Emily yelled at a cop in this hallway. "They took something from us."

Jimmy and Gerard both shot her simple glances that snapped her back into reality, into line with all she had been taught about involving strangers in general, and police in particular, in any family dilemma, no matter how much sense it seemed to make.

One of the Southport uniforms said, "We don't know what you're up to, Gerry, and we respect that we haven't had to come out here in a long time. But these guys say they got call to question you, so you need to come in. They can't hold you more than forty-eight hours, so let's not have a brawl about it."

Hannah and Madeline appeared under the archway, and Emily roared at her Boston-lawyer sister, "You can't help it but be a monster; you can't *help it.*"

Madeline was pulling Hannah into the kitchen as Hannah swore, "I did not call them. I didn't!"

Horace was already at the phone, Serena knew, to call the lawyer who had foolishly gone home an hour ago. But the second detective yanked the line out of the wall.

"Gentlemen," said Gerard, "you have no cause to be in my home and no cause to take me with you. As family men, which I believe some of you are, I am asking you to leave and allow me the privacy to sort our business."

Serena couldn't read whether it was a threat or an earnest appeal to their propriety as fathers.

That detective said, "We're rounding you up; it's that simple." He pointed out Horace and Jimmy to the reluctant patrolmen. "We have cause for them too—cuff them both. If the tip wasn't enough, we grabbed up your longshoremen an hour ago. They had an unmarked car, trunk full of pipes and knuckles, and the driver had speed in the glovebox." He took out his own cuffs as he said this and slapped one on Gerard's right wrist. "You're driving at some kind of turf war with the Italians! You'll thank us when you're still alive tomorrow."

Emily said, "You can't do this! Horace, tell them."

But Horace was in his own cuffs.

"Guys," Jimmy said, his hands in bracelets, "I'm telling you, not tonight. You pull this stuff tonight, and—" He was yanked toward the door, shouting they were flat on the wrong side of this.

Serena's eyes darted left and right. The detective turned Gerard by the arm to cuff his second hand, and Gerard locked his elbow. The detective stared. He slid his hand inside his coat. "Forty-eight hours to question you. I'd love you to resist. Think of all the time we'll have together." He smiled ear to ear. "We'll get to be friends."

"Dad," said Serena. Gerard looked at her through the cops, past the blaze of floodlights. She shook her head. She told him, with silence, what silence could say. When she wasn't sure if that worked, she spoke weakly: "I'm here."

The tall detective tried to turn him again, and Gerard let himself be turned. They marched the three men of the house down the steps and into squad cars while neighbors came out on their lawns to see them off, none surprised by any of it.

* * *

Sonia Maude turned curious folks in robes and slippers away at the door.

Emily got the lawyer back over who, hearing the story, drove straight from there to the precinct, and called an hour later to say they'd been taken to the Portchester Station. He also confirmed they'd arrested Brighton, the men in his car, and those in the car sent to Rispoli's hospital.

Serena comforted Madeline on the porch until she understood that Daddy would be home in two days, perhaps less, and, she promised, Beth even sooner.

When she got back to the dining room, Sonia Maude and Hannah were at the table, Emily on the phone. Serena lit a cigarette as Emily hung up.

"That was our foreman," said Emily, "the one car that didn't get arrested has gone home. They say the cops are looking for them. They have records and can't chance it." She picked up the phone and slammed it down. "Hannah, what are you still doing in our house?"

"I didn't call the police, Emily. I won't say it again."

"Sonia," said Serena, "can you go upstairs and sit with Madeline? She's trying to sleep, but I know she'll be crying. Please also call the hospital and check on Daphne."

Sonia left.

It was about an hour until sunrise. Serena blew out a trail of smoke, and it disappeared into the vaulted ceiling.

"Hannah didn't call the police, Emily," she said. "It was this guy Simon. This monk. He's playing with Daddy. He may even be afraid of what Daddy would do in the next two days if he wasn't locked up. I'm also fairly sure he was the one who gave Jimmy the tip that brought him to Rispoli's office today and started this whole thing. I actually think he planned it all."

Emily rattled the receiver and got to her feet, still staring daggers at Hannah. She let Serena's analysis settle in. "Even if you're right, how in the world are we going to get Beth back now? Brighton, Jimmy, Daddy, Horace, all locked up. Our workers are locked up. Or they went to ground. We've got one man out in the driveway. *One.* And we've got you and me, one sister on a ventilator, and one upstairs sobbing...and one sitting here wishing we would all just die already."

"Horace said Jimmy was about to get an address out on Long Island," said Serena. "Somewhere they may have taken Beth. Do you know if he spoke to anyone before the cops came?"

"I didn't see him take a call," Emily said. "He was doing laps around the house and then smoking outside. It's what he always does when he's nervous."

Serena walked out of the dining room through the kitchen. Hannah and Emily swapped a look and followed.

Serena went out the back door and into the side of the housekeeper's cottage. She knew this was where Jimmy liked to smoke and also that a landline ran to the kitchenette. She found his cigarettes and lighter on a garden bench. She went inside and flipped on a light. Next to the phone was a pen and pad with a Manhasset address scribbled on top.

***

The three of them returned to the main house and went into the den.

"We don't even know if Beth is at this location," said Hannah.

"Jimmy thought she would be," said Emily. "What else is there to go on?"

"We may have to reconsider calling the police," said Serena, seated exactly where she was when she spoke to Horace. The trust documents were still on the table, only partially signed. "Not telling them anything or even identifying ourselves—but getting Long Island cops to that address. These people who took her must be hired hands; they won't be mercenaries. They'll run sooner than shoot it out with law enforcement."

"We do not involve cops," said Emily. "That decision is mine to make, and it is final."

The den door opened, and Hannah said, "Sonia, please give us privacy."

"It isn't Sonia," said a man's voice. John McClusky entered the room. He wore a fur-collared coat. His overgrown brown hair was parted left. He looked at his wife. Her nose wiggled like an allergy had crept into her eyes. After a minute they hugged. Sonia Maude had called him, he said, and he'd tucked their son in upstairs.

Serena and Hannah greeted him warmly. As Emily felt their hellos drifting too near to small talk, she snapped, "John, don't interrupt, please."

"Do we know where they have Beth?" he said.

"Yeah," said Emily, handing him Jimmy's pad with the address. "But we have nobody. We're three women and you. And I love you, John, but what are you going to do to a Hell's Kitchen street gang?"

John set the pad on the table and took a seat. Serena averted her eyes from him after Emily's remark.

In the oyster bar that afternoon, she had told Emily she knew about what happened one night in New Haven. She didn't say how she knew, and Emily didn't ask.

That Emily was once a loyal and doting wife had lost its shock-value gradually in the intervening decade. She was not that same young lady, then so full of notions. She was now a woman with no compunction about not seeing her son a week at a time if life called for it. She was someone who could go to New Haven on business and get arrested at 3:00 a.m. for public indecency on the lawn of a model home, sharing a sentence of community service with her co-conspirator, an electrician named Eddie she'd met hours earlier at an all-night pizza shop.

Serena did not know if her father removed Emily from the trust before or after that call came from New Haven. Beth's reports were spotty in proportion to a fourteen-year-old's ability to recount adult ordeals.

Emily never really liked boys until John, Serena thought. She'd dated some, but nearly always with perfect indifference. Perhaps she discovered an infatuation with the opposite sex too late into the marital narrative. Or, maybe, Emily spent all the ammunition of her principles at the tender age of twenty. She stood so aflame with principle in that kitchen, so in love with the honor of war and the self-deliverance of wifely devotion, that like any perfect inferno, she was always bound to burn bright and blow out.

Hannah said, "Emily, if you won't let us call the police on Long Island, you have to accept the consequences of whatever might be happening to Beth right now. Daddy's gone two days. Think of what they might do for two days. And we can't get her out alone, and we can't do nothing."

"I'm not doing nothing," said Emily. "I am going to go see Rispoli in the hospital. It's 5:00 a.m.—by the time I get there, it'll be visiting hours. I'm going to make a deal on Daddy's behalf. If he doesn't like it when he gets out," she shrugged, "well, he didn't make it; I did. He can renege and go to war. But I'm going to get him to send Beth home."

"Rispoli is a pawn," said Serena.

Emily laughed. "You were shopping for push-up bras this morning. Getting ready to get noticed by sleazy congressmen. What do you know about business, Serena?"

"I know that Simon is in charge. Not some putz who couldn't take a punch. Rispoli's the voice. Simon's the mind. It's not a new dynamic. You read about it in all sorts of dominance hierarchies."

"In college," Hannah added.

Emily skipped that and asked, "So what if he is?"

"Let's go see him," Serena said, "this monk. Let's go to his house and ring the bell. Right now. I think I know what he wants. And I don't think it's Beth. I don't even think it's the land deal."

"Well?" said Emily.

"Do you know where he lives?"

"Yes."

John got up. "I'm driving."

Hannah shook her head and ran her hands through the roots of her dark hair. "I can't believe I'm going to be the one to ask: Is anybody going to bring a gun?"

John and Emily looked at one another, a husband and wife thinking domestically. "We have a rifle," said John, "but it's at home. I could get it."

"I know where one is," said Serena.

They went up past Madeline's room, past all their childhood rooms. They took down the hatch ladder and climbed the attic. Serena prodded a floor panel, and they saw a familiar secret.

"I'm not sure," said Emily. "I think we should leave it."

"*You* think we should?" said Hannah.

"If we go in there with a gun, it changes everything," said Emily. "If we use it, we'll be in the middle of Manhattan. We'll get caught and have to tell a whole story, and the gun will make any story hard to believe. Let's go talk to him."

Serena agreed. The others agreed. They went back down and told Sonia Maude where they were going and gave her the address where Beth may be. If they didn't call the house by noon, she was to give this address to the police. Then, they told their man parked at the top of the drive to back up square in front of the door and guard it with his life.

John had the car running when Emily said she had to give her son one last kiss. The others got in. Emily ran back to the house, past the room where he slept, took the gun from the attic panel, tucked it in her purse, and got back in the car. They crossed the George Washington Bridge at 8:00 a.m.

***

Liars made lousy killers. Killers often told the truth about everything else except who they'd killed. Thieves were quite likable, as a rule, and thieves were different from liars by nature, and many saints were not thieves or liars by an inch. Heroes died as pathetically as anyone. Leaders lost their way. Prophets were good at nothing practical, and a lover's heart could break a hundred ways, yet a true lover would learn no caution from pain.

These were convictions Serena would develop near the age of forty. Before then, she would, like now, wade timidly through the labyrinths of thugs and brutes, the same way she would later navigate intellectuals, columnists, and suits, manager types and the elite barbarians of California, Washington, and New England, not yet knowing their names, what to call them, but certain they were never who they said they were.

From the back window of John's car, she glimpsed graffiti tags on the rusted metal gates of unopened storefronts in southern Harlem. They weaved down First Avenue, cut over to Third, trekking toward the Upper East to skirt the rush-hour parking lot that had overrun the FDR.

At a red light on 96th, she saw a doorman, still in uniform from the nightshift, step into a crosswalk with a brown-bagged beer and a Parliament dangling from his jaw. He had gray curly hair that flooded his red cap, and his buttons sagged from loose threads, and he was truly a fat man. He didn't have a limp but walked slow enough and with enough anguish in his face that he must've thought he did. He got to the other side, took the cigarette out, and exhaled a cloud. There he took a long break, swigged his drink as a group of tiny kids murmured past. A homeless couple sat on the bus bench to his left. He took a seat with them. He looked up at the rectangle of sky that was his to see. He drank again and coughed until some of it came through his nose. The homeless couple got up and left. The light went green, and John drove on.

Serena had never spent serious time in Manhattan.

They found a spot outside Simon's building and looked on from the safety of the car. It was on 68th Street and Park. The front desk sat behind an extravagant revolving door.

"He's going to have people with guns up there," John said. "Right?"

"If we don't come back out," said Serena, "stick to the plan."

John said he couldn't let them go alone. Emily sided with Serena, and John banged his fist on the dashboard, then the wheel and the horn. The car shook. One of the men at the front desk, donning doorman garb, came out to their car.

"Good morning," Emily said lightly.

"Seems like a commotion," the building man said, his voice older than his face.

Emily batted some lashes. "Some of us are Irish."

The man smiled. He looked at John a while. He waved to the girls in back and left.

"Some element of surprise," said Emily, getting out of the car. "Come on. You too, John; my head can't handle another hissy fit."

They all went into the lobby. A janitor was buffing the reflective marble. Morning papers were fanned out smartly on a long wooden table between curved velvet couches. The same man who'd knocked on their car watched them advance on his station.

"Good morning again," said Emily. He didn't answer and his smile was a distant memory. "We are here to see Simon Hayes. I think he lives in 34B."

He asked that each person set their ID on the desk. He wrote each of their names on a clipboard, walked to the office area, and dialed a number on a gold-brick phone. When he came back, he splashed their licenses across the counter.

"You, you, you," he pointed out each of the sisters, "go on. You," he pointed at McClusky, "nothing doing."

John sighed. Serena rubbed his arm. "We'll meet you in the car."

The would-be Irish soldier watched from the edge of a thousand-dollar lobby carpet as the three sisters disappeared into the elevator, headed for the top of New York City.

***

Emily reached in her bag to check which way the gun was facing. The pistol-grip was still toward her. She stuffed her hands in her coat.

Back in 1970 when the local police confiscated the firearm found on young John McClusky's person in the Magic household, it took Gerard three months and a series of quiet favors to see it returned to him from the local evidence room, restored to its attic panel.

That incident would, Emily later found out, become the basis for several of Gerard's friendships with Connecticut lawmen.

People forgave him many things, Emily knew, because of the pleasures afforded them by his imaginative energy. Dinner guests left with ten new ways to view their own stale problems. He gave friends shortcuts they couldn't themselves quite see. He suggested force when he could see it hadn't occurred to someone and kindness if he thought the person had become too cynical, too selfish.

He was in love with their mother. And since she died, his next great affair was not with another woman but with the hidden perspectives of his own mind, which he knew he had to work to unearth.

Emily enjoyed the chess of their business affairs. But it took her time to make a move. She had to block all distractions. She knew that wasn't so for Gerard or Jimmy, or even Serena and Hannah. When Emily was a girl, she could give great speeches with no rehearsal, inspired by any injustice. Something about motherhood and the indulgence of her purest passions had robbed her of that easy affiliation with her genius. It was there. It was lurking. But it frustrated her to no end that it always seemed an inch out of reach. Drinking didn't fog up Jimmy. He used whiskey like mouthwash. Fatherhood had not muddled Gerard's instincts; it sharpened them. Everything her sisters went through seemed to christen their spirits. Emily knew she had a blade to draw and could not seem to wrap her skinny fingers around its switch.

She knew why Gerard removed her as executor of the trust. It was not because of an error in social judgment one night in New Haven. It was because she'd made too many business choices half-heartedly—not wrongly, not always, but without the gusto and follow-through that business demanded, that one's enemies looked for as a disincentive to invasion.

Her first responsibility, given when she was twenty-five, was to protect the family's lighting business. Gerard had started his career selling lighting solutions to restaurants, hotels, factories, venues up and down the coast, selling anything with a bulb in it to any place people had eyes. Emily protected their contracts. But there was a negotiation on the table to expand into Florida, South Carolina, and Georgia, and she'd fumbled it utterly.

Their competitors knew Gerard was no longer operating the company himself. They knew the lighting business was his biggest source of reported income and that he wouldn't fool with its propriety through strong-arming. They played by the rules and beat Emily handily.

Gerard had never told her he was disappointed. He had never pressured her to participate in his affairs at all. But she'd gotten a sense in those early years, the briefest indication, of how proud he could be when she succeeded on his behalf. She believed he loved having a daughter, his oldest, his first, who could be as enterprising and intrepid out of choice as he himself had become of necessity. She smiled at the way he looked at her when she was handing out assignments on those docks. He rarely permitted their mother to visit the docks, feeling it was too crude a place. Yet he relished Emily commanding the respect of the hard-boiled crew.

That was the first time she understood the fond contradiction of masculine pride: Men want their wives to stay home and be happy. They want their daughters to be president.

After losing the lighting bid, Emily did well for a while collecting debts from commercial tenants. She was wily. She was creative in assessing what a debtor owned that might be useful collateral. But she didn't have the same dispassionate view of violence that her uncle and father seemed to have grown up with. To them, becoming violent was an important willingness. Everyone had to know you could do it. But there was no joy in it. It was an imposition. A fight was a critical misery of the day. And when you saw, over many years, how casually a jaw can be shattered forever or how a guy's skull can get caved in under a boot on some sidewalk, you feared violence *even if you were good at it.*

Snake handlers know better than ordinary people the sizzling tingle of venom in the bloodstream. An expert on any scary thing knows the true fear one ought to have of it.

Emily was not an expert in violence but knew she commanded violent men. And as her responsibility grew, so, too, did her habit of delegation. As in the case of the ex–dock worker fit to sue their family, Emily's delegation became cavalier. Never but twice had she personally seen the violence she was ordering. Once she went out of curiosity, once out of malice. But it never hit home that it was a big deal to order someone's dignity stripped from them. Even if you won the day with that order, you became a sore spot in the memory of the man you conquered. In this way, Emily created many future enemies for her family. A lot of people who were weak in 1978 and '79 would be strong again in the eighties.

So Emily Magic's success in the family business would be best described as mixed.

Jimmy would tell you: It would be a mistake to think this girl wasn't tough. She was tough. She would go into any room and sit with any gangster and tell him how it was. She knew she was tough. She just wished it was easier to be brilliant.

When they knocked at 34B, it took a short time to hear footsteps. A man appeared. He held the door with his left hand and had a cane in his right. He was wearing a flannel robe. He was average height and balding. This was Simon. This was the man who used to be a monk.

"Come in."

Emily entered first. They showed their backs to him as they crossed his landing and took a short staircase to the sunken sitting room. Every window ran floor to ceiling. Central Park was a foggy green field far below. The kitchen appeared empty. Everybody sat.

"You don't dress like kids of the seventies," said Simon. He sat with them and leaned his cane on the arm of his couch.

"We were kids," said Emily, "in the sixties."

He apologized. "When Sid Vicious killed himself downtown, you couldn't get decent table service around here for a week. All the teenage waitresses were in bereavement."

Emily saw Serena looking at the rooms around them. She, too, expected to see the elbow of a henchman, the dress shoe toe of a bodyguard.

Emily tossed her hair. "We want Beth."

He looked at their feet, at their clothes a second time. "The new thing they are doing on the block: little devices that go inside your shirt. Record everything we say. I don't think your father would play a game with the cops. He's the old guard. I don't know about the new one."

"We haven't called the cops," said Hannah.

Emily looked over at her. She knew Hannah was the most frightened in the room. But fear alone didn't account for that strange moment on the ride into the city when they went through the first underpass, and Hannah reached into the front and squeezed Emily's shoulder.

"You can say something," said Simon, "that implicates one of you personally or your father in something criminal. Then we can speak openly." He rested one hand inside the other. To Emily, who had gotten to know certain kinds of men, he looked frail. "Or," Simon continued, "you can all take your clothes off. Whichever you find more hospitable."

Hannah provided the fear-frozen reaction he'd fished for.

Serena's eyes hadn't stopped searching the open parts of the rooms behind him. She said, "You're here alone, aren't you?"

Simon held out his hands, palms open, empty.

Serena said, "My father and uncle run laundering and bookkeeping operations in eastern Connecticut. They allow illicit cargo to pass through their docks—for payoffs. They use shell corporations to hide profits from these ventures; they regularly violate real estate law, anti-collusion, anti-trust laws, and use enforcers to commit vandalism and other violence."

"That's good enough," said Emily.

Simon beamed. "All right." He looked at Serena like an ace pupil. "Let's talk."

"What's the price for Beth?" said Emily.

"Fifty-one percent in the Jersey City land. *And*," he added quickly, "a fruit basket for Mr. Rispoli."

"And the price of leaving us alone forever?" said Serena.

He said, "I don't know what you mean."

"You were willing to kidnap a teenager for leverage in a real estate deal," she said. "Why won't you torture our father forever, now that you know you can?"

Simon clutched his cane and went slowly to the shelves above his TV unit. He took out a device. "Do you know what this is?" Serena said yes. "This is a Sony Walkman cassette player." He waved it around. It was blue and silver. "It cost me two hundred dollars, and it's the best thing I've ever owned. You see, I sat in a cave, or what felt like a cave, for eleven years and thought about who I was. They said I was a monk. I thought not of what the world said I should be, but who I really was, beneath every mask. Monks love talk of masks. All I felt was bitter." He paused. "What is your name?"

"Serena."

"All I felt was bitterness, Serena. Because the only sound I heard was silence. This," he stabbed the side of his head with his pointer finger, "isn't made for silence. It's made for voices. Pretty voices. With this device, I can go for a walk in nature and hear music at the same time. No one in human history has been able to do that. I look at flowers in the garden, and Mozart is in my ear…and suddenly Mozart is singing about the flowers, and the flowers and Mozart together are talking about me. And they're *for* me. I have them." He nodded fiercely. "My ancestors pined after beauty. I possess it."

Hannah, who knew more words than anyone in the family, couldn't match one of them against the breed of man Emily had taken her to meet.

"So," Simon said, mostly to Serena, "knowing that about me, if nothing else, what have you come to offer?"

Emily had a fiery rejoinder prepared but could sense Serena had something to say. She waited.

"Many men and women today are empire-building," said Serena. "My family, in its own way, is empire-building. But I don't think that's who you are. I think you want to run your business in peace." She let some silence in. "I think you want my family to kill Richie Rispoli."

Hannah and Emily stared at her. Hannah may have even said, "What?"

Simon, patiently regarding the young lady, said, "Mr. Rispoli is my partner. He is also my dear childhood friend."

"He's loud," said Serena, "and obnoxious. I learned a lot about him tonight. He has a reputation for recklessness and being a pig and a louse, and he does drugs and beats prostitutes. He's everything you're not. And his only success came when you joined him. Yet he has this Mafia cousin. And that, I suppose, keeps him protected. So what I think is you're going around causing trouble in his name. Waiting to find the right enemy who will get mad enough to knock him off. And you can be rid of him without making enemies of the Italians." Emily stared at her blue harness boots, cursing the simple sense life made a day late. "In a way," Serena added, "you chose Daddy because you thought he would kill for his children. You probably would've been right."

Simon said some things about Serena's wit before winding back around to her conclusion, offering only, "It is funny how relationships age. We never consider it when we are kids running through the fire hydrant, how likely we are to grow into the kinds of friends who'd be better off strangers."

"But it doesn't make sense," Hannah said, "you phoned the police and got Daddy and all the guys locked up for two days. Why would you do that if you wanted them out there gunning after Rispoli?"

Simon stared blankly.

Emily lifted her head, multiplying, dividing. "He didn't call the police, Hannah." She looked to her right. "Serena did."

Hannah bit her lip.

Serena leaned forward and told Simon, "Our offer is this: We'll tell my father the truth, and he'll find someone who has a good reason to do what you need to have done. But we want my sister home today."

"I have no reason to trust that promise," he said and drummed his cane. "Your father will commit to relieving me of my problem. He will call me and commit. In the interim, he will sign an agreement that grants me fifty-one percent of the Jersey City development. If he fulfills his obligation vis-à-vis Mr. Rispoli, we tear up the agreement and live in distant harmony, me in a tower above Central Park, operating my affairs my own way, and you with the talentless rich of Southport."

"And Beth comes home today," said Serena.

Simon nodded. "If your family welches, I shall simply take another. You have so many, after all."

Serena looked at Emily for a sign of approval. Emily shrugged. "Yeah, sounds good."

Serena stood up and said Simon would hear from their father. He shook all three of their hands. They let themselves out, and the monk put his music over his ears.

* * *

This was the year Jimmy saw *The Deer Hunter* eleven times in theaters.

It was the year a lot of thirty-five-year-olds decided to get sober and grow up, and a lot of disco romances turned sour under sunlight. People stopped putting feathers where they didn't belong. The seventies ended quietly, and boys and girls were ready to let the years go unlike 1969 when they dragged the spirit of December forward into the next wave of culture and into new mores, into the future forever.

Serena was berated on the long drive home for her antics and needless secrets. She apologized but pretended no regrets.

Beth came home in a cab around midnight. The next afternoon Gerard, Jimmy, Horace Eaton, and the others were released from questioning. The first thing Gerard did was drive Beth to the beach. They spent many hours alone. Serena never found out what was said.

Beth was quieter than was her nature for a couple of days but seemed to be telling the truth that she was left alone in Long Island and never saw the faces of her kidnappers. By the end of the week, she was more herself.

Hannah went back to Boston. John looked after their boy at home. None of the family seemed angry at Serena for her choices, and Emily spoke nothing against her so far as she heard.

Gerard signed the contract for Simon's 51 percent. And when the time came, and the ports were back in order, and the house was secured, and Beth was resting, and Serena was in the kitchen with Sonia Maude and Madeline making cherry pies, Gerard and his brother drove out to Hoboken for a sit-down with the Bonanno crime family.

* * *

Emily took a few days off. She went by herself to Atlantic City then Cape May. Alone on the beach, she saw families. She saw little girls her son's age. One of them stumbled close to her blanket. She removed her pilot sunglasses and smiled. The girl's mother came over and said she was sorry. She kissed her daughter's nose as she hoisted her up—a reflex kiss.

"I have one her size," said Emily. "A little boy."

"Oh, how nice. Isn't it going fast?"

Emily looked into the sun. "Flying."

She arrived home the same time as their sitter. John was on the front porch with lemonade and a friend from his school days. The sitter went in the house to tend to the boy.

"John, can we talk alone?" she said.

The men shook hands, and the friend told Emily she looked great from the sun. She took the open seat.

"I was planning on going to my nephew's ballgame tonight," John said. "I had the sitter come, I didn't when know you'd be back…"

"John," she said, "I want to be better to you." He broke eye contact. He looked at the weeds in their front yard. "I want to be like we were together. I know…listen, I know what you've gone through."

"Emily," her husband said, "I'm not ready for this. I don't think you know what you're saying."

"I do." She reached her hand out and covered his. "What you told me before…I'm ready to hear it now." She sobbed. "Oh, John."

His face was firm. He wouldn't look at her. "If you want to talk, you have to listen too. You have to hear everything I say and take it."

"Go ahead then."

"You've made me a coward. You've scandalized us. It would take years to even…" He looked at her. "My heart is hard to you." She took it. "That boy doesn't know you."

Now she nodded fast and spat, "I know—I'm Satan's spawn. Why not beat me, John?"

He got up and threw his lemonade on the lawn. "You can't hear it. I know you can't hear it. What's the use? You're perfect, Emily."

"I'm sorry, your *heart is hard.* Listen to the things you say! People in both of our families died from poisonous rat bites on steam ships just so we could live in this country and have these lives, and you talk like a housewife about your heart."

"You're a whore."

"Yes, I am. I like men, and lord knows they're in short supply." She caught herself and tried to stop. She tried to breathe. She dug her nails into her forehead and started again. "I know I need to change. But you can't talk like it's all misery here. Look at this house. I've given you a lot of pride as a man. I have. My father's given us…look, you were never going to any war. You're a sweet man. And without me, you would've gone to a technical college and learned to fix radiators, and old ladies would've made you sandwiches to take home. And you'd have an icebox. Life would be gray and short. Don't you ever get thankful it didn't go that way?"

He turned away from her. After a minute he went inside.

She walked over the plush lawn and picked up his broken glass. In the house her son was pretending he was a helicopter, and the sitter made credible propeller sounds. Emily went into their bedroom. John wasn't there. She found him in his toolshed. She stood in his presence as he worked on his coming-together projects.

She reached out and steadied his hand. He jerked away. She reached again and pulled a saw from him. She grabbed his face and kissed him. His cheeks quivered in her hands.

"Let's move away." She breathed into his mouth. Their foreheads were joined. "I'm willing to move for good. By your parents. Or to California or Kentucky. Anywhere you want."

He pulled her hands off. He searched her out. "I want to go to Ireland."

Emily's face sank. She wept until the past worked its way through her blood and its spirit was exorcised from her young, worn, half-Irish skin. "Ireland," she repeated, and as she shook, everything was ruined, and everything was possible. "I want to get to know our son in Ireland," she said.

* * *

Later that same day, Serena and Jimmy visited Daphne in the hospital. Daphne looked the most like Emily, and they both looked the least like their mother.

Daphne was sitting up in bed when they got there but sank deeper into the covers throughout the visit. Feeble lungs routed her energy; the ward air was lousy, and how this poor girl still would've killed for enough of it to get strong again, run in the yard, sing an anthem.

Medical wisdom was on the side of her recovery. But Serena hated the way Jimmy looked at her—like love and comfort were the most important things he could give her now.

"You see this," their uncle said, unfolding a single newspaper page. "In China you can only have one kid. Swear it. Government order." He showed the page to Daphne, then Serena. "Imagine them telling your mom and dad!" He put it back in his sports coat. "I saved it cause if I ever get shacked up with a broad that wants kids," he slapped one hand off the other like a jet plane off a runway, "we're heading right to China."

A hospital announcement interfered with Daphne's soft reply. She was smart and quick. She hadn't been to her school in nearly a year. She'd been under care, out of care, now hospitalized, and always tried to stay funny. Daphne was a Connecticut kid. Like Madeline and Beth, she didn't expect suffering.

"Serena," Daphne whispered before she fell asleep, "what is college like?"

Her face had this awful lime disguise.

"It's pleasant, Daph. You'll see yourself."

Jimmy and Serena had a late lunch in town, and when they got back to the house, Horace was meeting with Gerard and Emily in the dining room. When Serena joined, Horace explained that the Italians had sent a message.

This was flying closer to the sun than they had in the turf wars of years past. The Magics avoided the Five Families and their sprawling soldiers, and as a greater rule, steered clear of territories, industries, and trades that had official links to any organized crime—Italian, Dominican, Albanian, Asian, Russian, or Jewish.

But Gerard saw no way around it this time. They'd asked for a meeting at a restaurant in Hoboken. The Bonannos sent two men to accompany Rispoli's cousin, a made man named Vincent Tagletti. The soldiers were coarse. But Tagletti was decent. He was embarrassed by his cousin and said so. Gerard told him, with a mix of humility and candor, the story of the last seven days. The Italians, all of them, shook their heads with shame when they heard that his daughter had been taken from her own home.

Jimmy began to relay the offer they had come to make: a percentage of the Jersey City deal for the Bonanno family, rather than Rispoli and Simon, in exchange for Tagletti's formal protection.

But Jimmy never got the chance to say any of this. Vincent Tagletti was already on his feet, opening his arms to Gerard in remorse—in friendship. The two men hugged.

"Believe me," said Vincent, "as long as you and your daughters walk the earth, you have nothing to fear from Richie Michael Rispoli. You leave it to me now."

Now Horace told the room that Tagletti had sent a courier with a case of cabernet and a sealed note. Horace held it up to the window. The last line he read twice, laughing in between: *It is a family thing.*

"It isn't clear," said Jimmy, "that they straightened Simon out as well."

"If Simon isn't handled," said Serena, "he will come for us over and over. He doesn't think like other people. He'll find a way to hurt Daddy."

Emily looked at Gerard. "Did Serena just become a killer?"

"I don't want any of you to commit violence ever again," said Serena. "But if you think he's going to go away, you're wrong. I know it."

Horace reached into the envelope Tagletti had sent and took out Simon's copy of the land contract. It was torn in two, and Gerard's signature had been crossed out. "I think it's clear," he said.

Gerard said, "None of you girls will be in harm's way again."

Beth knocked and opened the door. It was her birthday. Serena got up and squeezed her. The others shouted merry noises. Gerard dismissed the meeting, and everyone filed into the kitchen.

Jimmy and Emily stayed behind. Jimmy patted his brother's arm. "If the worst thing that came out of this is that the Italians are planning to ask us a favor one day…" he shrugged, "it could've been a lot worse, brother."

"Yes," said Gerard. "Probably, yes."

Jimmy was quiet a minute, then broke out into that bombastic drinker's tremor he called a laugh. He hugged Gerard and said in Christopher Walken's voice, "A deer has to be killed in one shot!" and he strolled down the hall to make the party a party.

Emily hugged Gerard. "I am happy we're safe." He smiled, turning toward his study. "Daddy," she said, "I have to tell you about something John and I are planning."

"Tell me," he said.

"He wants us to move to Ireland. He wants…we both want to start over." She looked at the floor. "Far away."

Gerard blocked out the celebratory sounds from the kitchen. He went to his daughter and caressed her face. He finally said, "Is it final?"

She felt everything welling up behind her eyes. "No…"

"Emily," he kissed her forehead, "it is a good thing to do. You have my blessing."

***

It was 9:00 p.m. at the restaurant above the docks. Beth had a fifteen-candle cake on the table in front of her, and she was taking bites, dancing, taking bites, and playing pinball with Horace's nieces, and once, at Jimmy's behest, she tried to give a speech but quit halfway, and everyone clapped just the same.

On a whim, Hannah had come back for the party. Some people hoorayed when she came through the door of Henrietta's—a few did not react. Emily got up from her table where John had had his arm around her and embraced Hannah.

At the bar, Gerard, drinking neat Scotch, saw that hug.

Disgrazia.

That was what Tagletti's men had mumbled under their breath when Gerard finished the story of Beth's abduction. Richie Rispoli and Simon Hayes had disgraced themselves by threatening the life of an enemy's daughter—and by extension, Rispoli had disgraced his blood, his mother, his father…his cousin.

For the Italians, it was a "family thing."

Gerard had not counted on the ancient code of Sicily to be so sentimental in view of their modern world. But the mob was sentimental after all. What Rispoli had done was a desecration. Gerard would not find out for several years that Tagletti had already heard of him before that sit-down—that he'd already thought favorably of the family man in Southport whose tangled concrete roots were the same as his own. Whereas the Magics thought their run-in with the Italians was an isolated event, the effect of happenstance and the sociopathy of one sciatic Mozart lover, they would learn over the course of the next decade that, one, true Italian gangsters saw every odd meeting as the beginning of a new friendship and, two, nothing in the underworld happens by chance.

Even in their fifties, Gerard and Jimmy were still growing up.

Gerard saw Serena take a break from dancing with Emily's little boy and pour herself some water at their table.

"Hi, baby." He sat with her.

"Daddy," said Serena.

Her face was as soft to him then as it had been before she grew up. She had now looked into the eyes of people who sought to ruin her family. She had seen the world Gerard lived and worked in and heard the grief in his throat when they took his baby. Tonight she looked at him with love.

He put a scrap of paper on the table. "Sonia handed me this as we were leaving." Serena read it. "Message from a Mrs. Lawrence in Washington. Wants to know why you missed orientation. Whether they should plan to see you on Monday."

Serena read the scrap and folded it. "I don't know," she said. "I am not sure what to do."

"You could stay."

"I could." She looked around the party. She felt the breeze through the screened windows. "I Will Survive" played on the jukebox. The pier wore an unspoiled night. Only in this one big mahogany room dangling on stilts over the bluffs was there light and energy, the racket of celebration. "I might."

"Horace said you never finished signing the trust papers."

"The cops came and took you," she said.

"Do you still want to sign them?"

"I never wanted to," she said. "I don't want the money you made. I don't want to live the life it affords me. I don't believe in going out and conquering people—or anything else you and Emily believe. Maybe it was that way in the past, I don't know, but the world is different for us. I believe people have gifts, and we have to use those gifts, and that life is supposed to be sweet, not some terrifying war."

He said, "So why would you sign them? And why would you stay?"

Her eyes gleamed. "Because I love you so much."

That spilled them both over. He grabbed her hand, and her shoulders shook as she hid her eyes.

"Come *on*, Serena," Madeline screamed, "you have to do this song; we're all doing it. You're going to love it if you don't know it." She tugged at her arm, and Beth grabbed the other until Serena let herself be dragged to the dance floor. Emily was already up. Beth shamed Hannah until she relented, set her gin down, and got in line with the rest of her sisters, save Daphne and the dead.

Gerard turned in his seat as the song started. It was "Bad Girls" by Donna Summer. At first the older sisters didn't know how to dance to it, but Beth shuffled left and right, so they began shuffling with her, and soon the five of them moved as one unit, their belts and earrings sparkling each time the light touched them like the room was full of stardust.

Emily and Hannah waved their arms. Sometimes they bumped into each other and grabbed hands for balance. Serena put her arm around Beth. They all sang about bad girls, bad, bad girls.

Friends whistled. Serena's face was blood-red. And there was no war here. No one was terrified. There were no scared magic women on earth.

The group around the dance floor got bigger, fuller, and from his seat at the back, Gerard could no longer see his girls dancing.

***

The next song was slower. John and Emily swayed in the corner. As Serena stepped to avoid a rush of kids, she bumped the sharp elbow of Brighton Salk. He apologized.

"It was my fault," she said.

He smiled, and that was the first time, she thought, she'd ever seen him do that.

At the table, she fished through her purse for a small grain leather notebook and tucked the message from DC into its cover pocket.

Hannah came and poured champagnes. Emily joined.

It was a week ago that they'd drunk together under different circumstances with all the merciless perceptions sisters could muster. Tonight they were the same girls they'd been the day they left their childhood apartment on the Grand Concourse. They had known nothing about Connecticut or what to expect, or what it may be like to sleep with silence in the background instead of the reassuring ruckus of people just like you. These three girls and the late Jane Magic had held each other in the corner beside the furnace and promised that nothing important would be different. At this table at Henrietta's, the promise seemed to hold.

Emily told about Ireland. Hannah was loud in her endorsement. Serena said she'd visit.

As they drank, Serena, in an almost unconscious motion, opened her notebook again, removed the message from DC and tore it into small bits that drifted to the floor.

Emily didn't notice the bits, but the notebook caught her eye. "What's that?"

"Bunch of to-dos."

"No, it's more than that—look at those pages. You've got little markers everywhere." She reached, and Serena wrestled it back. "Rene, give it. I want to see!"

Grumbling, Serena gave it.

"What am I reading? Poems?"

"It's a songbook," said Serena. "It's not a very big deal," she said. "If I get an idea, sometimes I write it out; that's all."

Emily hadn't looked up. "This one is…this one is fantastic."

She showed Hannah. She kept reading. "Is this one about Mommy?"

"Let me put it away," said Serena.

"No," Emily moved to a bench a few feet away, "I am interested. Please."

Serena threw up her hands. She talked to Hannah for ten or twenty minutes. Jimmy came by and asked what Emily was reading. Emily didn't break focus.

When she was done, she set the notebook next to Serena's champagne. She looked around the room until her eyes settled on her husband and child. "Some of these are very beautiful," she said. She looked at Serena. "I think my son will be able to write songs like this."

Serena was in the middle of thanking her when Emily, slinging her heavy leather purse, excused herself to the bathroom.

Hannah raised her eyes. "Well. You made a stone heart shed some water. Look at you now."

Serena laughed. She flipped the pages. "It's really kind of silly, I just—sometimes I can't sleep and think of these lines. That's all."

Beth came to the table and asked for a glass of champagne.

"Fifteen," said Hannah, "is still too young. Try next year."

"A sip is OK," said Serena. "How about a sip?"

"I hate to break it to you," Beth said, "but I've already had two glasses."

The bang came in the middle of their laugh.

The girls first thought something had crashed down on the docks. The Magic men knew what a gunshot was. Jimmy rushed into the kitchen and rushed out, searching.

All the girls got up, shaking. Jimmy ran to the bathrooms. John and Brighton followed him, then Gerard.

In a few seconds John's wail traveled the restaurant. Serena and Hannah fought through limbs and the bottleneck of the tight hall and got a view of the bathroom. Gerard sat against the sink. He made no noise. Jimmy bawled into his sleeve, cursing them all to back away. John was in the stall with her. He pressed himself to her. Everything he said was crazy. He despised her for it.

Serena got one glimpse before some men set up a block, shoving them backward. She didn't see the silver attic pistol on the tile. She'd be told about it later. She saw Emily's boots, one pointed up, one sideways. John's voice was all anyone could hear.

When the crowd was shooed away, and police were coming up the port, and someone took John and Emily's son home, Serena saw an opening to go back in. She looked at the body. She knelt and rubbed her hands in the pool that had formed. The cops said she was polluting the scene.

She went back to the dining room. She sat in a far corner booth as everything happened, flipping each page of the songbook, trying to tell which ones Emily had read…which one had made her want to…

For the rest of her life, half the pages of that songbook would bear faded red imprints—the remnants of Emily Magic from a bistro bathroom floor.

***

They buried her five days later. The casket could not be opened at the wake, since she had shot herself in the temple. Vincent Tagletti sent a mass card. So did a lot of other people from the old neighborhood, and many of them drove to the burial site in Fairfield and embraced Gerard as he stood at the head of the family line. It was a rainy day, and the umbrellas, like the procession cars and the suits, shoes, and ties of the pallbearers, were black.

Serena asked to say a few words during the service and was told no. Gerard spoke briefly. John McClusky did not attend.

As Serena walked from the grave site to Hannah's car, she noticed the edge of her dress had run through some wet soil excavated to dig the grave. Her dress dragged the soil through each fresh track of grass as she walked. She pinched the dress and kept going—so the dirt would stop leaving a trail.

At the house, Southport townspeople mingled timidly with old neighborhood guests. The line of mourners there to comfort the family stretched to the top of the driveway.

Quietly Serena asked Horace Eaton to meet her in the den with the trust documents. She signed and initialed the remainder of the pages and left that night in Emily's abandoned Chevy for America's capital.

PART THREE

A Little Bit It Touches Us

In 1985, in a gray corridor of a gray building near Dupont Circle, Serena was casually offered a job with Tip O'Neil. It was days after Reagan had taken an oath for a second term, both parties were reconsidering staff, and some dusty fat men had come to respect Serena's ability to put Washington terms in her own words, to craft a story out of policy. She accepted the job with the Speaker's communications team on the spot. Ten days later she was told she had not passed a standard background check. The offer was rescinded. She heard nothing more.

A few weeks later she had another offer in Philadelphia.

There were experiments around the country in these years, as there have been in the years since, to diagnose how crime and fear had become ascendant in inner cities while wealthier people collected their winnings and sailed for the suburbs. A year or so earlier, Wilson Goode had defeated his opponent, former mayor and police officer Frank Rizzo, to become the first Black mayor of Philadelphia. He won largely on the promise of a renewed unity that he felt Rizzo had discarded at the expense of power. Under Goode's watch, a woman named Poppy Solnit created a public-private partnership to explore the root causes of inner-city homicide. Her mission statement called for a model that could be shared with other suffering cities across the nation.

Poppy Solnit hired Serena during their first meeting. Serena rented the English basement of a rowhouse in Penn's Landing the last weekend in March '85. She brought her books, records, clothes, candle-stick holders, her Mr. Coffee, and one sofa chair. Everything else she'd buy again in time. She was twenty-eight. As long as she lived, she would never miss Washington.

The first few weeks flew by. Serena was made to understand that each dime of their budget was precious and every contribution, or lack thereof, affected the lifespan they would have to achieve their mission. For the first time she understood the relationship between an organization's financial health and her own.

Poppy was a blunt teacher. She wanted her number two person spared none of the political or social realities of their work. They had enemies on all sides, she said, who would lose federal funding if their work proved that a better method existed to decrease homicides.

"It's all about bodies," Poppy said, walking nowhere in their tight office along thin, awful carpet, "drugs and everything else, and the kids and schools—it's all crumbling. But if we can figure out how to stop the bodies, we can work up from there. Businesses come back in; parents stick around. And no matter how many fed programs are cut, we'll have an idea, a sense, how to do this on our own."

In the beginning, Serena's job was to identify community leaders who could command the respect of young criminals. She would bring them in and explain the mission, be a saleswoman for the cause. In this phase Serena discovered she could inadvertently waste many hours of a day on "coalitions building." She stopped setting up meetings in their office and went out on foot to find people, pastors, coaches, rehabilitated dealers, storeowners, marchers, athletes who would listen to her. It was inarguable, her boss told the team every morning—two comms strategists, eight interns, and Serena—that all the city's problems were downstream of the body count. She taught Serena to present this vision to the people who had lived here their whole lives, to get them to buy into an idea of Philly that was not moralistic—they weren't judging crime or criminals. It was practical. Do what you want. *But don't kill anyone.*

Poppy was progressive by nature, and she'd marched for the nuclear freeze and rallied for Harvey Milk, but Serena soon realized her new mentor's hostility to ideology. What they were doing in Washington didn't matter to her and was as likely to be undone by the next gaggle of careerists and rubes as it was to touch the lives of people in need for the ten minutes it was certified law. Poppy was a source chaser. She prized efficacy over loyalty and preferred the perversity of the streets to gin-and-tonics debates at Old Ebbitt. She needed to believe her days mattered. Serena learned from her the beauty of a vision and, in more ways than one, the messiness of execution.

At the end of April, their organization, Safer Cities, hosted its first town hall in the cafeteria of a middle school in Rittenhouse Square; two hundred residents attended, nearly all of whom had already met Serena personally. Poppy didn't go in for rousing speeches, and she didn't give one then. She offered practical alternatives to murder.

Their enemy, she said, was this one statistic; it was not a way of life or anything greater. If they could shoot someone in the leg instead of the heart, smash a bone instead of shoot at all, they would slowly start to see systemic changes.

Some called her a racist. Some applauded. Serena watched her guardedly, not yet sure if she would be her best career example of strength or some twisted academic in love with a bizarre hypothesis.

The last day in April, Serena saw her first shooting. It was outside a deli a few blocks from their office, midafternoon, and a short man shot a tall, old one in the back of the neck and twice more in the head as he slumped. Serena was there passing out flyers stamped with mediation phone numbers. She hid with the others but watched the shooter's reaction to what he did. He hovered over the body, then rattled down an adjacent block.

A teenage girl who'd taken cover beside Serena said the shooter was an amateur. When Serena asked how she knew this, the girl explained, "He didn't know where he was running to. Stepping everywhere. He picked that block where there's mostly houses. You can't disappear into a block of houses." She shook her head. "Amateur."

Part of Serena's job was to assemble a volunteer squad of interns and doorknockers and college kids who could articulate the mission. She knew Beth was graduating NYU that spring and did not have a job yet. She called her father from Philadelphia to ask his blessing in recruiting her for a summer position. She promised Beth would be safe.

"How can you make that promise?" said Gerard.

"She'll be with me. The things we'd ask her to do would be in safe neighborhoods during the day. And don't you want her to see something of the world, Dad? You always said you were glad the older kids could remember the city."

Their phone conversations the past few years were cordial, often warm. She'd ask about his knee injury, his tension headaches. Gerard would ask about Washington and tease her evolving political convictions. They had a kind—if strained in the most ordinary way—father and daughter devotion and took pains to disregard, for those brief calls, the seemingly permanent distance between their daily lives.

They had never, not once, talked about Emily.

"Will Beth live with you for the summer?" he asked.

"Of course," Serena said.

"All right, she'll be there in two weeks."

"I haven't called her yet. I don't know if she's interested. I wanted to check with you."

"Two weeks." He told her he loved her and hung up.

* * *

Daphne would die at the end of that summer—August 29. It would be unceremonious and shamefully relieving to the people who'd watched her lungs degenerate over so many years. The family would make a collective decision to keep the funeral small and quiet.

Before that predictable tragedy took shape, in early May, Beth knocked on the door of Serena's English basement apartment. They held each other a good minute. Behind Beth, on the curb, her father's man Brighton Salk unloaded her large purple suitcases.

"Brighton drove you?"

"What? Oh, yeah." Beth watched him managing her wardrobe. "He's so weird to spend a car ride with." She ran past Serena, shouting, "Where will I sleep?"

Brighton got the contents of the trunk to the curb and from the curb down the short stairwell into the middle of the living room.

"Think it's mostly handbags," he said, dropping the last of it.

Serena couldn't remember how old he would be now—probably thirty-three, thirty-four. He wore the same dark casual blazer and gave a feeling he didn't know how to wear it, but any boy who changed many other outward appearances of his life was likely to wear something like this. He was still trim and tough in the shoulders and neck. He had a military crew cut, dark brown eyes, and ashy sunless skin.

She offered a cold water, and he followed her down the exposed-brick hall into the galley kitchen. Beth, from the bedroom, shouted for permission to take clothes out of Serena's closet to make room for hers.

Serena gave Brighton his glass and thanked him for driving Beth.

"Jimmy's been wanting me to take a meeting down this way, so it made sense. I'm going to Harrisonburg after this, then I'll head home."

"You mean Harrisburg?"

"Yeah."

"That's another two hours south. You staying the night there?"

"I'd like to get back tonight."

"You'll be driving into dawn," she said.

She meant to offer that he could stop back here and stay on the couch but for some reason couldn't manage to put it that way.

"I'd like to get back tonight," he repeated.

"How is everything at home?"

She sponged down the counter as he told some details that told her nothing, the kind of sparse, bloodless information you'd give a stranger or a snitch. She remembered him, who he was and where he came from, and tried not to take it personally.

"Your dad has to go to Italy," he said. "In the fall. Jimmy says maybe he's going, too, and maybe I will."

"Italy," said Serena. "Why?"

"Business," said Brighton.

She glistened the last stretch of pink Formica and dropped the sponge in the sink—a custom she would not be told until much later was recruiting bacteria of all kinds.

"I'm saying this for you, not me..." she said, facing him. "He's my dad, not yours."

This marked the first time in years Brighton's expression told a story instead of a rank and a serial number.

Beth came in holding one of Serena's dresses. "I was going to move this to the hall closet, but wouldn't it be better just to throw it away?" She looked around at the stillness she'd walked in on. "Oh, Brighton, do you have a girlfriend who might want it?"

He left for Harrisburg.

A few days later Philadelphia police dropped a bomb on a house that held occupants of a militant group called MOVE. Serena and Beth were at the Safer Cities offices, outside the evacuation radius, but had been, like a lot of people, forewarned of a blast. Eleven people died, all of them Black and five of them children, and sixty-one surrounding homes burned to the ground.

Philadelphia, and Mayor Goode himself, drew the ire and spyglass of national news. Serena's job—Poppy's mission—became, in many respects, more difficult, yet there had been a primal softening of the culture both in the city's bureaucracy and the community hierarchy, and while many people didn't have time to listen to Poppy at all, a crucial few listened quite carefully.

By the end of the summer, they had compiled data on all the neighborhoods where the Safer Cities approach had been enacted. Murders, they demonstrated, were down in proportion to which their alternatives were practiced. It was one of the only bright news items to come out of the city that year. The mayor, presumably, had been informed about their reported success but was preoccupied defending the choice to bomb his residents.

Serena was momentarily horrified by the entire city. Poppy said if she'd read more history, she would stop being so surprised by things. And without surprise, horror loses its teeth.

A few days before Beth was to return to Connecticut, she and Serena visited a man in Glenwood named Wayne Brixton. Wayne was sixty-three and had spent twenty-eight years in prison for murdering a store clerk in a robbery. Since his release four years ago, he'd been working with organizations like theirs to change the nature of his neighborhood "one block, one heart, at a time."

He had gotten to know the Magic girls and liked to tell them they lived up to their name.

"What we need is a group of people in the community to say what you're saying. You girls say it well, but we're not listening to you coming from Dartmouth and wherever, Yale, *New York*. We're a project for you. Nothing to be done about that. But you need people like me, in every city, to speak this message if you want it heard. No more murders. Hell, the first reason anybody out here is killing anybody is so it doesn't get done to them first. We need a murder truce. Then we can get to the other work. But you know, it starts with something more."

"What do you mean?" said Beth. "What more?"

"We have to tell these boys to forgive each other. It's not enough to say don't do it, or do this instead or start a boxing league, or whatever you got on your pad. They need to forgive. They had things done to them since they were four years old, most. I did. Half the time they're not even trying to kill the person they're aiming at—it's someone ten years ago they want. But this guy's here, so he'll do." Wayne rolled his eyes. "It's misery, man, but we can change all this. But we need to talk about forgiveness. You hear me?"

Serena said, "Does it really work? We are having success with practical things. We have mediators now, not cops or psychologists or anything, but community mentors. We give out their numbers, or we write them on the walls in places. People know we aren't telling the cops anything. Now I think...well, I wonder, we start saying 'forgiveness.' It sounds pseudo-spiritual. Does it really make a difference if you forgive anyone?"

Wayne had used the latter half of his twenty-eight years of incarceration to become fluent in the most respected literature around poverty cures, violence suppression, community corrosion, and the indicators that preceded a city's transformation. He could talk about ancient Greece or Carthage or modern Detroit or Chicago, and he would look and sound as natural in a snug professor's blazer as he did telling a tough kid on the corner things he couldn't imagine about prison. His voice was at once musical and serious, and he didn't speak without a declaration in mind, and the way he put it would become irresistible to your memory.

"Forgiveness isn't spiritual," he said. "Forgiveness is the most practical thing you got." He laughed some. "You girls think...if Marcus in Swampoodle kills Derek's brother in Fairhill, Derek's going to go kill Marcus's brother then Marcus himself. Then Marcus's *cousin's* going to kill Derek and Derek's cousin—and it goes. You're fighting retribution. Forgiveness ends the cycle. You want to attack this thing, so you attack it there. Derek has to look at his brother in a coffin and let all that rage out of his heart. Go home. Go to bed." He wiped his hands in the air. "One less murder war in the City of Brotherly Love."

On her last night in town, Serena took Beth to a nice Italian restaurant on Society Hill. While they picked at their ravioli, and Beth attempted to summarize all she'd seen, Serena spied on people about her age at the tables nearby. Jimmy or Brighton would call them yuppies. To the men who made livings the way they did, or to anyone who'd worked in a butcher's shop or on a building site, the concerns of her generation were doomed to seem silly and venal. Serena's last boyfriend's favorite film had been *The Big Chill*, mostly, he'd said, because "they nailed how things could seem like they were going so groovy, but you could still be so empty." Jimmy would've never known the word *empty* could be used for anything besides a gas tank or a Dewar's bottle.

The people Serena had graduated with had become as successful as they'd hoped to be—and seemed, on each successive visit, more insufferable for it. They liked appliances and loved to talk about the ones they had just bought or were to buy soon. They liked skiing. They missed New Hampshire but had moved to the nicest parts of big cities where things were happening, and they didn't go in for nostalgia beyond as a vehicle to discuss past achievements. They dressed immaculately, and a few still did cocaine but most merely drank, and they were all sure their bosses, or anyone who had authority over them, were either incompetent or megalomaniacal.

But she could not take away that they all worked very hard and had great taste in linens and dinnerware and did not pretend they were improving the world, merely their lots in it. She would not be able to say any of these things about generations to come.

"So how long will you stay at this job?" Beth asked.

"I just got here," said Serena. "It's hard to say."

"And is this what you want to do forever? It's a great mission."

Serena asked for the check. They walked to the Liberty Bell. Beth told a story she'd read about Benjamin Franklin and a prostitute, and Serena said she doubted it was true. They got rainbow cookies that were drier than at home, where they used more raspberry filling, and went to the museum steps and pretended to be Rocky.

***

Brighton's father was from Germany, and his mother was English, from Brooklyn, but she moved Brighton to the Bronx when her husband ran off with a candy striper after a jackpot at the track.

At nine years old, Brighton asked Gerard, whom he'd seen around the block and at the Crotona grocery, if he would pay anything for a street sweeper for his storefronts. Gerard brushed him off but soon saw him make a go of that deal with other landlords in the neighborhood.

"That pasty kid," Gerard's brother said one morning, "has a little thing going for himself. The other tykes have ideas, but that one goes up and asks."

Gerard started Brighton as a property manager. At the age of twelve, the boy was trusted to open and lock his storefronts and sign for vendor deliveries. At sixteen he ran security for all their businesses. By seventeen he'd gotten a few scars, one that intersected with his right eyebrow from a jagged piece of pipe. At eighteen Brighton stopped losing fights. He was calm if it went to the ground and could get leverage from below, and if it was only throwing punches, he never waited for anyone to throw first, and he never threw only one.

He didn't understand about the move to Connecticut. As far as he could tell, they'd won the lottery in the Bronx, and everyone they'd grown up with loved them and would die for them, and every day was a whirl of friendly faces and pride-earning work. But when the time came, he moved out of his mother's apartment and leased his own in Fairfield twenty minutes from the docks, where he was told he'd be managing a crew. His mother was about as displeased with his decision as she'd been when he took up with Gerard to begin with—or as she was with any news he'd brought home.

Gerard knew a guy like Brighton didn't get strong from the streets alone. His mettle had been tested before then. That woman showed him life was war. After ten years under her roof, Brighton seeing Gerard and Jimmy and Horace pull a few things over on their enemies was peacetime by comparison. Gerard's short answers and stony mentorship amounted to a sea of love. The Magics showed Brighton dignity was earnable, not a birthright. The day he fled the Bronx, Brighton gave his mother $2,000 and left her screaming in that stale hell in Woodlawn Heights.

After Emily's suicide, Jimmy took a long time off. Brighton expected Gerard to do the same, but he threw himself into business. Jimmy took it to heart and couldn't get through a conversation on the subject without losing composure and, Brighton thought, a bit of self-respect.

It was six years later, and nobody really mentioned her. John McClusky, the hapless widower, had taken his boy to Ireland, then to Tampa where his folks had moved. Gerard went to see him in 1983 and asked if he would move back to the area with his only grandson and take a supervisory role with his lighting company. McClusky said no at the time but returned the next year. He had been sycophantic toward Brighton ever since coming back. Brighton didn't know what would prompt a guy like that to return to this part of the world. McClusky mixed into any squad of hooligans like a prune in whiskey. But that's how Gerard wanted it, so Brighton brought John along where he could, offered him a beer if he was having one, and tried to listen to the guy talk. The big problem there was Brighton barely believed anything John said. He didn't think he was a liar. He just didn't think his words matched who he was. He thought John was constantly trying on a new set of traits, checking if it would fit, hoping no one would notice he hadn't yet found a set to keep.

None of them were at the hospital the afternoon Daphne passed.

Brighton believed Gerard thought he would have more chances to get there, hold her hand, speak alone. But Gerard didn't break down or throw anything when word came. His temper, nowadays, rarely showed itself. In the office at the port, Jimmy, Horace, and John stood up and paid their respects. Brighton walked up last and stuck out his hand. "Sorry, boss."

Gerard shook it firmly.

On the morning of the funeral, Serena came to the docks looking for her father and uncle. Brighton was in the middle of reaming one of their couriers when he saw her through the gridded window talking to a foreman.

"Go ahead," he told the guy.

"Am I canned or not?"

"You got one more life, but that's because Jimmy spoke up for you. Stop beating on the other guys just to find out if you can win."

"I beat on Shanahan because he talked about one of Jimmy's nieces, swear it. And I beat on Reilly because everyone working this shift knows he's got the virus."

"Shanahan's afraid of women. *You* talk about the girls; I know you do. And Reilly's got pneumonia, you dopy shmuck, not AIDS. You know what AIDS is?"

"Do you?" He held back a grin.

"Let me catch you again with your hands up," he got in front of him, "I'm gonna show you how soft Shanahan and Reilly really are."

Brighton went down the salt-ruined wooden steps, spit into the Sound, and crossed the planks to where Serena was clutching her hat in the breeze. He told his foreman, "I got it, Jimmy."

Serena nodded, then said to Brighton, "Does my uncle only hire men named Jimmy?"

"I hired that one," he said.

"No one's at the house. I thought they'd be at Henrietta's, but that's empty."

"Everyone's at Horace's. They're not doing anything at the church, just the burial, then back to Horace's for...whatever it is, a drink."

"Horace's house?"

Brighton shrugged. "Your dad didn't want people finding out, coming over. See how I called him your dad?" he said. She smirked. He could tell she was going to apologize, so he cut in. "I'm driving over now. I'll take you."

"I drove here," she said.

"You remember where his house is?"

"No," she said.

"So let's go."

* * *

Though she hadn't in many years, Serena said a prayer as the casket was lowered into the earth.

Back at Horace's, some shared memories of Daphne, most of which took place in the backyard when she was not yet a teenager. Past that age, memories were suffused with medical opinions and a warning she not "overexert."

Hannah had three brandies and told everyone Reagan was making their country into a respectable presence on the world stage. Madeline was mad whenever people went too long without mentioning Daphne. Beth, still sentimental about Philadelphia, would not leave Serena's side.

When Gerard and Horace went for cigars in Horace's garden, Serena slipped out to join them.

"You don't inhale it, Serena," said Horace. "*Taste* and let it out. Each one of these costs more than eighteen holes at Pebble Beach."

She came out with it. "I remember in the city," she said to her father, "you would sponsor parties for kids at Christmas, give to treatment centers and whatnot. Do you still?"

Gerard looked at Horace, then said, "We give to charities in New York and Connecticut."

"Can I ask what some of them are?"

"What's the upshot, Serena?" said Horace.

"I want you to consider contributing to the organization I work for in Philadelphia. We are...we have a model that's working to reduce violent crimes. Killings. If it keeps working, we're going to take it to other cities. I want you to think about helping us grow it."

"I know what you're working on. But I haven't heard anything about its success," Gerard played back at her. "Haven't read about it in any paper, haven't seen it on television."

"You will on Tuesday. I'm going on C-SPAN to talk about it."

The two men looked at each other through smoke clouds. "You're going on national television?" said Horace. He laughed and clapped his wooden knee joint. "I told you," he told his boss-partner, "I told you, this one was going to be busy, Gerry."

Gerard hadn't said anything.

Serena had held out her palm before to community leaders in Philly, donors in Washington, and headhunters on the Hill, but this was the most painful silence she'd endured.

"New York City had more than two thousand homicides last year," she said. "Imagine we could make this work in New York? Where we came from?" Still nothing. With his suit coat hanging open, and his tie tossed on a chair inside, she saw for the first time in his life that her father had developed the feeblest hint of a belly. "You know," she said, "I don't technically have to ask you for anything. More than half the family assets are still in my name. If I want to withdraw funds and put them into a 501(c)(3), all I have to do is call the bank."

A ghostly billow flew off his lips. "So why ask me?"

She sighed, her bluff crumbling. "Why wouldn't you want to do this?"

Late summer mosquitoes danced in the garden. The moon was low, clear, and crescent, and death's rank pollution was overflowing Horace's house, drifting into their mood here, where cigars were taken more seriously than the grim reaper himself.

"We're going to Rome in two weeks," Gerard said, "for business. None of us has ever been. Have you?"

"You know I have not."

"OK. So you'll come with us to Rome. We'll be gone seven days. You'll give me your assessment of the trip. When we get back, I'll give whatever you want me to give to this…murder group."

He stumped out his cigar.

"I don't want to go to Rome, and I don't have time to go to Rome."

"So don't go," he said, standing up. "You know the bank's number. Call them and get your money. And next time, don't pretend you need my blessing to save the world."

He went toward the house. Horace continued with his cigar in silence. Serena took hers, of which she'd had three puffs, laid it on the stone in front of him, and crushed the length of it under her heel. She spat on the remains, went inside, and told Brighton to take her back to her car.

***

Television made her nervous. She wanted to believe she'd been born superior to nerves, but all she could picture, as the tech with the headset counted down from ten seconds to live, was a big round table full of high school friends, Dartmouth English professors, crushes, and coaches watching and laughing at her every butchered phrase and malapropism.

Yet people who saw it said she was fabulous. Poppy Solnit was thrilled. And Hannah called and said lavish, supportive things. That's when Serena got the first clue how envious a person Hannah had become. She hoped it would even out, as other tendencies had in her other sisters, over time, through pain.

The day after the interview she took a connection to JFK. She met Madeline and Sonia Maude in the international lounge. They sat three in an aisle on an MGM Grand Air redeye. And each wore shoddy clothes they wouldn't mind getting smoke-ruined by ten hours of airlocked tobacco. They woke up in Rome.

Madeline lifted her shade as the plane began a descent. Serena saw what she believed was the Vatican. She thought of her Catholic mother. She asked Sonia if she knew what was special about the Vatican.

"It's where the pope lives," said Sonia. "You didn't know that?"

Madeline, twenty-seven, and Serena, twenty-nine, did not.

They collected their bags. A driver took them to where the whole family was staying, the Excelsior on the Via Veneto. They went to their rooms and took naps. When Serena awoke, she'd forgotten where she was. She stepped onto her balcony and wiped the exhaustion from her eyes. It was late afternoon. She looked up and down the Via Veneto and smelled the fall air. A sunset flirted with the cobblestones. An Italian love song played in the suite above. She had never been out of America. She ran to take a shower, furious at how giddy she felt head to toe.

***

Knocking on Gerard's door, Jimmy was already dressed in his tan suit and open-collar blue shirt, confusing, his younger brother thought, Rome's fashion for Miami's.

Jimmy sat on the bed. "Serena and the girls got here. They're coming to dinner."

"I know."

"Why you added on Serena I'll never guess, *hermano*."

"It's *fratello* here. *Mio fratello*." He took his own suit jacket out of a garment bag.

Jimmy looked in the bathroom, then at his sitting area. "You gave yourself the bigger room."

"The kid handed me a key. You want to switch?"

Jimmy seemed to be thinking about it. "No, but it's wasted on you."

As adults, Gerard and Jimmy did not argue. They could tell each other harsh truths in cold voices without offense. If you'd have asked them, both would say business came second to family. But only by putting business first had they found the dispassion and maturity to bury differences and never trade a cross word. In a most bizarre criminal way, this inviolable code of their business relationship—on which they believed their very survival depended—was the same thing that deepened their love as brothers year after year.

Success required respect; respect permitted affection.

"We need to sell lights on this trip. How many meetings do we have set up to sell lights?" said Gerard.

"At least two, but Horace is making calls from back home, trying to set another one."

"We need eight," said Gerard.

"It's difficult, Ger, with the language barrier."

"We need to be able to show why five members of our company flew to Italy for a business trip. Two meetings with midsize venues are not cutting it. We need eight, and one needs to become a customer. Don't work on anything else until we've set that right."

Jimmy picked up the TV remote and started flipping channels, forgetting he wouldn't understand a word. "Horace will come through," he said. "Besides, the girls are here. Isn't that the point? Show it was half business, half family? I also think we are getting ahead of ourselves that we'll be questioned about this trip."

"Tagletti will be in Rome tomorrow night," said Gerard.

Jimmy looked pointedly at him. "You kept that from me?"

"I found out an hour ago. I thought it would be his contact—but he's coming himself. So we need an alibi on both fronts. And we need it to be steel. I think we are going to be asked to explain this trip."

Jimmy paced the area rug. He appeared to be wondering several things and satisfying his own wonderings. He drew back the pink curtains and looked out at the eternal city. "The FBI's never heard of us, brother." He sort of laughed. "Listen to me, I'm supposed to be the cautious one."

Simple respect, the habit of dispassion, tenderness—they had practiced being perfect for each other.

Jimmy flipped on the TV again. Gerard went into his master bathroom to get ready alone.

***

Everyone was to meet in the lobby at seven to leave for dinner at a restaurant on the Piazza Navona.

Serena wore a blue sequin minidress. It had a deep neckline and was knotted at the waist. Guests in the elevator mumbled.

She walked into the decadent foyer, and the porter pointed out the rest of her party, the girls seated on a sofa, some of the men—Jimmy, Brighton, and two others who worked for her father—all at the bar with aperitifs.

Madeline whistled at her outfit. This drew the attention of the bar and some staff. The guys, shy if they weren't bloodying anybody up, stayed gazing into their glasses.

"We're waiting on your old man," said Jimmy. "They say this place is *molto bello*." He shouted to the bellboys to ask how his inflection sounded. They gave a thumbs-up. He looked Serena over. "I thought *I* was flashy," he tugged his collar. "You cut off half of that thing? Leave it as a tip for housekeeping?"

Serena shoved him. He made fists and jabbed the air.

Gerard came off the elevator and announced their cars were waiting. Everyone followed him through the golden doors.

Brighton waited alone for the bar tab. As he signed it, Serena idled. "You want to escort me to the car?"

He looked out to where everyone was shuffling into two black Pontiac sedans. "Escort yourself. I'm working."

"I'm going to tell my father you said that."

"Go ahead." He closed the checkbook and dropped the pen on the bar. "Everybody thinks you're a liar anyhow."

He walked ahead to meet the others. His grin made his cheeks so fat she could see them sticking out all the way back here.

***

The night of Daphne's memorial, he'd driven her back to her car. Serena hadn't asked him to walk her to where it was parked, past the "No Trespassing" signs and orange cones in Henrietta's private lot. Brighton said he could be in trouble if he didn't.

They took the path along the Sound. She couldn't bear the silence that she knew everyone else endured in Brighton's strange, cagey presence, so she filled it with grievances—about the burial plot, about the food Horace had catered—and eventually she let it storm out: Horace's supine wisdom;

Jimmy's indulgences and his cars; her father's emotional walls, miles high, unscalable.

When she got to her car, she didn't feel like leaving. The syrupy gentle night wasn't a match to anything in her mood. She turned on the ignition then turned it off. She slammed the visor mirror.

She got out and said, "What's wrong with any of them that they'd let me walk alone with some thug like you? Me in some abandoned parking lot with *you* to keep me safe. More likely you attack me than I bump into some Connecticut rapist hiding in Henrietta's dumpster."

He was about ten feet away with his hands in suit pockets. "Guess they think I'd be too scared to try anything."

Her breathing was everywhere. Her chest was up and down. She hated humanity and all signs of its triumphs. "Are you?" she said.

Brighton swallowed. "No."

The Piazza Navona was lantern lit and bustling with September tourists and Gypsies smarter and smoother than the three-card monte youngbloods of the East Village or Van Cortland Park. Gerard led them to the smallest of the Bernini statues where their local hosts, two native Italian men and their wives, welcomed the Americans warmly.

Gerard introduced his group one at a time, and the Italian couples embraced each person named. When this ceremony was over, they were led to a restaurant that looked more like a dining room, three blocks off the piazza. Serena had a risotto dish that would turn her into a snob anytime she'd try to describe it later on. Jimmy ordered a pizza and hated it.

After dinner, Gerard and Jimmy said they were going for a walk with their guests to a café for a digestif. Jimmy suggested that Serena, Sonia Maude, and the others walk the hosts' wives to the Trevi Fountain with Brighton Salk and his two security men. Everyone liked the idea except Serena, who stayed silent, and Brighton, who whispered something to Gerard. Gerard shook his head, and the four oldest men set off.

At the fountain Sonia Maude gave out coins for everyone's secret wish toss. Without comment she handed two to Serena. The fountain was brilliantly lit this time of night. The Italian wives showed off the statue with local pride and told stories, historical and personal, of the Spanish Steps.

Brighton leaned on a pillar where he could see everybody at once.

"What's the worst that could happen you and me disappear to a wine bar?" Serena said, not looking his way as she said it.

"I'm on the clock."

She saw Madeline hovering over the fountain edge, following Sonia's lead, tossing the lira over her left shoulder, and the coin glinted in the echo of crystal blue light.

"Did you make a wish?" she said.

He ignored her, calling over one of his guys and telling him to stand post on the other side of the circle.

Serena said, "Would you rather watch out for them or me?"

"I'm working."

"I'm walking down that alley alone." She pointed. "I'm going to find the first bar playing music, or whatever they call a bar, and sit alone and drink what I please. In about three hours, 1:00 a.m. local, I'll walk home, stumbling down backstreets until I find the way." She tossed him her lira, and he caught it. "Stay here if you think the Italian wives need more protecting than I will."

"Just," he said, puttering, "just wait ten minutes. Serena. Serena. I won't know where you go."

She shouted over the heads of sightseers, "First bar with music, girl in a blue dress drinking alone, smiling about something you'd have to be from New York to understand."

***

Before she'd left Philadelphia for Daphne's burial, Serena visited Poppy Solnit at her apartment on a Sunday morning.

"Are you telling me your father is a gangster?"

"I wouldn't use that word. He does things outside the law to further his legitimate businesses. The truth is that there's only so much I really know. I left home."

Poppy was drinking orange juice. She set it down. "And the question is, would I take his money to grow our organization?"

"I don't for sure know if he would give it. The question is," Serena said, "does it matter where money comes from? I know we've had donors who…I mean, in Washington, it's all corporate money from corporate actors who want the law to treat them some special way. I guess I wonder… my family has done things I think are despicable. I wonder if my thinking them despicable is good enough reason not to use what they can give to stop murders."

"Mayor Goode and the council," said Poppy, "sometimes tap into the city's utility budgets to fill police coffers. So they used nice traceable money to pay for that bomb they dropped on Osage Avenue."

"It's complicated with my family."

"With every family," her boss said, in her apartment where she lived alone. "Does your father pay taxes?"

"On some of his money, I'm sure, yes."

"Well," she said, "then the government is using dirty money to try to help people too."

"So you want me to ask him?"

"I don't want to know another thing about it," said Poppy.

She got up and opened the door for her guest, saying she'd see her in the office tomorrow. Serena walked into the hall and turned around. "Did you know what I wanted to talk to you about before I came?"

Poppy had green eyes that had a special way of calling you odd. "No, Serena. I thought you might be coming to tell me your sister's death was taking too big a toll on you, and you needed time off—or were maybe going to resign."

"Oh," Serena said, "no, I don't need any time off for that."

Poppy closed the door.

Tonight, in Rome, Serena found a place that played American jazz and blues, and she paid top dollar for a Barolo and watched the door. Her chaperone arrived in ten minutes.

He refused the wine for a while, then took some. It was lost on him, she thought, seeing how quickly he finished each glass.

Serena couldn't remember the last man who had inspired in her the role of aggressor, but with Brighton she seemed to relish it. She found him tormentable. She found a playground spirit on the barrel end of his boyish grins, this sore thumb of a silent tough guy clad in black, victim to her taunts. He struggled to make eye contact. He was never sure what he was going to say. His opinions were meek until eventually they'd land on a subject where one of the five or six things he already believed could apply itself, and he'd say it simply and with gravity.

They were dancing sitting down.

The first time he checked his watch was an hour later. "I can't believe we left those wives."

She smiled. "Why are we in Rome, Brighton?" She saw a notion pass cross his face. "I'm not playing you for information; I don't really care. But since we're sitting here, and you're nervous as a prom girl…"

He wiped the thumb smudges off the base of his wine glass. He didn't take long, she thought, to decide to trust her. "Did you hear about the Mafia busts in February?"

"No."

"Well, everyone else did." She waited. "They busted the heads of the Five Families in New York. They got 'em on a lot, drugs, gambling…what do you call it when you squeeze a guy?"

"Extortion," she said.

"Yeah. Lot of extortion. Anyway, nobody knows anything in the city, and people are protecting what they got, thinking now's when someone's going to move to take it."

"You need to use more nouns; I don't speak this way." She squinted. "What do any of you care what happens to the Mafia?"

"A little bit it touches us. Here's the thing.… A rat got into the Bonanno family around the time everything happened with Beth and Emily. That family lost a lot of their power, you know, on account of this rat. So those guys who were left, they were jammed, wanted to partner up with crews like us. They kinda needed to.

"A little while back, your dad and Jimmy, they went in on a construction project with a guy. An Italian. The short of it is: Now they know us. Someone over there, in the city, I guess they asked would we come to Rome. Since the busts, people here are running some of the business in

New York. For safety. They need to pass information both ways. And they need guys who ain't Italian, *brokers*, who the feds won't think to look at."

"You're *brokering* for the New York Mafia," Serena repeated. He lost his fluency, hearing her say it the way she did. "When did my father do this first special construction project?"

Brighton answered quietly. "Six years ago." She thumped the table. She looked around with fresh eyes. "It's not much, Serena. They know who we are; we know them. We ain't done much." He shrugged. "They leave us be. They asked us this favor, and there's an upside in it for the straight things Gerard has going. So he said yes. Honestly, I think it's also 'cause he wanted to visit this city. I don't know, but I think it reminds him of your mother."

"Don't talk about her," Serena snapped. "Who were those guys we just ate with?" she said.

"They're moneylenders, like shylocks, here in Rome. They have...power here."

"Mafia."

He didn't say anything.

Louis Armstrong blared a trumpet through the gravelly speakers. Cheerful, bombed locals laughed and touched hands, denizens of a city built on love and God and the skulls of gladiator slaves. Louis sang about nearness.

Brighton did something he never would. He reached across the table and took her hand. She let him for a second, then took it away.

On the promenade they saw a sign for *Ponte Sisto*. They took the bridge over the River Tiber. The black water swirled and reflected wavering lanterns.

Halfway along Serena said, "You see that?"

On the other side of the bridge, a man had shoved a Gypsy to the ground for trying to pickpocket him. The man's wife pleaded with her husband to hurry away.

"Mm-hmm," said Brighton.

"In the Bronx at least they were good at it."

He set his elbow on the banister. "How many murders did Rome have last year?"

"We don't study foreign cities," she said. "But I don't think many."

He looked with amusement at the Gypsy hustlers dusting their friend off. "They're not dumb," he said. "They're just a few years behind us." He pointed them out as he spoke, without regard for their noticing. "The first guy makes a mess of trying to take the husband's wallet. The husband gets rough; the wife doesn't know where she is." He pointed out the other. "That's when the second guy comes over, picks her bag, her bracelet, watch…the husband's so focused on hurting the first guy. He keeps his wallet, she loses a grand off her skin, doesn't know it for an hour."

Serena watched them and replayed the scene until it made sense. "Why do you say they're years behind?"

"I grew up running that. I bet you they're headed to a stoop somewhere, five other tiny crews like theirs, splitting it up and buying forties."

"Forties," Serena repeated, smirking at the one part he got wrong.

She hadn't noticed when the pickpockets began looking their way, during Brighton's seminar. Now they walked up on both sides, three of them—four.

She made to walk away. One of them blocked her. Two were quite short and no more than sixteen years old. Two were broad men. One had a face tattoo of a flame.

The closest said something vicious to Brighton in Italian. Serena looked around the bridge. There was a group twenty yards down the channel, but they weren't looking this way. There was a lady by herself across from them. She watched.

"OK," Serena said, "we're sorry, OK?" She stepped between Brighton and the first man. "We're sorry, and we go."

"*Cosa stai guardando!*"

"*Sei uno stronzo!*"

Serena looked the tallest man in the eyes. "You are trying to work. We interrupted." She motioned with her fingers. "We walk away. Leave you alone."

She had Brighton's suit sleeve. The Gypsies parted carefully, one still shouting in their faces. Serena led him swiftly through the opening. They were five feet cleared when Brighton snatched his sleeve back and grabbed the closest one, a kid, by the throat, squeezing it fast like popping a bag with air in it. The boy gasped, his eyes bulged, and he fell when Brighton let go. The tattooed face guy drew a wand from his waistcoat. Brighton took it on the left forearm then caught him by his collar and battered him with jackhammers five times, lifting his chin so each one hit clean. When he freed his collar, the tattoo sank. The other two tapped their feet, cursed, and spat, but neither moved any closer.

Serena screamed at him. Brighton felt his pockets, front and back, and said, "Check your jewelry and bag."

"Come *on*!"

"Check, Serena."

She checked and had everything.

He backed away keeping them all in sight, the two on ground and the two who didn't fight. At the end of the bridge, he turned and walked with her but refused to go any faster than they had on the way there.

***

It was 1:30 a.m. on the Via Veneto when they returned to the Hotel Excelsior, Brighton quiet as granite, Serena carrying her heels. The concierge stopped them. "You're wanted in room 600."

They came off the elevator. Jimmy was waiting in a chair at the top of the long regal hall. He looked at the signs of the night they both wore. "Strange days" was all he could muster.

They entered the suite. Gerard dismissed the two men waiting with him. The boss's stare drifted from his daughter to Brighton, his brain doing pirouettes behind thousand-pound eyes. "You were supposed to work! You know what work is, you ingrate?"

"Daddy," she began, and he took a fast step toward her.

She squealed and looked at the ground. Both Brighton and Jimmy saw it.

"Sir," Brighton said, collected, "I didn't want your daughter to walk the streets alone. I thought—I made a judgment call that you'd want her protected and that the boys could get everybody home. They had cars waiting; Serena would be on foot. I know it wasn't my call to make, but I had to make one."

"We don't ask you to make calls, Brighton," he said. "We ask you to show up. That's your job. *Show up.*"

Brighton looked to Jimmy to end the anticipation.

Jimmy said, "The Italian wives got separated from our group. Our guys lost them after the fountain. Now our hosts are spooked; they're running around trying to find 'em." He shrugged his Miami-suited shoulders. "It's not ideal, but…they're probably OK."

Gerard looked at his brother. "Oh?"

"I'm saying, Ger, the kid shouldn't have split, of course not. But things being equal, I'm glad Serena wasn't alone."

"No," said Gerard, looking again at his daughter, talking to no one, "she certainly wasn't alone, was she?" Gerard sat and said to Brighton, "You're bombed."

"I am not, I just—"

"Your face is red as a candy cane; you're hammered."

There was a firm, long knock at the door. Jimmy said, "I'll get it, I guess."

As he circled the sitting area, Serena said, "Daddy, we got jumped by some drifter kids on the way home. Brighton fought them off."

Gerard sized him up again. "And wasn't that impressive?"

Brighton twitched his head and walked to the window.

Serena heard the door unlatch and saw her father's face before she heard Jimmy's stilted greeting. She peeked around the corner. The man's suit was silver cashmere. His hair looked soaked. He opened his arms to Gerard.

"Mr. Tagletti," Gerard said.

The hug was long. Then he went around to each of them for a two-handed shake, repeating his name, "Vincent Tagletti."

Serena knew his name. It came back to her, the way it was spoken at her dining table, the days after Beth's abduction, when Horace Eaton voiced his concern that any meeting with a made man, even one that ended favorably for the Magics, would ultimately have a bad result. Now here they were, six years hence, representatives of a family-owned lighting installation business, in a Roman suite shaking the manicured hand of a mafioso after midnight.

Gerard said Serena was just leaving, but Tagletti covered up that idea, insisting he wouldn't be long. He sat on the edge of Gerard's bed, smiling.

"We were expecting to see you tomorrow night," said Jimmy.

"I'm early." He invited everyone to sit.

"You heard, I assume, that the men we met were separated from their wives tonight," Gerard said.

"I heard," he said solemnly. "And your men were watching them. I said, couldn't be, the Magics see everything. But no, it was true. My hosts here in town, my friends, *your friends*, they run around the city with no wives." He laughed and tried to conceal it. "It's either the start of a horrible tragedy or the earliest Christmas present in Europe!"

He let the laugh out. Jimmy joined.

Tagletti noticed Serena, unlike the others, had not taken a seat. He said, "We're being rude, talking business like you're not here. Let me explain: We have associates in Italy, my family does. We have enemies in New York, my family does. Just the same, our enemies in New York have associates in Italy. Would you figure that? So something goes wrong here, we wonder…is it the hand of chance? Or the long arm of an enemy, reaching across an ocean…"

"My daughters do not participate in my business," Gerard said.

"You mean not anymore," Tagletti said quickly.

Serena watched Gerard. He didn't react. She looked at Brighton. His hands had made fists in his lap.

Serena said, "What are you doing here if you hired us to come and do your bidding?"

Jimmy told her to keep quiet. Tagletti found this irresistible. "You remind me of my youngest daughter; may she rest in peace." He peeked at Brighton and whispered, "Moved to Iowa and married a Jew." He turned back to Serena. "I got a sign on my back, kid. The only people I can talk to are friends. Your father is my friend." He spun in a full circle and wagged his finger. "But your father's a dangerous man!" He said it like he was telling her how good Gerard was at a certain sport. "Do you know how dangerous? You know what he did? One time? She doesn't know?"

Jimmy was watching his brother. Serena knew he was hoping against hope Gerard played his hand without provocation.

"Hey, Vincent," Gerard said, "how many times did you smoke cigars with Donnie Brasco?"

Hopes dashed.

Tagletti's pleasant face turned to stone.

"We're here to close a deal for you," Gerard continued. "I think you should know: It's the last deal on our ledger. We'll close it. Then we're going home."

Tagletti told Serena, "A lot of people, you know, they think I'm…" he smashed his hands together, "*finito.* No more." He shouted, "Like Charlemagne!" He nodded around at them. "The paper says Donnie Brasco. The paper says what happened to Rastelli. The paper says about big shot Paul Castellano and his mansion. The paper says Bonanno who! *Mafia Commission* this and *Mafia Commission vaffanculo*!

"All because…this US attorney who thinks he invented the job, who turncoats on his own people…this son of a pizza maker from Brooklyn says *he's* going to wipe out the Five Families." He laughed like before, a slick gurgle. "Bonannos were kicked *off* the Mafia Commission!" He laughed and looked at them like he wondered why they weren't joining. "We were kicked off The *Commission*, Gerard. Can you believe it? We weren't welcome anymore. Now The Commission is indicted. And we're free!" He did a tap dance. "Mark my words, girl. My life…is just beginning. I'm sixty-three. Vincent Tagletti is the future of everything." He screamed in a hoarse voice and shook the walls, "And anyone who thinks this is a good time to make a move against me is gonna find out just how soon the future is coming!"

"We're sure you're right about that," said Jimmy. "The meeting tonight went well. They have your terms. When they left, they were going to think them over. And we're going to find their wives and get them home."

Tagletti hadn't looked away from Gerard. He waved his hand. "They were at a gelato shop in Trastevere. They're already home."

He went over to Gerard and held his hand out. Gerard shook it but stayed sitting. Tagletti grinned. He went to the door, opened it, and stopped.

"Hey, Serena," he said, "you know why Charlemagne's empire crumbled? It's not 'cause they got attacked from the outside. It's 'cause they couldn't rule it right. Couldn't get it right *within.* He did good for a while, Charlemagne." Tagletti looked at her old man. "Then he made something too big. Didn't know how to handle it. And it swallowed him whole." He tipped an imaginary hat. "Loved you on TV."

***

There was the question of what Gerard had done.

As Serena returned to her room that night, she realized it was something she was asking herself before Tagletti yelled it aloud.

In the years that divided the twilight of her girlhood—when she'd signed those trust documents—and the dawn of who'd she now become, she had this ungraspable sense that her father had turned one side of his face permanently away from her. There was a look, a clue of malice, he would not let her see.

His eyes were still those of a warm man, not cold like Simon Hayes's in that penthouse or Tagletti's or, she'd admit, Brighton's. Gerard Magic's great redemption was that he still wore the face of a family man. But in the long pauses on their infrequent calls, and in the eerie cruelty he'd revealed in Horace's cigar garden—when he concealed any hint of pride at the news she was going to be recognized nationally—Serena could tell there was a new dimension to his life he would do anything to stop her seeing.

***

There was the question of what he had done.

Would it change the color of the money she was prepared to take from him for her endeavors, her holy plans and high aims?

Family mysteries are intolerable. She was restless to know. Now and in the future, two things seemed to happen the same way every time she found out someone she loved had done something horrible. First, she felt furious and betrayed; then, often in the same minute, she would do anything to stop them facing consequences for it.

An hour after she'd gone back to her room, Uncle Jimmy knocked gently.

Madeline was asleep in the bed beside hers. Jimmy whispered through the chain lock. He apologized for Tagletti showing up. He was sorry she had to hear any of it. Then he said Horace had sent word that four additional sales meetings for potential lighting contracts had been arranged around the city. As the others would be busy with the Italian business, Gerard wanted Serena to take these meetings throughout the week and try to close a deal.

She thought of a dozen reasons to refuse; quickly she said she'd do it.

Jimmy nodded, then lingered. "Well."

"There's another thing?" she said.

"Yeah." She saw he was shaken at the inevitability of this next part. "Your father also wants me to tell you that Brighton did a lot of drugs growing up, that he uses call girls in Fairfield," he exhaled, "that his mother's a nut; his father was probably a rapist, that he may have something wrong with his brain, and he'll probably be in jail soon."

Jimmy had rattled the list off in a monotone voice, like a rap sheet recited by a jaded bailiff.

Serena unlatched the door chain and stepped into the soft red hall. "Why are we beholden to the Bonanno family?" Jimmy shook his head. "Jimmy, what did Daddy do after Emily died?"

"Go back to Philly, kid. Don't even worry about the meetings, just fly out tomorrow. I don't know why he brought you here. Get back to your life."

"Tell me what he did," she said, "after my sister killed herself." She searched his eyes. "Please, Jimmy."

Jimmy put his hands on her small shoulders. He told the truth.

When he was gone, she went out on her balcony.

She'd been wrong about something important. She thought Gerard had been trying to hide some new part of himself from her. That wasn't it. He wanted to show it to her. That's why she was in Rome.

***

Their second meeting with the Italian shylock group was two days later in a villa in Piazzale San Paolo, two miles from St. Paul's Basilica.

Gerard and Jimmy had, during the first meeting, presented an arrangement whereby the head of this moneylending operation would run the Bonanno family's Florida business for a 25 percent take of the profits. The moneylenders would be asked to send three men from Italy to Brooklyn to help expand the family's gambling trade and two to Staten Island to help consolidate their union position.

Neither Gerard nor his brother expected the Roman to go for these terms. They were asking him to send his most trusted and capable men to wade into a foreign crime business that was now actively targeted by the US attorney and FBI, and their principal explanation was that the work was too dangerous for New York's Bonanno soldiers, like Tagletti, to take on themselves.

It was a bad time to be an Italian gangster in New York, and the Italian gangsters in Italy knew it. They may have been second or third cousins to Tagletti or Philip Rastelli or any of the other capos. But they were going to want more money and more assurances than the Magics had been cleared to give. Nonetheless both brothers believed the first meeting had gone well, and they came today to close a deal.

Gerard and Jimmy hadn't spoken much in the two days since Tagletti's visit. Gerard knew Jimmy was angry with him for disrespecting Tagletti, less so with the Brasco reference, which could've been billed as rough chess playing, but more defiantly by refusing to stand to shake his hand. There were no two ways about that. Gerard was letting him know that this was the last piece of business he'd be willing to do with the Bonannos, and by not rising to his feet in that hotel room he was also saying he didn't think Tagletti was tough enough, just then, to oppose his exit.

Gerard never wanted a partnership, but Tagletti and his crew, while they were tougher and better feared, interceded on his behalf when Gerard needed them. Someone stood up for you, and you were in their debt: That was the way it was whether you were Italian or not—the old neighborhood way, the handshake doctrine.

Gerard owed them. They'd never strong-armed him or asked for an unfair split on any deal. They merely wanted friendship with a semi-legitimate enterprise and a family with a last name whose ethnicity wouldn't draw the prejudice of Uncle Sam's minions.

Jimmy never minded working with the mob. He thought they were reasonable, and the association was casual. But after the FBI indictments, he knew his family was risking everything in trying to help the Bonannos keep both hands on a vanishing fiefdom.

Jimmy got the sense that Tagletti and his people—their type—weren't fighting the feds, and they weren't fighting other families; they were at war with time itself. It was a fixed-ticket match. Jimmy wondered, on that morning drive through the short-hill villa town, if his family would ever have to fight that same enemy and whether they'd be wise enough to know Time could never lose—or if they'd start believing, like Tagletti, like long-dead rulers, like most New Yorkers, that Time is killable and men are not.

Their sedan pulled up outside the moneylender's villa. They were thirty minutes early.

Gerard asked the driver if there was anything they could see while they waited. He told them about Saint Paul's Basilica. In English, he told them it was very beautiful, very green; he stumbled through the word *monastic* and said it was built over the burial ground of Paul the Apostle. Jimmy said he'd rather walk around the block.

At five minutes to the hour, a courier with a mustache and straw boater hat walked out of the villa gates. He motioned to the American businessmen. They came over, and he spoke in impeccable English. He said his bosses had contemplated the terms and found them lacking. He said they had already communicated, through back channels, to the acting boss of the Bonanno family that they would have no part in assisting their operations from the old country.

When Gerard began his retort, the courier added that to demonstrate their seriousness, and show that threats or intimidation would be in vain, they had already issued a contract on Vincent Tagletti should he be seen on the streets of Rome. The Magics, the tidy Italian man with the mustache said finally, were free to enjoy three more days in the holy city, at which point the murder contract would extend to them as well.

***

Brighton hadn't said a word to Serena since the night of the scrape on Ponte Sisto.

He'd driven her to two sales meetings, but Sonia Maude was usually in the front seat, and he kept his eyes on the cabbies blaring their horns and speeding nowhere, reminding himself at every turn that the left side was right and right meant smash.

He overheard her reports to Jimmy on the meetings, neither of which seemed to promise a contract. At the third, he stood in the back of the room with another body man while Serena presented to two executives in cracked leather chairs.

One spoke in Italian, the other translated. "My colleague was hoping your father would be here today."

"He is indisposed," said Serena. "But any pricing he can greenlight I can too."

The Italian, then the translation, "We have no need for this service."

"Well. I won't waste your time." She collected her presentation items.

"Can you speak..." he continued, "for your father on most matters?"

She looked to Brighton at the back. He looked at their flashy shoes and rusty office. He nodded at her. "Well," she added, "most."

The two spoke natively for around a minute. Then, "We understand he is in town selling light. We also understand he is here to represent parties in New York."

Brighton walked to the front of the room, to her side. "Nobody knows what you mean."

The man who had spoken only in Italian now said in English, "We would like you to give your father a message."

***

A block behind the Pantheon there was an *enoteca* with a private garden. Jimmy paid for a bottle of Malbec and gave the proprietor twenty euros not to allow other patrons access to the garden for an hour. He sat at a small white table with Gerard and Brighton. Serena sat alone.

"Tell it again," said Jimmy. "I can focus better out here."

"There wasn't much to it besides that," said Brighton, soaked in sweat. "They were plain guys, knock-off watches; office was trash. But they had leather shoes. Had to cost a year's salary if that was their real office. So I figured we'd hear them. They know we're brokering for the Bonannos. They know folks aren't lining up to get involved in FBI business. So their offer is this: They can send men to New York to manage things. But they want a piece of *our business*. Not the Italians'. All our real estate, our properties, the books, cargo, all of it. They say the mob business is too hot. They think what we got—quiet, a little ways out from the city—they think that's the next thing."

"You think they were connected guys or independent?" said Jimmy.

"What do I know about that?" They sat in the stillness of the wine garden, listening to September birds and the shuffle of tourists who debated whether a gelato now would make them too full for dinner. "Did you make a deal with the moneylender?" he said. "If you did, we don't need these guys."

Gerard sat back in his seat. "Go get my daughter."

Brighton sighed, got up, and disappeared into the shade of the wine bar. He came back out with Serena. She pulled up a chair.

Gerard said to her, "Think about the room and the faces of the men."

"OK."

"Were they cops?"

Serena looked at the white pebbles under her feet. "I really don't think so."

Jimmy asked, "How much did they seem to know about us?"

"A lot," she said. "I got the impression—there's a feeling, all I can call it is a feeling—that there are people who know we're here. And that they're telling other people about it. I think these men knew that we..."

she looked at her father, "that *you* are under obligation to the Mafia and want to be rid of them. I think they meant to imply they would help achieve that. Take on the burden of helping the Bonannos in exchange for partnering with you in whatever else you're doing. *All* of what you're doing." She tried to let it sit, then, "Your business instincts have commanded the respect of scumbags all over the world."

Jimmy snapped and aimed a finger, "You want to go back out there again?"

Gerard wore a tan suit. He held a fedora in his hand, spinning it now and then. He sipped his wine.

Brighton said to Jimmy, "If you made a deal today, we can forget this. Did you make one or not?"

"No," Jimmy said. "They knew all of it. And they're not interested."

Gerard put in what his brother had left out for decorum's sake. "They have a contract on Tagletti. And if we don't leave Rome by Friday, there's a contract on us too." Brighton folded his arms and sat back, stretching his neck. Gerard said to Serena, "You want to sit in; this is sitting in."

"Let me break it all down," Jimmy said, after a while, rubbing the ridges of his nose, removing his suitcoat to show sweat pooled all over.

"Let me try," said Serena. No one gave her permission. They gave her silence. "Somehow people are talking about us. We don't know why." She spoke as though reading slowly the foreign subtitles of a tragedy. "Somehow…OK." She began again. "Vincent Tagletti is leaning on us to broker a deal that will keep his operations strong in New York. The moneylender you were set up with, who was supposed to be friendly to this cause, has put out a…*a hit*…on Tagletti. These other men, who may be Mafia related or maybe not, who may be cops but likely not, are offering to solve both of our problems—helping Tagletti in New York and us being rid of him—if we give up a piece of…everything.

"Now that way, all we do is trade one Tagletti for another. So that has to be out. And they weren't cops; they were bad men. They would be bad for us. That has to be out. But if Tagletti found out what they were offering, he would force our hand. Get his protection and give up our business, not his—what's not to love about that?" She picked up the Barolo bottle and set it in the middle of the table, her eyes moving along it as though tracing all roads in and out of a fortress. "We have to think… Does Tagletti know the moneylender people are going to kill him if he stays in Rome?"

Jimmy said, "I don't think so. They wouldn't have communicated that on back channels. That was a message for us to give him."

"Is there any…would there be any scenario where you or Daddy faced getting killed by anybody?"

Jimmy waited to let Gerard answer, and when he didn't, Jimmy said, "If Tagletti gets hit, and we could've stopped it, the Bonannos would have to kill us on principle. No matter what else they have going on or how long it takes 'em to get around to it…they'd have to. *Family thing*."

She thought of the hundreds or thousands of conversations she'd seen her father have with associates, first in their kitchen on the Grand Concourse, then in their elegant dining room with smoke clouds escaping into the hall. She grew up believing it would be impossible to participate in any discussion on the level they'd reached. Though never knowing their subjects, it was clear they were plotting, outthinking peril, and the right answer was always ingenious, and the man who uttered it would command several days' respect.

"What time did you leave that villa?" said Brighton.

"Exactly 8:00 a.m. local."

Looking at his watch, Brighton said, "It's a quarter to two. They're not going to give more than a four- or five-hour grace period. We better find Tagletti and get him off the streets."

"There's an answer here," said Serena. "There's a solution."

She said she was going to walk back to the hotel on her own and would meet them in the suite at six o'clock and not to act until then. Brighton looked to his boss to object, but he sat still as she left, gently spinning that fedora.

Outside the hotel, she bumped into Madeline and Sonia. They asked if she would join them on a bike ride through the Borghese Gardens. She agreed and was gone about two hours. She got back to the Excelsior, drank cold water in the lobby, then went to her room and scribbled out a note on stationery. She brought the pad to her father's suite.

"What is this?" he said, reading and handing it to Jimmy.

"It's a warning to the Bonannos that these men you met are threatening you as well as Tagletti," she said.

Jimmy laughed. "You can't put these words in writing, kid."

"Well, you write it the way you would if you needed to tell them." She tossed him her pen. "Use your code but send them word right away. This way, whatever happens to Tagletti, you did your part."

"You're saying we send off this note to cover ourselves," said Gerard, "then let Tagletti get gunned down in the streets?"

"You have no control over what one hoodlum does to another. This way, you…at least you know you're protected."

Jimmy smiled again. Just then the adjoining room door sprang open, and Brighton and another man came in. Brighton looked at Serena, then Gerard.

Gerard said, "It's fine. Speak."

"Tagletti was shot three times in the chest buying a newspaper."

Serena put her hands on her face.

"Dead?" said Jimmy. Brighton nodded. "What time?"

"Hour ago."

Serena leapt forward, "*Now*, Jimmy, write that note and get it in the mail to the Bonannos *now*—today!" Jimmy sat down and poured a whiskey tumbler. Serena looked at all of them. Brighton wouldn't meet her eyes. "You did it already, didn't you?"

"We sent the acting capo of Tagletti's crew in Riverside a telegram at nine thirty this morning," said Gerard, "warning them we feared grave danger—for us and for Tagletti too." Jimmy brought him a tumbler, and he took it. "It was the right idea, just needed it sooner."

Serena sat on the bed.

Jimmy said, "Now, Serena, we need you and Brighton to go back to these consultants you met today. Tell them Tagletti is dead. The New York deal is off the table. And, now this is most important, tell them the name of the moneylender who killed Tagletti—Brighton knows it. That's all you have to do is leave his name. We'll take care of everything else."

"Why?" she said, and she knew they wouldn't answer, and they didn't. Before she left, she said, "You're always going to face people like this, people who want what you have and think you're not strong enough to defend it. And you're always going to have to survive by chess moves, fifty-fifty shots!"

"We're here, ain't we?" said her uncle, lounging on the couch, a long shift behind him.

"Today you are," she said. "Some plan. Win one day at a time, then look out the window and see the day's almost over."

She went to the elevators and back to her room. Brighton called to say their car would be downstairs in ten minutes to take them to a second meeting with the leather-soled consultants.

On the way there, Serena badgered him about their plan and how come the moneylender got to Tagletti so quickly, so easily. All Brighton knew, he said, was that before they got to the wine bar, Jimmy had him grease the bellboy to cut off all incoming calls to Tagletti's suite from America.

***

At 5:30 in the evening on December 16, 1985, four assassins in trench coats and fur hats shot and killed Paul Castellano outside Sparks Steak House in Manhattan. Across the street in an unmarked car, John Gotti and Sammy "The Bull" Gravano watched the killing unfold as they'd planned it. The deceased Castellano was right then the boss of the most powerful crime organization in the country. A few weeks later, Gotti would take his place, marking the beginning of the most public, and perhaps final, chapter of the American Mafia.

To kill a boss like Castellano, someone would need the consent of the heads of all Five Families. John Gotti knew that was too risky. So he sought the agreement of middle management instead, soldiers of his own generation, made men in the Lucchese, Colombo, and Bonanno families who would go along and counsel restraint if their bosses, many of whom were then facing indictments, contemplated rash reactions.

The Bonannos, most, were traditionalists—and in any ordinary year, perhaps they would've been quicker to defend "Big Paul" Castellano. But '85 wasn't ordinary. It was the year of Tina Turner and every weird sophomore using *The Breakfast Club* as an excuse to go on being weird; it was grown-ups holding meetings over Bobby Knight throwing a chair; it was the year of a four-day siege on white supremacists in Arkansas—and the year Gerard waited in line for two hours on a cold winter's day to pay respects to Roger Maris at St. Patrick's Cathedral.

The Luccheses and Colombos tried, at different times, to avenge Castellano and go after Gotti. But the Bonannos went along with the new order. You could say, as some would, that Bonanno Underboss Joseph Massino talked them into it, given that he was Gotti's neighbor and chum. You could say that the Bonannos were busy picking up the pieces of five years' destruction at the hands of Donnie Brasco and the feds. Or you could say, as really nobody ever did, that they were taken advantage of, led sideways and pitted against forces from the old country in petty wars that lasted months and months...foiled by some faceless Connecticut businessman with a quiet manner and a talent for outliving his children.

The morning before they were set to fly home, Madeline apologized to Serena for something.

"Beth gave me this letter that she wanted me to give you when we first got here. I read it, and it's all personal and stuff, and I guess I didn't want you to be thinking about her the whole time, wishing she was here instead of me."

"Oh, Maddy, I would never. I've loved being here with you."

"Well, here you go."

It was handwritten on white loose leaf. Serena took it to the Borghese Gardens and read it under some shade.

Serena,

I cannot stop thinking about our time in Philadelphia. It was so magical, the days working and nights when we would watch movies and eat Bonkers and sometimes ignore the TV if we got talking instead.

I never really knew you when you lived here. I can't believe that. I know Madeline and I knew my Daph, and Emily—she was so good to me, so happy to see me. But you and Hannah left, and you were always the ones we all talked about.

For a while, I was mad at you for leaving. But I forgot about most of that in college, and then being in Philly, meeting guys like Wayne Brixton who told all those stories and said how we don't understand what forgiveness is…that's when I really thought I have to forgive anyone I can. I came home after that and hugged Dad, Maddy, Sonia, Jimmy, our cousins, and I even went to the hospital the day before Daphne died and told her I forgave her for not being around. But then I realized you can't go so far into forgiveness without thinking of the things you need to say sorry for. So I told Daphne I was sorry for thinking of myself all the time she was sick. For thinking how horrible it was of her to leave me alone without my best friend for the most important years of my life. And how even when she was around, she was always focused on her oxygen tank or something regarding herself and never being my sister the way she had been. Because, you don't know it, but when things got lonely in the house and everyone was focused on something we couldn't understand, and there was this sense of being so afraid even though we didn't know why, Daphne and me would go into the attic and set up a camping tent and bring out this big chest of flashlights, ten flashlights or more, and turn them all on and play light games on the ceiling. We used to fall asleep holding each other.

So I said sorry for feeling raw about her not doing that with me anymore.

I called Wayne in Philly and told him most of this, because I think people should know when they say something that changes some part of you. We talked for a short time.

Wayne says that absolute killers, the worst monsters on earth, have to learn how to forgive people, and the only way for that is: We have to forgive THEM first. We have to say it's OK to monsters. I think the reason people don't want to forgive isn't because they can't—it's because they don't want to get near enough to a monster to say it. You have to be only a foot away for them to hear it. You might have to say it more than once to show you mean it. What if they just eat you? What then?

When I got taken away that time, I saw monsters. They had evil faces. I was so close to them. I think about them in bed before sleep, and I have things I have practiced now to change the thoughts—certain lines from songs I recite over and over or prayers Sonia taught me. I scream the words in my brain until I can't see the images anymore. I used to just think of Dad's voice when I was scared. It was so calming. But after they took me, I couldn't keep on thinking he was able to protect me.

Anyway, I only wanted you to have this letter since I wasn't allowed to Rome, and since I assume you'll be back in Philadelphia after the trip, I wanted you to know it was the adventure of a lifetime seeing everything I saw with you. People say I didn't have a mother, but I had you, and I had Emily. I would never choose the way things have happened, but there's so much left to go. I don't want to be tricked into thinking it will all be bad just because some parts have been so far.

I love you,
Beth

The family went to a restaurant on the Piazza Di Spagna. Serena was quiet during the entrees. She was quiet as the table discussed the most beautiful things they'd seen, the hidden charms, the ages of the churches, the legacies of Michelangelo and Bernini. Sonia Maude asked if anyone had any regrets on the trip. No one admitted any.

Serena said, "Do you believe in God?"

The family waited. Gerard said, "Who are you asking that to?"

"All of you. Do you believe in—in the Christian God? The one who this city…the main attraction here?"

There was a clinging of forks, the noise of other tables. Sonia said proudly that she did. Madeline said she really didn't know what to believe.

Jimmy had a mouthful of arancini. He washed it down with a Scotch and said, "I do. Always have. And I'll tell you why." He wiped his mouth with a napkin. "That bit about don't covet your neighbor's wife. That was thousands a years ago… How'd they know I was always going to do that?" They laughed a long time; he went on earnestly. "All I wanna do is covet them all, friends' wives, neighbors, forget it. But really—how'd they know that? That's God right there." He ate some more. "That's how come he's real."

In the piazza, everyone said they were bloated, tired, and a young man offered to take their picture. They waved him away, but Gerard said he wanted one with his brother. That photo exists still today, weathered, overexposed, and Jimmy can be seen mid-laugh, poking Gerard's gut, squeezing his neck.

At midnight Serena knocked on Brighton's door. She came in still wearing her dinner dress. All his windows were open; his television and lights were on. She went past him onto the balcony and breathed in the night. Not looking over her shoulder, she asked two things.

"Did you ever sleep with Emily?"

"No. She…one time, she thought of it, but…no. Never."

She faced him. "Are you a killer?"

"No."

She went back inside and turned off the set and the lamp by the couch. It was near to dark, save the city's light. He took some steps in off the balcony. She got in front of him. He wouldn't peek up, so she took his chin in her hand.

"I'm a lotta other things, Serena."

"I didn't ask about those."

His chest rose and thumped. He kept his hands at his sides. She traced his lips with a finger.

"Why'd you go after those guys on the street even when they were going to let us go?"

He let his eyes be seen. "Because if you don't fight every time you're supposed to, you forget how. Then you're nothing."

She kissed him. "Show *me* you're a fighter."

***

The next day, Friday, the van for the airport showed at 9:00 a.m. A few hours earlier, Gerard borrowed a car from the hotel and drove out to Piazzale San Paolo, the site of Saint Paul Outside the Walls. The basilica was closed to the public at that time, so he roamed the colonnade, the green grounds.

He met a Catholic monk who had moments ago finished his sunrise devotion. He spoke to Gerard and answered some questions about the church's antiquity. The cleric's face had a certain serenity, a patience, which he seemed to present as an answer in itself to Gerard's meandering history questions.

When the cleric went back to his room, Gerard felt a deep restless itch. He looked around at the conditions of the interred. He began imagining himself waking each day to this place. There was no word for the kind of agitation the idea made him feel.

Horace Eaton had told Gerard, years earlier, about Serena's decisive question in the den: Had her father killed anyone? Horace was relieved he could tell the truth—*no*—and Gerard was relieved that when she'd asked it, that was the truth.

Emily's suicide didn't change him. It changed Jimmy, he thought, and probably the other girls. But he was the same man, and he would've been capable of the same things had anything similar provoked him one year, three years, or thirty years earlier. But it was Emily who unlocked that cavern and let out the person he'd kept secret.

Less than a week after her death, he'd had Jimmy bring him a senior member of the Westies. Gerard paid them to mutilate the hired hands who'd kidnapped Beth and incinerate their remains in a granary upstate. The Italians had planned to reprimand Richie Rispoli themselves, per their word of honor, but Gerard found himself unable to accept that arrangement. He shot the gangster the day he was brought home from the hospital, in his driveway in front of his caretaker. The Italians had let Simon off with a warning. For Emily, and no one but Emily, Gerard kept the ex-monk in a rented basement in Harlem, broke his spine and legs, chained his neck to the floor, and let him die over a few days from bleeding or starving.

But how could all this be for Emily, who took her own life?

That's what neither Jimmy nor anyone in his crew had had the nerve to ask. On some level, he figured, they knew the answer. His family's blood had been spilled. The world spilled it. So the world would spill some too. Enough so he could no longer tell which pool was hers, which belonged to his enemies.

1979 was the year that made Gerard a killer. He would never not be one again.

There was an open door to the basilica. He went in, finding himself on the right flank of the altar. Some churchmen were at the lectern, flipping pages of a book, perhaps a hymnal. Behind them was the sacristy. He didn't know it was called a sacristy. He just knew Catholics kept wine-blood somewhere under the cross. He went to the middle aisle. All the pews were empty, save a few men in brown robes, kneeling, their lips moving mutely.

He saw Serena.

He blinked, and she was still there. She was sitting, not kneeling, in a pew.

He went to her. "What are you doing here?"

She was in as much disbelief as he. "It was on my list to see. The concierge gave me a… What are you here for?"

"A cabbie told me about it," he said, "the day I came out here for the meeting."

She looked away, at the slabs, at the churchmen. She was as youthful and breathtaking as his daily vision of her mother.

He had already sat with her but now said, "You want privacy?"

"Did you come here to pray?" she whispered.

"I don't think so." He knelt his elbows on the pew in front of them, hunching. "I came to see it."

They were due at the airport. In a few hours the moneylenders' murder contract would extend to their family. They sat there like the last people at the edge of the world, the ground receding slowly before them, and if they didn't find some other world, they'd fall off the edge of this one.

"A lot of men like you," said Serena, "who came from your time and place, they do what they have to in life. Then they come to churches like this, in the morning when they're empty, and beg God to forgive them."

Gerard started coldly at her, their faces inches apart. "I don't need anyone's forgiveness, Serena."

"You need me, right?"

He trembled. "I will always need you."

"Then I forgive you."

She took his arm, and they left Rome together.

PART FOUR

Serena's Two Ways

Madeline was the only sister murdered.

Considering the world the Magic daughters lived in, and the people they let into it, one could say it was a blessing this fate visited only once.

Madeline was killed by two men not far from home. There was no rape and only a supposed motive. An autopsy would reveal how much fight she'd had in her all along.

Madeline, *who had a vision.* Nobody appended that line to her memory, not on her tombstone or in her obituary, but they could've. She'd had visions for everything—ideas for everyone's time, parts they ought to play in her prophecies. Reality was a bleary disappointment compared to her social imagination, a place where people were at their best and no potential for a memory was wasted.

Her death was a big turning point in the belief systems of Gerard's children. They went from lamenting a few unlikely tragedies to wondering whether they were all fated to die at some unnatural age. Madeline's last breath seemed to send a signal across the cosmos that the Magics had reigned long enough, that some other poor family ought to have a turn at becoming an empire.

The day before all of that, however, they had a party.

***

Poppy Solnit got off the Metro-North at Southport Station. The train platform was desolate. A tough June sun roasted gum wads on the benches. She was in no mood for Connecticut, nor to celebrate her protégé's engagement.

One of Serena's most irritating skills—and there were many that drove Poppy mad—was her capacity for receiving terrible news with grace and elegance. Then again, thought Poppy, how much of it had Serena really had? The girl was prosperous, young, brilliant, gifted with radiant hair, white teeth, and teeming breasts, and, ostensibly, madly in love.

These were Serena's good-news years.

What a day, Poppy thought, somewhat mournfully—trekking down the platform to find the car they'd sent—to test her protégé's gift for joy in the face of disaster.

Hannah Magic came around the driver's side and opened the trunk of her merlot red Mercury Sable. "Hi, Poppy. I don't know if you remember me. Serena asked me to pick you up."

"The lawyer sister in Boston." She stuck her bag in the trunk. "Find a new job yet?"

Hannah looked at the car keys in her hand. "Not yet, Poppy."

"Well, let's go."

Hannah took them through Southport's bustling downtown on the way to the house.

"Has the party started?"

"Yes," said Hannah, "about an hour ago, but people have been showing up all morning, caterers, a band." Some silence. "It's a nice day for it." The hum of the vehicle. "You came alone? I thought Serena said you were dating someone yourself."

"How was rehab?"

Hannah's hands tightened on the wheel. "It was a productive experience. Thank you."

"Living at home since you got out?"

"I am."

"At those big firms, I didn't know they could fire you if you'd made partner. You must've violated something in the equity contract." Hannah kept driving. "All the girls in your family, they don't seem to get far from home very long, do they?"

"We're almost there," said Hannah.

"Are you going to wear that sweater at the party? It's hot out. I'm hot looking at you."

"Can we drive in silence, Poppy?"

"Sure." She looked out the window. "I'll look around the town of Southport. This is my idea of a summer Saturday, Hannah. Driving around Southport on the way to your father's house."

Serena was forthcoming with Poppy about nearly everything, and Poppy, though twelve years her senior, usually reciprocated that trust and candor, however far it was from habit.

In the almost-four years since they'd launched Safer Cities, they'd aggregated data suggesting a 40 percent decrease in murders in the areas their community leaders mediated. They had received press attention from leading outlets and expanded operations into twenty cities nationally. Their headquarters were now in Westchester County, not Philly, spread along three floors of a restored tool-and-die factory, and they spent more time on calls than in the courtyards and classrooms of urban cities.

The new office also permitted Serena to commute from and live in Fairfield, not so far from home.

Serena now enjoyed the status of a cofounder. In 1988, the organization took in $8.5 million dollars in contributions.

On a typical workday in Westchester, the interns and regional coordinators and communications professionals pacing the halls of Safer Cities may see Serena coming in or out, early or a minute late for a development or strategy meeting. But just as often they would see her office empty.

In her early thirties, Serena was discovering many passions. The songwriting that was a discreet, undocumented part of her spare time had found a chance outlet. Poppy couldn't remember when—perhaps two years ago or a bit more—Serena came back from a fundraising trip to Napa Valley. Waiting in the San Francisco airport for a delayed flight, Serena struck up a conversation with a shaggy man traveling with a guitar case. He was a road performer who had been to every major city. He was older, diabetic, alcoholic, and half blind. No one in the entertainment business had heard of him or cared to buy him lunch. He played for Serena as they sat waiting for the plane. They kept in touch. A few months later, she sent him lyrics to a song she thought he ought to sing. He asked for more. Within a year, the record labels that had eschewed him began competing for his tracks. And in September 1987, a song Serena wrote in the bathtub played on the radio.

Safer Cities and Poppy Solnit were already competing with her family and fiancé for Serena's complete attention. Now they were competing with boom boxes, shaggy guitarists, and the muses that lived in the whorls of bathroom fog.

Hannah pulled into the circular drive. A valet took Poppy's bag to the porch and parked Hannah's car.

As she caught site of other Safer Cities board members by the hors d'oeuvres, Poppy was handed a glass of champagne. She finished it in two sips.

The stage was set left of the garden, facing five immaculate acres. An in-ground kidney pool, which Poppy didn't remember from her first and only visit to the estate, was put to good use by young socialites who flaunted everything and thrice-married capitalists with the decency to wear Hawaiian shirts over hair-encrusted guts. The band was giving it everything, and at least half the party danced. Every guest had a little plastic cup full of colorful nectar. Everybody wore sunglasses. Every child was confined to a play corner in the garden. If men weren't wearing swim trunks, they wore bright summer suits over white dress shirts. If women weren't drunk and sunburnt, they'd be both soon.

There was a guesthouse with a line to use the bathroom. Many people got in line over and over, laughing, twitchy, yelling *hurry*!

Poppy ignored the people who tried to say hello. She looked everywhere for Serena and finally found her, standing around a table of intellectuals, authors, and columnists she'd met all over New York, advocating the mission of Safer Cities, Poppy's project. Brighton came to her side.

Serena took his hand, and her engagement ring glimmered as their fingers intertwined.

Already in June, Serena had a vacation's worth of sun on her skin. She was beaming, cradling a pina colada, wearing an orange bikini top, a breezy white cover-up tied around her waist, sunglasses on, now coming toward Poppy, saying she thought she'd never get here.

Brighton greeted her next, polite but brief. He wore blue. She'd only ever seen him in ancient black suits. He was as comfortable at a party as Poppy or Albert DeSalvo.

"Serena, can we speak alone?"

"Sure, Pop. Let's get refills, and we'll go by the pool."

Poppy used her hand to guard her eyes. "Is that Linda Ronstadt?"

Serena blushed. "Colette, our producer, introduced me to Warren Zevon, and he introduced me to all these music people, and some decided to bring friends."

"Ronstadt," said Poppy, "is friends with Warren Zevon? What did he sing again?"

"She's friends with someone who's friends with him. He can't come though; he's in France. Colette's coming. She's bringing Tracy Chapman."

"I haven't heard of her. I don't want to speak by the pool, in the house, please, and now."

Serena handed Brighton her drink and followed Poppy in. They went through the kitchen and into the empty study. Serena leaned on the desk edge, and Poppy closed the door.

"We're being audited."

"I know that," said Serena. "It's…"

"It's not routine. Someone on our board reported us for impropriety under 501(c)(3) regulations. And the auditor came on Wednesday and had very specific questions. About you. About our money and how much of it comes from your family's business."

Serena adjusted the straps of her bathing suit. "OK…what did you say?"

"I told the truth; it's all public information. You donate—your family donates through corporations for write-offs. We can't hide who the donors are."

"Those are legal entities," she said, "and legitimate."

Poppy said, "The auditor came Wednesday. On Thursday I got a call from a reporter."

Serena ran her hands down her face. There crumbled that veneer of optimism.

"Why do you think it was someone on our board who reported us?"

"The auditor told me, point-blank," said Poppy. "I would guess Strauss or Monica Guerin. Neither of them has ever liked you."

"Monica likes me fine."

"She thinks you're a princess brat. Told me when I visited her farm." Poppy walked around the room. She scanned the bookshelves, surprised to see them filled with Greek classics, Euripides, Ovid, and verse—Skelton, Spenser, Marlowe, Wordsworth, Rosetti. In front of the books were trinkets and amulets her father must have accumulated over a career. Signed baseballs, statuettes, mementos of the fifties, a tiny war helmet, a toy train. The office had more feeling than she'd expected, more ambiance than she thought befitting Gerard Magic's daily work. "It isn't about what the audit will turn up. I don't know if those corporations are clean or not, and I don't know if you know. I'm sure money is laundered through them. Probably they won't find that out, and even so, I doubt they can tie it to us. But the press will write about this. It will taint our name. They've written about you, so now they'll write this. The decent thing," she said, "is for you to resign."

"You came to my engagement party to fire me."

"I came to ask you to put the mission before yourself. Otherwise, the headline is, *Crime money used to fight crime.*"

Serena rubbed her naked arms, chilled by the temperature drop in the house. She said she could find the board member who made these allegations. She said she could work with their accountant to face the IRS, and she knew, above all, she could charm the press and get the best of their coverage.

"Don't throw me away before we even know how bad this is, Poppy. It isn't a death sentence; it's a fight. I'm a fighter. Are you?" The party was stentorian. "I have represented this mission for four years, and, with you, I've *built this organization*."

"You've been checked out for over a year. And it isn't just your music. How involved are you in your family business, Serena? Because I think you've gotten very involved. And I think a reporter or a government agency that asks questions is going to find repugnant answers." She shook her head. "I don't think you even work for me. This work has given you the moral permission to do your other work. Your *family* work." Her voice simmered. She felt herself fighting sentiment. "You were wonderful to get to know, sweetheart. I'm glad I met you. But you're out, Serena."

Poppy expected, in keeping with the pattern of their prior confrontations, Serena to walk out, sigh heavily, brood a day or so, and come back with an appeal to friendship and values. Instead: "My family gave $1.2 million to our organization last year. That's the single largest contribution we received. I've personally solicited in excess of $18 million in funding since I've been here. I'm a legal partial owner and recognized cofounder, and the only reason anyone writes a story or does a TV spot on what we are doing is because *I'm involved.* So you're right, Poppy: I don't work for you. You work for me. If you want to go to court over it, say when. In the meantime, I'll let you know when I find the leak on our board, and I'll handle the IRS." She walked past her. "Now get out of my family's house."

***

Madeline and Hannah were up in Emily's childhood bedroom in front of a vanity. Only someone who lived here would think to wander this far down the hall to disturb them.

Maddy had her makeup neatly laid out on the caraway desk. Hannah borrowed one item, rethought it, took another.

"I had an idea of this day," said Madeline. "I thought we would be taking family photos all morning on the lawn, and then Daddy would toast Serena, and she would be standing shoulder to shoulder with us, not with some group from the city."

"Party's just begun," said Hannah. "It could happen."

"It won't," said Madeline. "We all woke up hungover—well, not you. How are you feeling with everybody partying?"

Hannah hated her lipstick. She wet a tissue and rubbed it off. Her eyes were surrounded by sallow ovals. Her nose was running every so often, a constant cold she couldn't root out. "Day at a time."

She stood up and took her party dress out of a garment bag. She took off her sweater and looked at herself in the vanity. She was petite, skinnier now than she'd been as a preteen on Jones Beach. She slipped the dress on.

"That's nice, Hannah. Have you seen what they're passing out down there?" She drew a copy of *Rolling Stone* from her bag. "Beth bought two hundred copies straight from the printer."

Hannah read the profile headline that she'd already seen, "The Balladist Combatting Homicides." Serena's photo was altogether flattering even if Hannah thought the editors chose one with a smile that seemed more mischievous than compassionate.

"I liked the song," Madeline continued, "I really did, but it was *not* her best song. It just wasn't. She's very talented, and they put this one on the radio. And now she's some crime-fighting Dolly Parton. I think celebrities are calling her because they like that she does more than one thing—like all the political types, they wish they could write songs or play a cello, and all the music or actor types wish they were doing something real in the world. Serena has both worked out, doesn't she? And now she'll have a husband."

"Let's not get bitter, Maddy. I don't think that would be good for me."

"You don't think it's a little annoying how perfect they are together? I never even thought Brighton was cute; now suddenly, I look at them standing in that garden, and they're breathtaking. They're always laughing together, *always*. And anytime they're in the same room, they're touching. She's on his shoulder, or he has his hand in hers. Is it really love or just a big security blanket?"

"It's love," said Hannah. "When they split that time, that one Christmas she thought it was over...she came to Boston. I've never seen her...it's love."

Madeline looked at her sister's face in glossy print. It was 1989. Experts still mattered greatly. Journalists were writing twenty-thousand-word pieces with poetic turns and full-throated ideas, exploring secret human grottos through quotidian subjects. The elite circles were small, and if one knew someone who knew someone who danced a foxtrot with a celebrity or had a cousin out in Hollywood or was a sound engineer on *Live at Five,* this was an anecdote worth sharing at a large dinner table. Serena was neighborhood-famous, city-respected, and relevant to a changing world.

"I can't believe Serena is the first one to get married," said Madeline. "Well, not counting Emily." She shoved the magazine in her bag. "At least forty feels far away."

"Not to me," said Hannah. She smiled. "Emily always said I would marry a dentist and live in New Jersey."

They both laughed a long time.

"Oh, goodness," Madeline said, looking through the blinds into the yard. "Norman Mailer is here. I mean, gag me with a spoon, Hannah."

"Daddy likes his writing."

"Dad reads everything now; I bet he won't give him the time of day. Twenty bucks Dad doesn't shake his hand?"

"No," said Hannah.

"Twenty bucks and I'll pour a martini on Linda Ronstadt."

"Do I have to pour a martini on Linda Ronstadt if I lose?"

"No, just twenty bucks."

They shook.

Sonia Maude knocked and said, "It's Sonia." She poked her head in and said Hannah looked lovely.

"We'll be down in five minutes."

"Poppy Solnit needs you to take her back to the train."

* * *

Serena dodged guests long enough to bring Brighton up to speed on Poppy's news bulletin. They stared, from the galley of the cottage, out the window at the Safer Cities board members convened around a tray of crab cakes. Brighton asked if she thought it was Monica Guerin who contacted the government. Serena said she didn't know, but it was probably Monica or Kristoff Strauss. She didn't know how they could find out or what difference it might make if they did.

Poppy was correct: This battle would be with the press, not the government. They adored Serena at this moment, but if they got to theorizing that the inner-city movement with which her name was synonymous was being steadily funded by criminal enterprises in Connecticut, the green room elite would turn on her. They'd call her a fraud and a con, lobotomize her reputation for sincerity, and probably disgrace her songwriting.

She was invited, with her diabetic guitarist, to go on *Johnny Carson* next month. The music press was abetting nonprofit press, and nonprofit success was emboldening her reputation as a poetess, a creative. Her career was in bloom. Now someone wanted to pluck it at the root.

Brighton suddenly said, "Look, can you cover up? You ain't been near the pool; there's no reason to be busting out like this."

She looked down at what she wore—or didn't. "You know, you get uncomfortable when I do anything lately."

"I'm happy for what you do, Serena. I'm happy for the songs. Just put your clothes on, OK?" He went toward the yard. "I got an idea how to figure who's the fink on the board."

Alone she wandered into the guest house's sitting room. Two people made out on the couch. Two others fidgeted with the record player.

Serena saw Beth through the back window and called her in.

Beth laughed and danced over. "What a riot!" She hugged her neck. "What a day!"

"Mr. Heneman is out there," said Serena. "He's going to put in a word for us with City Hall in New Haven. I doubt he knows what to say, but that city contract is aces for us. I want you to sweet-talk him, get him confident he's getting involved in a sure thing."

"Serena," said Beth, "it's a party. I haven't heard Dad talk about work all day. He's playing chess over there with Horace, drinking diet sodas. Let's not work today, come off it."

The kissing couple was closer than she'd wanted them, so Serena pulled her baby sister toward the bathrooms. "Beth, we put you in charge of the entire lighting business. You're a twenty-five-year-old CEO. It's the oldest business in this family, and it shows our most on-paper revenue. You want to act like a kid, or you want to act like a CEO? Go out there and schmooze Heneman. And tell Madeline I'm looking for her and to come find me."

One of bathroom doors opened, and Beth's friend, snickering with ferret lips, waved her in. Beth grabbed Serena's arm, "Come in quickly, then I'll work; I promise."

Serena took her arm back but followed. Beth did a line off the rose ceramic sink. She handed a rolled bill to Serena. "So childish," said Serena, and Beth's friend spilled out some more, and Serena snorted one, then a second. She dropped the bill in the toilet, and they cursed at her as she went back to her engagement party.

***

Serena sat with her father, Horace Eaton, and Emily's widower, John McClusky.

McClusky had proven loyal to the family time and again. He was a good friend to Serena and a swell father, and he encouraged the relationship between Gerard and his grandson when he had no special reason to condone it at all. The Magics had caused John a lot of pain beginning at a reasonably young age. It was either a perverse form of Stockholm syndrome bringing him back year after year, or, Serena thought, like in a lot of families, love was tangled up with malice, resentment with dependency, and this Irish widower felt closer to them in all their brokenness than he ever had to his own folks or anyone else who claimed to love him but never told him he needed to be better.

Horace was ten months recovered from a hemorrhagic stroke and could no longer manage the family's affairs. Until they found someone of his caliber they could depend on, Serena had taken a more active hand in operations, at times enlisting Hannah's legal expertise to bridge gaps in her knowledge—with Hannah cooperating to the extent the questions were hypothetical, nonspecific....

Serena was a support to Hannah when she decided it was time to get sober. Hannah was in no state, after said sobriety was achieved, to moralize with her sister or condemn Serena's instinct to help family at all costs.

Without that same instinct, Hannah would have faced the darkest part of her life alone.

Horace's facial muscles were having a good day. He smiled at the bride-to-be from under his wide-brimmed wool hat. Their table sat under a dogwood tree as far from the band as the acreage permitted. Their chess game was nearly over. Gerard would win.

Serena caught her father up on Poppy, the IRS, Mr. Heneman, and which business acquaintances had come and which had sent gifts, whom he should take the time to greet personally, and whom she would receive in his stead.

"Why don't you put your cover on?" Gerard said, studying the board.

Serena averted her eyes from McClusky's. She got up with the faintest groan, untied the cotton shirtdress from her waist and slipped it over her head.

She saw Madeline and Hannah at the edge of the pool, staring past the guests and servers at her.

Now Gerard said, "There are two men whom Brighton brought on at the ports. One's named Ramirez; one is Miller. They have a business; they told him what it is, and he told me. He'll tell you—or John here will, he knows. They're coming today to meet you. Whatever they're going to be making off their cargo, we're going to take fifty-one percent. Not fifty, not forty-nine. You're clear?"

"They're running a business off our docks, we get fifty-one. Ramirez and Miller. I'm clear."

Gerard moved a rook. Horace's hand quivered as he reached out and tipped his king.

Colette, Serena's producer, approached the table singing the chorus of their shared hit. Serena giggled and hugged her.

"This is my father."

Colette patronized him for his great looks and wonderfully scary smile. "What are you reading?" she said. "Oh, wait," she turned and yelled, "Norman, come here! *This* is Serena's father."

A man in a plaid suit with sharp cufflinks, budding jowls, black-gray hair, and a veiled smirk that may as easily have been Jewish as Irish stalked over to them. He shook Serena's hand first, said he'd loved the *Rolling Stone* profile and that she had a real gift for verse. He looked, she noticed, more than once at the swaying V-neck of her coverup. He turned to Gerard, spotting the paperback beside his soda.

"What do we have here? Longfellow!" He jabbed Serena. "So this is where you get it?" He held out his hand to Gerard. "I'm Norman Mailer. Thank you for having me to your home."

Gerard looked at the writer. He looked at the foamy producer and at his own daughter. He picked up Horace's fallen king and pressed it into Mailer's open hand. Mailer studied the piece as Gerard took his Longfellow book and headed toward a hammock behind a row of cypress trees.

***

At 3:00 p.m., they cut the cake. There were hoorays and jokes. Sonia Maude worried they would be running out of food before nightfall and recommended a few dozen pizzas for safety.

Ramirez and Miller showed up during Beth's champagne toast. They were dressed like hands-on cargo men coming from a day at the docks, and possibly they had. They ate ravenously from the buffet.

Brighton told Serena, "The cargo guys are over there; I'll take them in the house, and you come in when you're ready."

"All right," she kissed his cheek.

"The board fink is Strauss, not Guerin."

"How do you know?" she said.

"I told them both the IRS was at your office. Guerin said it was probably routine and kept eating. Strauss said we need to lawyer up, and they got nothing on us, went on blabbing ten minutes how the government's corrupt."

"Hmm." Someone snapped their picture. They smiled before the flash. "All right, ask Strauss to meet us in the dining room and take the cargo importers to my father's office. Have Madeline sit in with Strauss and ask John if he'll wait with the cargo guys."

"All right."

"Wait. Switch that."

"McClusky in with the suit; Maddy with Ramirez and Miller?"

"Yes."

Brighton went off.

Serena went to the bar. She heard Norman Mailer's table arguing about the flag-burning case, Mailer on the side of civil liberties and the like, and at the music table where Colette spoke fastest and loudest, someone suggested a toast to the now-late Roy Orbison, so they toasted Orbison, and Tracy Chapman said how about Chet Baker, so they toasted Chet Baker. The bartender filled Serena a rocks glass full of Glenlivet. She savored the first sip. Behind her a fat man with glasses asked a skinny man with glasses, "What'd you think of *Rain Man*?" The skinny one said, "It was good, but I don't know if it deserved to *win*."

She went to her room and changed into a blouse and summer khakis. Madeline spotted her on the stairs and asked if Daddy really shook Mailer's hand. "Sort of," said Serena.

"Please elaborate—there's a lot on the line here. It looked like he just handed him something."

Serena finished the Scotch outside the study and left the glass on a cherry breakfront. She went in, and Madeline followed.

Ramirez stood up to shake her hand. Miller nodded from his chair. Madeline and Brighton stood in front of the bookshelves, and Serena took her father's seat. "Tell me about your business."

In the long winter to come, she would think back to this meeting. She would think about the way she dealt with these strange men. Searching for what she could have done differently, she wondered if she should have ever been in that room at all.

Men in the music business and men in politics and men in philanthropy were diminishable with a look after any time in a room with men like this. At first Serena merely appreciated the contrast that these brushes with the underworld afforded her, returning to the smart air-conditioned world like a bar brawler who'd spent a week in the ring with Roberto Duran. But before long her fondness grew. She relied on these encounters, out of her element, to be superior to the element everywhere else. She relied on them to feel strong. She relied on them to feel anything.

Ramirez said, "It's a cargo business, I'm not going to say what it's in the cargo, but it's your port; you can find out if you want."

"Stolen cars," said Serena. "Contraband."

A beat went by. "Yeah," said Ramirez. He had a smirk like she'd seen on Andy Garcia in *The Untouchables.*

"Guns," she said.

Ramirez looked at the backs of his hands. "Yeah, there's some guns in the boxes."

"We don't want guns," said Serena. Madeline snuck a look at Brighton. "If you want to bring in minor narcotics, cars, jewels, that's your business. We don't want guns with no serial numbers coming through our ports that will be sold in our cities and used to kill people."

"Serena," said Brighton, "we have a deal almost finished here."

"No, we don't," she said. She looked at Ramirez. "We won't take illegal guns. As far as I know, we never have before. Brighton, did we do their paperwork already?"

"They're W-2s. Journeymen wages plus OT."

"OK, so fifty-one percent in our favor on everything but guns. We have a deal, or do we need to fire you on day one?"

Ramirez kept going with that baleful Garcia grin. Now Miller spoke—and he spoke like a sidewalk kid. "Nobody told me I worked for you." He popped a switchblade but didn't do anything sudden with it. Serena held up her hand, steady. "You ever seen anything like this?" he asked her.

"Put it away, man," Ramirez told him.

"I'm asking the girl a question. You, lady. You ever seen this?"

"Have I seen a knife?"

He smiled. "I know this's bad for business, but I got a feeling I need to show you this." He jumped across the desk. "Let me show you!"

Brighton leapt off the shelf and caught the knife hand, twisted it from Miller's wrist, and it fell on the rug. Madeline screamed and kicked at it. Brighton locked up Miller's neck, and they tumbled backward together over the chair.

"Get in here!" Madeline screamed and started banging the walls.

Ramirez hooked Brighton's arm, stopping his throwing a punch, and Miller squirmed out. When Serena saw the two men had the upper hand, she charged Ramirez, who threw her off easily. Her wrist banged against the granite column of a chest.

The room filled with John McClusky and other men, and they pinned the two importers to the wall. Brighton got to his feet. He picked up the knife, held it to Miller's cheek. "Let me show it to you now."

"Don't!" Serena said. "Look at me. I'm fine. All he did was threaten me." She was gripping her wrist.

Brighton held the knife at the incisive angle to pare Miller's face, pressing it in enough that some blood was already pooling. Serena knew one wrong word from Miller, and he'd be carved.

John McClusky said, "Come on, Bright. It's bad if they leave cut up."

Brighton closed the switchblade. He said, "Sixty-forty our way on everything you bring in. And there won't be even a cap gun in them crates, like she said. Now shake my hand and go over and shake hers. And I beg you...do something funny."

They did as Brighton said. Miller moved slower than Ramirez. He moved so slow he had to be thinking of anything else he could do besides what he'd been told. Then they left.

John iced Serena's wrist in the kitchen. She said it was fine but winced anytime he pressed it. "You need to tell someone if you're going to change terms."

"I didn't know the terms until a few hours ago. If my father wants me involved, he needs to bring me in earlier."

"That's what you want?"

In 1968 they'd stood in this same room, McClusky and small, trivial Serena, as he iced her opposite wrist after Hannah and Madeline conspired to tip her lawn chair. He would've been nineteen, a sweet boyfriend to Emily. His face was fuller today but not much different besides.

"It's not about what I want," she said. "It's how I can protect us."

Brighton came in. "I'll handle Strauss about the IRS."

"I'm fine," said Serena. "Let's go."

She set the icepack in the sink. They went to the dining room.

She knew it would be an hour at least before Brighton got his blood pressure back to balance. He didn't talk about how he felt when she was in danger—or how he felt about anything—but she'd learned to receive his cues, when he was anxious, when he was feeling really grateful for her and wanted to take her to the beach, when he wanted to fight for no sane reason and needed to be talked down, when he was mad with her father or sappy over Horace's health, when his long memory wouldn't let him sleep, and when he was exhausted by one of her habits but couldn't bring himself to ruin an afternoon over it.

It was her idea to meet his mother. It had gone as well as he'd told her it would. His childhood Bronx kitchen smelled like tomato soup and molded crumb cake, mixed, in the week-old garbage, with scratch-offs and TV guides.

She asked Serena questions that insulted her son. He tried to smile through it. In defense, Serena said more to her about why she loved Brighton than she'd ever told her fiancé himself. It wasn't their way, vowing, gushing. She respected his introversion, understood it as both a professional necessity and a by-product of sincerity. Her friends and family had no idea, she often thought, what a thrill it is when big words break free from a man who says so few of them. *Marry me.*

In the dining room, Kristoff Strauss said, "I heard one hell of a commotion and a girl's voice. I tried to come out, but..."

"A longshoreman threatened me with a knife," said Serena, "so my fiancé threatened to pare his face."

"Good lord."

"Why'd you do it, Kristoff?" she said. Brighton stood behind her, arms at his sides. John McClusky loitered in the doorway. "Your money is tied up with ours. You dropped a dime to the IRS, but it was the wrong agency. You wanted FBI or maybe DOJ. The IRS is going to put you through hell along with us. My sister Hannah is going to write out a letter, and you're going to sign and send it to them."

Kristoff sat at the table. "Or you're going to...what? Have your boyfriend beat me up? What a den of thugs." Kristoff was lean and impeccably dressed. He'd made his money in Washington and Texas and thought

Safer Cities would make a colorful addition to his beneficiaries. He was on nine other boards, and there was only so much due diligence one could pay one's lawyer to perform before overtime fees cannibalized one's lake house mortgage. "I won't be investigated because I'm not an accessory before or after the fact. And if you want me to call the DOJ, say the word, princess."

"No one's going to beat you up, Kristoff. We're businesspeople. I write music. Perhaps you've noticed my friends on the lawn—musicians, journalists, writers. I'm not in here to threaten you. I'm asking you to send another letter to save us both a bureaucratic nightmare." She fought a lightheaded sensation. "And everyone I know out there, I'll introduce you to. And any project you have, any organization you need funded, those concerns will become mine."

Serena could see he was trying not to laugh.

"You think I need bribes? You think I need your *friends*? Serena, I suppose I'll be the first one to get to tell you this: Those famous New York people aren't here to get to meet some one-hit songwriter with a bleeding heart. *They know about your family*. They're here because it's...beguiling." He spoke this next bit so slowly: "They want...to have a story... about gangsters." He shook his head. "Boy, kid, since I met you, you really stopped seeing things the way they are."

He got up. She was staring past him at the wall art.

He paused next to Brighton and said, "The IRS called *me*. They were already onto you. Try any of your strong-arm nonsense, and I'll call 'em back."

He walked past McClusky who tailed him out.

Brighton put a hand on her shoulder. "He's scared. He's rambling."

Serena said, "We have no leverage. We need leverage on him." Her voice was weak.

"I'll just talk to him."

"No," she barked. "Can't be that way." She squeezed her temple. "We need...we're not just beating up the world, Brighton. *Think*. I'm not going through life that way. We have to...outsmart people." She breathed and said, "I came in here without a plan. I'm drunk."

He put his arms around her. She cried into his crisp blue shirt. It left a stain.

***

When Hannah got back from her second trip to the Southport Metro-North, they were just cutting the cake.

She refused champagne from a server for the third time that day. Brighton walked away from the cake and escorted two men not at all dressed for the event into the house. John McClusky jogged in after them.

Why that poor bastard wanted to work for her family after all Emily had put him through confounded Hannah.

Emily and John's son was eleven or twelve now. He didn't look like much on the baseball field, but Gerard was often spending whole afternoons with the boy, probably instilling a code of action beyond what the modern playground kid required. McClusky himself never seemed to mind. He liked the time Gerard spent with his son.

Hannah had never heard John speak of Emily but knew he visited her gravesite. He'd been aging well enough and could've remarried—now though, he was forty or forty-one, his hair thinned, a gut teasing his belt buckle, and the future promised him no vanities.

He was a good man, Hannah thought. He really always had been. He was scared of many things but tried to face them anyway. He was courteous to all her sisters, even after twelve-year-old Serena dashed his hopes of war glory. John adored Serena these days and was proud of her music. Around the lawn on an odd Sunday, while his boy played with Gerard and Jimmy, John would ask her to read him anything she'd written lately, anything she had hopes for. Serena always indulged.

When Serena visited Hannah's rehab center in Des Moines, she tried to distract the patient with tales of home. One thing she shared, apropos of nothing, was that the prior week she, Brighton, and Maddy joined McClusky and his son for a canoe ride across the Sound. At one point she and McClusky were wrestling the oars, laughing; she thought, if they were alone, John would've tried to kiss her. She shivered in that visitor's room, and Hannah enjoyed a merciful laugh.

Gerard was kinder to McClusky than before. He let him as far into the business as John wanted to go. Then again, Gerard was letting them all in lately. He told only the plain truth in response to questions. He avoided meetings and appointments. He spent most days reading in that hammock—on the study chaise during winter—and playing with or teaching Emily's son. He was quiet during dinners, but he hugged them all if he hadn't seen them in more than a day. He never judged Hannah's addiction—to booze, uppers, downers, or daytime TV—and he cooked her an omelet the morning she came back from rehab.

Now Hannah saw the same two ill-dressed men leaving through the side door, escorted by some of Brighton's juniors. She got a better look at their faces and caught a shiver not unlike Serena's remembering John's near kiss. They were ugly. They were dangerous. She was sure.

Madeline came out, spotted Hannah alone with her iced tea, and told her about the scrap in the office, the scoundrel with the switchblade. She said she'd never seen anyone get violent around here and had had a vision for what she'd do if it happened, and she was mightily disappointed that instead of what she'd imagined, all she did was yelp.

When Serena finally came out, the sun was its dying color. Hannah pointed to the cottage, and they went in there and found Beth. Madeline asked the living room crowd to go have some cake. The four sisters were alone.

"Are you OK?" Hannah asked.

Serena said she was fine.

Beth handled her wrist, and she winced again. "This is going to swell."

"Like you know that," said Serena. She looked at Madeline. "Why did Linda Ronstadt just run out of here soaked?"

Hannah spit out her iced tea.

"It's complicated," said Maddy.

Beth told them that everything went aces with Heneman, and they needn't worry. Madeline asked about Kristoff Strauss, Poppy, and the board.

Serena said, "Poppy came this morning to tell me the IRS visited Safer Cities. She wanted to fire me."

"Can she?" said Hannah.

"No. But we had it figured that someone on the board dimed to the auditors. That was wrong. The IRS contacted Strauss. We're being investigated by at least one agency, maybe more. Maybe the nonprofit is their only target. Maybe all of us."

"Does Daddy know yet?" said Beth.

"No."

Hannah sat on a couch. The others took her lead and sighed as they sat on chairs or stools, the tension of smiling and lying all day deflating from their lungs.

Madeline looked at the furniture. "Did anyone ever bring a boy in here when Sonia was out?"

Beth laughed, "Sonia's never out."

"Remember Mrs. Wolinsky?" said Hannah.

Serena said, "I liked her better than Sonia, frankly. She would cuddle with me after Mommy died."

"I barely remember her," said Beth. "Why did she leave again?"

"She had wicked back problems," said Hannah. "She couldn't take care of this place."

Outside the band announced a break.

The sisters sat in relative silence a moment. The presence of their decisions and collective past made itself known in the room, like the ghost of a loved one.

One by one, Gerard had let them understand who he was. One by one, he let them touch the business, understand it, and participate by degrees. He let them find pride in it.

Hannah looked at her soft, brilliant sister Serena and thought it was rather inevitable that she would wind up in this bunkhouse with a garish party in her honor just outside, a thousand pounds of family stress on her pointy, tanned shoulders. When any father, loved by his daughter, violates his daughter's ideas of goodness, she can either give up the ideas or give up the love. This bride-to-be was full of love.

"Have we ever been investigated before?" said Beth.

"I don't think so," said Serena.

"Well," Beth lifted her drink. "Here's hoping." She drank.

Serena was staring at Hannah. "What is it, Hannah? You want to tell me something?"

Hannah nodded. "I wasn't ready to talk about it."

"What?"

"Someone from the FBI visited me in Des Moines."

"Oh."

"I'm sorry, Serena. I didn't know anything. I was so out of my mind. I didn't say anything because I didn't know anything. I just dismissed it as a longshot. But now if the IRS…someone might be onto us after all these years."

The band started up, and Madeline asked who was going to tell Dad. Beth volunteered, but Serena said she'd better.

They all went out, and Hannah took Serena's arm. "I'm sorry I didn't say it sooner."

"It's all right. I love you, Hannah."

"Serena, are you sure those two men are nothing to worry about? They had these faces…"

"No, no. We have to focus now. They were nothing," she said. "I think they were afraid of me."

***

Ramirez and Miller had become killers young: Ramirez when he knifed a man in Staten Island over what he thought was a bad split on a run of bodegas; Miller at fourteen when he beat his father in their family kitchen. He beat his head in, and when he wasn't sure if he was dead, dug through the bedroom closet until he found a Ruger .38 and shot him four times.

Miller teamed up with Ramirez in 1986 on a munitions run in Miami, and they'd been thick ever since. Ramirez went out and got them business, and Miller decided when someone needed killing, and Ramirez didn't interfere after that decision got made.

It didn't matter which of the Magics they got to. They'd been messed around, first on the specs of the deal, then by a pale fella with Miller's own knife, and like little boys they were made to say sorry to the teacher. It only mattered which of the family came out of the house first. That would be the one they took.

Later, Serena would tell herself they mistook Madeline for her, that she herself caused it, with her gun morals and rehearsals of toughness, knowing she would never face men like that without Brighton to throw at them. But Miller didn't care if it was Serena, Brighton, McClusky, or Gerard Magic himself. He was flesh-mad and wouldn't be a chooser.

They waited seven hours in an alcove at the bend in the block, went to a motel, ate, came back, waited more. All the party guests left that night and some the next morning. But they didn't finger anyone from the Magics until the next day at sunset.

Madeline drove out alone. She looked ruddy, simple, beat. They followed her to a restaurant on the water where she ate with people about her age and grabbed her going back to her car. It wasn't terribly drawn out. She fought well, and they strangled her.

The cops knew all of this, even the identities of the killers, before anyone in the family. Miller left her body there in the parking lot, and someone in the restaurant had already called in their plates. Fairfield Homicide identified Maddy's body and put out a search for the wagon, registered in Ramirez's name, all before some uniforms drove to Gerard Magic's house and told him.

Sonia Maude answered the door and cried out of instinct before the cops said a word. Everyone else cried soon—absolutely everyone.

***

Two days went by where no one left the house or answered the door. They ate leftovers from the party, mostly pizza and finger sandwiches. Uncle Jimmy came back from Hawaii and seemed to be the only one who wasn't too broken to talk vengeance

He was in the study, pacing the room, smoking and crying and saying he wanted them both and there was nowhere they'd be safe.

Gerard sat on the couch, not in his desk chair. Hannah sat beside him and held his hand.

A little later, Sonia announced Sgt. Emory Prince.

The sergeant held his hat in his hands. He glanced around the room. He shook Gerard's hand. "My father's here too."

"He is?" said Gerard.

Sgt. Emory Prince opened the door, and the former Sgt. Kenny Prince, who once wore his son's badge, came in and offered the same respects.

"My son has come here of his own conscience," said Kenny, who had aged gracefully and had character in his face, a stout voice.

Emory Prince said, "It's times like this there's no dead right thing. My father's always sung your praises, Mr. Magic, and all your girls have always been kind to us. I went to school with Maddy...." He tapped his gun-belt, toeing squeamishly the line between a man's judgment and the dogmas written by other men who lived now in dirt. "I was part of a conversation about an hour ago with my captain. Fairfield is getting help trying to find these two scumbags—Ben Ramirez and Dice Miller. There are federal badges in our squad house. They're looking to catch these guys fast before anything happens to them on the street. They want to find out what those boys can tell about your operation, about the docks. Since it's clear it went bad between you and them, they figure these guys will spill if they take the death penalty off the table for what they did to Maddy."

Kenny Prince stepped in front of his son. "These filth deserve to hang, Gerry."

Gerard stood up. He hugged the father and son.

Before Sgt. Emory Prince left, he said, "Find these guys yourself, sir. They may not get justice from us."

***

Jimmy Magic was sick. He had thrown up on the flight home and again in a pail in the cottage.

He couldn't think what sign Serena or the others had given these men to make them think they could get away with this. Gerard Magic had been left alone by petty hoods and true gangsters for many years. There were racketeers in Jersey, Brooklyn, the Bronx, even in New Haven, who wanted a piece of these docks yet wouldn't risk tangling up with Magic, not by now, not after everything.

Gerard was seen to defend his territory too well. He was seen, in recent years, to have bested Tagletti and shirked the Bonannos. The Westies in Hell's Kitchen knew what Gerard was capable of and had let word out. When a Westie is out there telling your enemies it's just not worth it, the message is going to get heard. In three decades on the map, the law had never stopped him and no heavy had ever bent his knee. The Magics were owed many favors, were personally beloved in every thug-owned saloon from there to White Plains, and had won the loyalty of enforcers.

This affluent Connecticut family was feared and respected and left to itself the way any private family ought to be. But two sewer rats didn't know the score. They weren't told or forgot or were too drunk and stoned to remember. Jimmy didn't care which. He was going to kill them.

He was seventy-two and had a bum prostate, an orphaned liver, and a daily sadness around 4:00 p.m. But he was going to do this one last good thing—a thing he'd never had to do before—to show these girls how much he'd always loved them.

His brother's life was now filled up with his books and that grandkid. Never was Gerard a reader, not through sixty-five years. Now at sixty-nine he was reading Longfellow, Eliot, and he would talk about it, too, if you asked. Gerard was a killer as of 1979. He didn't kill anybody growing up, but he did those killings he had to do after Emily. They thought leaving the Bronx would save them from becoming those kinds of guys. The stinking, champagne-soaked wealth of this coast town couldn't save them from killing. As soon as they agreed to love people, they had to know they would always end up killing others.

Jimmy had sent all the men he knew, anyone who would take his call, to the trains and to the old warehouses on Monroe Boulevard and to the dives in Bridgeport. He had a .38 at his house, ten minutes away. He was about to go get it when Brighton came with news.

Together they went to the dining room. Jimmy told Hannah, "Wake Serena up and get her down here." Then to Gerard, "We got them."

"What?"

Jimmy nudged Brighton. "Tell him."

"Our foreman spotted them at the port. They were parked under Henrietta's. They came back for their stuff. Must have had something in those lockers."

Beth was at the table beside Gerard. "You're kidding me. Did he stop them?"

"He chased them onto the dock with four other guys on the crew. They got them pinned down next to a pontoon."

"Can anybody see them?" said Beth.

"It's pitch-black out there," said Jimmy. "There's no floodlights anywhere. We can drive right up onto the dock. Come on, Gerry."

Hannah came in with Serena behind her wearing a gray robe. Jimmy told them everything.

Serena instinctually took a step to the door, then rubbed her eyes and said, alarmed, "The cops have to be watching the dock."

Jimmy rushed them. "There's nowhere to watch the dock from—we've got crates for half a mile out front, and they're low near the water. Henrietta's is closed; the gate is up. We're leaving now. Girls, stay behind." Hannah told them to hang on. She said she had to think. "It's not for you to think about," said Jimmy. "We all know what needs to happen, and it's up to us to go do it. The car is leaving now—who's coming?"

"I'm coming," said Brighton.

John McClusky came in from behind Serena. "I'm coming too."

"Guys," Serena said, "I want them to suffer as much as anyone. But think about what they really know: They know we take payoffs to let things pass through the pier, but they can't prove it. We never did even one deal. The FBI is here. In our town. And they're trying to charge our family. You want to go out and do this, knowing they could be around any corner?"

"You want to chance the feds getting their hands on these guys?" said Jimmy.

"It's not about that," said Brighton. "It's just not. It's for Maddy."

Jimmy patted Brighton's arm. He looked at Gerard. "Are you coming?"

"No," said Gerard.

Jimmy nodded. "We'll do it for you."

Gerard said nothing, and Hannah took one more shot at getting them to slow down as Jimmy, Brighton, and McClusky stormed down the long hallway and piled into the car.

***

Three hours passed.

Serena, Gerard, Hannah, and Beth sat in the front parlor staring through the window. Serena was the only one having tea. She thought it might calm her, but it was bland and cold now, and her stomach rumbled.

It was about 4:00 a.m. They hadn't spoken much. The overhead lights were off, though no one was asleep. Their eyes had adjusted to the darkness. A car would pass the drive every half hour or so. Serena's chin would rise, thinking it would turn in, until it kept on going.

"Are you awake, Dad?" Beth said.

"Mm-hmm."

"You can go up," she said. "We'll come get you when they're back."

"Don't be worried, honey," he told her. "It's going to take them a while to do everything that comes after the first thing."

Hannah's face was in her hands. She peeked out. "You ever do that, Daddy?"

"Let's not talk right now, baby."

"It's OK. I know that you did," she said. "I understand."

Gerard scratched his face. He settled further into his seat. "Let's not talk right now. Let's think about Madeline. Let's think if she's with your mother. It would be something if she was."

"I don't know if Madeline believed in that, Dad," Beth said.

"Well," he said, "whatever someone believes about something doesn't change much about whether that thing is real. And if that thing is real," his voice started to crack, "you better believe that beautiful little girl is with the angels tonight."

Hannah covered her face again. Gerard clutched the arm of his chair and stayed quiet.

It was daylight when the car pulled in. All but Hannah had eventually fallen asleep in their chairs. She told them to get up, *here they come.*

Serena's eyes adjusted. She saw the guys' blazers pass the window. Jimmy came in the house first and looked at them. John McClusky came in behind him and closed the door.

"What happened?" said Gerard.

Jimmy looked a hundred years older.

"Where's Brighton?" said Serena. Jimmy went past them to the stairs and started climbing. She got off the couch and yelled after him, "Jimmy, what?" Slowly he went all the way up. She turned on McClusky. "What happened—did you do it? What's Brighton doing?"

John looked at the floor. He inhaled. "They got away."

"How?" said Gerard.

"By the time we got there, they had gotten a drop on the crew guys. They knocked two of 'em senseless and got hold of a shotgun the foreman kept in the office. We, uh..."

"Speak, John," Hannah snapped.

"We pulled up, and they put the gun on us. We were...they had us out of the car, and it looked like they might shoot. Brighton charged them, and Miller caught him, and the two of them..." His voice caught and tears fell. "They fought...and Ramirez, he kept the gun on us and said he'd shoot if we stepped in."

He started hyperventilating, and the words were all garbled.

Serena smacked him. "Speak! Where is he?"

John sat back against the door. He shrieked and slammed his fist into a glass frame, shattering it. Serena ran up the stairs, three at a time, and passed two doors before she found Jimmy in the guestroom, sitting on the edge of a made bed.

Serena shouted in tears, "Tell me, you stupid bastard. Now." She sat on the floor in front of him as he got his nerve up. "Is he dead?"

Jimmy whispered, "No." He said, "Ramirez kept the gun on us. Miller put a beating on Brighton. He got the best of him, and that was fine—it was done. Then Ramirez kept us back, and Miller kept working on him. We said he'd had enough—and they could just leave. But the son of a bitch didn't stop."

She was cradling her neck in her arms, rocking. "Say it."

"Miller got hold of a wrench and cracked his head open."

"Please."

"I'm sorry. We took him in…they got him on tubes…" Jimmy almost threw up again but stopped it. He slid off the bed onto the floor with her. "He was the devil, this Miller. He was just the devil."

"What hospital?" She tried to catch her breath, gasping, snatching her uncle's suit. "Jimmy, what hospital is Brighton at? Tell me, I beg you."

Jimmy held her to his heart. She bawled. "You let it go, honey. He won't be much good for anything to anyone."

***

The government came in November. It was the Monday before Thanksgiving. The case had taken over a year to build, and they indicted everybody, even though many wouldn't stick. They overshot, knowingly, serving all foremen; the night crew; some VPs at the lighting company; Horace and his wife; Poppy Solnit; even Sonia Maude, who had offered lemonade to the detectives. The ceremony of arrests was undignified and purposefully public, but all were out on bond before midnight. A lawyer, a new one with an office in downtown Southport, said the rudiments of the case were flimsy. But the kids were worried, and they could see Gerard was too.

He had become a man who loved Tennyson. He had accessed parts of himself, these last years, that he never knew about, that you'd have been bludgeoned for discussing on the Concourse, where men had a shift coming up, a Schlitz in the icebox. He read, the morning of his arraignment, Sir Walter Raleigh:

> *The flowers do fade, and wanton fields / To wayward winter reckoning yields, /*
>
> *A honey tongue, a heart of gall, / Is fancy's spring, but sorrow's fall.*

When he was released on bail, he walked over every inch of grass in his yard, plucking some up, smelling it, letting the blades dance in the wind and sun.

In 1991, he was sentenced to twelve years for racketeering, bookmaking, extortion, and conspiracy to import contraband illegally. The details of worse offenses were made public at trial, but the prosecution felt they were on sturdier ground without adding those charges. There was no direct evidence of Gerard's violence.

Jimmy got about the same time plus another five years for his 1976 participation in an auto-theft ring, which a key witness attested to. It was something of a compliment that over a multi-decade span of a career, the feds could only find three people to testify against the Magic family: Jimmy's old Bronx roommate, who'd worked with him on the car ring; Angelos Lykaios, who gave mostly hearsay but had a few proofs of their bookmaking; and Poppy Solnit, who had done nothing legally wrong and knew they had nothing on her but cooperated from a sense of a citizen's duty and an irrevocable woodchip in the center of her heart.

Beth and Hannah were never charged. Horace died awaiting trial, and Brighton they never even served the warrant on.

Serena Magic received a suspended sentence of eighteen months for conspiracy to money launder, though they never demonstrated Safer Cities returned any dividends to her family's businesses. All the people in New York City who had written pieces about her and sent her letters now wrote new pieces and sent new letters. Thus began the years of Serena's disgrace.

But in fact those began even earlier, before the trials concluded and the '91 sentences were handed down. They began on that Thanksgiving of '89, a few days out of lockup, when she saw she had only two paths—two lives—still left to choose from. And like a lot of boys and girls in their early thirties, she was profoundly shocked at how recently the future could have been anything.

***

Brighton's doctor visited the Magics' house on a weekday morning that December. He was not his full-time doctor, but a great one, a neurologist out of Mayo, and Gerard had pleaded with him to review the case.

"He's already communicating," the guest said, steaming tea in front of him. "That's a spectacular sign." He looked at Serena, not Gerard. "He's a tough nut. A basilar skull fracture is the worst thing that can happen to the human head, there's no question. I don't want to diminish that. But he's making some sense in what he's saying. Now it's been five months. We're talking about this playing out over many years. To see him speaking, now, is a win."

"You call that speaking?" said Gerard.

The doctor stayed on Serena. "He had so many things happen. He had two infections. He had meningitis, sepsis. We know the frontal lobe was damaged. I'll tell you what another doc might not: It is a crapshoot. He is medically paralyzed right now and may stay that way. But you see guys like this, and they're fighters, and first they get their fingers back, then their arms, then…it's not impossible that one day he's zipping around in a wheelchair, speaking clearly, being himself."

"Himself," Serena repeated.

"Well. Some version of who he was," the doctor corrected. "But you say he knows you, right?"

"He knows me," she said.

"Well, then, if there was memory loss, it wasn't total. Can you give me an example of something he's communicated to you?"

It was beginning to snow. Serena looked at the dead grass collecting it.

"He touches my engagement ring. He says the word *marry*."

The doctor walked over and comforted her. She didn't cry in front of him. Gerard showed him out.

Serena went to her mother's piano and tried to remember a complete song. She got most of the way through "They Can't Take That Away from Me." She fumbled the climax and slammed the fallboard.

Her song, the hit she'd ventriloquized for the airport guitarist, would probably be called folk. But verses came to her in all forms: Some were rock and some punk, some blues, and some could only work against a jazz melody. She thought of the first time she went to a jazz club. She was twenty-two. It was the week after she'd moved to Washington. Her first local friend, a self-reported anarchist from Montana, took her to Georgetown, to Blue's Alley.

The girl spoke to Serena during the set, and Serena eventually, nearly unwittingly, asked her to please quiet down. She didn't know what she was feeling, watching the trio work to understand one another, to volley a rhythm she believed they were inventing. An old man with a hoarse voice took the mic and sang about an old café. She knew the old café as well as he did, she felt, without ever having been to one or knowing what traits an old café was supposed to have. She knew what he meant because he'd transmitted it without any descriptions, using the currents of the trio, the feeling in his refrain that he had only this one chance to tell them what he meant.

Anywhere she'd lived or would live, clubs like that promised an enchanting contradiction. Jazz was privacy in public. It was a whispered secret in a room of noise.

That's what Brighton was to her. He would hold her hand in a crowd. They were in the world but in dream. They kissed on that balcony in Rome, and they were alone with the moon even though Italians cheered on the boulevard.

Hannah and Beth came into the den. They were each holding tea mugs. Beth offered to make her one, but Serena refused.

"What did the neurologist say?" said Hannah.

She swiveled on the piano bench. "Nothing substantively different from what the regular one says. He's from Mayo, so we're supposed to hear it differently."

Beth sat on the couch, tucking one leg under her. "We've been reading up a lot, babe." Her voice was gentle, motherly, like it had all just happened yesterday, not five months ago. "The paralysis is the worst of it, but do you know some of the other things he could face?"

"I know them all," she said. "Please don't list them."

"Even if he gets some motor back," said Beth, "even if he remembers you now, that may get worse, not better. Think of the kind of life you'll have, Serena."

Serena rose off the bench, and Hannah said, "Sit down. *Sit down, Serena.*" She submitted. "You never want to hear this, but now's the time. They're going to have to make long-term plans for him soon. If the feds start impounding assets around here, Daddy won't have any money to help him. You should go to Daddy now: Ask him to set up an account for someone else to take care of Brighton. I can help him establish it in a way that it won't get touched. And Brighton will be…he'll be better off."

"You're talking about the man I am going to marry," she said.

Hannah set her tea down. She sat next to her sister at the piano. "That man is gone, Serena. I loved him too. He's as gone as Maddy. All that's left to decide is whether you're going to lose the rest of your life like they have. For God's sake, there are only three of us left. Daddy had all these girls, and they're dead." Hannah cried, and Serena's innocence took her over completely, and she herself cried like she had for Maddy, like she had for Brighton. "You owe it to the dead people in this family to have a life."

They held each other. Beth came over, and they held her too.

"I can't leave him," Serena said, after a few minutes.

"But you can," said Beth, standing up. "You can marry John."

"What?"

"John McClusky," said Beth. "He'd love to marry you, and you know it. He would dote on you, and he can help the family get through this next horrible chapter. That lawyer is making it sound like we'll all be OK, but it's going to be an ordeal. John will take care of you, and more importantly, you won't have to spend every second taking care of him. That's barely… that's not even natural, Rene."

"Your solution," said Serena, "to my fiancé's brain injury is for me to marry my dead sister's husband?"

"Yes," said Beth.

Serena looked at Hannah. Hannah wiped her eyes clear. She nodded.

Serena let out a laugh full of hate and shoved off the bench. She ignored their calls to come back and whispered under her breath that they didn't know the first thing about jazz.

***

When you take care of someone, you learn how much you love yourself.

Your energy, attention, hunger: Concerns intervene in your hourly thoughts not as they once did, passively and patiently, but with fire-needle points, aching to be gratified.

Serena's early mistake was in trying to ignore tedium's power. Tedium is a matchless force on the human psyche, and she pretended otherwise at her peril; rather than understanding and grappling with it, she thought herself above it.

She spent eight hours a day that summer in Memorial's trauma wing, and more in a long-term clinic as Brighton fought to recover speech. Nurses pulled Serena aside and said to pace herself, that the road was long and arduous, and she'd need her strengths. But she laughed at them and said look what he was going through—did they think a tired body, a restless brain, was anything in the face of that?

What they didn't point out, but could have, was that she had never gone through *that*, so to think she would derive strength from a comparison to a condition she could only imagine was not prudent but arrogant, not sweet but stupid.

Her standard of comfort was high and her pain threshold low, and now she was sleeping in a chair three nights a week and eating Jell-O, string soup, or carton egg whites for breakfast and dinner.

She noticed, by September, a recurring numbness in her legs when she napped in the guest seat. A nerve in her neck was now pinched, and she became conscious of a cavity. Her eyes were always sagging. Hospital air had a taste, and somehow its flavor triggered her lethargy. The food caused constipation—or its opposite. She found her skin, in the cerulean mirror, pallid as a patient's. She often wore the same socks and slacks several days in a row and began to loathe her own hygiene.

She was in near-constant search of more things to do for him. She played cards to stimulate his attention, read him novels, changed dressings, bathed him, checked and rechecked settings on his vitals monitor as its plaintive beeps burrowed into her forehead.

Yet with each considerate act she felt a pang to remind her of some equal and opposite need in her own body, her own brain. The more she threw herself into his care, the louder the voices of self-concern blared in her brain. She told herself to ignore it, that the happiest people forget themselves utterly and give, give, *give* to another. She was determined to suffer with him. She knew she deserved to. She knew that some time, somehow, she would be shown that suffering was right and that there was not only honor in it, but peace.

The nurses tried to be kind, and many were, but their faces returned woefulness as they changed bedpans, their chins and cheekbones drawn down by the laws of hospice gravity—you see, these were faces that had witnessed the true ending of all stories, after the parts writers use to end books, after the many victories of life, after dark and before dawn, when hell sings.

By December, Brighton had been speaking with significant slurring for several weeks. He had relearned a smile, though it was tough to distinguish from a wince. His fingers moved. He could lift his arms. He was beginning to get range of motion in his neck. He was giving his fiancée all the hope she needed to endure the rest, to lose many battles against tedium yet win the long war.

A few days after the visit from the Mayo neurologist, there was a snowstorm, and she couldn't commute to the clinic. She put on her boots and walked into town. Most places were closed. There was near a foot on the ground. She walked toward Jennings Beach, craving a view of the ocean under snowfall. It was many miles. She wasn't dressed for it. A truck beeped at her, and John McClusky pulled over.

They sat there on well-covered sand watching the surf make sense of a blizzard all under the carnage of a silver sky.

He made his speech. It never became clear whose idea it was originally, Beth's or Hannah's or John's himself, perhaps conceived one day at Emily's gravesite, mixing up, as was his wont, notions of grace and grief, sacrifice and matrimony.

"I'll never forgive myself for that night, Rene. Brighton was so brave, going right at them even though they had a gun. Me and Jimmy—all we could see was the gun on us. I wish I wasn't that guy who only sees a gun. I could feel the bullet in me if I took a step. Meanwhile, Bright fought and fought. He's a hero. I'm some fat piece of nothing who let his wife get so broken she shot herself, some guy who left a hero alone in a war. I thought God made me a solider, Serena. I ain't that.

"But I am a father. I've taken care of that boy. He loves me. You know, you can be valiant in a fight, once, in this big great way, and that's really something. But then there's being valiant quietly, every day, when no one can see, and there's something in that too.

"Since Emily, I've learned how to take care of people. I know I could take care of you. It wouldn't have to be—you wouldn't have to love me like you do him. I know it's not going to be that. We could just be together. I would make every day easy and good for you. For him: I let it happen to him," he cried. "The most good I can do is make it so you never want for anything."

Jennings Beach was abandoned, and only a few winter crows and song sparrows overheard his confession.

Serena said, "You are betraying him."

"You could see it like that, if you think having you meant more to him than you being all right. I think you being all right came first."

She didn't shake the blankness from her face for a second. She'd learned it from those nurses who knew everything. It was her new mask. She'd cling to it.

"I don't want you, John. I love you like a brother, never a lover." She mashed some snow. "You aren't even speaking as a lover, but like some martyr. You think giving your life for me every day," she said, "will give you some peace about Emily and Brighton. It won't."

"It might," he said. "But there's something more in it than that." She didn't ask what, so he told her. "I would get to marry the most perfect girl I've ever known."

On Christmas Eve, she decorated Brighton's room with garland and tinsel. She read him two chapters of *Great Expectations,* then flipped through a poetry collection she'd brought from the study. She thought he understood some of them.

She hunted for one that might be about winter or Christmas or some morsel of warmth. She found one from an Englishman! His name was Ernest Dowson. But she stopped halfway when she saw it was about none of those things. She put the collection away, shut off the lights and held his hand, and the gaudy-colored Christmas lights made it so she could still see her ring.

She got home at midnight. Everyone but Gerard had turned in. He poured her an eggnog, and they sat on kitchen stools.

"I know what Beth wants you to do," he said. "I know what McClusky wants and Hannah, Jimmy, and the rest. I'm your father. I've lived a full life, Serena. I want you to hear me now: If you leave that boy alone to be a cripple, you will regret it until you die.

"There are a few times when the right thing to do demands everything. I know I'm not suited to this speech. I know it, and you know it."

"You are, Daddy. It's OK."

He gripped the counter. "I'm not. But it's the truth whether I have the right to say it or not. You have a chance at a simple way. You go move somewhere with Brighton, marry him, give yourself to the marriage. It will be a difficult life, but it will be better than the one I've lived, than any of your sisters have. It will stand for something."

She looked at her feet. She couldn't stomach the forces at work in her. "Jimmy says I haven't made a promise yet. That if I walk away, it isn't a betrayal. And that the alternative is…it's too awful to say." She sobbed and said it. "That the alternative is I just become a mother to a corpse."

"Brighton's not a corpse. He'll be a man still. Serena, do you know what I would give," Gerard asked, "to have your mother in the next room hooked up to machines, *mumbling, smiling,* holding my hand?"

The schemes of the poets had broken Gerard worse than the grifters had been able to over seven decades. He was ruined for crime. He could not hide. He now had to tell his daughter a truth of the cosmos he never wanted to believe: Everything matters.

"It feels like he's gone, Daddy."

"He's not gone." He grabbed her. "Be strong, Serena. This is what strength is. *Be tough*. This is the moment—not some other. Don't pretend this isn't your test. You gave your heart to this man."

She pushed him off. "I don't want to hear it. You child-beater. You scumbag," she sobbed and fell into his arms. "You hit me. I was a child. How many times, Dad? How many?"

He held her as she convulsed. "Too many, honey."

"Why?"

He held. "Because you knew the truth about me."

She wrestled herself closer, even though there was no closer to get. "I loved you."

"That was the worst of it."

***

Had they not been busy with lawyers, civil and criminal, and money managers trying to protect what assets they still could, the Magics or someone close to them would've paid a princely sum to have Ramirez and Miller tracked and killed. But they were under the weight of indictments and grief. The edifice they'd built was facing demolition one brick at a time. From strength they retreated to protection and from there, Gerard knew, would falter backwards into fear.

Maddy's killers got out of Connecticut and probably out of the country.

Serena asked Beth one night, "Did Madeline ever tell you, when we got back from that trip to Rome—did she ever say what she wished for in the Trevi Fountain? She made this big earnest wish. I remember her face as she threw the coin. But I never asked."

"I don't remember anything about that," said Beth.

Serena took care of Brighton. She faced down her selfishness and let her father's wistful commands penetrate her heart. She hugged her fiancé often and told him he would never be without her—in some sense, *never*. And in late March, when spring birds began to return north, joining the crows and song sparrows of Southport, Serena Magic and John McClusky were married on Jennings Beach.

The ocean breeze taunted her veil. Hannah and Beth stood up with her. John read his own vows. The reception was at Henrietta's, and only about a dozen people were invited and only half came.

They spent their wedding night at a hotel in New Hampshire, not far at all from Dartmouth and the oyster bar where Emily had once lied about Daphne's health to get Serena home.

They stayed two days at the hotel and didn't take a formal honeymoon. For the next few years until the trials concluded, Serena would visit Brighton every morning, spruce up his room, change his bedpan, and talk to him about what was in the news or the weaknesses in the DA's case. At noon on the dot, she'd go back to the family house, serve lunch and tea, and help Hannah and the paralegals in the dining room fortify their defense. At 5:00 p.m., she'd go home to John. He usually cooked a healthy supper, and they'd eat in the garden while she'd tell him the same new things she'd told Brighton, and if there was nothing new to tell, they would sit in silence, and he'd reach across for her hand. And she'd let him have it.

The Dowson poem she dared not read to Brighton that Christmas Eve was really very sweet, as Englishmen can often be. She'd read out the first stanza but stopped herself here:

They are not long, the days of wine and roses:

Out of a misty dream

PART FIVE

I Let a Song Go Out of My Heart

September 7, 1997
Dear Hannah,

I am not bitter about the eulogy. You were the person to give it. I'm glad you did.

It was hectic, Hannah. I can't believe we got through it, period. That you were up there instead of me was not an issue. But I appreciated your letter. It was sweet and sensitive. You haven't always been that way, but I like it. You went through a lot of brutality and came out gentle. I wonder if you would say that about me.

This month it will be three years since John and I moved to Florida. Next month I'll be forty-two. I still *feel* young. My face is young. I get that from Mommy. Bizarrely, I have the most energy I've ever had. But my legs don't look young. They feel like trunks. John doesn't like to hear that. I bounced back from both pregnancies so quickly I thought my body would never change. It's starting to.

John is well. That man Gerard Huxley finally retired at the insurance company, so John is a full supervisor now and is excelling. We are hoping he will receive a substantial raise soon. We joke about how he went through another boss named Gerard. A mixed bag, those Gerard bosses...

It was wonderful having you and David visit last year. I wish you would come again. Our house, and our town, is not as close to the beach as our house was in Southport, but the drive to the shore isn't bad. (Like John says, we live near nice places but not in one.) My boys loved seeing you and hearing our old stories. Eric still plays with the magnet tiles you gave him. Henry is young, but he smiles when I show him your picture.

John's son comes over every Christmas and Fourth of July. He really turned out to be a good man. He loves the boys. He will get married next year himself. Emily would like the girl, she's original and somewhat mean.

David is a good man, too, Hannah. I'm thrilled you found him. He is like Daddy in a few ways, but mostly not at all. I loved when he did that Al Gore impression—I told so many people about it. He really can relax and not take himself completely seriously, which is such a gift in successful men. Strong women are the opposite; they are the funniest people in the world. A really strong woman has a perfect sense of humor. Proof of that is I used to be much funnier.

Anyway, I'll answer some of your questions as best I can.

Let's start with the incident when you were here. "Incident" seems a strong word, but it was the word you chose. I don't remember it unfolding exactly as you do, but I will admit it was as uncomfortable as you say. I understand why it sent you "straight to bed." It is a new pattern, but a pattern anyway, that something nags at John and starts out innocent, then turns him red.

Another couple saw something like this between us and didn't understand it. They had lived in Florida forever and didn't know about Irish couples born in apartments.

Well, here's my memory of that night: We were all four sitting there enjoying a glass of wine—you, a ginger ale—and John saw what a mess the plates were. He said why don't I clean them now. I said, more rationally, the kids were finally asleep, and the four of us were having fun, and I'd clean them after. He gave the speech you say he gave, and he did smash the glass and say how horrid I let the house get and the rest. That's fair and true. But the fight did NOT continue after you went to bed. He went to the yard and collected himself. When he came back in, he apologized and cleared the sink himself. Then, as you admit, he apologized to you the next morning.

You are fit to judge him, I guess. Go ahead. I'm sure David hates him. But you have to remember, I put him through the worst, Han. I think in some ways I was worse to him than Emily was. I never cheated, but I loved another man instead. Emily cheated but loved him. Neither of us treated him like a man; none of you did either. It caught up with him here, in Florida, that feeling of having gotten old and not being sure you did it right.

By the time Daddy was fifty, he had built a kingdom. Sure, he was rotten about it. But he did it. John had to start us all over, after they impounded everything and the lighting co. finally went under, and he had to support a convicted wife and two kids with his GED and weak knees. He feels the dagger of fifty like we would never understand.

I'm not making any excuse for that night or the others. But I'm trying to live with my part in it. He is working on himself.

It all came to a head over the summer.

I had gone to a Chili's for one of Eric's friend's mom's birthdays. They were all drinking blue cocktails and talking about how Versace got killed. (They said his name, VER-SOCK-IE. I'm sorry—these are good people—I'm horrible.) I got home, and my boys were upset because John had snapped at them and locked them in their rooms. He never hit them and never could, and I swear to you on Emily's grave, he's never hit me. But that night I found him in our room. He stunk of gin. He looked so much older. I turned the light on, and he was holding a pistol.

I never knew we had one in the house. He said when he moved here, the guys at the company told him how easy it was to go buy one in Florida. He said he got one that looked just like the gun Daddy kept in the attic. The one that Emily used. He said he felt drawn to it. I tried to get him to put it away, and he gave me the same kind of litany he'd rattled off that night you were here. How he'd slept through a whole life, how dreadful and selfish I was, how I secretly planned to raise our kids to treat him like dirt.

I swore he was wrong, that I had grown to respect him—to love him. He said I merely needed him, nothing more. I was quiet for a while. I should've kept talking and reassuring him, but I was quiet because I wanted to really think what was true.

I can't change how we began. I never felt the tug of affection. But now we've settled into this companionship, built a home, had these kids. I take pride in John. He had never had to start over and get a job and rise up, and he did all of that for us. I think other marriages that start with explosions of passion must end up somewhere close to what we have anyway. So what's the difference what road we took to get here? We're here.

But before I could tell him any of that, he moved over on the bed and asked if I would always listen to him. It was such a strange word, *listen.* I thought he said *love* at first, so I quickly said yes, then realized I heard it wrong. He cocked the hammer on the gun and held it out. I didn't say anything. He said if I ever wanted him to trust me, I would hold the barrel to my head.

I stared at him. I wanted to do it for him but couldn't bring myself to. I tried to cry, so he would drop it, but I couldn't do that either. I just sat and waited. He got that I wasn't going to do it. He threw the gun at the wall and left until morning.

The next day he said he'd do whatever I wanted: therapy or meditation or medication. He felt like a heel. We had a lot of good weeks with the kids after that. It's not been perfect peace ever since, but what is?

After Princess Di, I felt sluggish for a week. I didn't think it was related, but...that young royal girl whose family couldn't save her no matter how royal they were...I got a script for some meds that are supposed to clear some of this up, this fog, so we'll see. I don't like the neutral feeling. I've never been neutral. My brain feels incapable.

Honestly, if you didn't give that eulogy for Jimmy, I don't think I would've been able. I haven't written a song, even a lyric, in—I was going to say months, but now it's years.

I love the way music is going. I'm not critical of it like other people my age or John's. I like Bryan Adams and Fleetwood Mac. I think we've arrived at a wonderful time for music. And I have nothing to contribute. Even after the trial, producers would get in touch. I could ghost write if I kept my name out of it. I wouldn't make a royalty, but it was a quick payday—and an outlet. I think my best work was when I was thirty-six and thirty-seven, the house was taken, and everything was changing around us. I made men and women famous with some of those songs—or at least I like to think. Then they dropped me not because I was some tough guy's daughter, but because I started to stink at it.

Is it motherhood? You wouldn't know.

It may have taken my best energy. My energy used to swirl up and burst out. Now it takes the form of efficiency. I pack lunches and think how we can save money. My old energy is still there, but I fear it is being used to sharpen my nightmares.

The morning after that episode with John in the bedroom, he recited his apologies and went off to work. Eric was at school, and Henry took his nap. I went back into our room and found the gun, made sure it was loaded. I went to the same spot on the bed, held it up like someone else was holding it and put the barrel in my mouth. I sat there for ten minutes, until my tongue was numb to the copper.

You will ask, was it suicidal or sexual, and I don't think either. I think John wanted me to stare at the past. And that gun, which wasn't the one that killed Emily or that I'd used to get him arrested as a boy, *was* the past. All guns were the past for us, and I owed a reckoning.

I got away, Hannah. At the time, it was all I wanted. I didn't deserve jail, and I didn't get it. I wanted some money but knew I didn't deserve that either and didn't get it. I wanted to keep you and Beth, but you went back to Massachusetts and found David, and Beth is in New York, and at least she seems to be doing well for herself. I wanted to keep Daddy and Jimmy. In their seventies those poor men had to face jail. You could see even the judge didn't want to do it to them. He wanted to let bygones be.

Jimmy died in a damn prison infirmary. He must've wanted a drink so badly. Daddy looks like he'll get parole next year. I know it makes John nervous, the idea of him getting out and coming to live with us. Where else can he go?

Last I visited, he looked gaunt. He still reads.

I will share a secret with you. You know the song from a few summers ago, "Sidewalk Royalty?" I'm sure you heard it on the radio. "They rule, then perish; topple orders, then fall to the next kings. They drink in fancy rooms, defend tradition just to make enemies.... Sidewalk royalty, men who die joyously."

The singer says she got the idea reading some book about a breakup. But I wrote it. Every word. It's a song about Daddy and Jimmy and the grown-ups in our dining room.

You may not believe me, and I signed a bunch of documents saying they could sue me if I told anyone. But I'm just telling you. And if they sue me, they can have my dishes, my 1,300-square-foot house with yellow wallpaper, my sewing kit, and John's gun. We'll claim you as the rightful owner of Eric's magnet tiles and maybe those will escape seizure.

I really wrote that song, and it felt great. Now...

Do you think I write with any color anymore? I feel I forgot my colors. I used to hear a song, and it would poison my day, absolutely poison it. The only cure was to curl up with my songbook and write something, anything, that could equal up to that feeling, drain the poison, show myself I could still touch the roots of time.

Most of my best never got sung. That's the gremlin of songwriting; I need to find someone else to complete the work—someone with a voice that tells you something, and of course I have no control over that.

What I wouldn't give for one studio hour with Billie Holiday. Floridian therapists talk of melancholy; Billie invented it.

A lot of people think their heroes would like them. I'm no exception to a lot of people. But I think more than like me, she would fondle the verses, let them into her heart, and the new blood would seep into her chords. Everything she sang was drenched in blood.

The other day I was drying a quilt. I was hanging it outside because it was too big for the dryer. John was helping Eric on the bike, cheering him.

Henry was crawling in the grass. The radio played "Have You Ever Really Loved a Woman?" by Bryan Adams.

He has no words we haven't heard before, but he brings them all up like he's discovering them. I'd heard it and thought it was good, but this time it just broke me. It broke my breastbone in two, and I had nothing to answer it. I stood there like an idiot holding the quilt, thinking how Mommy dried our things on clotheslines along the fire escape on the Concourse, probably never feeling some phantom pain in her chest she couldn't explain, doing what life asked of her in exchange for living it.

Do you think I am a bitter woman, Hannah?

Beth calls me and tells me about parades in New York City, how crime is down, how Central Park is crisp again, how Fitzgerald said life starts all over when it gets crisp in the fall. She said everyone she knows is making money. She goes to the Minetta Tavern and the Oak Room. She dates brokers and curators. She said everyone loves Julia Roberts and Will Smith and Italian food, that she kills whole afternoons at The Strand, that they've hosted nights in Union Square to honor the Beats, that *The Lion King* is overrated, but *Saturday Night Live* is finally peaking, and everyone on Fifth Avenue is dressed as sharp as they were in *North by Northwest*, and no one cares much about OJ anymore, and the best of everything is free for young women who take it. It is a warm, creative season in America. And I'm in Florida drying quilts and sucking guns.

Do you ever think it is funny how some of us came out of Mom's womb with so much to do and prove, and others wanted a cold milk and a funny TV show?

Emily suspected magic in herself. She was trying so hard to find its form. As a kid, she thought it would be spectacular romance and the trials of a war wife. Then she thought she could find it with crime and Daddy. Then she quit trying to find it and did those other things. The search takes so much out of us. Maddy, Daphne, Beth—they never cared for magic. They liked boys, spaghetti dinners, fireflies, parties, shoes: things that make life a straight line, not a mountain. I loved them for that. Jane was magic. I remember it even now. She died when she was fourteen, but that girl gushed poetry and ideas and charisma. She would've scaled skyscrapers. She died in a turned-over bus fire. She died a firework.

I'm the most obvious case, not because I'm special among us, but because I was loudest about it, and for some reason I haven't died.

But you, Hannah. Everybody would count you in with the professionals. You weren't born in a business suit per se, but you ran for class president at ten and chose a law school at thirteen. But I want to tell you: I am not fooled. I think you have more natural magic than any of us. I think you have so much that it terrifies you. So you buried it under a courthouse.

All valedictorians are at secret risk of gruesome suicide. They have discovered that the surest way not to kill themselves is through visible and indisputable success.

You haven't taken a full breath since you were a girl. You are afraid of what you will notice if you calm down and look around.

I don't begrudge you the safety of your life. Look at mine. But I want you to know that you walked through this world with magic up your sleeve. And it showed itself more than you wanted it to.

It is so grisly, isn't it? We would be better off with nothing driving us. We would be better off as Beth and Maddy than as Shakespeare and Princess Di and Billie Holiday.

Some people are charmed to feel relevant to history. Some are merely doomed to feel they should've been. And the happy many feel neither.

Boy, I should try to find someone to sing that for me.

* * *

I put the pen down for a day to travel. The Florida airports are quite nice actually. They are spacious and bright, and their flights never much delayed.

It isn't true that it's only old folks down here. There are many young people coming in who can't stand any longer the bustle of tough cities. They pass you at the supermarket, sense that you, too, are from New York or somewhere like it, strike up a conversation, and end with things like, *It's another day in paradise!*

Atlantic City is nowhere near here. I can't drive to Philly; I can't drive to Boston. I can't have pastries on Arthur Avenue. I don't meet flashy gents in gabardine suits who have stories from the Copa days and imply they've played cards with gangsters. I can't ski at the alumni events at Dartmouth. I can't go to Vermont. I can't find a jazz club, though some drifters play guitars at beach combers and croon into Miller Lites. They don't have cocktail parties in Florida yet. It's a social innovation that hasn't gotten here. Maybe in Boca or Miami, but we don't have them here, in our town, twenty minutes from the beach—thirty-five if I'm honest.

I don't know why I care anyway. I am a mother.

That reminds me: One of the last things you asked is if I thought I was a good mother. What a Hannah question.

I can be very good. I love them endlessly—more than I ever have you. I put it that way, so you understand what love is for a mom.

Do you remember watching the Academy Awards with Daddy, Jimmy, and Mommy growing up? Mom's brothers would come too. (I haven't thought about them in ages.) At a certain point, between awards, they would have the *In Memoriam* part, and the orchestra would play over images of everyone who died that year.

I never recognized the names. But I would watch Mommy and the others. They would get so misty after each one. We were having great fun guessing the winners up to then. But when the dead came onscreen, Uncle Johnny or Dad or Tommy or Jimmy would say, *No, HE died?! My goodness.* And we would sit quiet, and they would get small tears on their cheeks.

I felt so left out. I wished I could know who these actors were and why they were so great. But that wasn't why they were crying. They were remembering where they were when they saw their movies. They were remembering their own parents. And they were thinking they themselves would be dead someday. Now we know they were right.

Well, that's my answer to your question. I'm a quite good mother until I get to watching some *In Memoriam* section. And I stop thinking about what my boys need. and I start thinking of Jimmy Stewart and Red Skelton, then the Minetta Tavern and the gothic lampposts on street corners around New Hampshire. I think about magic and the constellations and myself, and not at all about the kids on my living room floor.

Living rooms are better than the constellations. I try hard to be a gentle woman in a living room and turn the energy of music into a love I can pour out on these sweet kids and that sad, good insurance man.

Trying so hard at something I'm no good at makes me realize how hard you tried to be there for all of us when your nature was to forget us forever. It makes me realize how hard everybody tried—even Jimmy, who was so naturally tender yet so bad at selflessness.

This is my season of silence. When I want to sing or write, I will think of you instead. I will think of how tightly you hugged me when you couldn't find words or even when the words were cruel. You were strong as a protector, not as a monster. I will think of how you went into every room ready to fight. Fighting was so hard for me. I will think of you how I always see you: when we shared a room in the Bronx, and you thought I was asleep, and you prayed one prayer over and over: *Never let me hurt anyone, God, never let me hurt anyone.*

Love,
Serena

***

Serena rented a car and drove from Logan Airport to Forest Hills Cemetery in Boston. She read this letter aloud, then sealed and buried it in some fresh soil, under tulips and burgundy dahlias, before the tombstone of Hannah Magic.

PART SIX

We Were Merchants

Gerard got out of bed. Catherine was asleep. Sun-dust floated over the naked lump in her belly, half-covered by an itchy yarn blanket.

The floorboards creaked under his feet as the Bronx woke up below and above him. Outside, past power lines, chimneys, and morning smolder, it had never slept.

He went into the kitchen, and Jimmy was passed out upright in a kitchen chair. There was a lit Viceroy next to his coffee mug.

"Wake up, you bum."

Jimmy's eyes snapped. His voice was full of a dream. "You chain-locked it again; I had to wake the kids up. Quit doing that." He wiped his mouth and smoked. "I came to get ya—the Tullys are across the street."

Gerard looked in on his daughters; five of them asleep in one room, three in one bed, two in another. He closed their door. "Now?"

"Your wife's family," said Jimmy, "is part of that nice Irish line of night owls. In a lotta parts of the world, it's still nighttime."

Gerard got his long coat and put it on over his white undershirt and bed leggings and stepped into slippers. The furnace clicked.

They went down four flights of stairs, Gerard saying morning to everyone in his building and rubbing the head of Mrs. Wolinsky's dog pissing on the stoop. They crossed the street and met three of Catherine's brothers, the Tully boys, none of them yet in their police uniforms at this early hour.

"Hiya, Gerard," said Johnny Tully.

"Johnny," said Gerard, nodding, "Tommy, Patrick. Early enough for ya?"

The three brothers were stomping their feet to keep warm, hands deep in their trench coat pockets. They were unshaven, and their eyes were fat from sleeplessness and ale. Gerard could tell they had all been laughing.

Patrick Tully was eyeing Gerard's legs, naked beneath his overcoat. "Don't go getting fancy just for us, Ger," he said and looked around fast, and they all cackled. "Having all these girls is making you a bit delicate, no, Ger? Can't you pop out just one lad for the sake of fairness?"

"Now, boys," said Jimmy, "you followed me back here and said we ought to do our talking now, so those with something to say, get to it."

"The man's got no trousers, God's sakes," Patrick pointed. "I mean, you have to pay for this kind of thing in the village!"

Gerard turned to leave. Johnny Tully stopped him and told Patrick to pipe down.

"Ger," said Johnny, "we want you to put an end to this business with our brother."

"I can't put an end to business I didn't start. I got no quarrel with your brother—besides that, he won't leave me be."

"We understand that," said Johnny, "our brother Aiden, well, he's, uh…," and all three of them looked at the ground in sudden-onset shyness, "he's taking himself a bit seriously as he gets older. It's a misfortune for all of us, really."

"Let's call it what it is," Jimmy Magic said. "He doesn't like us because our parents came from England and yours from Ireland. The rest of us have moved on, but not him."

"I wish it was easy as that," said Johnny, "at least that I could respect."

"Last week," said Patrick Tully, "he tried writing a fine on O'Doyle's down the street. It's a damn cop saloon. It's all our kind in there. Said they had too much trash outside. Can you believe it? Too much trash outside a bar? Hell, it's better keeping the trash outside than in, stinking up the potatoes..." he looked at Tommy, "and competing with Sally Wilson."

Another round of laughs. Jimmy joined this one. Even Gerard grinned.

Aiden, Johnny, Tommy, and Patrick were Bronx cops. Their father had been a landlord, and their mother died young—and their sister married Gerard, and he was writing his name in the streets, just like these mirthful police, making a lot of friends and being serious about helping them.

"Aiden's knocking on all the old ladies' apartments in the rooms over our office," said Jimmy Magic. "He's asking questions he shouldn't be asking, wants dirt on us. Dirt on his own family. Besides that, he's a beat cop trying to play big-shot detective. I've got a mind to tell his sergeant how he's spending his shift, get him stuck on a desk."

"Now, now," said Johnny, "there's no cause getting sergeants involved and all that. How'd that look, you suppose, the Tullys and the Magics taking their beef to the station house? We settle it here, among family.

"Gerard, Aiden's had quarrel with you ever since you married our sister. Personally, I've always liked you fine. Hell," he looked at Jimmy, "any brother of this sorry English good-time-Charlie can't be too far down hell's way." Jimmy smiled. "And when it comes to some of your dealings, well... I'd as soon rather you didn't put my sister or my nieces in harm's way by shaking hands with degenerates. But...it's what's in a man's soul that counts. That's our way.

"But Aiden's got the *important* bug. Wants to be an important man and put that over a laugh and a friend. It's a shame, and it ain't our father's mold. But he's my brother.

"So what I'm proposing to you is this: There's a Golden Gloves in Pelham next Tuesday. They're in need of an opening bout. I want it to be you, Gerry, against Aiden. Six rounds, thick gloves, nothing rotten. You slug it out—if you win, Aiden leaves off your business. If Aiden wins, you stop running hot items out of that lighting shop. And that's that."

"Aiden will agree to this?" said Gerard.

"Aiden's a damn tree," Jimmy yelled, his words showing up one at a time in the frosty air. "His neck's as thick as Patrick's head. What kind of a fight is that?"

"You're not afraid for your kid brother, are you?" said Patrick. "Everybody on Fordham Road says Gerard Magic's a tough fella. Though maybe they haven't seen what he wears to bed."

He looked around and again got his sniggers.

"Aiden will agree," said Johnny. "I suspect he's been wanting a reason to get into a slugfest with you, Ger. This'll do as well as any. Though one thing: Don't mention it to my sister, OK? She's got enough to manage, five girls up there and another on the way, and a pack of brothers who don't know how to mind their own business."

"I won't tell Catherine," said Gerard and stuck out his hand. Johnny shook it, smiling. "Patrick," Gerard went on, "a man with all daughters wearing leggings in the street may be delicate. But he's still the man who screws your sister."

As they went back across the street, Jimmy told Gerard he would be crazy to get in the ring with Aiden, who was a child in many ways but a giant in the one that would matter on Tuesday.

"There comes a time," said Gerard, patting the dog again and heading into the stairwell that smelled of ancient linoleum and phone books, "when you have to fight your wife's family. It doesn't much matter who wins. It matters you fight 'em."

"Those boys love you," said Jimmy. "It's this Aiden who's the problem. There are other ways, Ger."

"It's Johnny's idea, the fight. Not Aiden's. This is all of them trying to get me to stop making a better life that will take us out of here and leave them behind. May as well be all of them in that ring. Aiden's nothing but the patsy." He started laughing. Jimmy asked why. "I've waited ten years for this."

***

Catherine Magic, formerly a Tully, was mixing pancake batter when Gerard and Jimmy came back in the apartment. The girls were waking up slowly, and the radiator clicked softer.

Gerard put his hands on her belly, under her robe, and asked if she thought this would be the one.

"Alice upstairs says her brother had twelve girls and each time thought it would be a boy," said Catherine. "You let it in God's hands, Daddy." She kissed him. "I know that's not easy for you."

Jimmy dealt them both cigarettes. "What do you say, Catherine?"

She jiggled the stove until it lit. "Radio says Eisenhower says we can't be nice to Cuba anymore."

"Ha," said Jimmy, "1961's off to a swell start. Hey, that's what your husband was just telling me on the stairs. *No more diplomatic relations.* See, Gerard, you voted for Kennedy, but you and Eisenhower were thick all along. Nixon should've been your man."

Gerard stared, and Jimmy dropped the act. Hannah came in and asked for a cigarette.

"No!" Catherine and Jimmy screamed together.

"I'm going to be ten soon, Mom. Deloris has them every day."

"That's cause Deloris's family has no class—you look awful when you smoke, and it stinks up the house."

"We don't have a house," said Hannah. "We have an apartment, and it already smells 'cause all you do is smoke, and all anybody who visits us does is smoke and drink iced tea or whiskey."

Gerard said, "Get in the living room and help Emily watch after your sisters."

"If Maddy falls off the couch again," Catherine added, "you won't eat for a month!"

Mrs. Wolinsky knocked on the door and let herself in.

There were apartments that kept the chain lock on during the day and those that only used it at night, if then. The Magics were a night-chain family. During the day, neighbors and friends came and went, shared records, sipped tea, and told a joke they'd heard ten minutes before. Their one apartment was its own home, but it was also one room in a tall, grungy house; they had responsibilities to the whole and reaped the energy of the big home as well as the intimacy of their small one.

Their two bedrooms were getting crowded. Yet life was pleasantly automatic. Each day pulled them forward into it and through it, tiring them out with its fullness. It would've been cruel, Catherine thought, and offensive to God, to make abrupt and casual changes to a life full of blessings.

The new baby was due the beginning of February. Catherine had a girl's and a boy's name picked out. She had named them all, except one: Serena. Gerard picked that name. It had been his mother's.

Mrs. Wolinsky put a tray of cheese buns on the table. "Eat up. Harold doesn't feel good today. I made them for no one."

Catherine called the kids in, gave them one each, then plopped their pancakes down and said yes, Hannah could mix chocolate milk for the lot.

The kids ravaged the table as the adults went to the living room. Catherine opened the windows and let the icy air mix in with the heat, the stove smells, and Viceroy clouds.

"Maris versus Mantle," said Jimmy, crisping the paper. "I'm going to get us in opening day."

Mrs. Wolinsky said, "All we talk about is baseball—it's winter."

"It's a game of anticipation, Mrs. Wolinsky," said Jimmy. He tipped some ashes. "You see these two guys right here?" he showed the page. "They're both gunning for the home run record in the American League—heck, in the history of baseball. The record is sixty home runs in a single season. You know who set it?"

Mrs. Wolinsky said proudly, "George Herman Ruth."

"The Babe! Now, just about every working-class Moe in New York wants this handsome guy right here to be the one to break it." He pointed to Mickey Mantle's newspaper face. "But one man, who happens to be my brother, wants this other louse over here. What do you think of that?"

"I think it makes no difference to my water bill or to Harold's heart condition which of those two men hit more baseballs over a fence on 161st Street."

"Ah, but it makes all the difference, Mrs. Wolinsky," said Jimmy. "It's the spirit of New York those boys are playing for." He got up and walked around the tight room. "You stroll down the street the morning after the pinstripes clinch playoffs, or Mantle *belts* one over center field in the ninth, man, oh man—" he slapped the tube "—your bus driver's holding his head a little higher. The girls playing jump rope, their father's in such a good mood he gives them ten cents for candy, and they run around screaming, laughing. Bartenders are pouring free rounds, the meter maid don't give out no tickets, not to a fellow New Yorker, not here in the Bronx." He took a deep, sweet breath. "It lifts the whole city. Sixty home runs—well, sixty-one—that'll get us to the moon this year!

"Of course," he looked at Gerard, "only if it's the right man for the job."

"Maris is a slugger," said Gerard, seated on a stained, crooked-spine sofa. "It's not sentimental. Mantle may be a better player. But Maris is…I see something in his eyes that's not about New York at all. It's cold. He's a winner."

"You're the only Yankee fan," said Jimmy, "who doesn't like other Yankee fans. You like it to be some private thing, don't you?"

Gerard smiled. Catherine got up and sat beside him, cozying under his arm. No one could tell what about this conversation reminded her of her fondness for her husband, but there it was.

Serena came inside with syrup on her chin. "Mommy," she said.

"Yes, bumblebee."

At four years old, she spoke beautifully. "I was thinking. Why do you love Daddy?"

Everybody laughed.

"Because he's big and strong and handsome," said Catherine.

"I'll take that one, kid." Jimmy's sleeplessness was making him dance. He spun little Serena around. "You see, there's us—the folks in this building and all up and down the Concourse. And then there are other people who make the rules, pass the laws, decide who gets how much money. And there's a big wall between them and us. Now, I know that. Your uncles know it. Mrs. Wolinsky knows it. But your father doesn't believe it. He thinks it's a myth. And your mother loves him for that." He stuck the ink-bleeding paper in her little hands. "She loves him because he roots for Roger Maris."

Mrs. Wolinsky said she'd better check on Harold. "If he sees a roach, he blames me."

"Oh," Catherine waved, "everyone seems to have those; don't be embarrassed." She tussled her hair. "Just luck they don't visit our house, I guess."

Emily shouted from two rooms away. "What are you talking about, Ma? We caught three roaches this morning!"

***

In America, in New York, most of the English and Irish made their truces in the 1940s and '50s because they came through the war together—and peace, the end of rations, and a new lightness on the faces of seventeen-year-old boys conspired to make them bury the past, bond over this new idea, a fresh start in a fair place with people on the street all day, selling something or playing handball.

For Aiden Tully, in 1961, the good feeling of ethnic equilibrium had worn off. And he went to McGovern's Gym on Tuesday night after his shift ready to pummel the royal devil out of his brother-in-law.

In the metal folding chairs outside the ring, from Gerard's side, were Jimmy and about twenty good men from the block who wanted to see Aiden get what he had coming. On the Tully's side were the Tully brothers and their hordes of cousins along with thirty cops, most of whom also thought Aiden could use an ass-kicking but was unlikely to get one.

Gerard took his shirt off. The boy who worked the gym, about Emily's age, helped lace up his gloves. Aiden came over, his gloves already tight, a beam on his cheeks, and said, "I'm not much for dancing, Ger. But if you see me doing a jig after this, don't take it too personal, eh?"

Gerard didn't answer.

The crowd made a lot of noises and drank a lot of beer, and the cops started singing Irish songs, and some of the Italians in the back booed harder than the English. It all got Aiden's blood up.

Aiden was six-foot-four. His skin was whiter than his eyeballs. His hair was auburn; his face ugly with freckles and moles. Walking the beat, he wore his tidy policeman's cap and mirrored shades and swiveled his nightstick, and you wouldn't see much of him under all that. Here in the ring, he wore nothing but grass-green trunks. The furry red patches under his arms stood up and danced each time he threw showman punches at the air.

Aiden was a history man, had had more schooling than any of his brothers, and felt connected to his ancestors by way of a long-channeling misery. He wasn't likely to forget the snobs and overlords who kept their boot on the throat of his people who sought to decide where they should live, how they should work, what God they should believe in, and how much of their country they could keep. Even if Aiden himself never endured these atrocities—born as he was at Calvary Hospital on Eastchester Road and not in some subdued province of Ireland—he kept up reasons to hate his colonizers both as an Irishman and an American. He thought it a damn pity, the day he could no longer avoid shaking his sister's boyfriend's hand, and sure enough it felt coarse as the country it belonged to—that snide, gray, charmless wasteland, home of Oliver Cromwell and King George, Darwin and the daft queen, ignorant, lazy, and joyless, the country that forever changed religions over a mistress.

Aiden couldn't bring himself to understand how his brothers or his sweet little sister Catherine could tolerate the company of that family, American in name only, not a dash Irish. Jews or Germans would've been better. And to top it all? They were crooks.

Someone rang the bell. "Fight!"

Aiden came hurling a wide right. Gerard ducked it cleanly and served a spell of punches to his guts. Aiden felt a few but used his reach to step Gerard back. He fired a quick jab, and it slid off Gerard's right eye. Gerard got in three more body shots that round, which proved to be his best, and didn't feel much hurt until the end of the second. The third and fourth rounds were bloodbaths with Aiden finding his tempo. Gerard was knocked out in the fifth.

The Irish songs came back louder; the Italians went home. The few English who'd come, and the pals of the Magics who hoped against hope to see a stodgy beat cop get his due, filed out to the bar next door as the lads screamed "Four Green Fields" in their faces, singing that sweet melody with rage.

Jimmy hosed water over Gerard's face and toweled him down. "You fought 'em, brother."

Mrs. Wolinsky appeared where she didn't belong between two rows of chairs, screaming how they'd better come: Catherine had the baby early.

Jimmy made to lift his brother, but Gerard's strength returned at once, and he charged ahead of them, racing through the double steel doors. The Tully brothers wailed from the middle of the ring:

But my sons had sons, as brave as were their fathers,

And my fourth green field will bloom once again, said she!

***

Mommy was coming home today.

Mrs. Wolinsky promised Hannah. Daddy had been back and forth the last ten days. Today he was bringing her with him.

Emily loved when her mother kissed her. It was soft and on the corner of the lips. Her father's kisses were firmer, and his scruff scraped her cheek. She didn't mind it always, but sometimes felt he didn't deserve it if he had worked many nights in a row or broken a promise to play. Mrs. Wolinsky once told Emily she was lucky she had a father who, when he said he was working, was actually working and not "off getting into trouble."

For a while, Emily thought Daddy was as much of a drunkard and voyager as the other fathers in the building or as Uncle Jimmy. But she heard Mommy telling Uncle Johnny one night in a storm that he wasn't half the man Gerard was because of those same things that Johnny always did and Daddy never would. Emily knew Uncle Johnny had enough to say about Daddy that if there was something to say back to that, he would've said it. But Johnny took the insult in silence, so that must've meant it was true.

That made Emily hold her head a little higher in school and down on the sidewalk. She had wondered if Daddy would ever cheat on Mommy and leave her behind the way Deloris's parents had split. But after hearing Johnny stay quiet like that, she realized it would never happen.

Every morning as he left for the office, the girls would yell the games they wanted to play when he got home: hopscotch, Candyland, Park and Shop, Uncle Wiggily, Concentration, marbles. He would collect the names as he put on his coat and hat and tell each one what order their game would be played that night. The girls would hop around when theirs got called. But only Emily seemed to notice that on the nights when he got home early enough to play at all, he would sit down and make a big show of starting the game. And within ten minutes, he would remember he had to make a call and would say he'd be back soon. Ten minutes was the average length of time he could play. The girls, by then, were invested in the game, so they went on playing.

Then again, maybe every few months, he would stop at the door on the way to work, throw his hat and coat in the corner and decide he was staying home all day, and the kids were skipping school. They would build a big cushion fortress around the TV set, drink chocolate milk, and pass the day teasing one another or making fun of the soaps.

He was a tricky dad. It was too hard for Emily to decide what to feel about him. Mostly she let the question sit and enjoyed the TV days and felt proud he wasn't a cheat and hated him if he showed he cared a bit about the world outside the Concourse.

Mrs. Wolinsky had the kids smooth their beds and clean the sink, the cupboards, and the kitchen table. It seemed to Emily that all she'd wanted to talk about on the nights when she stayed with them was how many words different women in the building could type in a minute. Alice O'Malley was up to eighty-five a minute, but Kathleen Herbert, whose husband was on "hard times," could do a hundred, and her dictation was second to none. Mrs. Wolinsky liked to talk about what everyone else was talking about and liked to be better at it—not the thing itself under discussion but better at talking about that thing, knowing more, and showing she knew it.

She also felt that kids shouldn't know anything. That wasn't Mommy and Daddy's way, but she couldn't help it: She shooed them off if she was on the phone, hearing news, and denied if they guessed right. Daddy had told Emily and Hannah everything one of the nights he was home, and they weren't supposed to tell the others yet because it was sad for little girls to hear that another little girl, just born, was now gone.

Emily didn't talk about it with Mrs. Wolinsky because she knew the poor lady couldn't handle that. But she didn't think Jane and Serena would just forget about the baby Mommy had promised.

It was 10:00 p.m. when they came home. Mommy was still in her hospital clothes. Mrs. Wolinsky arranged the couch cushions for her and made a show of helping her sit.

Daddy said, "Mrs. Wolinsky, thank you. We're going to take some time as a family now."

"Oh, oh, sure." She stumbled around looking for her overnight bag. Emily saw it had been the furthest thing from her mind that she might be asked to leave when they got home. "I'll be out of your way. Catherine, dear, one day at a time. I'll be down in the morning to help with arrangements and all that. We'll give that girl a...well..." She got to sobbing in the hall, and Daddy walked her to the door and used the chain lock when she left.

To her oldest daughter, Catherine looked changed in the space of time they'd been apart. In a few weeks, she would be herself again. But now she smelled of the sick place she came from. She gave the kids a speech about how some precious things get taken out of the world. And how that's what happened to their family.

"So where is the baby?" Serena said, and kept saying it no matter how well they explained it.

"Mommy had a baby," said Gerard. "Only she had it before she was supposed to. And it died."

"Why did you do that?" Serena asked Catherine.

"No, no," said Emily, stroking Serena's hair, "it wasn't Mommy's fault. That happens sometimes. God controls when babies come, not mommies."

"Oh. Why did God do it?" she said.

Gerard went to his chair and sat down. Catherine talked a lot about God and his ways. Gerard typically went to his chair and waited when she did that.

"Did you name the baby, Mommy?" said Jane.

Catherine said, "We named her Brianne. We thought she would die right away. She held out nine days, the little thing. She was so wonderful. You would've loved her right away." She didn't cry. Her voice got light and strange, but that was it. She held them all on her lap even though Gerard said she should be careful in her state. "I'm surrounded by my sweet, strong girls. You fill me with such love." She went around and told them each what special gifts they were born with. She got to Serena and told her hers, and added, "Your gifts make you eternally innocent. No matter what hard, awful things happen, your gifts make you a child again."

Emily said, "What are your gifts, Mommy?"

Catherine's wonderful laugh filled the house. Everybody in the Bronx referred to their apartments as houses. "I have two: I have a belief in God that runs through down to my toes; he visits me and loves me and gives me extra love to spread around, more than anybody should have."

"What's the other?" said Jane.

"I can make people happy with the way I play the piano."

"Even on a sad night like this?" Serena said, and her eyes looked like they were watching Santa, hoping he would turn out to be the same man legends promised.

"Even tonight," said Catherine.

She got up and led them all into the hall. She lifted the cover on the spinet, rubbed her hands together, blew on them. She played.

Her daughters put their arms around one another in a line, blocking the room from one wall to the other. Catherine sang with a rasping sadness that somehow, by the end, became severe joy. She smiled in between every lyric. Her shoulders bounced as she struck the keys. The kids had no idea what losing a sister was supposed to feel like because Catherine played over it. There was sugar in her voice. Along with God. And little girls loved sugar, and from their mother they borrowed God.

Behind them, Gerard leaned on the doorway of the kitchen. His face was still marked from the fight with Aiden. Emily looked back every few minutes and caught him smiling. It wouldn't be so bad, she thought, right then, if he came over and gave her a kiss.

***

The day after the funeral Gerard went back to work.

Waiting outside the lighting office on Walton Avenue, he found Johnny and Patrick Tully, this time dressed in full uniform. Patrick's blue collar was tugged up around his neck to stem the chill. Johnny, the oldest Tully brother, smoked and rested his free hand on his gun belt.

Johnny said and Patrick repeated, "Hiya, Ger."

"Boys." They were standing in front of the padlock on the office gate. "Well?"

Johnny tossed the cigarette. He had thirty pounds of a spare tire around his waist, and his teeth were as tinted as the sun. He muttered more than spoke. "We don't like being here on account of…well, on account of what you've been put through already and…"

"What is it, Johnny?"

"You lost the fight," Patrick chimed in.

"So?"

"So," Patrick's hands fidgeted in his pockets, digging for warmth, "you lost means you stop running a front out of this office."

Jimmy Magic arrived for his workday, lunch bag in hand and winter coat over his arm instead of on his back.

"We wouldn't put this on you today, except for Aiden," said Johnny. "He's got a real bug about it and says if he finds out you're still moving hot items in here end of the week, he's going to dime you out to his sarge, and they'll run a party on the whole joint."

Jimmy barked about the lost child and the callous hearts of men who called themselves family. Gerard patted Jimmy's shoulder and handed him the padlock key. "Open us up for the day," he said to Johnny. "If Aiden wants to come knock down my door—I'll open it for him."

As he made past them, Johnny snapped, "Now come on now, Gerard, a man's word is what it is. You lost in that ring."

Jimmy got the gate up. The fruit vendors were out now, stocking crates of Georgia peaches—Georgia fruit, all the way up here on the sidewalk of Walton Avenue. Gerard said, "I said I'd stop, and I will. I don't need your brother's help deciding when."

He got inside and watched Johnny and Patrick through the glass argue over what to do next and end by storming down the street.

To call the lighting company a *front* was not truly fair, and the Tullys well knew it. The Magics supplied lighting fixtures and solutions to over a hundred local businesses. On occasion, they used the storeroom to hold products, "hot items," that a third-party vendor delivered from out of town. Sometimes they were fireworks, sometimes cigarettes, sometimes German chocolates. There were never drugs or weapons. They were delicacies hard to come by or free of tax, and they'd hold them overnight and have them couriered the next day to the private rooms of pawnshops or trade markets under the bridge or at the piers. Gerard never stole these things, and he never directly sold them on the street either. He paid near-wholesale value to the vendors and sold them at near-market value to street peddlers. The only thing Aiden Tully could ever really suspect him of was keeping some stock on hand a few nights a month here at the office close to home. For that, he got in the ring. For that, the Tullys visited him the week after his baby daughter's death. For fireworks and bubblegum. For the curiosity shop of the old Bronx.

Jimmy put on the coffee. "Ger, we stopped moving hot products in and out of here over a month ago. Why not just tell 'em?"

"What fun is that?"

Jimmy laughed and said he'd thought Gerard might be forgetting about fun. "And if Aiden brings a raid on this place? Well, I guess that'd embarrass him pretty bad, wouldn't it?"

Horace Eaton came in and offered his condolences.

Gerard shook his hand and said, "Have you thought over our offer?"

The three of them sat at the conference table in the backroom. There was no art on the faded green walls. The popcorn ceiling was frayed at the corners, and exposed pipes sometimes leaked wet rust. They drank coffee out of Styrofoam.

"Let me say, Gerard, you're no Ralph Kramden. You make a life out of your ideas. Everyone on the block has come to know that."

"Let's skip this part, Horace," said Gerard.

"It's a gamble on my end," said Horace. "I was a kid during the Depression. It's hard to think of wanting more than I have now. And the laundry business is on the up. We've got janitors, and a tailor comes in twice a week. I got the best spot on Morris Avenue."

"Neighborhood's changing, Horace," Jimmy said. "In ten years, this won't be a safe place. It won't be a place for your girls or my brother's. And maybe people will be able to buy laundry machines. Like they have now with TVs. We used to all go to one guy's house to watch a ballgame, and now we all got 'em."

The small business owner with a taut wooden leg took a hard candy out of his pocket and unwrapped it with ceremony. He reached into his briefcase and took out an accordion folder. "I did my study of your numbers. You want me to close the doors on my little business, join your big one. But what you've got isn't all that different. You've got a lotta little businesses sewn together. And they're making you money instead of costing you by an *inch*."

He held up his thumb and pointer finger to show what an inch was.

Jimmy said, "We made six hundred thousand dollars last year. Name me one other Moe here to Riverdale bringing in that kind of dough."

"All together," Horace replied, "your properties and your lighting company reported five hundred ninety-two thousand dollars. You *profited* sixteen thousand dollars. All your money went to expenses."

Gerard got up and opened the blinds. The light was full of a city gloom. It was February, and a New York winter never used ten words when one would do. He shuffled around the table and sat in the chair beside Horace.

"How much did you make with the laundromat last year?"

"Eighteen thousand."

"Net?"

"Seven."

"See, that's not half bad. That's why we need you, Horace," said Gerard. "I think a fella like you could find ways to turn our sixteen thousand dollar profit into thirty or fifty. My brother and I, it's no secret we've been runners on a book. But we want to get out of that racket. There's more to the world than the bums around here throwing bad dollars on a flyer. In order to go after the really big things in life, you need to be seen as a big man." He pointed at the accordion folder. "Six hundred is a big number. It doesn't matter that we don't keep it; that it goes into making it all work. It matters that people think we're rich. We take money here and pass it over there, keep a little each time. And after a while, people think you're strong and smart; you start to get shots at a whole lotta dough at once."

"We call that *the ticket*," said Jimmy.

"You can't get the ticket," Gerard said, "being a bum. You've got to show something. You've got to own things, land and concrete and a business. It's not the point whether you're making money—it's whether it looks like you are."

Horace Eaton said, "If the whole country thought like that, we'd be in a heap of trouble—and the most dangerous part is, we would never know it until it was too late."

"Horace, I promise you: I'm only thinking about a decade or two ahead of the country."

Horace missed trolley cars and the simplicity of hunger. He got a sense, sitting there with smart men, that if he sold his business and joined theirs, very little would be simple again.

"What's the ticket?" he said. "You want everyone to see you get big. Then what do you want to do?"

Gerard and Jimmy traded a long, relieving smile.

"You ever been to Connecticut?" said Jimmy.

"I can't drive," said Horace. "I don't leave the neighborhood if I don't have to—and I don't."

"Here's a question you'll know the answer to," said Gerard. "How does the mob make money in Red Hook, in Hoboken and Newark, in Staten Island?"

He thought a minute. "Well, in some of those areas, they used to own a piece of the longshoremen. But a lot of that's been cracked down on..."

Jimmy took a brochure off the shelf and spread it out in front of Horace. "What if we told you there was a little patch of harbor—no more than a few miles—where the Maritime PD never bothers to look too close...where the mob has no hooks in, where cops are sweet old men who go home early. And municipal laws make it so private citizens can landlord them docks."

Horace looked over the tristate map. He glanced up and said, "It would take years to win this contract. You'd have to fill the posts with men you could trust, and what kind of men do they even make in that area? And how in the universe could you run a port in Connecticut from the Grand Concourse in the Bronx?"

Gerard smiled. "The Bronx is prologue, Horace."

***

There was one other Tully brother: Father Gregory Tully. He was a father with no sons, only family, friends, and a flock of sinners. He was the funniest of the clan and knocked, that Thursday, on the Magic's apartment door after his weekday service wearing a face that hid a taunt.

Catherine took her brother's coat, and they engaged in one of the great mid-twentieth-century northeastern pastimes: sitting at an old table in the middle of a day and talking about nothing.

The Irish, Catherine suspected, invented the practice to give relatives a wide berth to arrive at an actual point and overcome the reticence, evasiveness, and guilt that had long prevented confrontation, healing, and emotional depth. Although Catherine would not have put it that way. She would've said, if *pressed*, "Sometimes it takes a while to get things squared away, and you've gotta go around the block a few times before you find the door."

They were always close, the Tully kids, and loved one another painfully, but it was easier and more sincere to tell each other that through talking about Mr. Dixon's shameless affairs or raising a glass to Harold Wolinsky's liver cancer or signing the cross whenever an ambulance blared. They loved one another by agreeing about everything and understanding the basic morbidity of the world.

After about an hour Father Tully came to his point. "How is your heart, my sister?"

She tapped a Viceroy into a brown crystal tray. "I barely knew the girl."

"You knew her better than anyone did," he said. "Like all parents, you had dreams for her."

Catherine considered the question. Had she had any dreams for the infant girl who died after nine nights? She'd confined them to one: that she see a tenth.

"So many people," said Catherine, "were joking during the funeral. And after at the pub. There was more laughing in that pub than on a Friday night. It was so loud I had to take Serena and Maddy outside; they were frightened. You'd think those clowns would have more respect is all."

She allowed herself some small crying.

"Think of when we heard about the war when we were kids," said Father Gregory. "First thing Mommy would say was, you know, it's the crazy ones from bad families who die. They have death wishes; they run out on the front line! They want to die, I tell ya!"

They both laughed a while.

When the last chuckle fell from the table, he added, "How can we expect people to face what it really means? Their lives are hard enough without you telling them about that poor little baby, born without a chance."

Catherine said, "Were you at the fight between Aiden and Gerard?"

He raised his eyes. "You weren't supposed to hear a thing about it."

"Right, lot of subtle men running around my life: Gerard with balloons on his face, and Johnny and Patrick giggling like Doris Day."

"Ah, Catherine, I would never go to a barbaric display like that. Among family no less. No, sister."

He adjusted the felt of his Roman collar.

She said, "You place a bet on it?"

He laughed and said, "You have some nerve! Talking to me that way in my own home!"

"You're in my home, Father. You bet Aiden, didn't you?"

"I got it near even money; what's a man in my position to do? Even money on our Hercules brother against your business-minded Englishman! Pass on those odds? I can't very well *throw money away*. I'm not a Jesuit for heaven's sake."

She shook her head as she cleared the crumb-spotted dishes. "Well, you enjoy your winnings; I know he got licked. But I don't think he thought it would go any other way. So if there was any respect in that ring, in my book, it ought to belong to my husband."

"Respected he was," Father Gregory nodded. "Right through when he kissed the canvas. Look, it's all a silly business. But he is going to have a problem with Aiden if he doesn't quit poking the boy in the eye."

"Aiden thinks the kids flagging the Good Humor truck are poking him in the eye."

He nodded again. "Right you are. But Gerard is choosing a certain road, Catherine. Are you ready to go along it with him?"

She was letting the sink run over the dishes. She shut the faucet and toweled off her rough hands. "And where's the other road lead?" she said. "Although it's not a road at all, that one, is it? It's a parking lot. And we all sit in it and eat Entenmann's."

Father Gregory Tully got up smiling. He was due to hear confessions. He got his coat and hat and kissed his sister on the cheek. "Sunday's mass will be offered up for the soul of your little girl. May she be in heaven. And may she be the last one you ever lose."

***

Catherine finished folding the last day's laundry. She hand-washed clothes four or five times a week so that it felt that she wasn't ever really not doing it. Gerard went through socks and undershirts like Aiden handed out summons or Johnny smoked Luckies.

Catherine's life was bookended by the sexes: men above, women below.

In a few months, the day after Emily's birthday, Catherine would turn thirty-two. She was nineteen when Gerard proposed. He was ready. She felt ready. Her classmates were engaged. It had seemed like a fine notion, and it disturbed her brothers irremediably. All of that added up to a thrill and a dream. He spoke about his plans—not his ideas, mind you, his plans—and called them *plans*. There was never a trace of doubt in his voice that any of them may not come to fruition. Over time, her reflex skepticism began to seem sort of...pointless; he wasn't talking about things that may or may not happen to them; he was discussing the future they would forge through acts of the will.

Catherine had never heard anyone talk that way. She was a member of a class of people to whom things happened, most of them unfortunate, some hilarious. But they were all passengers together on an aimless and unnavigable voyage through time, and the smart rovers latched onto buoys: pensions, double-overtime, disability insurance, union membership, a sergeant's test, journeyman status, conductor, cabbie, civil service, ShopRite supervisor, one hundred words a minute, automobiles, ponies, Luckies, the pinstripes.

Gerard wanted to build something. It made her family sick. It made Catherine curious.

The men in the Tully family, through their compromises and pacts with society, felt protected; what she didn't expect them to understand was that there was no greater feeling of protection that controlling one's own outcomes. They couldn't imagine how secure she felt talking a problem over with Gerard and realizing, slowly, she could solve it. Father Gregory would say give your problems to God. She wanted to tell him that God hands quite a few back.

It was a gradual process, leaving behind her inherited idea that the major events of life happened without her consideration or consent. But most days she did it successfully. And if ever she felt truly beaten down, as perhaps she did in the weeks after she lost her baby, she turned back in secret to the family tradition of duty. One's duty, she felt, was a fail-safe. It didn't matter how you felt about it; you did it. But this was 1961. It was before anxiety. It was before "career" and "vocation" and "Zen." And people like Gerard and Catherine, totally unbeknownst to themselves, were inventing a new chapter in America. It would be filled of a lot of things, and one of them was magic.

On Friday, Catherine took Emily and Serena to the doctor while Johnny's wife, Theresa, sat with her other kids. Afterwards Catherine brought them by Gerard's office. It was unseasonably warm, and she caught him coming out of a conference with Jimmy and suggested he leave early to join them at the park.

As Gerard packed his bag, Catherine heard the slamming of several car doors out front.

Jimmy peeked through the blinds. "It's that demented brother of yours, Catherine. And he brought playmates."

Gerard and Catherine took a look. Aiden was rounding his squad car. Three other cars were lined behind his, about eight men in uniforms getting out, blocking the street.

"They've come to raid our lighting fixtures," Gerard said. Jimmy laughed.

"Let me go out and talk to him," said Catherine.

"My dear," said Gerard. He followed her out, and Jimmy kept the girls in the doorway.

Catherine walked up to Aiden's car. Johnny Tully crossed from the far side of the street at the same time.

"What do you think you're doing, Aiden Tully?" she said as she closed the gap between them.

"Your husband is running a lawless operation out of that office, and we're shutting him down."

"You mean unlawful, you ignorant snob," she said. "If the office was lawless, it wouldn't matter what laws he broke, would it?"

"Catherine," said Johnny, "Gerry's had every chance to set this right. He gave his word, and now he's leaving Aiden no choice."

"There's nothing but stacks of lighting catalogs and some secretaries in that office, Aiden," she said. "You want to embarrass my family."

As the spectacle grew in the middle of Walton Avenue, and folks came out on their fire escapes, and vendors sat on cartons to have a view, a thought visibly invaded Jimmy's complexion, and he tiptoed to Gerard.

"Um, say, Ger."

"Hmm?"

"You know, I'm thinking it over. Even though there's nothing hot in there, it may not be best to have them raiding the office."

"We got everything out weeks ago. Let 'em at it."

"Well, that's the thing."

Now Gerard looked at him. "What, Jimmy?"

"I got you something, and I forgot to give it to you. It's in Trina's office under the torn-up rug. What, with the beef we had with the McCarthys last month, and then…"

"Say you got me a gun, Jimmy."

Jimmy tightened up his eyes. "I meant to give it to you weeks ago, but then the kid happened, and I kind of…ah, brother. Say, why don't you just stay out here and distract 'em, and I'll sneak it out through the alley."

Gerard looked around the block. "I bet that stiff put a car back there." He sighed. "Jimmy."

"I know," he said. "I know."

He shook his head and walked over to his in-laws.

"Your time's come," said Aiden, seeing him.

"Maybe, Aiden," said Gerard, "maybe." He looked down the street. "Tell you what, your brother Gregory has lunch around this time at Dolan's, yeah? What do you say you and I go down there and join him. You can leave all your boys right here in front of my building with Officer Johnny. If we can't work anything out in the presence of a man of the cloth…of a Tully, no less…then you can come back here and put a raid on my place."

Aiden objected and said they were through talking, but Catherine made a sharp plea, and Johnny brokered the rest of it. Gerard and Aiden set off for Dolan's on the corner. Jimmy, Johnny, and Catherine stood around with the crew of beat cops. In a few minutes, Jimmy had them crying with his Grace Kelly voice.

When they weren't looking, Emily and four-year-old Serena took off after Gerard and their uncles. The office boy, worried about them, chased after. Little Brighton always thought himself a protector.

***

They walked into Dolan's and stomped their feet on the long, thin rug running over a flagstone floor. Father Gregory Tully was at his usual lunch table, polishing off a skirt steak, fingerling potatoes, and a Guinness.

"Gerard Magic," said Gregory, cheery under his collar, "in the company of the law! Could my eyes be drunker than the rest of my face?"

Gerard and Aiden sat in the empty chairs.

"He wants you to play peacekeeper," said Aiden, sliding the baton off his belt so he could sit comfortably, setting it on a bench beside the brick fireplace.

Gerard laid out the circumstances that had gotten them from distant and discordant brothers-in-law to a boxing bout to an afternoon in which a bevy of cops sat outside his office—he spoke as if Father Gregory would have no idea about the workings of the peasant class on either side of the law.

When he was through, Gerard added, "We don't much care for each other, your brother and I, but there's no reason we can't find some civility. The truth is, I stopped running inventory out of there before the fight even started. Aiden, I suppose I didn't tell you because I didn't want you to have the satisfaction. But there it is. We don't run that operation anymore. If you want to come in yourself and take a look around, I'll show you. But here, before your brother, let's find some way to move forward in peace."

Father Gregory wiped his chops. He said amiably, "Well, what do you say, Aiden? That doesn't sound so reasonless to me."

Aiden stared. "No deal."

Gregory laughed. "You're serious?"

"Yes, I am. No deal. Even if you're not running items out of there, you're running them someplace. I know you use strong-arms to buy up properties cheap around here. I know you and Jimmy have been runners for the Belmont bookmakers for years! Cowards, you don't even run your own book; you get cash flow just from finding suckers and sending them over to Belmont. And I know other things, and I'm sure I don't know the worst! If you don't want my boys in that office, it's probably cause you got something hidden. Now I'm more raring to go than ever. So I'm going back there, and I'm going to have my raid party. How's that?"

Gerard kept his face.

"Now," said Father Gregory, "let's not be foolish as all that. Why don't we have a drink and sort this? I'm done with this," he slid the empty glass forward, residual foam gliding down its neck. "Let's drink as a family."

He got up and rubbed the indents of Aiden's absurd shoulders. He went to the bar, spoke to Dolan, and came back with a bottle of Redbreast Irish Whiskey. Dolan brought over some short glasses.

"What do you suppose my brother's problem is with you, Gerard?" Father Gregory said, pouring them all a few ounces. "If you had to suppose."

"I would suppose he doesn't like that his sister married an Englishman. That I have never been to England, don't attend a Protestant church, and talk much the same as either of you doesn't seem to matter to him. Then I'd suppose a close second is my business habits."

"You don't talk the same as us," said Aiden. "Let me call out the lies when I hear them. We say *tell you somethin'* and *get things straightened out, how's it goin'.* You say everything more careful. Pronounce it big-shot like. You may be half a crook, but you talk like a pencil pusher. About the worst of both worlds."

Father Gregory sniffed the whiskey. "What my brother means, Gerard: You think of yourself as better than the rest of us around here, and you like us to know it."

"A sin," said Aiden. "Pride—right, Greggie?"

"Oh, sure is. Pride before the fall. *He who exalts himself*, Gerry. *He who exalts...*"

Gerard took his glass from the middle and sipped. He said, "You're a church man, right, Aiden?"

"Every Sunday. I see you come with my sis once a month."

"And you do what the church says?"

Now Aiden paused. He looked at his brother. "I'm a sinner. I do the best I can."

"But you want other people to do what the church says, right? You and your brothers are OK; you're sinners. But everyone else, they should listen."

Father Gregory said, still smiling, "Takes a man of faith to talk faith. Are you that man?"

"Your nuns slap kids around. You couldn't care less. Johnny and Patrick are brutal to the Negroes. Father, how much did you gamble last week? Aiden wants to torch my book—good thing you don't bet with me—but don't tell him who you use. He's going to knock over all the honest crooks in town, and then he'll have a clean neighborhood, right? And it'll just be you Tullys slapping each other's backs and having a pint, chanting nonsense about a country you'll probably never go back to again.

"You're Catholics. Sinners. *Absolved.* And you go to Mass, but you don't look at God."

The barkeep came and dropped a dish of sunflower seeds in the middle of them. This gave Aiden a minute to unclench his teeth.

Father Gregory looked around at the few regulars along the bar. "Tom," he called. "Tom, come over and sit with us a minute, would you?" A tall fellow with a wispy and receding hairline wearing a blue doorman's uniform collected his cap and Budweiser can and came over. "Take a seat, Tom, and put away the Bud, look what we got here." He poured him a Redbreast. "Gerard, you know Tom Collins?"

"No."

"Tom Collins, this is my brother-in-law, Gerard Magic."

"That your real name?" said Gerard.

"That yours?" said Tom.

Father Gregory laughed. "Tom, how's tricks?"

"Eh, can't complain." He set his cap on the table and took a drink.

"Well, you can't complain, how about that? Three of us, all we're doing is sitting here complaining. See, Ger, Tom used to work at the Ascot. They closed it down to...what'd they call it, Tom?"

"Renovate."

"That's right," said Gregory, "*renovate.* Gerard knows these words; he's a building man himself."

"Oh, a super?" said Tom.

"Bigger than that, Tom. Gerard's got it so the supers work for him! Anyways, Ger, Tom here went quits with the Ascot, and now he's a doorman at the Carlisle. About how long it take you to get down there in the morning, Tom?"

"It's not so bad, maybe forty minutes, door to door."

"You take the D?"

"The 6."

"We've had some cold mornings, Tom. How is it out there on that subway platform some of these mornings? One day the radio said it was one degrees. Believe that? One! I don't know even if I should say *degrees* if it was only one of them. Ger, you would know: Is it just *degree*?"

Tom laughed. Aiden craned his head between his brother and Gerard, scorekeeping.

"See, Gerard," said Father Gregory, "Tom has four kids. Three girls and a boy. Tom, Ger has five girls. The man can't reproduce males; don't hold it against him. But Tom here, he doesn't think one way or the other about what he has to do. He loses a job, he goes out, gets another. It's all pretty simple. Because his burden, you see, is being a good man and taking care of a family. That's what a good life is, Ger. It's a simple one. How simple is *your* life?"

Just then they heard a scuffle by the bar, and Dolan called out, "Are these mutts with you, Tully?"

They looked over, and Dolan had Emily Magic by the ear. Serena was close to tears beside her, and Brighton was staring at Gerard, baring his teeth, looking for the command to attack.

Gerard got up. "They're with me. Let go of her ear, Dolan, or that twelve-year-old boy's going to maul your hand."

Dolan let go. Gerard took the kids and put them over at a bench by the hearth. "Sit here, the three of you, and don't make any noise. Dolan, call my office and tell Trina to go out and tell my wife the girls are down here."

Another neighborhood boy in ragged overalls ran down the steps from the pub's landing and joined the kids' table. "Perfect," said Aiden as Gerard returned, "look at that, Big Johnny McClusky's boy is mixing in with the Magics and that sewer rat. Wonder who'll rub off on who."

So ten-year-old McClusky and eleven-year-old Emily sat on one side of a bar bench that stank of Jameson, ash, and ale, and four-year-old Serena and twelve-year-old Brighton Salk sat on the other. And the four of them stared blankly at and through one another, nothing between them except the hope of a laugh and half a chance to reveal who they were.

Meanwhile, at the adults' table, they finished their first drink and poured a second, and the talk got going again, and they were honest today: the priest, the cop, the doorman, and the crook.

"You ask me if I have a simple life," said Gerard. "What's simple about the Bronx? We wake up to noises that haven't stopped for a half a minute all night. We hear people, crazy people, screaming through the walls at each other. Some of them are like Tom here, but some of them have the worst things wrong with their brains. My kids play down in the street with the other kids after school. But you know what they tell them at school? There's nothing good in the future. It's misery. You better learn how to type. Meet someone in Manhattan who can help you. Latch on to a supervisor, a foreman, get him to like you." He shook his head. "I want my kids to be strong, Greg. Not street tough, which is important and fine, but strong here." He thumped his breastplate.

"That sounds good," said Tom. "I'd like that."

"Tom, you are strong," said Father Gregory. "Don't you see that? You're strong quietly. Day in and out. That's what a hero is; he isn't some guy in a boxing ring or cashing in on his neighbors." He looked plainly at Gerard now. "Tom is a man who serves. My brothers are men who serve." He gripped his collar. "I am a man who serves. That's all we can do, Gerry: serve. It reminds us of our place. And after we've served for the day, we get together and laugh. The two most beautiful things in the world, service and laughter, and I don't think you know either of them. That's what breaks our hearts—mine, anyway."

"It ain't just that," Aiden was seething, worked up and over the top by his brother's brimstone cadence. "It's that he wants to take them all outta here because he thinks we're rotten. I *know* he's planning on leaving. All those sweet girls, they'll never know what a normal life is."

"Normal," Gerard repeated, not adding anything to the word, just uttering it.

"Gerard says," Father Gregory said to Tom, "we go to church, but we don't look at God."

Tom Collins laughed. He had a good-willed laugh. "That's a good one."

"See," said Gregory, pointing, "he can't imagine you don't mean it as a joke."

"Ain't it?" said Tom.

"No," said Gregory, "it wasn't."

"Oh."

"Do you go to church, Tom?"

"Every Sunday, more or less." He took a sip. "I guess your next question is, do I look at God?"

Nobody said anything, so Gerard said, "Do you?"

He looked down to really consider it. He looked up. "When we have a hard time."

"Does it make any difference to you," said Gerard, piling on poor Tom, "what a man does with his family? If he wants to take them away and try to change what they think of as normal?"

"None at all," said Tom.

"But suppose," said Aiden, "some fella married your sister, Connie. Shows himself a good guy. Then they have some kids, and he wants to take them away. Then what?"

Tom thought some more. "Well. I don't know."

"Normal," Gerard said again. "They won't know how normal it is, sitting at someone's busted kitchen table at 4:00 p.m. on a summer day, sweating through your shirt, tobacco smoke poisoning your eyeballs—waiting for some guy to finish his story, so you can laugh at something that wasn't even funny. You guys waste your whole lives at these tables. I won't waste mine. I won't waste theirs. My girls are going to live."

Father Gregory looked over at the kids playing on the bench.

"Say," said Tom Collins, "ain't you the fella lost the baby?"

"Yes," said Gerard.

"God almighty, I'm sorry for it."

"Thanks."

"What a thing, to lose a child."

"What a thing," said Aiden, staring back at his drink.

A mourning Irish silence quelled their moods for a short time.

Father Gregory broke in, "All the men on the block come in and confess to me. You hear them through the walls. I hear them close. I know better than any of you—even you, brother, who walks the streets—what grief and madness they carry. Your share of it is accounted for, Gerard. We stood witness when they put that poor little thing in the dirt. But don't be telling me or anybody that working class lives are wasted. They are full of richness. Good and evil are at work on them all day, and all they want, crying before God, is for good to win by the tiniest little bit. That's plenty enough to satisfy them. And they pray in shame that it's enough to satisfy their maker."

"I don't know why," said Aiden, "we're all sitting here justifying ourselves to a crook. A crook, Greg."

"No meat for Lent," Gerard murmured under his breath. Then he turned the thought into a sentence. "On Fridays during Lent, you tell them all no meat. So the mothers, they snap at their kids when they eat hotdogs. They shout at them in the street: *No hotdogs, you brat—Jesus died, and you're eating a hotdog.* And they belt the kids across the face. So what happens is, they don't eat meat, and instead, they hit their kids."

The jukebox was cooking now. The tune was low and old and hoarse, and it reminded the boys that the big band days were so recent yet lost forever. Aiden looked at Father Gregory, awaiting his answer, and none came.

"Last year you bought the storefront on 190th and Hoffman," he said to Gerard. "Next month it goes on fire. You remember that, Gerard? Mechanical fire, right? It was a bad deal you got because you didn't know druggies were moving in on that whole corner. So you sent your brother over there to light it up. So happened nobody got hurt. But not because you cared if they did."

Gerard looked over at Tom. "How much they pay you at the Carlisle?"

"Eighty a week."

"You make ends meet with that?"

"We do all right. My kids got jobs. My wife sells cherry pie."

"How do they like you at the Carlisle?"

"They like me all right."

"What's something wrong over there? Something sloppy or that your boss isn't happy about?"

Tom hooked his thumb in between two buttons on his uniform, and his fingers played an imaginary saxophone on his shirt. "There's homeless outside the door in the mornings. Sometimes they sleep in boxes out there. The guests don't like seeing that. Then I guess they're not pleased with how many folks come to the jazz night. They got that on weekdays, Mondays and Wednesdays, so it ain't a crowd."

Gerard nodded. "Where'd you work before the Carlisle and before the Ascot?"

"A&P."

"What'd you do over there?"

"Supervisor in the stockroom."

"You work with numbers?"

"Sure."

"All right, here's something I bet you never thought of, Tom," said Gerard. "You worked with numbers at A&P, and now you open doors at the Carlisle. Why don't you tell your boss over there—why don't you tell them this: You've got a plan to get rid of the homeless, and if you do it, you want an extra ten-spot for every week there's no one out in front of the building.

"You get them to say OK. If it was my building, I'd give you twenty. But ask for ten. Then, once they say OK, you get to know the homeless guys. You shake their hands, treat them with respect. After a few mornings of that, you say, 'Listen, I know a spot a few avenues over where heat drifts up from the subways, and it's a heck of a lot warmer than here in front of the hotel.' Plus, you'll bring them each a coffee and a pastry once a week if they get set up over there since you've been ordered to clear the curb anyway. So they all go over there—because why not, what's one street against another, and now they're making a return on it—and you, you're getting another forty dollars a month, and your expenses on that forty are whatever the pastries cost—what, four, five dollars? You pocket thirty-five."

Tom was grinning. "All right, but—"

"Hold on. The jazz nights. You tell your boss not only can you shoe away the boxes out front, but you've got a way to get their jazz nights heated up. What's the bar make over there on somebody coming in?"

"Well," said Tom, "depends. A big drinker could spend thirty dollars. On average, a cover charge plus a drink—ten?"

"Let's stay conservative; let's call it ten. You tell them you want an extra dollar a head that *you bring in* on that ten. On your lunch break, you go to the print shop. You lay out a buck to print up a few hundred flyers. You have it say *Carlisle Jazz Night, Mondays and Wednesdays*. You go to Columbia, the college up there. They've got buildings all over that area. You tell the registrar—that's the person who does the kids' schedule—you tell her you want these flyers slipped under the doors of all the kids who have no classes Tuesdays or Thursdays. You give her whatever she wants: a ten-spot, flowers, a backrub. You get her to give you that list. You see those kids start to show up for that jazz. They think the only jazz is in the Village. They'll come. They'll tell professors. They may not spend as much as the bigshots, but the buzz starts with the kids and trickles up.

"Even if it only works a little bit, you're making something on it. You're out on a start. And you think of another idea and another. And soon you're full of them. And your boss, he can't stop you having ideas, and soon he sees, this guy's no doorman; he's a bigshot in a doorman's uniform. He takes you off the street. Now you're inside. Once you're in, there's nowhere to go but up. And that's a tall building, the Carlisle.

"See, the Tully boys here, they'd have you do your hours, go home with sore feet and a headache, snap at the kids, fall asleep watching *Carson*, do it again, again. Why? So you can serve. Be one of the neighborhood boys. If you spend near as much time thinking about how to change things as you do thinking how hopeless they are—you pull ahead of everyone. Then you see," he looked back at the priest, "how many friends hate seeing you pull ahead."

Tom Collins said, "Hmm." He was about to take a drink and paused. "That bit with the homeless, it's not half-bad. You give me something to think over, Gerard."

Father Gregory smiled. "The Devil beckons, Tommy. The self-made man who worshipped his creator: That's what we call him. The Devil always wants you thinking you can do anything alone. Being crafty. You're no crafty man, Tommy. You're a decent one. Cling to being decent. Let crafty boys like Gerard Magic have the fun. It won't last them but one lifetime—I promise you that."

Aiden, restless, slammed his glass down empty. "I'm going to have my raid."

"You're not," said Father Gregory. "You had your laugh in the ring, Aiden." He looked Gerard in the eyes. "And there won't be any changing this man."

"But Greggie, I gotta do what I said—"

"That's the end of it. Take your boys home."

Aiden sat back in his seat, huffing, narrowing his eyes at the crook. He snatched his baton and left. Tom Collins shook hands with Father Gregory, then Gerard, slinking off toward the bar and looking behind him every few steps as though checking was any of it real.

"It really is your neighborhood, Father," said Gerard. "I own more of it. But it will always be yours."

"There's a poem that goes 'It's Not Always May.' That's the name of it. Do you like poetry at all, Ger?"

"Never read a poem in my life."

"Well, I'd like to say this poem for you, if I could."

Gerard stared at the priest a long time. He was a skinny man, like all the Tullys were skinny, and that white square patch of collar floated under his chin every time he put a flourish on a point. Gerard sat there, a drop left in his glass, wondering if Gregory believed in God or if he believed in being a good Bronx Irish boy in 1961. He wondered for the longest time, turning over the evidence. By the end, he believed Gregory himself wasn't sure of the real answer. And if he wasn't, how in the hell could Gerard know?

"I told you," said Gerard, finishing the drop, "I don't like poetry."

He slid his glass to the middle. He made the sign of the cross over his head, heart, and shoulders and went home to his family.

***

A man who loves to kiss his kids' soft faces but does not enter into their games only takes from them.

Shortly before he died, Gerard's father told him that. It had seemed, when he said it, he was relaying the kind of lesson one finds at the end of life, looking back—sifting the dross and grime from the solution of memory, scrutinizing wistfully the particles that remain—rather than imparting his own sacred practice. Gerard would have remembered if it had been the latter.

At the end of September, Roger Maris had tied the home run record. One of the next few games he was bound to break it. People were mad at him and mad at anyone rooting for him, and security traveled with him due to hate mail and death threats. Gerard got a kick out of it.

Sunday, October 1, Maris and the Yankees took the field against the Boston Red Sox. The Magic family went to the 11:00 a.m. Mass, sat in the pew across from the Tullys, and Father Gregory kept the whole show to about forty-five minutes. When it was over, everybody skipped conversation on the sandstone steps in front of 181st Street and went straight to Dolan's to watch the game. The kids played on the rug by the hearth. Gerard and Jimmy sat in prime bar seats beside the four Tully brothers with what felt like the rest of the city packed in behind and around them. You could hear Red Barber's voice calling pitches and plays in between someone's shouts for another draught, but if it was someone besides Red Barber, you wouldn't have heard a thing.

Catherine snuck up and squeezed Gerard's shoulder. "Today's the day?"

"Feels it." He looked at the small brown box and its round dials as the screen broadcasted, with twitching effort, nine good pinstriped men taking the field.

The others ranted about the bad hand Mantle had been dealt, fifty-four homers and an injured hip. They clapped and spat, *Let's go, baby,* if something good happened for the Bombers, but there was bitterness and grief all over the air. Maris got up to the plate for his first at-bat. The weight of his number sixty was plain in his black and white gait, his slender farm-boy cheeks.

According to the papers, Maris was losing hair by the clumps, hated as he was by so many New Yorkers whose pride and tradition he was poised to eviscerate and rebuild. The Boston rookie pitcher Tracy Stallard threw a pellet with all the venom of youth; Maris popped out to left. Gerard caught Father Gregory, three seats over, smirk to the sour right side of his face.

Brighton snuck in at the end of the second and whispered something to Jimmy, who turned to Gerard, "Kid says Horace is waiting for us at the office. Wants to tell us something."

"It's Sunday," said Gerard.

"What do you want me to say—he's waiting for us. Come on." Jimmy dropped a quarter on the bar and shouted, "Dolan, hold these seats; we'll be back in five."

Patrick Tully shouted at them as they cracked the bar door, and the crease of daylight betrayed the trick of eternal Irish night. "Working on a Sunday! Just like the Devil!"

Horace waited in the conference room of the lighting office. When the Magic brothers came in, he said, "Southport, Connecticut, is a hell of a town."

"You went?" said Jimmy.

"Sure. Took my wife on Friday, got back about an hour ago."

"Well?" said Gerard, holding his hat, still in his Sunday suit. "What'd you make of it?"

There were pink and yellow papers spread across the table. "I made it out to be a dream," said Horace. He shook his head. "You boys have been buying up property for more than two years now. You collect good rent. You pay it back out to your debtors. You've got cash flow but no cash. And these buildings you got—it's not 1935. It's the sixties. You're buying in the wrong spots; you're facing rent control, redlining, crime, bad loans. You're not thinking like investors. You're spending money like kids in a Monopoly game." He fished out the pamphlet they'd given him with photos of the Connecticut shoreline. He slid it across the faded cherrywood. "You're going to have to pay off a lot of people to take control of that dock. Even a little dock like that one. Your cash, it doesn't support it. You're dreaming big. But you're years away. Listen, I'm sorry to be so straight with ya."

Gerard dangled his hat from his fingers. He looked around at his small damp office.

Jimmy said, "Years? How many years?"

"Jimmy," said Horace, "you couldn't even afford to live in that town right now. Let alone purchase the pier, pay off patrol, hire a crew…I don't know. At your current profit margins? Ten? Twelve?"

"Ten years," said Jimmy. He looked at his brother. "Ten more years."

Gerard had been breathing steadily through his nose. He flipped his hat around and clutched it over his head. "Jimmy, I want you to find good men to work those docks. Bronx boys who'll move with us." On his way out, he held up a single finger to Horace, "One. One year. Not a day more."

He got to the office vestibule, turned and went to the secretary's office. He pulled up some shaggy carpeting and found the silver pistol Jimmy had forgotten to give him.

***

An armed man, he walked down Walton Avenue back toward the pub.

On a sunny day on this street, a person could find anything. All the storefronts boasted gaudy bulletins high above their awnings with words tinted to suggest the shop owners invented them: CURTAINS — MEATS — SLIPPERS — DO-NUTS — GAS — NATHAN'S. Everybody was selling or stealing and had a story about it.

Who couldn't you meet here? Irish, Italian, Jewish, French, German, Polish, Black, Hispanic, Puerto Rican: They lived along the Concourse or near it. But rarely would you meet an Englishman. Not a full one or one with any pride about it, and Gerard was not that man either.

He started laughing, thinking of it, of the faces of his neighbors when he tried to explain it: The English *developed* the Bronx. Their British visitors, overlords, ruminating on how to make the most of their colonies, realized this patch of map had a strategic advantage situated between New York and New England. They put up a king's bridge, gave it to a lord to manage and collect tax, to scrounge farmers for what they may be fearful enough to forfeit. Today merchants marched around these corners like they were themselves responsible for every advantage the streets provided. Gerard was certain, if drunk and pressed, Johnny Tully would credit his father or uncle with adding that revering *The* to the borough's holy call sign "The Bronx."

It was another of Gerard's measureless frustrations with the working class, his class, that they claimed to be students of history, lovers and defenders of it, yet had no respect for what history really was: old. The Bronx barely existed before the beginning of the century they were in. Bronx County was established a decade before Gerard was born. The immigrants were still sorting out who would stay and what to build if they did. The Tullys, like the Magics, like Horace Eaton and little Brighton Salk and the other cops, crooks, clergy, and supers of Crotona and Walton and Bruckner and the Concourse, were enrolled not in the inheritance of anything but in the momentous task of beginning something. None of them understood that. And the ones who did were obligated to do something about it.

Gerard went back into Dolan's and found his stool. He ordered a Cutty Sark. Johnny and Patrick recounted the plays he'd missed. The pistol poked his belly as the inning changed, now top of the fourth, no runs. He spotted Officer Aiden Tully, having abandoned his prized barstool, crouching among the children, coaching them in their phantom batting stances, elbow up here, shoulders straight, chin tucked… "*There's* a slugger!"

He squared Jane and Emily, then Serena grabbed an orphaned wooden spoon from Dolan's shelf and pretended it was a bat. Aiden laughed at her and patted her head. "Come here, squirt." He fixed her up with a stance using a menu as home base. "Now you stare straight into the soul of the pitcher as you think about how you're going to smack the macaroni out of that ball when he sends it over the plate. You, kid," he snapped at one of the others, "go be the pitcher, over there. Serena, stare at him, mean like the Babe, but also like the Babe, you don't care about anything. You just know when he sends that ball over, you're going to sail it. Let me see how you mug at him."

Gerard watched as Serena narrowed her eyes and pursed her lips, staring across the floor at some sort of dwarf Boston devil. A wave of hilarity tore across the line of Tully barstools. They clapped and called the little girl a *pisser*.

Serena asked Uncle Aiden to tell her about Babe Ruth. Aiden sat on the dusty floor and curled his long legs up like getting ready to talk to God over a fire. He told her the legend. She looked at him with a mix of awe and fear, her imagination fired by learning more about what had been in front of her every day. Gerard saw that Aiden was taking pains to enchant his daughter. And it was working. She was enchanted.

Gerard felt a pang of conflict about his surroundings. He had come to take it for granted that this was a place worth leaving behind, one that a man who coveted a nobler future *must* leave behind in the name of conquest.

The words of Father Gregory came back to him again and again: service and laughter, the supreme of all callings. Could Gerard be wrong to stake his life on a mission instead of, say, on a pleasant hill with a view, in the path of a cleansing breeze…

If you caught him in the right mood, Gerard would admit he loved that the walk from the office to the drugstore took fifteen seconds. And that the druggist knew his order—ham sandwich, lemonade, Hershey bar to take home for the girls to share—and called him Ger. He would admit a pride in his brother Jimmy for being truly beloved. He would admit a pride in his wife for being respected and his girls for being known as graceful, precocious, inclusive of losers and freaks, and reluctant to murder insects if they could as easily be set free.

The sound of kids playing in the streets in front of buildings, taken as a chorus, could stunt sanity. But the spectacle of it, when you stopped and watched: It was poetry in development. Tic-tac-toe and handball and boxball, punchball, stickball, and a jailbroken fire hydrant melded to create a symphony of adolescent potential, a chalk-strewn canvas for the discovery of one's skills and deficiencies.

Over the run of one whole childhood, boys and girls got a chance at one miracle each on those sidewalks. One chance to become a legend. They played every day waiting for that chance, knowing it would come, and they'd have to face it, ready or not, and the waiting charged the borough with an invisible charisma that even adults could not escape.

They all lived together in the space of that elusive potential—simple people who got up every day suspecting for no reason at all that they may be destined for unthinkable greatness and carrying that hope with them onto buses, into drugstores, letting it color in a *Hiya, Tom*; a *How's things*; or a kind word about a dead rambler.

There were so many colors in the Bronx. No one outside knew that. There were pastels and mosaics, walking sticks with gold crowns… You pull off the Whitestone Bridge and bear right, and you're smacked with 'em: baby-blue Fords; candy-pink Lincolns with their swollen fenders and glitzy hubcaps; green Chevy Camaros; brown and orange Corvairs; Mini Coops Laguna beige, smoke blue, Alaskan blue, taupe, stone; sharp red Caddies with snowberry-white tops. Boys in blue jeans and high white socks clutched onto the backs of the M4 bus. Women waited for crosswalks with fuzzy blonde hair that had hosted curlers three patient hours the night before. Unlike in Manhattan, the sky still featured everywhere. Turn on Hunt's Point, Throggs Neck, City Island, Orchard Beach, you could see way out in front of you. To the west, Alpine, Tenafly, and Englewood housed suckers who thought they had it figured out but would soon discover the song of the cricket was a poor substitute for the vitality of your fellow man, the echo of car alarms, the subway eek, domestic spats, and protests to closing time.

The glimpses of sheer greenery were made more powerful by their contrast to sprawls of cement, like a saint stands out in a war. Gerard loved the Botanical Garden, Van Cortlandt Park, the woodlands of Mosholu, the cappuccinos on Arthur, the pungent vestibule at Alexander's, the opulent windowpanes of Sears on Fordham Road; he visited Woodland Cemetery and told himself stories of the dead constructed only from hints on their tombstones. He took Catherine to Loew's Paradise Theater every month and knew she thought more of it than the Met. Giant steel trunks sprouted into twin yellow streetlights a hundred feet into the sky. They were the hallmarks of important boulevards along with powerlines precariously knotted and window AC units blemishing brick edifices, leaking rust-water in the contours of distant countries.

The enterprisers of all this, city planners working off New Deal grants and European inspiration, enlisted geniuses that erected architecture to make working men feel like both ants and giants. Regal and insignificant. Gerard couldn't fathom that they knew what they were building here. He doubted very much the city planners knew their own role in fostering generations of an inimitable American whose children would go on to span the range of industries; travel parts unknown; become intrepid, spoiled, or kingly; and take with them, if nothing else, that refusal to say a kind word when a morbid one would do, and grumble "Not for nothing..." before shattering everything you held sacred.

Serena loved the smell of bakeries. Emily loved the Tullys; Hannah loved pancakes, sunflower seeds. Maddy loved Bungalow Bars. Jane loved hopscotch and punching holes in old newspapers. Catherine loved her family. Wouldn't they all be just fine here? Wouldn't it be fine if Gerard could calm down and find a spot on a hill?

The smack of the bat snatched his privacy. Red Barber called, "There it is!"

"WHOAs!" and "LOOKs!" convulsed the bar, and people mashed into him for a clean look. Maris had hit it hard and high to right. And boy, was it gone.

He sprinted the bases, his puffy pant legs lifting in rhythm with the dirt clouds at his heels. Red Barber said, "And here is the fella with *sixty-one*.... You're seeing a lot today."

Sixty-one flashed on the screen. It disappeared, then came back. Maris went into the dugout, came back, and took off his cap. *The fella with sixty-one.* The number flashed, and you heard the whistling of folks in the stands. Dolan twisted the volume all the way up. Everyone in the bar murmured; some clapped and screamed. The Tullys clapped calmly.

Gerard stared into that fading black and white number. He leaned over the rail and called Dolan over. "What is it, Ger? I can't hear nothing in here..."

"Put your towel on the bar."

Dolan spread his towel. Gerard palmed the pistol from his hip and slid it cleanly under the towel. "There's a piece under there. Wrap it and leave it for me under the bar. I'll come get it soon."

"I don't want this in here."

But Gerard had gotten off the stool and turned to the row of cops. "Aiden!" The shouts of the patrons were deafening, and the whistles of sixty-one kept on. Jimmy was back now aside Horace and Brighton.

Jimmy yelled, "What gives?"

But Gerard ignored him and screamed over all of it. "Aiden! Aiden Tully!"

Patrick noticed him first, then Father Gregory. Finally Aiden, along with everyone else from the neighborhood crammed like Depression-era steamboat passengers between them, paid mind.

"What?" said Aiden.

The faintest smile flickered across Gerard's square face. He aimed his thumb at the door. "I want you outside."

"What?"

"I say I want you outside!"

"What for?"

"I'm going to beat the living hell out of you."

The bar released its second howl of the afternoon, longer and louder than the victory hymn for the Bronx Bombers and Maris himself. And Aiden smiled.

In the messy rush of limbs to the exit, only some had the sense to mind the kids while everyone else jockeyed for a good angle on the sidewalk. As he hit the street, Gerard took off his suit jacket and rolled his sleeves. He'd expected Catherine to be at his side, saying something angry, anything, but calmly she filed out with the rest and arranged the kids in an untidy perimeter, each one close enough to keep a hand on.

Johnny Tully got hold of his whistle and stopped traffic, closing off the north side while Patrick took south. Everyone cheered for a start. Horns blared. People on windowsills screamed *sixty*-one.

Now Aiden was down to his undershirt on the other side of the loose circle. He had the same fighter's face from the night at Gold's Gym, and his eyes were not different from little Serena's, imitating the Babe.

Johnny Tully walked into the middle and started shouting rules. Gerard shoved him out of the way. "It's not a bout," he said. "It's a fight." He walked up to Aiden, his eyes level with the cop's chin. "How about it?"

Aiden was in the best mood of his life. "Say when."

"When," said Gerard, swinging with the might of the Bronx a right fist at his brother-in-law's eyes.

"Daddy!" Emily screamed.

Aiden shook off the punch and charged Gerard into the middle of the street, driving him into the pavement and pulling back to set him up for a blow. He reached into the sky, balled his fist, and drove it down.

Before it could land, Gerard got hold of the hand Aiden was pinning him with and twisted two fingers until they broke like number two pencils. Aiden shrieked, and his punch went wild, landing with half its force. Gerard pressed. He shouldered Aiden to the side, took some hits to the gut, and brought his knee up into his opponent's chin. It was a clean hit. He felt the jaw rattle. Aiden rolled away, got right to his feet, and stormed back at Gerard, swinging and spitting.

Gerard took a lot of pain. He went down, got up, went down.

Emily and the girls kept their faces buried in Catherine's dress, peeking out every time they couldn't hear anything. Jimmy and Johnny screamed at each other that no matter the outcome, both sides would walk away. There would be no neighborhood brawl today. They both were shouting violently and repeating the same thing, not able to notice they were agreeing.

Aiden got two hands on Gerard's throat and was hurting him. Horace screamed it was unfair—he may kill him.

Gerard finally found Aiden's mangled fingers and pressed them until he could slip the grip. He got momentum behind one leg, tilted back to get space, and fired it up into Aiden's solar plexus. That bought him some time, seconds really, to breathe new air.

He took four or five deep gasps before Aiden was back. Gerard saw him coming and saw he was unsteady, that his hands, for the first time in either fight, were not directly guarding his face but balled in front of his chest: a lazy place to keep your heads.

Aiden threw one, and it caught Gerard's shoulder. He threw another, and Gerard, not waiting to see what it felt like, threw his own and caught the Irishman purely on the tip of the nose.

"Yes!" screamed Jimmy. "Press it, Ger. Go! GO IN!"

Aiden swung dizzily with his left while his right, his strong hand, clutched the blood now leaking down over his lips. Gerard took the pain from the left, which was nothing too bad, and got close enough to work his guts. When Aiden brought his right arm down to guard his body, Gerard started laughing aloud, seeing the opening every fighter knows to wait for, even an unseasoned one, a businessman with sharp pronunciations.

Aiden's bloody head was wide open, lolling in the Sunday breeze. Gerard held him still and clobbered his eyes with short, fast jabs, six, seven, eight of them. Then he pushed him to see how steady his knees were. They wobbled. Gerard opened up a full arc and fired through Aiden's cheek. And that bastard dropped.

More folks cheered than had been rooting for Gerard. More folks than had known either of them.

"All right!" yelled Johnny Tully. "You made your point. Walk off. Walk."

But Aiden was standing up. Gerard walked over, waited until he was all the way up, and laid him out again.

The street went wild.

The Tullys came over and lifted Aiden, crying the things losers cry. Jimmy lifted Gerard's arm into the sky.

He walked in a daze through the parting crowd—his shirt torn, his face newly ugly, Jimmy steering him—back into Dolan's. The street chanters bottlenecked at the entrance, elbowing each other as they inched in, eager to get near the gladiator himself.

When enough people were inside, the chant began: *Sixty-one! Sixty-one! Sixty-one!*

They'd be connected forever, Gerard knew then, the legend of Maris and the legend of his fight with a stuffy, drunk Irish giant. That was the thing about Bronx legends. You never knew when your chance at one was at hand, but you could be sure it would play out the same place the others had: on the street or sidewalk, with everyone you'd ever known calling your name.

Aiden didn't come back in that night. Patrick took him home, patched him up. He didn't see Gerard for about a month after that. When he did, he nodded, usually from across the street under his policeman's cap and blues ensemble. He didn't threaten the Magics' business interests again.

It was an hour later—with the Yankee game still on but no reason left for paying attention—when Father Gregory sidled up between the Magic brothers.

"Father!" Jimmy screamed. "If you're here to take confessions, my brother has a whopper."

Father Gregory nodded solemnly, the trace of the smirk never far, as though it were all gravely ironic, ironically grave. "Fair enough, Jimmy, fair enough." He turned to the victor. "Gerard, have you had a chance to read the poem I recommended you?"

"Not yet."

"Well, I figured as much, so I went home and got my copy." He handed him a small chapbook. The hardcover was rotted. Its spine read Longfellow. "I marked the page for you."

Gerard finished his Cutty. He took the book, flipped to the page, read it, and closed it. "*It's not always May,*" he repeated. "What of it?"

"You won't always be king," said Gregory. He let the celebratory noises punctuate it. Gerard handed him back the book. "Keep it," said Gregory. He went round the bar.

Jimmy said, "They can't win in the street, so they're trying poetry." He laughed. He talked about the precious moments of the fight. He reenacted Gerard's greatest moves. He talked about Connecticut, about the docks, their plans.

Catherine came over, and Jimmy danced with her. She got free of him and kissed Gerard's cuts and bumps. The kids came over. Gerard teased them, and they laughed with ridiculous relief.

He nodded to Dolan. "I'll take it back."

"Just don't hit me," Dolan joked. He snatched the towel bundle and laid it out. Gerard unwrapped it, stood up, and hooked the pistol back into his belt.

Everyone he loved kept the party alive until night fell over their bloody Sunday. Gerard looked around at how immersed they were, each one of them, in the present. He danced. He drank another Cutty and another. He told Horace to get ready. He told Brighton to get tougher. He dipped his wife and kissed her, and their girls cried, *Awww*.

He went to the deep part of the bar where Father Gregory was still chatting and drinking steadily with sinners. He laid his hand warmly on the priest's shoulder. "Say it again."

"Say what?"

"What you said over there."

Father Gregory fixed his eyes. "You will not always be king."

"I am tonight."

PART SEVEN

The Last Death

A makeup artist studied Serena's flaws.

A man with a headset and clipboard, who looked like he'd never gone anywhere without running, popped into the dressing room. "Serena, since it's live to tape, there's no rush, but Charlie is going to be in a rush starting at 2:00 p.m., so it would be better if we were at least halfway through, so when he does get rushing, we have a lot in the can that shows him calmer, you know? *You* know."

"When he starts rushing," the makeup artist added, "you can always tell when it airs."

"I'm ready when you are," said Serena.

The makeup artist and producer laughed in unison. "Well, you're not ready, sweetheart."

On the thirty-fifth floor of one of the tallest buildings in New York City, Serena waited to go on national television and discuss some of the things people had been wanting to discuss with her these past six months.

It would have made sense when she was thirty or thirty-five, these polished media professionals courting her for a drink or a book deal, but now, at fifty-three, she felt she had misplaced her ability to play their game.

She didn't understand what anyone *from the world* would think she could give them.

She had flown with John out of O'Hare Airport at 5:50 this morning, their driver taking them from JFK to their hotel on the East Side, then taking 63rd Street west to Fifth and doubling back to 58th, past Equinox and Bloomingdale's, Tiffany's, and the Pierre and the transparent mega cube of the Apple Store, pulling up on the curb outside the Bloomberg atrium, where Serena stepped out of the car.

She had been to New York more this year than in the last ten put together. It was less terrifying each time, the icy steel and reflective tower glass, the lazy chaos of every pair of eyes that caught her own, for an instant, before finding their phone or the sidewalk.

Through security and the preinterview, she flipped a few times through the notes she and John had prepared on the plane.

"You look great!" The producer had returned and ushered her out of her chair, down the wide white hallway and through a heavy metal door with a blinking red light overhead. "He's a very good guy, and he's interested in you. He's been talking about it all week. It's just a conversation. If you stumble or start over, chances are we're going to cut it, so don't sweat. It's not live. Just keep saying that to yourself: *It's not live; it's not live.*" He laughed, and she smelled a village of coffee and cigarettes behind his molars. "Go get 'em—you're an incredible woman."

As quickly as she'd entered the studio, the lights were dimming, and a second producer was showing her to a chair at a brown table with two glasses of water filled to precisely the same height. The host came out, shook her hand, and sat. He was too kind to be accused of arrogance. If he was faking it, he still deserved the reputation for it. At that rate, what was the difference between such dedication to the artifice of human sincerity and sincerity itself?

"Charlie, we're rolling."

He turned from Serena to the camera tree, nodding once into the blackness around them and modifying his voice ever so slightly as he read off an introduction, taking you into his oaky private confidence, turning the present into history.

He finished and spun toward her, "Serena Magic, thank you for being here."

She imitated every other guest she'd seen, murmuring like an elegant French actress, "Thank you for having me, Charlie."

He scooped up a handful of publication clippings and magazine covers from his note pile and let them fall messily about the table. "So you are the talk of the town—well, this town anyway, and I imagine some towns in California. Now, you've agreed to come here and talk with us, and there are any number of areas you can't legally get into, and we've spoken with your lawyers and know what those are. So as generally as you can, tell us what's been happening in your life these last three, six months."

"Well, that's a broad question, Charlie."

He laughed. "It sure is."

"Well...I'm...I have a son who's applying to colleges. My husband recently got promoted to vice president at his company. But I don't suppose those are the things you want to discuss." He sat with his arms folded and a smirk on his big-city jaw. She said, "I've been accused of some flattering things. People are saying...there was this one magazine piece that alleged I was a writer on a famous song. Then after that, there were some other pieces that said I had written on other songs that had also...became popular."

Charlie took up a magazine cover and shoved it at her. "Modesty may be in your contract, so we aren't going to fault you for it, but let me just read some of these things, and you sit there and stay inside yourself." He flicked the hinges of his cheaters and stuck them on. "Here's Tim Winters writing for *The Atlantic*: 'Serena Magic was a two-hit wonder songwriter who fell from grace in the nineties for the crimes of her family. She was herself indicted on several counts of conspiracy, though served no jail time. In the nearly two decades that followed, she may have ghost-written, in part or in full, the lyrics to some of the most celebrated tracks in recent memory, including'"—Charlie peeked up—"then he starts to name names."

He grabbed another clip. "Here's Ellington for *New York* magazine: 'Serena Magic, now in her fifties, is a stoic and unassuming presence at her PTA meetings, a doting wife, and nimble baker of the kinds of pastries you'd find on Hanover Street in Boston or Arthur Avenue in the Bronx. But like a lot of people who've moved around a lot and snap out of trances to answer superficial questions, Serena has a past. Study the lyrics to "Pardon in Rome" or "Letters from Fairton Prison" or "Wayne Tender" and you may find biographical clues that hint at a writer who goes uncredited by the labels, production companies, albums, and recording artists alike.'" He skipped ahead and held up a finger. "'The problem with the denials of the singers and the labels teaming up to take legal action against Ms. Magic—or as she goes by now in Chicago, Mrs. Magic-McClusky—is that none of them will be able to falsify, in the pasts of the singers, the autobiographical details that show up in the lyrics and belong squarely, effervescently, in the sordid and color-filled past of Lady Magic.'" Charlie yanked off the cheaters and smiled. "Well, son of a bitch. What do we do with that?"

Serena placed her hands on the table. "I was asked one question by one reporter about a year ago. He was a gentleman doing a profile piece on Huey Lewis. Now I've never known Huey Lewis or written anything for Huey Lewis, and I told this man as much. He asked some other questions and said he'd heard a story he wanted to share with me. I said he could, so he told me this story—this long, drawn-out fable about a mythical songwriter who had an ignominious kind of reputation. And because of that reputation, nobody wanted to work with her on paper, so she was commissioned in secret to...well, to punch up lyrics for record labels or sometimes to write them from scratch. He wanted to know: Was I this person?"

"And?"

"And I said I was under contract with some companies—and I named them since as far as I knew and know now, I've signed no nondisclosure agreement regarding the companies I've contracted for. But that was the most I was willing to divulge. Everything after that happened on its own."

"In that same piece for *The Atlantic*, Winters says in LA, they had a code name for you. He says when you came up in discussion, the industry folks would call you 'the basement poet.' Had you ever heard that term before?"

She shook her head. "Not until I read Winters's article. You find out a lot about yourself when the press notices you're alive."

Charlie scoffed. "The basement poet. I assume that means you were like the ugly stepchild—they kept you hidden down there, and when they needed something, like say a hit song, they came down to get it." She didn't give him anything but a patient glare. He went on, "This is a hell of a list,

Serena, the artists who may not have written what they said they wrote… there are a few legends on here. Powerful men and women. You wrote your first song in '87. Now we're sitting here in 2010. Let me ask you something and see if you can answer: Some of these songs…are there are any details you recognize in them from your life?"

Serena said, "There were some, yes."

"For instance?"

The producers were running back and forth behind the semicircle of cameras pointed at them, each twinkling tiny lights like alien crafts coursing over a desert night.

"Well. Some of them are about generic things that could've been part of anyone's life: love and tragedy…shame. But there are others that I suppose are similar to things from mine."

"'A row of tombs under a rainbow,'" said Charlie, "'six sisters hold hands through the dirt.'" He paused. "You suffered the loss of sisters, is that right?"

She held her chin up. "Sure, that's right."

"How many?"

Neutrally she said, "All together, six."

"Mm-hmm." He glanced off camera, as though checking whether other media creatures would be rushing toward them with bludgeons. "'In Letters from Fairton Prison,' there's a long verse—well, the whole song seems to revolve around the correspondence between a daughter and her father in prison. Now, famously, your family was…you come from a family that committed crimes."

She inhaled the frigid studio air. "Whatever has been written is…not entirely accurate, but somewhat."

"Did your father commit crimes?"

"He had a longshoremen's operation in Connecticut. He was convicted of racketeering and extortion."

"And he went to jail?"

"Yeah."

"Is your father still alive?"

"Yes, he's eighty-four. He lives with us in Chicago."

"So he's no longer imprisoned?"

"No, he got out more than ten years ago."

"And obviously, he is not involved in criminal"—he gestured with his hands, indicating his meaning was plainer than his words—"no criminal activity currently."

"Well, I wouldn't tell you if he was, would I, Charlie?"

He laughed. "Eighty-four." He shook his head. "So you grew up with this dad doing these things you probably didn't understand. You lost your mother when you were thirteen, and six sisters died—was that all of them?"

"I have one left, my sister Beth."

"OK, all but one die in different ways, some in truly terrible ways, which the articles get into that I won't make you relive here. So you go through all this, and you turn some of it into this beautiful music, and you never tell anybody. And it comes out through no fault of your own, and now you might get sued for it. Trouble seems to follow you around, would you say?"

"I don't know," she said. "I've had a quiet life for a long time."

"A quiet life..." he said, "and *Esquire* is calling you the 'Voice of Generations...'" The studio blackness sat there. "Here's what I have to wonder," he said, his voice more intimate than a lover's, "I'm not saying these articles are true, but if they are, why not just violate the NDA, take the hit in court, go out and start your second act? The public is with you. People think you got a raw deal here. There's going to be more than enough interest in hiring you on the other side of this. Whatever the whole thing costs, whatever you're liable for, isn't that a small price to pay to take the credit you deserve and keep doing this, this *thing* you were born to do? I mean this is your life!" He ruffled the papers. "And other people are out there calling it theirs. Don't you want your life back?"

"It's a very good question. I'll have to think about the answer." She craned her head around to see the producers looking at her. "Maybe I'll write a song about it. And when someone famous decides to sing it, you can find out."

The headset clown yelled, "Cut!" and a school bell rang. She waited in the wings while Charlie recorded teasers and voice-overs. He shook her hand afterwards and held it while he said some things about her brilliance and beauty, and it got to where the longer he spoke, the less she was able to believe him, and by the time she walked out of the building, the whole day seemed a lie.

He had left it incomplete, that lyric he'd quoted on air. Like any writer, Serena felt the incompleteness of her expression bedeviling her sense of order. She repeated it to herself in the elevator, the words alone, divorced from song:

A row of tombs under a rainbow, six sisters hold hands through the dirt;

Three died sweet and lovely, three broken and hurt.

Out on the street it was prime Manhattan noon. Everybody ran everywhere saving themselves from a single, sad thought. Serena got in the car where John had been waiting, handling business calls and emails, and they went to the hotel to rest until dinner at a place she hadn't been in a long time: the Plaza.

* * *

The last few months in Chicago, the parents of her kids' friends had shown a new curiosity about Serena. They didn't tend, before now, to ask her opinions.

John's friends were investors and developers, chess and brandy lovers, and she had to admire—because he wanted her to—how much he'd fitted himself into their idea of a good fellow.

So she played her part in the tepid unfurling of a mother's destiny, being all things to her boys, retaining her attractiveness to flirts and egotists, speaking unfiltered thoughts to no one, and every once in a while, slipping off to some solitary space to scribble a song.

In the four years since moving to Chicago, following another of John's promotions, they'd become part of a true community. That she kept her opinions to herself was a small trade-off for the livelihoods they'd rebuilt, over two decades, out of the carnage of Connecticut. Everything that winds up any way is missing things that would've come from some other way. But things needed to wind up, she knew, otherwise you die wondering what an ending would've looked like.

As much peace as she'd made with the navies of wifehood, menopause, and anonymity, she could not curtail a thrill at the sudden changes of expression on the well-heeled faces of those Chicagoans.

"Is it true?"

"You—wrote—*that*?"

"All this time…you never even peeked at our vinyl collection."

The women pretended they had always been as close as they now sought to become. The men who'd made passes at her redoubled their efforts and thought nothing of arguing with her rejections. (She'd never cheated on John.) Her sons' friends begged stories from her. Her town-house neighbors came by after the press trucks pulled off the curb. They said they'd always suspected something about her, something different…

John and the boys had known everything all along. They told her to own it all—that they'd stand with her and behind her. John now trusted her enough and had made of himself enough of a Chicago industry skipper, to support her flowering, her great at-bat—Serena's justice.

She didn't have a plan beyond agreeing to the interviews. She spent hours with her lawyer deciding on language that would keep her just on the side of cooperative with anything she'd signed. But it was difficult not to notice the phenomenon her television host had articulated that morning in the city.

The people were behind her.

More than behind her, they were mad on her behalf. They didn't care that she was the daughter of some Bronx guy who'd risen, for a short time in the amber seventies and eighties, to the status of powerbroker in some spellbinding netherworld. They cared only that she'd suffered for her songs. They cared that impostors took them and used them to earn silver and gold and the worship of legions. They wanted her to fight them—to set history straight, *music history*, the history of the soul and marrow, not the mind and bones.

She had been thinking, since that first article printed her name, about what it would look like to take a stand, to reclaim her words…

She had been thinking lately about the past.

"How's Dad?" said Beth.

Hours after the interview, Beth and Serena waited for their table at the Plaza, their husbands sent to order drinks from the bar.

Beth, forty-five, looked beautiful, slim, licentious in the grape-cherry glint of the Oak Room's chandeliers. She lived with her husband on the Upper West Side. They'd been married twelve years and had one child, a son.

"He's OK—he gets around," said Serena. "He only stays with us half the year, then he goes to that condo in Florida. I think he prefers it there."

"How does he afford to keep it?"

"We pay."

Their generation seemed to have boys instead of girls—John and Emily's son, now in his thirties; John and Serena's two; Beth's one. The coin flipped with prejudice.

Beth was a partner at a public relations firm. She did the bidding of rock star entrepreneurs, TED Talkers, philanthropists with a message, and had grown a reputation for her ability to weave a narrative over which publications would salivate. She'd said often how she loved it and wouldn't think of quitting. Her husband was a tech lawyer. Hannah had met him a handful of times before she died of ovarian cancer in '97 ("me and Gilda Radner," Hannah had quipped in hospice). Beth always swore they would've grown very close, the two lawyers, both skinny, dry, skeptical. But this was not a testable hypothesis.

"Well, I wish he would've come with you," Beth said, about her dad. "I would've loved to see him. I wonder how long he'll be mobile."

"He's slowing down. It won't be long before he stays with us full time."

"John is a saint to put up with it."

Serena shrugged. "Daddy's been better to him. It's John's house he's living in. John has—he's gotten tough."

Serena and Beth looked at their husbands carrying their drinks over, concentrating not to spill them. "John McClusky," Beth said. She laughed in a way that meant, *I'll be damned.*

Soon they were shown to their table.

"When will it air?" asked Cal, Beth's husband, a few years younger than Serena, a few older than Beth.

"Tomorrow," John answered for her. "Investors in Chicago want her to start her own record label."

"Which makes no sense at all," said Serena. "Or as much sense as a novelist being CEO of Barnes & Noble."

The waiter brought a square plate of surf and turf dumplings, French onion mini boules, and Scottish salmon. Cal and John used the proper forks; Beth used the dinner fork, and Serena used her hands.

Beth repeated what she had told her sister on the phone—that everyone she knew and had spoken with thought this was the story of the year, and like all great stories, there is a window for telling what happens next. Soon it would close, the story-window, and her supporters and acolytes would be unable to remember what became of her, that woman who wrote those songs and never admitted it.

Serena said, "I like my life, Beth. I don't need a new one."

Beth looked around at the cocktail dresses and blazers, at the regal Bavarian frescoes, the lighted beams. She cradled her martini. "Somehow you pulled it off," she said to her older sister, her only sister.

"What does that mean?" said Serena.

"You're a legend who's never done anything."

***

Six weeks later was St. Patrick's Day. John and Serena were back in Chicago where their son Eric awaited verdicts on early college applications. Henry was a liberal arts kid and had a few years to figure out where he wanted to go—but Eric wanted to go into business, like his dad, the insurance executive.

Eric was one of those boys, Serena often felt, who could keep one foot in with his peers, camouflaged in normalcy, and the other someplace else entirely, where he was not like them at all. He drank beers. He had told at least one girl he loved her; he played soccer and had an exclusive friend group. But she could see he ultimately couldn't care a cent about any of it.

It gave her an idea for a song called "Purple Teen Twin Worlds," but she hadn't found time to write it.

Henry, their younger son, was a contrast. He had a penchant for tantrums and had exacting ideas about how a night should unfold, which reminded Serena of Maddy. He loved music—his mother's included—and reading and all the best shows like *The Sopranos*, *The Wire*, *The Shield*, *Deadwood*, and *The West Wing*. When people in Chicago paid attention to Obama's inauguration or the Cubs' filing for bankruptcy or Tiger's infidelities, Henry watched the news only when John Updike died or Roman Polanski got arrested in Switzerland. He, too, had managed to secure a perimeter of friends whom he likely felt little in common with but enjoyed as a sort of sociological experiment in the price of community.

This gave her an idea for a song called "The Spy," and this one she did write but couldn't find a melody to pair with it.

Henry and Eric had been taught from infancy that everything around them was a variable except one another. They may live in other places, they may be called many names, but loyalty to this family was to be their constant. So the two brothers never spent any time not being as close as they could be. It wouldn't really occur to them. They had all been prepared for a life much more difficult than the one they'd ended up with.

There was some Irish music on the street that day, and Eric and his friends came to the house after school to hang out in the recently finished basement.

Serena poured Tostitos chips into a few bowls and asked Henry to take them down to the older boys. When he came back, she poured more into a smaller bowl and said, "Take these up to the loft and see if your grandpa wants any."

As she folded up the bag, she heard the front door open and was happy to think John had come home early. Then she heard a patter along the hall that indicated a greater number of feet.

Beth came in first, then Cal, holding two leather bags, John last.

"Pardon," said Serena, "what are you doing here?"

Beth gave her a hug without answering. Cal set down their bags. Serena asked again.

"Came for the weekend," said Beth.

Serena looked at John. John said, "Your father asked them to come. Cal called me this morning and said I had to pick them up at the airport. They won't tell me anything, but now they're in my house, so maybe they have to."

"Where's Dad?" said Beth.

"Upstairs," Serena answered.

Beth looked at Cal, then at John. "John, can you go get him?"

"What's going on?" Serena demanded.

"Dad got a letter, Serena," said Beth. "He wanted me here when he showed it to you."

***

John told Eric to take his friends somewhere. Henry went early to band practice.

In the living room, John and Serena sat on one couch, Cal and Beth on the other. The shuffle of slippers began on the loft upstairs, rhythmically swishing, then found the last step and turned into the room. Gerard Magic wore a sport fleece and sweats, probably Eric's, and held a walnut, single-point cane in one hand and a once-folded slip of paper in the other.

"Gerard," said Cal.

Beth got up. "Daddy."

She hugged him, then walked with him to a sofa chair.

He looked around. "Family," he said. His Adam's apple was a sharp stone in the loose skin of his neck. His face was pale, vaguely blue. His eyes moved along each of their middle-aged faces. "We could've done a lot worse than to wind up together in some townhouse in Chicago." He looked around some more. "All this furniture."

"What's going on, Dad?" Serena said.

He seemed to still be agreeing with himself. He unfolded the paper and handed it to Serena, saying, "This letter was written a month ago, but it reached me last week." She took it. Gerard added, "It's from the fella who killed Madeline."

No one really moved.

"What's his name?" Cal said.

"There were two," said Beth. "Dice Miller and Alex Ramirez. They caught Ramirez; he's serving life in prison. Is it from Ramirez, Dad?"

Serena answered, reading, "It's from Miller."

Cal said, "Is he the one who…"

Beth nodded.

John said, "Serena, let me have it when you're finished."

"Just tell them what it says," said Gerard.

Serena cleared her throat. "It says… He says that he saw me on TV. That he's sorry about what he did to Maddy and…that he's sorry." She read on in silence another minute. "It says things about who he was then." She looked up. "He's unburdening himself." She passed the letter to John. "What's the point of showing us this, Dad? You want to give it to the police?"

"No."

"Well," said Serena, "I don't see the use of showing us. They never caught him, and they won't now. He says he's been living abroad."

"He wouldn't have seen you on TV," Gerard said, "if he was abroad." Gerard leaned on his cane to stand up. He limped to the mantel and stared at the framed photographs perched between candlesticks. One was of Catherine. "I think he's in Arizona. Or in a state close to it—New Mexico or Colorado. He routed the letter through a courier service; I found out the service is based in Tucson. I know at one time he had family in Sedona. That got turned up when it first happened. So…I think he found his way back there. I think he's working with a church. Certain things in his letter… Well, I told the courier service everything, and they said they had no information except that the guy gave the name Francis. So I think he's working with a church or a youth ministry in Arizona, New Mexico, or Colorado, and going by the name Francis."

"OK," said Serena, "…well, good work, I guess. We'll call the police and tell them."

Gerard faced them again. "I want you to find someone who will find him."

"And do what?" said Cal, his voice rising.

Beth looked at her hands. Gerard stayed looking at his kids, then at John.

"You've got to be kidding," said Cal, standing up. He looked at Beth. "What conversation are we taking part in here?"

"You can wait outside," said Gerard.

"The hell I will," Cal shouted.

"Cal's right," said Serena. "Please don't say anything else about it, Dad."

Gerard went back to his seat. He leaned on his knees, the way he would've in the days when his body's movements were slicker. "He didn't just kill Madeline."

"We know what else he did," interrupted John. "First, we would never find him. That's got to be a fake name if he gave it to a service. Second, there are thousands of churches in those three states. Third," he waved the letter, "he says he's abroad. I believe him. I don't think he flirts with his life like this. He's been on the run twenty years. And you know what else, Gerard? We aren't killers. You're…you're having a fantasy about a different life. That life is gone now."

Serena had her forehead resting on her fist.

"Read the letter again," Gerard told his son-in-law. "There are a few clues that he's lying." He smiled weakly. "I've read it thirty times a day for a week. You know what he's doing? Do you know what he's doing, John?"

"What Gerard?"

"He's telling us where he is." He lifted his cane to tap the letter unfurled on the sofa. "It's in there. If we send someone down there, we will find him. He wants to be found."

"So give it to the police!" Cal was the only one shouting his contributions to the discussion.

"Serena," said Gerard, "I don't have any money, otherwise I wouldn't involve any of you. This is something I need to see done before I die. Simple as that."

"How has it gone so far, Gerard," said John, "getting what you need the way you need it? Do you feel peaceful?"

"Come on, Beth," said Cal, "we're going back to New York."

"We just got here," Beth said.

"I don't care; I don't want a part in this. I told you that the day we were married."

John stood up. "I'll take you to a hotel. Come back tomorrow, and we'll talk everything over." Cal objected, and John said, "You're part of the family, Cal, whether you like it or not. So I'll take you to the hotel."

Cal stared at him a while, then reached for his bags.

Beth said, "I want to read it. Let me have it." She read the note. She kissed Gerard on the cheek and followed Cal and John out the door.

Alone with her father, Serena said, "You can't be serious."

"You know I'll find a way to do it with or without you. You may see a shriveled man here, but I'll see it done. That man will leave the earth before I do."

She leveled her eyes at him. "You put us through hell our entire lives."

"Is this hell?" He pointed at the nicely furnished room. He looked at the carpet. "Don't live in the past, Serena."

"Miller is the past."

He shook his head. "Miller is now. He's in every room I've ever been in. He was with me eight years in a cell. Killing him will be the last... The rules are different for everyone. Men like John and Cal, if they never do anything to hurt anybody, that'll be good enough. If I have a shot...it'll be because a man as wicked as me has the guts to kill men wickeder. If you tell me you can't understand that, I won't believe you." He hobbled away.

***

Beth's husband, Cal, was a modern man.

If he had a new idea, it was often quite new. It was an idea one could only get in 2010, with everyone nearby talking like they were part of 2010 and discussing the developments and trajectories of 2010. It would have made little sense to Cal, the notion that most great new ideas are at least somewhat old.

When they were first married, Beth suspected he would have affairs. His restlessness gave clues that sedating his demons would be more critical to him than his vows. But she had seen no signs she was right about that. Instead, she found herself married to a man who was faithful for the same reason he was agitated—because he was too busy to be otherwise.

Cal couldn't have been more different from her father, and yet in their love of their projects they were alike. They both navigated the law. They both thought over plans after hours and on Sundays. Only Cal was unlikely, thirty or forty years hence, to call his family into the sitting room to help him plot a murder.

"It gives me the chills that we were a part of that conversation," Cal said to his wife. "If we go back tomorrow, we have to start by insisting the subject not come up. Already as we stand here, if anything happens, we are criminally liable. Do you get that, Beth? We have prior knowledge."

They'd had a silent dinner in the hotel restaurant. Back in the room, the windows were pitch dark, shielding from a single-digit temperature.

Beth sat on her side of the bed, facing away. "I can't believe I'm forty-five."

Cal made a frustrated noise with his breath. He sat next to her. "How old do you feel?"

She thought about it and said, "I feel fourteen. And I just got home from being kidnapped." He took her hand. "Everyone is so happy to see me. I'm the only one in my family who got to see everyone look at me after they thought I could be dead. They held me so tight." She started crying. She stopped to say, "My dad took me to the beach and sat there with me for hours. He told me everything."

"What's that mean—everything?"

"Everybody should be kidnapped once, Cal, so they can see what they mean to people when they get given back."

His voice got deposition-serious. "A lot of them don't get given back, Beth. Look at Madeline."

"Don't talk about people you've never met."

He let go of her hand. He got up.

"I'm sure your father has good things about—I'm sure there are redeeming things about him. No one is all bad. But we can't go back tomorrow. This is about our family now. We must go home."

Beth said, "I'm the youngest. I was barely there for any of it. I don't romanticize my father, Cal. He was a bad father and a bad man. I've never asked you to get close with my family. But we remember family when terrible things happen. This is terrible that that monster would send my father a letter."

"You don't have enough fear," he said.

"I fear flying and the bacteria of hotels, and I've confronted both those things today. You can face one of yours. I'm going back tomorrow, and you're going with me. And if I decide we're going to help them, you're going to do everything you can to stop us getting caught. I don't think it will go that way, but if it does it won't be this big deal. It will be a sweet thing, and I'll be a grateful, loving wife to you and mother to our son. And if you don't, I will divorce you and leave you broken and alone."

***

Serena was asleep.

John McClusky rolled over and saw her chest rise in even beats. He used the bathroom—again. The neighbor's light threw a beam off his mirror. He walked softly into the hall and took the steps to the loft. He heard the TV as he climbed. Gerard was in his recliner.

"Can you lower that a second, Ger?" John said.

Gerard picked up the remote and turned it down. John sat.

"You can't sleep?" Gerard asked.

"No. You?"

"I'm always up at this time."

John wiped the fatigue creases off his face. Gerard's brown suede recliner was new and had already begun to look old. It was, John knew, where Gerard ate and slept.

Gerard said, "You're thinking of doing it, right?" He nodded. "I practically raised you, John. You married two of my daughters—fathered three of my grandkids. I know that brain. You're going to do right by us."

"I'm not going to kill for you, Gerard."

"You won't do it for me. You'll do it for her. Because you know, no matter what she tells you, she wants him dead. And it's her protector who will do it. Whoever that is."

"Why not stop there? Why not kill Miller's family and everyone he ever loved? Isn't that the way? Won't that give us the most peace? And if I end up in jail for a decade or so," he shrugged, "it won't be like she's not used to it. You think I'll win over my wife by following her father's footsteps. Look where those steps lead, Gerard. They led you to my attic."

"There's only the right thing and the wrong thing. Any other words are excuses for being a coward. But you know who would do it, John, if he were here? You know who would kill him? If he were here this afternoon when I read that letter, he would be on a plane to New Mexico right now. And he would find that rat scum and end him."

"Serena didn't choose him."

"You're right," he coughed. "I'm sure she never regrets that. Let's wake her up and ask."

John stood up. He breathed through his nose.

"You were a peaceful man when you went to prison. You had this look on your face. That it was all going to be OK. Now you just look so lonely, Gerard.

"You know—you still live in a world where the only thing people can do is prove themselves to one another. Everything is some defining moment. You can't imagine that a man and wife simply love each other. That they don't need to prove themselves every day. You can't imagine what love really is because you've never had it." He poked himself in the chest. "Serena is mine. I'm hers. That's forever."

"If that were true, you'd have been asleep hours ago." Gerard reached for the remote. "You didn't come to tell me that, son. You came to ask if I thought you could get away with not doing it. And my answer is no."

He reclined further and turned the volume loud again.

In the kitchen, John thought of all the other things he wanted to tell Gerard. He walked to the foot of the stairs several times, intent on going back up and letting them out. Each time he caught his breath and returned to the counter. He ate a few cookies. He brewed himself tea. He knew it wouldn't do any good, twisting a knife into a dying man. All eighty-four-year-old men were dying. Gerard would have deathbed recollections that blew his mind. He would know, finally, that he robbed something from each of his daughters and more, what each specific thing was. He would be too sickly to focus on the television or recline in his chair. He would have to face it, on that night, each thing he took and the face of the person he took it from. John started laughing at the thought: It would be eight heart attacks that finally killed him.

***

Everyone read the letter many times. In April, John used a third party to retain a private investigator in the Midwest to search for Gary "Dice" Miller. Gerard had not been wrong that the letter left clues. By the middle of May, John got word that the investigation was successful. Miller was the head of facilities services at a Baptist church in Flagstaff, Arizona, going by the name Gary Francis.

The family reconvened in Chicago. It was two weeks before John and Serena's oldest son would graduate high school.

"This is Edward Cantone," said John, introducing a man in a lame brown suit to the rest of the family. "He operates a private investigation service. I asked him to come and tell us what he found."

Gerard was seated between Serena and Beth on the living room sofa. Cal hovered in the doorway. "Thank you for your time, Mr. Cantone," Gerard said respectfully.

The man sat in the wooden rocking chair. "I am glad to be part of this investigation. You can imagine a lot of times I get brought in to help investigate marital strife or blow the lid on an insurance claim, things of that nature. In this case, nothing was murky about who's right and wrong. This guy's as much of a scum bastard as I've come across."

"Can you tell us what you found out?" said Serena.

"He's in Flagstaff. Been there over a year. He was in Latin America before that, possibly Brazil. There's an open warrant for him, but it's so low priority that nobody was going to recognize his face coming back. He's gone by a lot of different names. He's twenty years senior to the picture they have. There are thousands of people wanted for murder from the '80s and '90s. They're just…it's rare you have a manhunt that…stays a hunt."

"Have you ever worked for law enforcement?" Cal asked.

Edward looked up and caught the lawyer's glare. He asked John, "Is he family?"

John nodded. "He's married to my sister-in-law, Beth."

Edward answered, "In a word: yes."

"How about in ten words?"

Edward smiled. "Anyway, this guy got back in. Fugitives go back and forth. They think enough time has passed; they take a shot at coming back. Sad truth is, a lot of times, they're right. They often do just what this Miller did. Find a town where a lot of the people are passing through and take a job nobody looks at."

"So he's working for a church but not in any religious capacity," Serena said.

"He's a glorified janitor. But it's a big church. He does a lot. He knows the community. I spoke to someone who said he's...he's got them thinking he's a parishioner. He gets room and board. He's set himself up pretty good, I'd say. Then he sends Mr. Magic this letter." He produced the letter. "It's full of tells."

"It's your opinion," said Cal, "that he wants to get caught."

"It's my opinion that he wants to get found. That's different than caught. He wants you, Gerard, to know where he is. And obviously," he tapped the address on the envelope, "he knows where you are."

They sat around for a minute. Their silence was grim: the silence of profound confusion about where to go next and what vocabulary one might use to seek directions.

Finally Gerard said, "Did you see him with your own eyes?"

"Yeah."

"Did you take a photograph?"

"No."

Gerard rubbed the scruff under his neck. "What can you tell us about where he lives?"

"It's an attic room in the annex of the church. The church is huge. Its southern wing connects to an office building for pastors. He lives above that. I didn't see the room, but I saw him enter the building and leave early in the morning to unlock the church. The floor plan shows it's small. Room for a cot and a sink. No windows. It's just him there at night; there's nobody else living on the grounds, and security leaves at midnight. This is the address and all my other notes."

He laid a few sheets of notebook paper on the coffee table. Beth picked them up, looked briefly, and handed them to her father.

John said, "Thanks, Edward. Do you mind waiting down the hall for a couple of minutes? I think we'll have more questions, but I don't think we know what they are yet."

Edward got up quickly, nodding. "Absolutely, that's reasonable, John. You just holler. Coffee out there?"

"It's brewed."

"Great."

John looked at his wife a while. She took the collection of Cantone's notes from Gerard.

Beth said, "It's troubling he didn't take any photos if all this is true. How hard is it to snap a photo to validate what he's saying? And I hate to ask this, John, but how did you find him? Is there any evidence he's any good at this?"

"John and I found him together," said Gerard. "He's fine. Miller is right where this guy says."

"OK," said Beth, "but now he knows as much as we do. It's going to be…I mean, suppose something happened to Miller. Edward becomes… what does he become, Cal?"

"An accessory before the fact."

Neither Gerard nor John gave a fast response.

Beth said, reading their stillness, "So he's not a private eye."

"No," said John.

"Oh, God," said Cal. He walked around the room. "What in the hell am I doing here?"

"Stay calm, Cal," said John. "Take a seat."

"You've got me ten feet from a hitman!"

John got up. "I don't like it any more than you do, and I've got a career and a family all the same. But you weren't there, and you didn't know the girl. You don't know a thing about Connecticut or the Bronx, and you don't get an opinion on how strange and unusual the circumstances are because you've got nothing to compare them to—because nobody does."

"I tell you what I would do," Cal replied, "if I was Edward Cantone, sitting down the hall, drinking your Colombian coffee. I would take your money to kill Miller. I'd kill him. I'd lie low about six months, make sure

I got away with it. Then I'd come back here, and I'd say—*I can prove you paid to have a man killed. So unless you give me every red cent you've got, I'm going to burn you up.* And you might say back: *You can't blackmail me, you're a hitman.* But of course he can. You don't know a thing about him, including his real name. He's going to have proof against you. Tons of it. He's been in your home! He knows your life, and he's dangerous—he's a killer. Are you a killer, John? No."

"I am," said Gerard. Cal looked over at his father-in-law. "I am, and you're not. Don't pretend to understand men like Edward Cantone any more than you've understood me. Hitmen make their living killing, not blackmailing. It'd be difficult for you to grasp this, but that fella in the kitchen is a stand-up guy."

Cal snorted loudly. "You're right, Gerard. That is difficult for me to grasp. Beth, tell me we're ready to leave."

Beth said gently to her sister, "Where are you in all this, Rene? You're hardly saying a word."

"I don't know," said Serena. "It's surreal." She thought some more. "John, can you bring him back in?"

John went and got Cantone.

"How's everybody doing?" Cantone said. "It's normal to have the shakes."

"Mr. Cantone," said Serena, "is he reformed?"

"Pardon?"

"From what you found out about Miller, from what's here in your notes, there's no mention of what he's like now. Is he still a criminal? Do you know if he has killed anyone else?"

"I wasn't able to find those things out, but I can tell you that Flagstaff church is a multimillion-dollar honeypot. Would not be the first time a grifter convinced a congregation he was some repentant sinner, a child of God. Give it a few months and he's found out where they keep the loot."

All, including Cantone, could tell this conjecture had been unsatisfying to Serena.

He added, "If the question is about the state of the man's soul, I don't know the answer, and nobody but Miller and Miller's confessor is going to be able to know or tell it. Seems like you're asking me, does he still deserve it, after all these years…that right? Well, I don't know. I'm sure no number of years passing has made your sister more deserving of what she got. Seeing it that way, no number of years should make him less deserving of justice. I know there are other ways to see it. I just can't help see it that one way.

"But I promise you, I'm not angling here. Plenty of folks think they want to go down this road and find out they don't have the stomach for it, and in my business, you want to find that out now, here, before we start traveling together, and my fate gets tangled up with yours. So I'd just as soon go home and leave you in peace if peace is what you have now. But if it's not, and if this could help even one iota, I'd be honored to do it."

"I vote yes," said Gerard. "It used to be mine was the only vote that counted around here, Edward. But I'm an old man, and I don't have money. So mine's not going to be the one that decides this."

Edward nodded and smiled at Gerard. "I understand that, sir."

Gerard looked around the room.

Beth said, "I won't pay toward it. But I'm fine with it happening. That's as much as I can say."

"Well, you sure said enough, honey," said Cal, shaking his head.

"Are you staying married to me?" Beth said to him. She yelled, "Answer," when he wasn't answering.

"You know that I am."

"Then we—*we*—said enough."

Cal rubbed his closed eyelids with his thumbs. "We," he whispered.

Gerard said, "What's it going to be, McClusky?"

John looked at his wife. She didn't nod. She didn't move. John said, "Kill him."

***

Eric's high school graduation was moved indoors on account of rain. The rain had stopped by the time the principal read down to the Ls, so they filed back out to the canopied stage for the remainder of the roll, which meant Eric McClusky would walk in style.

The spring moisture had made a pleasant mess of the air. John and Serena used their light coats to dry their seats and prepared to cheer for their boy.

Serena had slept well throughout the whole of the last few months, spanning the decision about how to proceed against powerful foes in the music business as well as the arguably weightier choices around Miller. She had even been served with a second lawsuit from a record company, alleging defamation. But it wasn't until last night, the eve of Eric's graduation, that she found she was unable to quell her brain.

There was this one day in 2003, seven years earlier, she spent a lot of time reliving.

They were still living in Florida, but Serena had gone to visit Beth in New York. Beth was in her late thirties then. Everything was at it should've been for a woman near the end of her youth. Beth had an adoring husband, a powerful job, and was four months pregnant, barely showing a bump. She took Serena to her office and told her all about her work life. They ate glorious Italian food together. It reminded Serena of Philadelphia in the '80s when Beth had come to visit, scarcely out of college, terrified of the world, and Serena showed her how to take the first steps into reality. Only this time it had been Beth showing Serena things about a big scary city, and Serena, the Floridian mom, who felt out of place at every crosswalk.

On the third day of her visit, Serena asked if Beth ever traveled up to Southport and looked at the old house. Beth said she had gone once, that an Indian family owned it now and had made substantial renovations.

Without much discussion, they agreed to a visit. A few restaurants were the same. Some antique places and the diner remained where they'd always been. Some things were new. Henrietta's was a bowling alley.

They drove down their old street and pulled up in front of that ancient Connecticut manor. There were some elegant cars in the driveway. Beth had said changes were made, but to Serena it looked the same. It was gigantic and inviting. The great green backyard peeked out behind the façade. Kings had lived here. Serena was then immersed in a season of life in which something like this would make her cry, so she did.

She pleaded with Beth to take her through the Bronx on the way home. They'd be passing it anyway. Beth relented, despite how exhausted she felt, and they got off at Mosholu Parkway and drove down Fordham Road and then East Tremont and around Van Cortlandt Park, eventually passing their old apartment. Serena was sappy the entire afternoon. They visited all kinds of places she claimed to remember, many of which Beth wondered had she really even been.

They stopped in Woodlawn where Serena said she wanted to buy them a proper pub dinner. Pubs were few and far between across the Bronx now, but some remained. As they ate, Beth couldn't help noticing Serena's eyes glued to the door.

"You keep looking over there like you're expecting someone."

"No, I'm trying to think if we've ever been here."

"In Woodlawn? Serena, we hardly ever came back to the Bronx. What's going on with you?"

Serena sighed. "You drive home, Beth. I'll take a cab later."

"You're expecting to see someone. What's going on? Has all this been a trick?"

"I'm not trying to trick you." She pushed her plate of cornbread away and set her elbows on the table, rubbing her hands together. "I'm looking for Brighton."

"What?"

"I spoke to Patricia Sheridan last year. She said she saw someone who told her that he lives here in Woodlawn. That he spends time in the pubs here. I guess…I don't know what I was hoping for, a glimpse or something. God, I'm humiliated."

"Is that why you flew here?" said Beth.

"No, of course not. I put it out of my mind completely, but then we were driving around, and one thing led to another…it's ridiculous."

"Look, it's natural to want to know how somebody's doing you spent all that time with…why not call him?"

"Let's go home."

"He goes to the pubs—does that mean he's out of a wheelchair?"

"I don't know! That's what I want to…" she breathed, "I don't know anything. If I let my mind wander, it devours itself. His mother lived in Woodlawn back then. It made some sense that he would come back, I guess. I just wanted to see him once more. When I say it out loud, I realize how selfish it is."

The waiter came over to clear their plates.

Beth said, "Do you know Brighton Salk?"

"Beth, stop."

"Yeah," said the waiter, "I know him." Serena looked up.

"He comes in here?" said Beth.

"He has. Mostly he hangs next door at Murphy's."

"Is he there now?" said Beth.

"You see me standing here, right?" He took the plates away.

Beth handed Serena her coat. "Come on."

"No. This is ridiculous."

"He's probably not there, but let's just check. You came all this way." She yelled after the waiter. "Hey—does he walk?"

"Huh?"

"Brighton. Can he walk?"

"Looks like walking to me."

Beth left some money, dragged Serena by the arm out to the street and around to the entrance of Murphy's. Serena yanked her arm back. "I can't breathe, Beth."

"It's OK. Look at me: *You* brought us here."

Serena rested her hand on the tavern door a second, then pulled it open and went in quickly. Beth followed.

Murphy's was a little smaller than the first joint. There were some men throwing darts and two bartenders talking to off-duty cops or firemen. There was a large group of coworkers that had smooshed tables together in the dining area, laughing belligerently.

"He isn't here," said Serena, having carved a circle around the barroom. "Let's go home."

The bathroom door swung open and shut before the sisters turned around. That gave him a few seconds to see them first.

Beth said, "Hi, Brighton."

"Hi, Beth." He blinked. "Hi."

Serena said something. He started past her as she spoke. He walked simply and fluidly across the room. He wore a sports coat and jeans. He was thin.

"Timmy, I think someone clogged the toilet in there," he called to the bartender who thanked him. He sat on the stool where his half-filled beer had been waiting with a coaster over it. He turned to Serena. "What are you doing here?" He smiled formally. "It's nice to see you." He peeked at Beth. "You too, Beth. Are you pregnant?"

"Yes," said Beth, "just found out it's a boy."

"That's great. Turning the tide."

She laughed mildly. "Yeah, looks like it. I'll wait—I'll just sit over on that side, Serena."

Nobody said anything. Beth walked to the other end and sat alone by a loud television.

"You look so…" Serena whispered, "so healthy."

Brighton took a sip of his dark beer. "It took a while."

Her voice caught, and she had to shake it loose and start again. "I'm so happy for you."

"I heard you and John have children. Come here, you can sit." He slid out a stool for her.

She had been standing in the middle of the floor in her long coat, her purse dangling an inch off the ground, the strap clenched in her fist. She made her way to the stool.

"What did you say?" she asked.

"I heard you're a mother."

"I have two boys."

"That's beautiful."

"Brighton…"

"Whatever you think you need to say, you don't."

Tears fell from her. She nodded, trying to stem them. Brighton handed her some square bar napkins. "OK," she said, trembling. "I never thought I'd find you here." He didn't answer that. "Why did you move back here?"

"I moved in with my mother after…after everything. Eventually I got better, but then she was sick. So I took care of her for a lot of years because—well, because she'd taken care of me. She died in the winter."

"I'm sorry."

"It was time."

"Now?"

"I mean I've got good work here. I'm a super on some properties. Pays all right. I've got a few friends, you know. Maybe someday I'll move to a beach town somewhere, like in Connecticut. But I'll tell ya, it's hard to leave the Bronx," he said lightly and picked up his beer. "I don't know why, but it is."

Her hands crumpled the napkins. "You left once before."

"Look how that went." He laughed and sipped.

The bartender stopped by. "Bright, who's your friend?"

"Timmy, Serena Magic. Serena, Timmy Boy the bartender."

"Hi," she said.

"Hiya, lady—you can't be from these parts."

"I was born on the Grand Concourse. But we moved to Connecticut when I was a girl."

"How do you know this hump?"

She looked at Brighton. He was older than sixty. He answered for her. "She once thought of marrying me."

"Ho!" Timmy yelled. "Dodged the biggest mistake of her life. I knew just looking at you," he wagged his finger, "that you had some set of brains. Good for you, honey. Here's one on the house for good sense."

He poured two ounces of Redbreast into a deep glass and left it in front of her, wandering off to kid the regulars.

"You don't have any anger toward me," Serena said.

Brighton shrugged. "I got to square things away with my ma. We got on pretty good terms. You know, I mean…maybe a guy should do more with his life than just get sick and get better and get on good terms with the woman who brought him into the world. But in my case, maybe that's enough."

Serena drank the Redbreast in a gulp. "Maybe." She set the glass down. "I can't believe you're, um…I have a lot of things I've thought about saying, but it doesn't feel like you want me to."

He shifted his stool, so they were face-to-face. He took his time thinking. "I went out and…I tried to have it all and you with it. You"—he kissed her hands, and she felt that his hands were cold and shaky—"you who were perfect. And the world knocked me right out." He clapped hard. She startled. "It was my lesson. Not yours." That coworker crowd was laughing loudly again behind them. "Most days I just think about the lesson. It's a good thing to think about. But sometimes, if I just can't help it…I think about how sweet it was for that little while in that beautiful little town when it looked like it was all going to work—and that God was weaker than tough guys."

His eyes clouded over, and they cried together silently, not touching.

Beth came and got her. Serena clung to her, and they walked out, no one uttering any decent words like goodbye.

Today the weather cooperated for the rest of Eric's graduation ceremony. Serena and John cheered and shouted joy when he marched across the stage and lifted his diploma. Serena whistled. She made all the noises you make when you love someone and something great happens for them.

***

The day all the important music people were set to get together in search of settlement terms in a large room in California, Serena was at her window in Chicago.

Her lawyer called once, twice…she let him leave voicemails. She read the print versions of articles about her. She compared them to the now-faded and twice-creased print articles from the '80s. Her face had changed. Her posture was less imperial but still sturdy, proud. She was, on balance, a Connecticut girl, and Connecticut girls do not fix toilets, and they don't say *rad*iator, and they rarely slouch. Emily would have slouched all over *Rolling Stone*.

The twin lawsuits were the first wave. There would be others. She would possibly win. She had written the songs. The truth was with her, in her heart and marrow and carpal tendons. But what appetite she still possessed for the gore of a fight she could not say.

And there was the question of: to what end? The music had been released and adored, in many cases, by millions. Her job as a songwriter had been done. Her attorney would be alone in that important room just now making the case that Serena had been duped all these years, that she'd been intimidated into signing away rights and accepting a pittance as a hush fee. The truth was twofold: Yes, she deserved credit. But yes, she had accepted their deal. If they let her be a songwriter, she was willing to do it shamefully. She was willing to be a basement poet if it meant she could whisper up through the grates to the townsfolk, share a sewer lullaby.

John came into their bedroom holding his phone. He said her lawyer, not getting through, had phoned him.

"I don't want to hear it," Serena said, standing.

"I think you should," said John, pressing a button. "Rick, I'm back; I have Serena."

The attorney's voice garbled the speaker.

"I am sorry, Rick," said Serena. "I couldn't make it."

"It isn't!" Rick shouted. "But listen, lady, I think I brought the whole thing off without you. First thing we have to do is renegotiate my involvement. I was there without you, and I laid out the precedents and pulled every thread of this thing until they saw it the way I did."

John said, "Rick, tell us what happened. You have our word—we'll do the right thing."

His laugh garbled the line again. "Oh, boy, John, Johnny my friend, oh boy. Sit down. Better yet, lie down! Serena, the label is showing me its belly. They don't want to go to court; they don't even want to threaten it anymore. You played that media tour like Yo-Yo Ma. They are terrified. All they're getting is nasty press and hate mail. They are willing—are you ready? They are willing to side with you over the artists. They want to embrace you publicly, release all the terms of the contracts, and have their head of talent do a press tour with you where you tell the story together. Obviously, some things need to be smoothed out: You're going to have to dance a little, maybe some things you shouldn't have said, blah blah. But the upshot is: They aren't joining the suit. If one of these has-beens wants to sue you, it will be an independent action. After the label embraces you, no judge will hear it! Baby, I don't know what lady victory looks like if this isn't her pretty face."

John and Serena locked eyes intermittently throughout his rant.

"Wow," said John. "Rick, you did a great job."

"The remunerations provision, John..."

"Are they opening up the royalty agreements?"

"Every single one. Serena, it's been a long time since you've been rich, sweetheart, so dust off the gown and get that chariot out of the garage...."

John hung up and tossed the phone on the bed. "How about that?" he said.

Serena had chills. "Yeah."

"They're going to acknowledge you, Serena. Did you hear him?"

"I did."

He laughed. "Are you in shock?"

Henry and Eric came in. They could tell by the weird voice Dad was using something had happened. John laughed and told them. "Your mom is about to be a legend. Or—now the world will know she's one."

They went out for dinner and dreamed aloud.

Afterward, on the walk to the car, John held his wife's hand. He said, "You know I'll do anything for you."

"But do you know I would do anything for you?" she asked.

He put his arm around her. "For a while I thought I knew it. Now I do. I know it."

It was midnight when Beth called. Serena woke up to the tremors on the end table. She took the phone downstairs.

"I spoke to Daddy," said Beth.

"I'm still processing it," said Serena. "It's strange to win like that. I feel like I didn't show up for the fight."

"What do you mean?" said Beth.

"Oh...the music...what were you referencing?"

"The situation in Arizona. It's happening day after tomorrow."

Serena turned around in the downstairs foyer as though she'd felt someone behind her. She was alone. "Daddy said that?"

"Yeah. What were you talking about?"

"Nothing. I didn't know this."

"Serena, I'm at the airport."

"Why?"

"I'm going to Arizona. I want to see this man before it happens."

"Beth, listen to me." She spoke slowly. "This is the difference between jail and freedom. Go back outside, get in a cab, and go home to your family. If there is a record of you being anywhere near there…"

"I need to see his face. I don't have any peace about this. None. Cal keeps saying… He works in a church. He's old. It feels suddenly wrong and wicked. Like when we all made the choice, we were drunk. We'd forgotten every lesson about revenge and why it doesn't work." In the background Serena heard loudspeaker notifications for boarding flights. "You and me and Cal and John, we're happy. Happy people don't do these things. We're agreeing to it because Daddy is unhappy. He's miserable and thinks this will fix something."

Eric came in the front door.

"Hold on," said Serena.

He had been at another in a string of friends' graduation parties. His eyes were glazed from beer. Serena blew him a kiss and pointed to the phone as though to say she would talk to him in the morning. He waved, looking relieved to go straight to bed.

"Even if we wanted to stop it, Beth," she said, stepping out in front of the house, "there would be no way. What do you think you're going to see in Miller's eyes? You're going to look at him and know if he's still a bad man?"

"Yes. I think I'll be able to tell. I know what a good old man looks like. That night years ago when we saw Brighton in Woodlawn. His eyes were good. He was resigned to every awful thing he went through, and he came through it with peace on his face."

"Shut up, Beth."

"If Miller is good, he'll look that sort of old. And if he's bad, he'll look like Daddy."

***

Gerard,

I saw your daughter Serena on TV. They say she got screwed out of a lot. She should've been famous. Sorry she went through that.

I am also sorry about what I did to your other daughter and the other man the night after. Mostly for your girl I am sorry. Nobody should die that way. I had voices in my head those days. They were mean as hell. I'm still mean, but no more voices. A pastor man showed me a trick to get rid of them. I learnt to shut them up. After a while they stopped going on.

None of that is help to you. You were in it with us but she wasn't. Just I wish I did not kill her. I killed my own dad. I killed a lot of guys who died afraid. I know I am not all bad because I still hear them being scared at night. I would not care that they were scared if I was all bad. But I do. You have that with anyone you scared?

On the news Serena said you were still alive and that you were 80 about. That's pretty old. I feel old, but I am not that old. Not like 80.

I lived in Mexico all this time. People treat me pretty good. I wished I had kids or a wife but never did. You did. It looked like it did not fit well with your life. I guess I could be glad I never had none.

There's one thing I can't explain to people around here. I was a piece of dirt. I did things wrong. But I can't go all the way their way, because they got it wrong to. You can't be some guy. Everyone wants me to be just a weak little guy who prays and cries. I tried it. All these folks sing and look nice. And then monsters decide everything. If you can't beat a monster, you can't decide nothing. You know that. These guys don't. But no one listens to me because I am horrible and killed people who were scared, like your girl.

Sorry.

Miller

***

It was minutes from nightfall, in Flagstaff, Arizona, when Serena's rental car pulled into the Hilton. Serena had told John she was going to New York to see Beth, and she'd told Gerard nothing.

She parked and found Beth's room. No one answered. She called her cell—voicemail. She sat in her car and began to doze until Beth knocked on her passenger window.

The western desert air got in with her.

"I kept thinking how you said you won the fight you didn't show up for."

"Well, I showed up this time," said Serena. She looked out the windshield at the brightly lit hotel.

"I know I've gotten us in hot water. But even if it's documented we bought plane tickets out here…if it's going to happen tomorrow night, all we have to do is fly back tomorrow morning."

"That will still make it look like we're involved."

"They would have to investigate us to even know we were here. This many years later…you think anyone will really look into it?"

"I don't know. I don't know, Beth, but here we are. Did you go see him?"

"I went to the church. I drove around it three hours, hoping he'd come out or go in. If you want to turn right around and leave tonight, we can. But…"

"What?"

"Don't you want to get a look at him?"

Serena's hands rested calmly on the wheel. "Yeah."

They agreed to sleep and attend a church service the next morning. Beth's hotel room had one queen bed. They shared it.

***

They didn't see anyone, in the bright, modern Baptist church, who they immediately thought was Miller. They had both seen his face in person only one time before and in a mugshot many hundreds. They looked for faces that could have been his, plus time and sun.

When the service ended, they stood in front of a ceramic fountain in the courtyard. Beth had that mugshot photo in her purse. If, however, she were to ask anyone if they knew him, people would be sure to remember that if something happened to him later. They couldn't seek help in identifying him or ask for him by any name. They simply had to wait to spot him yet could not be seen to be waiting.

They left and had breakfast and coffee and returned for the service at 11:00 a.m. During the chorus of the first hymn, the silver-framed doorway that fed a corridor popped open to admit an elderly lady with a walker. In that corridor behind her, a heavyset man with haywire black hair was stacking boxes. The door eased shut. Beth immediately believed it was him.

Serena said, under the storm of the choir, "He saw me on TV. I can't go up to him and check."

"I don't see why it matters. I mean…all right, I'll go. Stay here."

Beth disappeared into that hall. Serena's heart leapt higher inside her chest every second she was out of sight. Finally she dropped her songbook and followed the wall toward the door. As she approached, Beth came back through it. Serena took her hand, and they backed away, behind the pews.

"Is it him?"

"I don't know. I asked him where the restrooms were. He just pointed. I looked at him, but I can't tell. It might be."

"This is crazy. Was it him or not, Beth?"

"I think it was."

The choir peaked. Serena went through the door. The man was now using a box cutter to slice the tape off a shipment. He wore baggy workman's pants and a blue T-shirt. Serena got close. His back was to her.

"Miller," she said.

His cutting hand stopped moving halfway across the box. He turned around. She let him look her over.

He whispered a word that meant many things to many people. "Magic."

***

They were surrounded by pastoral staff and delivery people. A strong western sunlight sliced through the hall from the delivery gate. Miller looked behind Serena. He asked if that was another sister. Serena nodded.

Miller looked around at people taking note of them.

"Want to talk?" he said. He looked suddenly uncomfortable to Serena, like he was afraid she would let out some trivial bit of gossip that would ruin him before peers.

"Where?" she said.

"There's a kitchen there. They got coffee."

Beth and Serena followed him to it. He sat down. Serena steadied her hands. She and Beth sat across from him.

"You got cops with you?" he asked. Serena shook her head no. "How'd you find me?"

"My father thought you wanted us to."

"I don't know about that." He laid his hands flat on the table. They were large, weathered. He had a pouch around his waist, but his back was broad. His facial hair was a neatly trimmed thing, at odds with the chaos of the hair on his head. "What do you want?"

"Why'd you write that letter?" Beth said.

"Felt sorry. Said so."

Beth opened her mouth slowly. "Do you still do things to people?"

Now he watched them. He let his mind work on them and the day. He came back into himself. "You found someone to kill me."

"No," said Beth. "I just want to know."

He looked at Serena.

"Yes," she said, "we did." His eyes fell. "Did you want that?"

"It crossed my mind." He sat back in his seat and folded his arms. "When's it going to happen?"

"Sometime. Maybe. Tonight probably. If you don't think you deserve it, you can always run."

He nodded. "Anything else?"

"You can answer my question," Beth said.

"I ain't killed anyone in a while. I did some other things. Not in a while."

"Is this real?" said Beth, motioning around the room. "This whole thing."

"It's been real so far. Now you're here. Now it don't feel that real. Feels like me again."

Some people had been at a table in the kitchen's corner, out of earshot, but watching. They got up and left.

Serena said, "We can't stop the man coming here tonight. Even if we wanted to. It's too late. But if you leave here and get running, we can make sure he doesn't come after you."

"I ran a long time."

"Well, a few more miles won't kill you. But staying here tonight will. That's your choice."

Serena got up and Beth with her. At the door Miller called, "It's extra mean, setting this up, then making it my choice. Why not let me go quick and scared and alone, like your damn sister?"

Beth shook. Serena faced him. "You could never die like my sister because you never lived like her. You lived like a dog. And I hope you die like one. I'm just not willing to become one to see it happen."

They left the room and heard him slamming his fist on the table, then louder crashes as though perhaps he was throwing things. The farther they went into the hall, the more they heard crazy noises from that kitchen.

The delivery door to the street was now locked, so they exited through the front of the church. On a bench in front of the courtyard fountain, Edward Cantone was reading a King James Bible. He pretended not to know them. They found the rental car. It was three miles before Serena realized she was speeding.

***

At the hotel, they packed frantically as Serena's phone lit up with a third call from John.

"He knows," she kept saying. "Cantone called him. We've got to get out of here."

They finished packing. Now Beth's phone rang. John.

"You have to talk to him, Serena."

Serena took Beth's phone and answered. "John, it's a long story—"

"Serena, you both need to get back here."

"I know. We're coming."

"You know?"

"Yes, I'm sorry. I'll explain everything. Let us get to the airport." There went a beat. "John?"

"Are you in New York?"

She looked at Beth. "I thought you…we're in Arizona."

"Arizona!"

"John, we're leaving."

"Serena, get home. Your father had a stroke. I don't know what you're doing. But if you want to say goodbye, you'd better get home."

She sat on the bed.

"John, this is Beth. He's still alive?"

"Right now he is, yes. We're at Northwestern Memorial. I would hurry up. And just—I don't know what to say right now but get the hell out of there."

"We're coming," said Beth.

Serena repeated it. Then, "Tell Dad to hang on."

***

They landed at O'Hare after midnight and took a twenty-minute cab to Northwestern. Gerard was nonresponsive when they entered. Eric, Henry, and John were in chairs beside his bed. Serena hugged her sons. John asked the boys to wait in the hall.

Serena sat on the edge of her father's bed and took his hand.

"It was my fault, John," said Beth. "All of it. I had second thoughts, and I went there to try to see him—Miller—and Serena came to get me, to bring me back. I put her on the spot. I did it."

John took Serena's arm. "You may have sent us all to jail."

Serena shook him loose. "Let me say goodbye to him, OK? Then you can yell at me the rest of our lives."

John ran both hands along his scalp. He walked to the other side of the monitors.

"Has he talked at all?" said Beth.

"A couple hours ago. It wasn't clear."

"What was he saying?"

"It wasn't clear."

Serena looked at him. "What was it?"

"He wanted to know if it was done yet."

Beth and Serena sat on both sides of his bed. They ate ice chips and told him stories. They told him the stories they remembered most vividly. They talked about the nice feeling that being from a big family gave them, one that still lives in them. They became completely sentimental and told him everything they could about what had gone well in their lives.

Around 3:00 a.m., John took his sons home. He came back at ten the next morning. Gerard was still alive, opening and closing his eyes faintly like a newborn. John woke Serena and Beth, who were sleeping crookedly in purple cushioned visitors' chairs. He brought them into the hall, walked them to the far end of it.

"Miller killed Cantone last night."

"What?" said Serena, her voice frail from sleep.

"It's on the news now. National. Cantone went to the church's attic room, and Miller slit his throat open, then took Cantone's own gun and shot him four times. He stole a pastor's car and drove away. Two cops pulled him over in Prescott, and Miller shot them both: One's critical. He's driving south, and there's a statewide manhunt."

Serena leaned on the beige wall grip that rehabilitating patients used to walk. Beth grabbed her stomach and sat on the floor.

John didn't give them any time. "Did you see Miller?" Neither could talk. "Did you see him, Serena?"

"No."

"That's a lie. God help me if the cops come to us. Cantone should've burned anything that led to us, but I'll bet anything he didn't. I'll bet he had articles on Maddy's death in his car, his office, his house. So they will come, won't they? And it won't be you, the celebrity songwriter, they arrest this time. It'll be me who found and paid a hitman. It'll be your patsy. God help you, you monster."

"John," Serena grabbed after him, and he pulled away. She sank to the floor and held Beth.

In time they made their way back to Gerard's bed. They sat with him. Serena stroked his wispy hair. "It's OK, Daddy."

Beth cried. She bawled.

A few minutes after noon, Gerard kept his eyes open for a long spell. Serena waited and waited for them to close. Finally, she gave him his lie. "We got him, Daddy. Miller's dead. He's gone."

The muscles under Gerard's saggy English cheeks relaxed. He died.

***

The first hint of Gerard's stroke had come while eating popcorn. He'd microwaved a bag and put on the Turner Classic Movies channel. His first hope was that it was an anxiety attack.

There was a time, as John had pointed out, when Gerard was resigned to many fates of life, one of them being its end. Before he went to prison, he had aged into a kind of harmlessness. His girls were grown. They had come to know him. They had, some of them, stepped inside his world. The zeal of aiming at something that society intended to hold back from Gerard had worn off completely. He had become gripped instead by the notion that a man could squeeze two lifetimes into one: He could be both a builder and a sage, a dealmaker and a philosopher, a killer and a grandfather.

But prison demanded the full faculties of his will all over again. He lived for eight years in a medium-security facility and was reminded every day that the men around him were those that society would compare him to so long as he lived.

He saw his brother Jimmy six times in those years. They wrote long letters to each other trying to square everything—how it all went wrong and why and when.

Jimmy died in 1997. The last letter Gerard received from him was the angriest. He had confessed to a near-constant bitterness, spanning decades, about being second in line, never being trusted to lead and being treated as a glorified secretary by some of his nieces. He wrote that Gerard "never wanted to trust him" because Gerard never wanted anything accomplished that he didn't do himself. Gerard, for his part, didn't believe Jimmy had harbored these feelings across years, but that the tedium and agony of prison life had cast his brother's memories in a rotten light. He thought Jimmy needed someone to be awful to.

When he found out Jimmy was dead, Gerard burned that last letter. He had kept that picture of them from Rome, laughing in front of a piazza fountain, taped to his cell mirror. He left it there for another six weeks, and one night he burned that too.

The only way to understand himself, nearing the end of everything, was to maintain the same regard for the past he'd always had: none. A man whom society calls a prisoner is a man who must work to change his future, to make it different than the present. Prison returned to Gerard his gift for envisioning an improbable outcome and doing anything in human power to bring it to life.

When he went to live in John and Serena's attic, he tried to be a grandfather again. The boys were kind to him, but they were grown. He was in Chicago, where he had never been before, and no one knew anything about him except that he'd ended up broke and broken, a beneficiary of a son-in-law's charity. He tried to read Longfellow again. He couldn't. He binged television and junk food. He limped around the block if it was warm. When he got the letter from Miller, he saw his great chance to use his only gift again, his talent for being a man of will. It was so sweet and precious to him to plan it and bring it to life that he let himself fall in love with poor Madeline all over again.

The night Miller was to die in his attic, Gerard had a stroke in his.

His grandson Eric called the ambulance. The next thing he heard was John's voice in the hospital. He moved his mouth but didn't think John could hear him. He moved his lips and asked the question over and over. Had it happened—was it done? Please, tell him it was done.

When he woke up again Serena was with him. He couldn't feel it, but he thought she was holding his hand. Beth was on the other side. They were speaking softly, too softly to hear. He needed them to speak like they did when they were kids. He needed them to yell like they were in that hallway on the Concourse, screeching what they felt. It had to all become urgent to them again.

They disappeared.

He opened his eyes and only the white ceiling was before him. Where were his grandsons? Where was John?

Then his girls were back. Beth and Serena, they wouldn't leave him again. Serena was shaking. She told him something.

He tried to use all his muscles, all his will, to beg them to scream it—like they were girls. He would have served eight more years in hell if he could have gone back and stayed home from work one more day when they were young, if he could have said yes to reading one more story. He would go to hell now if he could go back and not rush.

Serena, he said, but couldn't speak, *tell me, please, if we got the bad guy.* She told him the answer, but he couldn't hear it. He squinted until he couldn't see the white ceiling at all.

***

The cops did come. What they found in Cantone's files was never clear, but they knocked on the McClusky's townhouse door seven days after the murders in Arizona.

John spent no time on a dance of wits. He retained a stellar criminal firm. They examined the timeline and facts and fastened his story tighter than a noose. He had yet to pay Cantone for anything more than expenses incurred during his private investigating. By either sheer ineptitude or a miracle of grace, the police never placed Beth and Serena in Flagstaff on the morning of Cantone's death. Serena had not used a credit card to book her flight, and they were alibied by hospital security records when the episode in the church attic took place.

The detectives openly suspected the truth: that John and Gerard had hired Cantone to kill Miller, and Miller killed Cantone first. But they could not disprove the narrative that John had merely hired a private investigator with the intent of turning his findings over to police, and Cantone was acting in his capacity as investigator when Miller killed him.

These and other chess moves, legal and civil, played out over six hellacious months, but in the end no charges were filed.

In 2014, Beth and Cal died in a plane crash over Tuscany. There was a brutal storm, and their pilot thought he could handle it and could not. The obituary would blame the plane and the pilot, but it was Mother Nature that took Beth. Mother Nature willed her dead.

Serena and John became legal guardians to their son, Fred, then twelve. But it was John's first son, the one he'd had with Emily, now a man in his middle thirties, who offered to take Beth's boy into his home and raise him up with his own young family. Serena gave her blessing.

Eric and Henry McClusky went through college and graduate school—Eric for business, Henry for the fine arts. They came home often and retained, throughout their entire adulthood, the kind of relationship all parents wish to keep with their kids as they age.

And no one ever caught Miller.

***

The record label tried its best to keep the promise to Serena that her lyrics would be hers again. The day after Gerard's funeral—weeks before she and John made up and pledged their undying love all over again—Serena read over the terms of the legal truce. She would not have to concede much at all to have her rights and royalties restored. Foremost, they wanted her to accept their apology. They wanted to embrace nationally. And from then on, they would conquer the music business together.

Serena, alone in the attic loft that was until recently her father's, finished reviewing their terms. She took out her phone and returned a call from one of the dozens of reporters who'd contacted her that past year. Even as someone picked up the line, she still did not know which outlet she'd reached.

"This is Serena Magic."

"Serena, I'm glad to finally get you. How have you been?"

"Fine. Well, my father died."

"I'm so sorry. Was he sick?"

She thought about the question. "I want to give you a quote."

"OK."

"I didn't write any of these songs. I wish I did, but I haven't the talent. I am sorry to all the great musicians and songwriters whose work I tried to steal. One day I'll know why I did it."

There was a length of respectful silence. "Is—is that all?"

"Yes."

She took a long walk around her house. In the basement Eric and John were hosting friends, roaring at the flat screen playing their video game.

In the dining room John sat with the lawyers. They had a pot of coffee in the middle of the table. Her townhouse was a fourth the size of that Connecticut estate, the back lawn of which sat hopelessly still as seven girls trampled it summer after summer until one at a time they began to disappear.

She went to the storage room behind their study and turned over boxes until she found where she'd stowed her old songbooks. She sat on the floor and thumbed the first little notebook she'd ever written anything in, the book Emily had read at Henrietta's before taking her life.

There was one song she had written about Emily. She wondered, as she had many times, if this was the one Emily read. It wasn't about much. It was about the day they moved from the Bronx to Southport.

To distract the younger kids, their mother had sent them down to the stoop with crayons and paper. Emily had drawn a lovely picture of a house, the kind she imagined they were moving to. It was a marvelous little work, full of bright colors and flowers. Jane held it, mesmerized. Their father walked by carrying the record player to the car. He saw the picture and, thinking Jane had made it, told her it was beautiful—that he was proud of her.

Hannah informed him that Emily made it, not Jane. When Emily saw Jane's face fall, she lied, "That's not true. It is Jane's. Jane made it, Daddy." Gerard stooped, kissed Jane, and kept on.

Serena's song about this was the kind of thing a first-time songwriter might write. Technically she thought it was a poor effort. But sentimentally she loved the ending which celebrated her big sister for using pain to create beauty and *giving away the glory.*

Now John came into the storage room. "The kids are making too much noise; we can't work in there."

"OK, I'll tell them."

John left without another word. He would be curt with her a few more weeks before softening again. By the time she turned sixty, they would never fight again.

She told the boys to take their friends out. She gave them some money for pizza. Sitting on their Chicago townhouse stoop, she watched the young guys skip and holler down the street.

She told herself she could still write songs if she pleased. She could put pen to paper. No one could stop that.

In the years to come she would have a lot of ideas. Occasionally she would sell them to a label but always on condition of anonymity. It became more important to her to work in secret than it had ever been to the giants who'd stolen her lyrics. In this way, she enjoyed perfect freedom. She could create anything. She could love or hate or apologize to anyone, and no one would know it was her doing it. No glory would be Serena Magic's, and maybe that would be penance enough, she thought. If they weren't going to remember Emily or Jane or Maddy or Hannah or Daphne or Beth or Brianne, they weren't going to remember her either. If all those lovely girls could create beauty with no glory, she would do the same.

On some days Serena would think about fashioning a song from Miller's letter to Daddy. She could call it "Monsters Decide Everything." She was torn because it would make a great song, but she didn't think it was true.

ACKNOWLEDGMENTS

I have written stories, with minimal notoriety in distributing them, for most of my thirty-seven years on earth. Along the way, I've gotten more encouragement and kindness than I've deserved. I think there are probably more talented people who have been less encouraged and thus remain unpublished. So in a very real sense, I owe this book, and many of my other creative projects, to those who have patiently journeyed with me.

In no certain order: A special thanks to my agent and friend Scott Kaufman, who is maybe the last honest person in New York; to my friends and constant readers Elise Daniel, Nathanael Yellis, Will Sanderson, Pete Kane, Danny Griffin, Rosalie O'Connell, Nicky and Damian Bell, Sam Curphey, Josh Schwartz, Chris Quagliata, Kev Coleman, and John Reed; to my partner in business and war Brendan Nardozzi; to the excellent team at Post Hill Press for their faith and guidance; to my glorious extended family of true characters and heroes, Tommy and Tommy Collins (Sr. and Jr.), Kathy and George, Mary, Chris, and all.

Many of the characters in this book draw from the humor, candor, warmth, and originality of a special enclave of New York—a species I fear will vanish from future generations—but that is embodied by my family and the people who loved them.

I am indebted above all both to the family I grew up in and the one I've now created. To the former, my brother Ryan has been my constant check on reality and my best friend; my mother Eileen has been the heart-beat of anything true I've done and the strongest person I've ever known;

and my father, Robert Slingsby, no longer with us—he taught me how to write.

As for the latter, I thank my five children, Cecilia, Noelle, Mary, Susanna, and Robert, who teach me the moral of all stories; and my wife Julia, who I love so much that nothing else seems important.

ABOUT THE AUTHOR

Zachary Slingsby is an award-winning writer, filmmaker, and the creator of the comedy platform and brand entertainment studio King Jester, featuring some of the best comedians and satire online. He lives in Nashville, Tennessee, with his wife and five children.